Burnt Black Suns

HIPPOCAMPUS PRESS FICTION

W. H. Pugmire, *The Fungal Stain* (2006)
———, *Uncommon Places: A Collection of Exquisites* (2012)
Franklyn Searight, *Lair of the Dreamer: A Cthulhu Mythos Omnibus* (2007)
Edith Miniter, *Dead Houses and Other Works* (2008)
———, *The Village Green and Other Pieces* (2013)
Jonathan Thomas, *Midnight Call and Other Stories* (2008)
———, *Tempting Providence and Other Stories* (2010)
———, *Thirteen Conjurations* (2013)
Ramsey Campbell, *Inconsequential Tales* (2008)
Joseph Pulver, *Blood Will Have Its Season* (2009)
———, *Sin and Ashes* (2011)
———, *Portraits of Ruin* (2012)
Michael Aronovitz, *Seven Deadly Pleasures* (2009)
Donald R. Burleson, *Wait for the Thunder* (2010)
Peter Cannon, *Forever Azathoth: Parodies and Pastiches* (2012)
Alan Gullette, *Intimations of Unreality* (2012)
Richard A. Lupoff, *Dreams* (2012)
———, *Visions* (2012)
Richard Gavin, *At Fear's Altar* (2012)
Jason V Brock, *Simulacrum and Other Possible Realities* (2013)
S. T. Joshi, *The Assaults of Chaos* (2013)
Kenneth W. Faig, *Lovecraft's Pillow, and Other Strange Stories* (2013)
John Langan, *The Wide, Carnivorous Sky* (2013)

Burnt Black Suns

a Collection of Weird Tales

Simon Strantzas

Foreword by Laird Barron

Hippocampus Press

New York

Copyright © 2014 by Hippocampus Press
Works by Simon Strantzas © 2014 by Simon Strantzas
"Dig My Grave" © 2014 by Laird Barron

Acknowledgments: See p. 308.

Published by Hippocampus Press
P.O. Box 641, New York, NY 10156.
http://www.hippocampuspress.com
All rights reserved.
No part of this work may be reproduced in any form or by any means without the written permission of the publisher.

Cover art © 2014 by Santiago Caruso.
Hippocampus Press logo designed by Anastasia Damianakos.

First Edition
1 3 5 7 9 8 6 4 2
ISBN13: 978-1-61498-083-4

Contents

Dig My Grave, by Laird Barron 7
On Ice 13
Dwelling on the Past 47
Strong as a Rock 64
By Invisible Hands 84
One Last Bloom 102
Thistle's Find 170
Beyond the Banks of the River Seine 185
Emotional Dues 201
Burnt Black Suns 235
Acknowledgments 308

Dig My Grave

A couple of years ago I spent the end of winter in the mountains of western Montana. Even at the close of March, snow piled among the pines hip-deep to an elk. At night the wind moaned through the canyons and the forests and played a ghostly melody on the chimes. Out there in the dark, the coyotes chorused as they prowled. Around the witching hour on the bitterest nights, the old Siamese barn cat would cry in that hair-raising note only felines can hit as she ghosted toward the light in my cabin window. If I could perfectly describe the tenor of this new collection by Simon Strantzas, it might be something like that. This is a book that resonates with familiar themes and classical tropes and reintroduces them as feral changelings.

Some ask, what is the value of horror literature? Of what profit to the mind is the weird? I say, here it is, Exhibit A, in your hand or transfigured upon a screen. Here is a mirror, a microscope, a soot-blacked canary at the bottom of the shaft. Here is the morality play and the cautionary tale. Here is the delivery mechanism for that jolt of frisson that does more than stimulate the primitive self. It is the very signal that alerts us to our atavistic stirring. The human primate has evolved, but we still grow canines, we make fire, and keep our weapons and our dogs close to hand. We dread the unknown and in so doing attempt to make sense of it.

This is the dawn of a new golden age of dark literature. Horror, dark fantasy, neo-noir, and the weird have proven not only resilient, but resurgent. The trend isn't always reflected by the *New York Times* bestseller list, but it's been in progress since the new millennium and Simon Strantzas has carved a significant niche in recent years. A great deal of his power lies in accumulated effect, and as with the best artists, he is relentless, a shark constantly in forward motion. That's an admirable quality in a horror writer, especially one who is rooted in the classics. His early stuff was a bit of Ligotti, a dash of Aickman, some classical weird cross-wired to the postmodern. Austerely ornate. Elliptical. His tales spoke of ague and estrangement, urban derangement of a crumbling empire and a jaded commonwealth.

With *Burnt Black Suns*, Strantzas continues a trajectory into deeper darkness like that probe sailing out of the solar system into the gulf of night, and in some respects the odyssey has brought him closer to the primal core of the tradition and its rawest, purest essentials. I'm a sucker for the natural world in literature—whether it is Blackwood's "The Willows," London's *The Call of the Wild*, or the Yukon poetry of Robert Service, give me a glimpse into the primeval landscape, a life-or-death struggle upon the tundra, or a scorching trek through badlands, and I'm hooked. Strantzas's wilderness doesn't discriminate. It swallows up doomed Arctic expeditions, weekend mountaineers, forlorn suburbanite wanderers out of their depth, and it waits with implacable hunger in the caverns beneath cities. To this mix of pulp and brutal naturalism there's a prevailing undercurrent of his trademark weirdness, a gradual raveling of the threads binding prosaic reality, the disintegration of social bonds, the map of the known world blurring into terra incognita.

But there's another striking mutation in evidence—an unsettling foray into the realm of body horror that echoes the decadent phantasmagoria of literary master Clive Barker and filmmakers such as Takashi Miike and David Cronenberg. Strantzas has incorporated miserablist sensibilities and honed them into a steely edge encrusted with the verdigris of tradition yet possessed of real cutting power. *Burnt Black Suns* is an altogether menacing experience, much more visceral than his previous offerings. What you get with these new stories is a shovelful of dirt to the face.

As I write this, it's winter again and I'm in the Hudson Valley as far eastward as I'll ever come without falling into the Atlantic. This room is cold. My window overlooks a gray wood. The ground is silver from last night's hard freeze. Snowflakes skate across the glass, forerunners of a storm rolling out of the north. Recently the sun wobbled and reversed and stood upon its crown. Soon the planets of our solar system will align in a conjunction. Physicists chuckle about the possibility of five minutes of zero gravity on earth. Cattle mutilations continue apace. A devil-painted clown stalks the highways and byways of Massachusetts posing for photos before vanishing into the underbrush. The Smiley Face Killers remain at large and largely unremarked.

These items are fitting, evidence of synchronicity, tendrils of the cosmos insinuating themselves between the bricks and sending a shiver through the foundation. Each represents another microfracture in the smooth eggshell barrier between us and the dark. The fractures occur everywhere all the time. Journalists record these phenomena in articles of science and crime. Most of us nervously chuckle or scoff over drinks. The numinous and ineffable can be dismissed by the simple act of toil. Each day we trudge through factory gates and lean into our traces and forget. Death and worse are easily dismissed over dram and darts while the lamp shines warm and cozy. It's only at night during the small, desolate hours that the phantom groans of our subconscious gain primacy, only in that wasteland do we acknowledge the pitter-pat of feet trampling our graves. Then we fall through the trapdoor into the oblivion of sleep and forget why our hearts are troubled, why the flesh between our shoulder blades tightens, why we fear the shadows and the dark.

Let these stories be a kind of alarm, let them bridge the dusty spectral light of dead stars and the false permanence of our waking selves. Stoke the fire and shutter the window. Pour yourself a glass. I find that bad news is best taken with a dose of scotch. Charles Simic once said that when you lean over to lace up your shoes, you "look into the earth." Simon Strantzas knows the truth of it. He's come with shovel and pickaxe to show you the way.

—LAIRD BARRON

Rifton, NY
February 1, 2014

Burnt Black Suns

On Ice

The bearded Frenchman landed the plane on a narrow sheet of ice as expertly as anyone could. It wasn't smooth, and the four passengers were utterly silent as the hull shuddered and echoed and threatened to split along its riveted seams. Wendell closed his eyes so tight he saw stars, and clung to what was around him to keep from being thrown from his seat. When the plane finally slid to a stop, part of him wanted to leap up and hug not only the ground but the men around him. He didn't, because when he finally opened his eyelids the first thing he saw was the thuggish Dogan's disgusted smirk, and it quickly extinguished any lingering elation. Isaacs, for all his faults, was not so inhibited. Instead, he had his hands pressed together in supplication and whispered furiously under breath. It caught Dogan's eye, and the look he and Wendell shared might have been the first time they had agreed on anything.

"The oil companies have already done a survey of Melville Island, so there shouldn't be too many surprises ahead," Dr. Hanson said. "However, their priority has never been fossils—except, of course, the liquid kind—and it's unlikely they saw much while speeding across the ice on ATVs, doing damage to the strata. So we have ample exploring to do. We'll hike inland for a day and set up base camp. From there, we'll radiate our dig outward."

Gauthier unloaded the plane two bags at a time, and his four passengers moved the gear to the side. They packed light—only the most essential tools and equipment—so the hike would be manageable, but seeing the bags spread across the encrusted surface, Wendell wondered if he were up to the task. It took too long to load everything on his narrow shoulders, and when he was done he suspected the pack weighed more than thirty pounds. Dr. Hanson looked invigorated by his own burden, his face a smiling crimson flush. Isaacs was the opposite, however, and visibly uncomfortable. Wendell hoped the goggle-eyed boy wouldn't be a liability in the days ahead.

They walked across the frigid snow, and nearly an hour went by before Dr. Hanson turned and looked at the breathless entourage behind him.

"So, Wendell," he called out, barely containing his anticipation and glee. "Have you noticed anything peculiar so far?"

Wendell glanced at both Dogan and Isaacs, but neither showed any interest in Wendell's answer. Even Dr. Hanson seemed more concerned in hearing himself speak.

"For all the research the oil companies did here, it looks as though they made a major error in classifying the rock formations. It doesn't really surprise me—you said they weren't here looking for rocks. Still, they thought all these formations were the result of normal tectonic shifts—that these were normal terrestrial rocks."

There was a pause.

"And that's not the case?"

"No, these are aquatic rocks. The entire island is full of them."

"And how do you account for so many aquatic rocks on an island, Wendell?"

"Lowering water levels, increased volcanic activity. The normal shifts of planetary mass. It's unusual for something so large to be pushed up from the ocean, but the Arctic island clusters have always had some unique attributes."

Dr. Hanson nodded sagely before catching his breath to speak.

Wendell noticed that the dribble from Hanson's nose was opaque as it slowly froze.

"These islands have always had a sense of mystery about them. The Inuit don't come here, which is strange enough, but they have a name for these clusters: *alomerk*. It means 'the deep land.' I don't know where that term comes from, but some claim it has survived from the days when the island was still submerged."

"That would mean either Melville Island only surfaced sometime in the last ten thousand years, or—"

"Or there was intelligent life in the Arctic two hundred million years before it showed up anywhere else on the planet."

"But that's impossible!" Dogan interrupted, startling Wendell. He looked just as confused. Dr. Hanson merely laughed excitedly.

"Yes, it's the worst kind of lazy science, isn't it? I wouldn't put too much stock in it."

They fell back into a single line quickly: Dr. Hanson leading the way, then Dogan, Wendell, Isaacs, and finally the pilot, Gauthier. Wendell made a concerted effort to keep close to the front so he might hear anything Dogan and Dr. Hanson discussed, but the sound of their footsteps on the snow had a deafening and delirious effect—at times he hallucinated more sounds than could be possible. The constant crunch made him lightheaded, a problem exacerbated by the cold that worked at his temples.

But it was Isaacs who suffered the worst. Periodically, Wendell checked to see how far behind his fellow student had fallen, and to ensure he hadn't vanished altogether. Yet Isaacs was always there, only a few feet back, fidgeting and scanning the landscape. Gauthier likely kept him in place. The two made quite a sight, and Wendell was amused by how little Gauthier did to conceal his contempt. Isaacs was a frightened rabbit in a cage. Gauthier, the snarling wolf beyond the lock.

"This feels wrong," Isaacs whined, and Wendell did his best to pretend he hadn't heard him. It did not dissuade Isaacs from continuing. "You can't tell me this feels right to you guys. You can't tell me you guys don't feel everything closing in."

Wendell glanced back. It was reassuring to see that even an expensive jacket couldn't prevent Isaacs from being ravaged by the weather—his eyes bulged, his color was pale.

"Isaacs, look around. There's not a wall or anything in sight. Nothing to box you in. The idea you feel confined—"

"I feel it, too."

Nothing about Gauthier's face betrayed that he'd spoken. Nevertheless, Wendell slowed to close the distance between them. Isaacs did the same, eyes wide and eager.

"What are you talking about?"

"Don't you feel it?" Isaacs said. "I feel it all over my body. I don't like being here alone."

"You aren't alone. There are five of us, plus a plane. And Gauthier has a satellite phone, just in case. The only thing boxing you in is all your protection. You're practically surrounded."

"Then why are we so alone? Where are all the animals?"

"They were probably on the shore. Gauthier, we saw some birds or something when we flew over, right?"

The pilot shook his head slowly. It spooked Wendell nearly as much as Isaacs had.

"Well, I'm sure there are animals around. They're probably hiding from us because they're afraid."

"I don't have a good feeling about this, Wendell," Isaacs said. "I don't have a good feeling about this at all. We should get back on the plane and go."

"Wait, did Dogan put you guys up to this?"

The look of surprise did not seem genuine, though it was hard to be certain. Wendell wanted to press further, but he heard Dr. Hanson's voice.

"Wendell! Isaacs! Come, you must see this!"

Wendell turned to the men before him. They looked confused.

When the three reached Dr. Hanson and the visibly uncomfortable Dogan, Wendell didn't immediately understand what the concern was. Before them lay ice, just as it lay everywhere. Dr. Hanson smiled, but it held no warmth. It was thin and quivering and echoed his uneasy eyes.

"Do you see it? Right there. On the ground. Where my foot is."

There was only ice. Wendell kneeled to get a better look, but a pair of iron hands grabbed him and yanked him back to his feet. He stumbled as Gauthier set him down.

"Don't," was all the pilot said.

"Are you really that much of an idiot?" Dogan asked, and Wendell felt once again the butt of some foul trick. Had it not been for Dr. Hanson's distinct lack of humor, Wendell might have stormed off into the snow. Instead, he tamped his irritation and looked again.

He wasn't certain how long it took, but slowly what the rest had seen resolved. Isaacs, too, spotted it before Wendell, serenading them with a litany of "oh, no," repeated over and over. Dr. Hanson tried to help by asking everyone to back away, while Wendell wondered why no one simply told him what he was missing.

Then he realized it wasn't him who was missing something but someone else, because trapped beneath the sheet of ice was what could only be a severed human finger.

The flesh was pale, verging on white, and beneath the clouded surface it was barely visible. Wendell inspected the hands of the party to be sure it hadn't come from any of them.

"I don't like this. I don't like this at all."

"It's not going to leap out and grab you, Isaacs. Get a grip on yourself."

"But where did it come from? Dr. Hanson, could it have come from Dr. Lansing's party? You said they were here for a few days. Why else would they have left after finding only those three small ichthyosaur bones?"

"I asked Dr. Lansing that very question, Wendell. He simply responded by asking me how many bones beyond three I thought would be necessary to collect to prove his point. Five? Ten? Fifty? He said all he felt necessary were three to prove ichthyosaurs travelled this far north. I'll grant you: that makes little sense, but that's Dr. Lansing for you. Even he, however, wouldn't be foolish enough to waste time poring over this discovery. More than likely, it was due to some accident involving the oil men here before us. There's nothing we can do for the fellow that lost it, and we have more important discoveries to dig up, discoveries beside which this will ultimately pale. Let's march on. We still have a journey ahead of us."

Dr. Hanson resumed walking, Dogan trotting after him. Isaacs looked as though he was going to be sick, but before he could Gauthier shoved him.

"Keep moving. Standing too long in the open like this isn't a good idea. You never know what's watching."

Wendell looked around, but all he saw were hills of ice in every direction. If anything was watching, he had no idea where it might be hiding.

Wendell couldn't stop thinking about the finger as they continued on. Maybe it was the sound of their footsteps, or the dark beneath his parka's hood, but he felt increasingly isolated from the group, and as they travelled he became further ensnared in thought. He'd never seen a severed body part before, and though it barely looked real beneath the ice, it still made him uncomfortable. Someone had come to Melville Island and not only lost a finger but decided to leave without it. How was that possible? Wendell shivered and tried to get his mind on other less morbid things. Like water.

Water is the world's greatest sculptor. It is patient, careful, persistent, and over countless years it is capable of carving the largest canyons out of the hardest rock. Who knew how long it took to carve the shapes that surrounded the five of them as they walked? It was like a bizarre art gallery, full of strange smooth sculptures that few had ever seen. Wendell reached into his pocket and fished out his digital camera. As he snapped numerous photos, he realized he was the only one doing so. Dr. Hanson barely slowed his pace to acknowledge the formations, and the sight of the towering rocks left Isaacs further terrorized.

"Do you have to take pictures? Can't we just keep going?"

"Dr. Hanson said to document everything."

"Then why didn't you take one of that finger?"

It was a fair point. Why hadn't he taken that photograph?

"It's not really part of the history of Melville Island, or the life that was here, is it?"

Isaacs shrugged, then spun around like an animal suddenly aware of a predator. Wendell stepped back.

"What is it?"

Isaacs took a deep breath, then exhaled slowly.

"Nothing. I guess."

He wanted to say more, but despite Wendell's prodding Isaacs remained quiet.

They trudged along the ice, keeping their heads down as they followed Dr. Hanson. He had studied the maps for months and was certain that their best bet was to set up base camp about twenty-five miles in. From that point, they could radiate their survey outward and see what they might discover.

Wendell wondered, though, if it wouldn't have been better to remain nearer the shoreline where remnants of a water-dwelling dinosaur might be more evident. He kept his opinion private, not wanting to contradict a man capable of ending his career before it started. Which was why Wendell was both surprised and irritated when Dogan posed the same question. And even more so when he heard Dr. Hanson's response.

"Good question, Dogan. I like that you're thinking. It shows a real spark your fellow team could learn from. However, in this case you haven't thought things through. Don't forget that during the Mesozoic area we're most interested in the Earth had yet to fully cool. Melville Island was more tropical than it is now. The greatest concentration of vertebrates will likely be farther inland.

It shouldn't take us more than a few more hours to get there."

The thought of travelling a few more hours made Wendell's body ache. The cold had already seeped through his insulated boots and the two layers of socks he wore inside them.

"Maybe we could stop and rest for a second? I don't know how much longer I can carry this gear." As Wendell spoke the words, his pack's weight doubled in tacit agreement.

"I suppose it couldn't hurt," Dr. Hanson said, and Wendell wasted no time slipping the burden off his shoulders. Immediately relieved, he then sat on the snow to give his tired feet a rest. Dr. Hanson, Isaacs, and Dogan all followed his lead. Only Gauthier remained standing, one hand on his belt, the other in his frozen beard. He looked across the horizon while the others used the moment to eat protein bars and contemplate what had led them to their seats at the top of the world.

It had been days, and overfamiliarity combined with sheer exhaustion was enough to keep them quiet. No one spoke or glanced another's way. They simply kept their heads down and tried to recuperate before the next leg of the journey. Dr. Hanson's eyes were wide as he plotted their next steps. Isaacs experienced jitters, which continued to multiply as the group remained stationary. Dogan, however, was the opposite. With eyes closed and arms wrapped around his legs, he appeared to have fallen asleep. Until Gauthier delivered a swift kick to his ribs.

"What was—?"

The pilot shushed him quickly. Dogan, to Wendell's astonishment, complied.

"Did any of you see that?"

They all turned. Around them was the vast icy expanse, wind pushing clouds over the snow-encrusted tundra, eddies dancing across the rough terrain. But Wendell saw nothing different from what he'd already witnessed. A glance at the other men revealed the same confusion. Wendell looked at the towering Gauthier, waiting for the answer to the question before them, but the pilot was silent. He merely continued to stare. Isaacs could not bear it.

"What? What do you see?"

"Shut up," Gauthier hissed, and Isaacs cowered, his breathing uneven. Dr. Hanson flashed an expression that was buried so quickly Wendell didn't have time to process it.

Gauthier raised his arm and pointed away from where they had been walking, off into the distant vastness that flanked them.

"I think something's been tracking us."

"What do you mean?"

"I mean I've been watching while you four were stumbling along, and I saw something—a shadow, keeping pace with us. It's been there ever since we left the runway."

"Where is it?"

"There. Do you see it? In the distance. It's not moving now. Just a shadow. Watching us."

Wendell squinted, but still saw nothing.

"It's likely a polar bear," Dr. Hanson said. "I've been warned they come to the island, looking for seal. No doubt he knows we're here."

"Should we be worried?" Isaacs asked.

"It's not going to come after us," Dogan said. Dr. Hanson was more hesitant.

"Well, I don't know if I'd go that far. But there's enough of us that it should keep its distance."

That failed to reassure Wendell. And if he wasn't reassured, then Isaacs—

"So you're saying a polar bear is following us, and we shouldn't be worried? Nothing to worry about at all?"

"It's okay, Isaacs. You'll be okay. Gauthier, tell them not to worry."

"Don't worry. It's moving now. It looks too small to be a polar bear anyway. Probably just a pack of wolves."

It wasn't long before they were moving again.

* * *

They successfully made it to the camp site without further report of being trailed. The lack did nothing to calm Isaac's nerves, but Dogan reverted to his old ways, insinuating himself between Dr. Hanson and Wendell any time they might have had a moment to speak. It was infuriating.

The five of them had been awake and travelling for well over twenty hours, and as far as Wendell could tell the sun had not moved an inch. The clouds, however, were not so bound, and he suspected their speed had as much to do with Hanson's decision to camp down as did the coordinates Dr. Lansing had provided him. The last thing Wendell wanted to do when they finally stopped walking was set up the tent, but Gauthier helped them all find the motivation through the promotion of fear.

"The way this wind is breaking? There are storms brewing ahead, somewhere beyond the ridges. The weather here is unpredictable. If we don't get cover and fast, we might not be around long enough for you four to start digging up bones. Get ready for what's coming."

"But what *is* coming?" Dogan asked. Gauthier laughed.

"A storm, man. A storm."

In the time it took to tell them, thick smoke-like clouds had rolled across the clear sky, casting a long shadow across the top of the world. Somehow, from somewhere, the men found the energy to erect their shelter, and Wendell silently admitted it felt good to have Dogan as an ally for once.

The storm arrived as the last peg was hammered in place. The five of them huddled beneath the tarpaulin tent, one of the tall water-carved rocks acting as both anchor and partial shield from the winds. Inside the enclosed space their heat quickly escalated, but Gauthier warned them to keep their coats on in case the wind wrenched the tent from the ground.

Strangely, Isaacs was the most at peace during the ordeal. While Dogan and Wendell held down the edges of the tent, their knuckles white, Isaacs had his eyelids closed and head tilted back to rest on his shoulders. He sat cross-legged, his body moving with the slightest sway. Wendell thought he also heard him humming, but convinced himself it was only the wind bending around the sheltering rocks.

They stayed hunkered for hours, wind howling outside, pulling at the thin barrier of canvas standing between them. The sound of it rippling back and forth was a terrifying thunder, and even after hours enduring it, the noise did not become any less so. Each clap was an icy knife in Wendell's spine, and as he shook under the tremendous stress he used every ounce of will he had within him to maintain his rationality and tamp down his fear. Deep breaths, slow, long, continued until the knot inside his chest slackened. It was only when he felt he could look again at his fellow captives without screaming that he dared. Isaacs remained blissfully distant, his mind cracked, and he was simply gone from it to another place. Gauthier and Dr. Hanson spoke among themselves, planning and debating the next course of action, all at a volume that was drowned by the howls and ripples. Only Dogan noticed Wendell, and the scowl across his face suggested that whatever truce the circumstances had negotiated for them was fleeting at best. He stared directly at Wendell with a stubbly, twisted face and did not bother to look away when Wendell caught him, as though he wore his disgust with pride. Wendell took a breath to speak and tasted the most noxious air. Dogan shook his twisted face, but it was no use; the fetid odor filled their lungs. Wendell covered his nose and mouth with his gloved hand. Whatever it was, it was sickly and bitter and smelled not unlike dead fish.

Outside there was a long sorrowful howl that sounded so near their shelter that Wendell prayed desperately it was only the wind echoing between the stones.

Sleep did wonders for Wendell's demeanor, and when he emerged from the battered shelter a few hours later he stepped into a world canopied by a cloudless sky punctuated at the horizon by a single glowing orb. Gauthier was already awake, and Wendell found him prepping their equipment, beads of moisture frozen in his unkempt beard. He did not look pleased. Something was wrong.

It was only once outside the tent Wendell noticed it—something in the post-storm air, some excess of electricity, or maybe a remnant of the foul odor that stained his clothes. Whatever it was, it was troubling.

Dr. Hanson emerged a few minutes afterward with an eagerness to meet the glaciers head-on.

"You're up early. Good man! Why don't you hand me one of those coffees?"

Isaacs, too, joined them, and when the thick-set Dogan finally emerged from the tent, the look on his face upon seeing the rest of the team gathered made Wendell certain any ground gained the night before had been lost. Dogan was the same man he'd always been, and Wendell did his best to deal with it. He was frankly too tired to keep caring.

"After we've made our breakfast," Dr. Hanson said, blind to the turmoil of the students around him, "let's start our search for some ichthyosaur fossils. Right now, we are most concerned with locating those."

"Dr. Hanson?" Isaacs said.

"We should start at those ridges." Dogan pointed into the distance opposite, where a slightly elevated ring circled the land. "Water would have receded soonest from those areas, leaving the earliest and most complete fossils for us to find."

"Good thinking, Dogan. I applaud that."

"Dr. Hanson?" Isaacs repeated.

Dogan may have gotten the Doctor's attention, but Wendell was not going to be outdone.

"Maybe, Dr. Hanson, we should use a grid pattern closer to where Dr. Lansing and his students made their discovery? I mean, it makes sense to me to start with a known quantity and radiate from there."

Dogan shot Wendell a look, and Dr. Hanson laughed at them. "Both good ideas, men, but don't worry. I already have a plan. You see, based on my expectations, the fossil—"

"Dr. Hanson?"

Hanson sighed.

"Please don't interrupt me, Isaacs."

"Dr. Hanson? Can you come look at this?" Isaacs was kneeling by the tent, staring into the ground.

Immediately, Wendell was certain it was another finger. Another pale white digit trapped beneath the ice. Or perhaps it was a whole hand. Something else lost for which there could be no reasonable explanation. Dogan approached, as did Gauthier, both alongside Dr. Hanson. Wendell remained where he was, worried about what they would find, though their faces suggested it wasn't anything as mortally frightening as a severed finger. But it was also clear no one knew if it was far worse. Wendell hesitated but approached Dr. Hanson, his heavy boots crunching the ice underfoot. When he reached the four men, any conversation between them had withered.

Something impossible was caught in the tangle of boot prints surrounding the tent: an additional set of tracks in the crushed and broken snow. They differed from the team's in size—they were smaller, hardly larger than a child's, and each long toe of the bare foot could clearly be traced.

"Is it possible some kind of animal made them?"

"No," Dr. Hanson said. "These are too close to hominid."

"They *can't* be, though. Can they?"

"I thought this island was deserted."

"More importantly, what was it doing standing here in front of our tent?"

"I don't like this," Isaacs said. For once, Wendell agreed with him.

"Dr. Hanson, what's going on?"

"I wish I knew, Wendell. Gauthier, what do you think?"

Gauthier looked at them over his thick beard. It was the first time Wendell had seen puzzlement in the pilot's eyes. Gauthier looked at each of them in turn as they waited for him to offer an explanation, but he had none to offer. Instead, he turned away with a furrowed brow.

"Where is everything?"

Wendell didn't initially understand what he meant, not until he walked into the center of the camp. He looked back and forth and into the distance, then pushed the insulated hood off his head.

"It's all gone. Everything."

It had happened while they slept. Someone or something had come into the camp and stolen all their food and most of their supplies.

Things became scrambled. The men spoke all at once, worried about what had happened and what it might mean. Wendell was no different, a manic desperation for answers taking hold. Dr. Hanson did his best to calm them all, but the red rims around his eyes made it clear he too was shaken.

"I don't understand it," he repeated. "There aren't supposed to be any visitors here beyond us."

"It looks as if you were wrong. There *is* someone here. Someone who's been following us."

It sounded crazy, and Wendell fought to keep from falling down that rabbit hole. Perversely, Dogan was the one Wendell looked to for strength, and only because he could imagine nothing worse than falling apart in front of him. Isaacs on the other hand suffered no such worries. He was nearly incapacitated by terror.

"We can't stay here. Didn't you guys hear it? Last night? That muffled creaking? And the crunch—I thought it was something else. I thought it had to be. It couldn't have been footsteps, but all I see on the ground are thousands of them, and all our stuff has vanished. We can't stay. We have to go. We have to go before it's too late."

"Calm down. Nobody's going anywhere," Dr. Hanson said. "This expedition is a one-time event. It took all the grant money to send us here. If we don't bring back something, we will never return to Melville Island."

"Good," Isaacs said, his whole body shaking. "We shouldn't be here. There's something wrong."

Dr. Hanson scoffed, but Wendell wasn't certain he agreed. Dogan certainly seemed as though he didn't, but said nothing. After the journey they'd taken and what they'd seen, they had to trust Dr. Hanson knew what to do.

But what he did was turn to Gauthier for an answer, only to receive none. The pilot was more interested in sizing up Isaacs. When he finally spoke, it startled all of them. Isaacs almost screamed.

"The kid is right. We can't stay here. Even if we wanted to. Our supplies and rations are gone. We wouldn't last more than a few days."

Dr. Hanson shook his head. Wendell could see he was frustrated. Scared, tired, and frustrated.

"I told you: we can't go back. This is it. There's no time to spare, not even a few days. Not if we're to complete our tasks in the window. We have to stay here."

"Do we *all* need to be here, Doctor?" Dogan asked. His voice wavered with uncertainty.

Dr. Hanson hesitated a moment. "No," he said, "I expect not. At least, not all of us."

Dogan looked directly at Wendell. Wendell swallowed, outsmarted, and prepared himself for the inevitable. Instead, Dogan surprised him.

"Send Gauthier back to replenish our supplies while we stay here and work. It's only a few days. We can hold out that long, but we can't go on forever without food."

"Maybe Isaacs should join him," Wendell added, nodding when Dogan looked over. "He sounds on the verge of cracking, and for his sake as well as ours he should be off this rock if he does."

"Yes, we should go. Can we go? Can we?" Isaacs looked ready to swallow Gauthier. His bug-eyed face was slick and pallid, and Wendell wondered if Isaacs was too sick to travel. Then he wondered if it might be worse if he stayed.

Dr. Hanson did not seem entirely convinced. None of them did. None but Isaacs. Wendell had to admit, thinking about the strange footprints in the snow outside the tent, he wasn't sure if he'd rather be the one leaving.

"Maybe we should vote?" Dogan said.

"No point," Gauthier said. "I'm leaving. The kid can come if he wants."

Isaacs looked as if he were going to dance. Hanson nodded solemnly while Dogan said nothing. Wendell wasn't sure what he felt.

They split what little food they had left among them before Gauthier and Isaacs loaded their packs and left. There were six energy bars, a bag of peanuts, and four flasks of water. The two men took only half a bar each—as little as they could to get them back to the landing strip while Wendell, Dogan, and Dr. Hanson kept the rest to help them last until the plane returned.

"I want you to get back here as soon as you can," Dr. Hanson said. "We can't afford to be down this many men for long."

"We'll be back as soon as we can," Gauthier said, then handed Dr. Hanson a small leather bag. "Take this. In case of emergency."

Dr. Hanson looked in the bag and shook his head.

The two men waved at them as they started back—Isaacs nearly bouncing on the ice, while Gauthier's gait remained resolutely determined. They passed the tall, smooth rocks without trouble, and the crunch of their boots on the icy snow faded quickly once they were out of sight. The three remaining men stood in uncomfortable silence. Wendell worried they had made a grave mistake.

"I'm sure they'll be back before we know it." Dr. Hanson tried to sound upbeat and reassuring; Wendell wondered if he was as unconvinced as he sounded. "But in the interim, we have the equipment, and we're at the primary site. I know the situation is not as fortunate as we would have liked, but let's see how much we can get done before Gauthier gets back. We are here for another three days, so let's take the time to gather the information necessary to salvage this expedition."

The three of them trekked out from the base camp on Dr. Hanson's suggestion despite all they'd seen, right into the bleakness of Melville Island. Trapped, they needed something to occupy their minds, distract them from disturbing sights like the severed finger, like the worrying sea of bodies that had mysteriously surrounded them as they slept. The only thing the three could do was resume their search for the elusive evidence of ichthyosaurs in the Arctic Ocean. They spent what hours remained in the day scouting those locations Dr. Hanson highlighted, turning over rocks, chipping through ice and permafrost, doing their best without tools, a researcher, and a pilot. And with each hour that passed they discovered nothing, no sign of the ichthyosaurs they were certain had once swam there. Dr. Hanson grew increasingly quiet as he brimmed with frustration, and Wendell decided to stay out of his way until they finally retreated to the base camp. Dogan, however, was the braver man. Or more foolish.

"Dr. Hanson, I have to tell you, I'm concerned."

"Oh, are you? What could possibly concern you?"

Dogan didn't hesitate.

"I'm concerned for our safety. I'm concerned our emergency transportation has left, that we're undermanned, and that neither Wendell nor I truly have any idea where we are. We're just following you blindly. I'm worried about our safety."

"Well, don't be, Dogan. Let us return to the base camp. We will reassess our plans there. Perhaps you and Wendell can help determine our next course of action. There is something on Melville Island worth finding no matter what the cost. I intend to stay until we do."

But when they finally reached the base camp they discovered what that cost was. It had vanished. Along with it, any trace of their presence, including their footprints. It was as though they had never been there.

"Are you sure this is the right place?"

"Of course I'm certain. Don't you recognize the shape of rocks? Or the nook we used for shelter? This is most certainly the right place."

The three stood watching the snow for a few minutes, as though the sheer force of their collective will would make the camp re-materialize, and when that too failed to yield results Dogan sat down on the snow, spent, a heavy-browed doll whose strings had been cut.

"Maybe we should go back to the landing strip," Wendell suggested. "Gauthier and Isaacs may not have left yet."

Dr. Hanson shook his head. "We've barely begun, we can't leave."

"But, Dr. Hanson, our camp—look around us. We can't stay here. Whatever it is that's—"

"Enough!" Dogan said, struggling to his feet with a concerning wobble. "I'm not waiting to be hunted by whatever is out there. At least at the landing strip, we'll be ready to leave once Gauthier gets back. I don't give a shit about ichthyosaurs or Mesozoic migration patterns or just when the hell Melville Island formed. All I want right now is to get off this iceberg and back to civilization where it's safe. And Wendell, I'm betting you feel exactly the same. So, are you coming or not?"

Wendell liked neither solution. Dogan was right: staying seemed like idiocy—something was watching them, stealing from them, and had left them for dead. And yet, his solution made no sense. How did he know whatever was following them wouldn't track them to the landing strip? How did he know when or even if Gauthier would be back to rescue them? Wendell wasn't convinced, but to blindly ignore what he had seen so far and continue to explore Melville Island with the same willful ignorance as Dr. Hanson seemed ludicrous.

"All I know is that whatever we do, we can't stay here. We need to keep moving."

"I don't think the two of you understand the importance of what we are doing here, or the costs involved. This is not simply a trip to the shopping mall. This is not something easily aborted. We must stay and complete our expedition. We have found nothing so far to justify the cost, and without that we will never be granted the opportunity to return. My tenure at the university will shield me from losing my position, but likely I'll never complete my work. Isaacs, he'll get by on his father's wealth, but the two of you? Your careers will be irrevocably damaged. Your graduate studies will have become a waste. This is the moment. This is the place where you both have to decide your respective futures. I already know what needs to be done. I implore you both to stay with me and discover those secrets hidden long before man's eyes could witness them. Stay with me and discover the true history of the world."

But Dogan wouldn't. And Wendell reluctantly concurred.

The three men split what remained of the food and set a timeline for Dr. Hanson's research. They agreed that he would keep trying to contact Gauthier via the satellite phone the pilot had given him, and when he got through he would let Gauthier know that both Dogan and Wendell had returned to the landing strip, and what his own coordinates were so the party could return to meet him. If before then anything should occur that might suggest Dr. Hanson was still being followed, he would immediately set out for the landing strip and join the two men there. Wendell didn't like the idea of leaving him alone, especially with little more than a half an energy bar and overburdened with excavation equipment, but there was no choice. Hanson insisted on completing the expedition, no matter what the cost.

Dogan, on the other hand, was not so committed. He and Wendell took the rest of the food and began their long hike back. Clearly, it wasn't lost on Dogan that he had chosen to retreat with his worst enemy; Wendell certainly felt no better about it.

The trek across Melville Island was as quiet as it had been the first time, the two men walking single file over the uneven terrain. But Wendell's dread made the journey much worse. They had been numbered five before, not two, and they hadn't carried the suspicion they were being stalked by a predator. On the occasions the two men stopped to rest, they didn't speak, sharing an overwhelming fear of what was happening. Wendell hoped if they remained silent the entire trip would simply be a hazy dream, one from which he'd soon awake. But he didn't.

His stomach rumbled after the second hour of their journey, and the sourness on his tongue arrived after the fourth. His head ached dully, letting him know his body was winding down. Dogan, too, seemed to be having trouble concentrating on the direction they were supposed to go, and more than once he stopped to ask if Wendell wanted to take the lead while he plotted their next steps.

They took a rest after a few hours to eat a portion of their reserves. It seemed so little once Wendell saw it through the eyes of hunger, and it took immense willpower to keep from swallowing it all. He was exhausted, and Dogan looked no different, his eyes rimmed with dark circles against pale skin. His voice, too, was throated.

"Who would have thought it would be you and me, trying to keep it together?"

Wendell wanted to laugh, but just wheezed air.

"I don't think anyone would believe it if we told them."

"I'm not sure I believe it myself."

And like that, things had changed between them. Wendell didn't know how long it would last, or if it would survive their return to civilization, but at that moment they were bonded, and Wendell would have done anything to keep Dogan at his side.

It was unclear how long they sat, silently building their strength for the journey ahead, but their stupor was broken by an unsettling howl. Dogan and Wendell straightened, eyes wide and searching the landscape in all directions for its source.

"There!" Dogan shouted, and went off running toward the sound, his feet sinking into snow as he dashed, his limbs flailing for balance. Wendell followed blindly in Dogan's footsteps, hand pressed against his pack to ensure nothing was spilled. When he finally caught up, both he and Dogan were panting, barely able speak.

"What did you see?"

Dogan pointed.

There was nothing there, but that wasn't what caused Wendell to shiver uncontrollably. It was instead what *had* been there, and the evidence it left in the crusted snow—a flurry of footprints, none larger than a barefooted child's. They proceeded in a line, leading back in the same direction from which Wendell and Dogan had come, as though whoever or whatever had made them had been keeping a steady watch on the two students since they left Dr. Hanson. It was no longer possible to avoid the truth: something was following them, something that wasn't a wolf or polar bear or any other northern predator. It was something else, and they knew absolutely nothing about it.

"What are we going to do?" Wendell asked. Dogan's eyes teared from the cold.

"What else *can* we do? We get the hell out of here right now."

They didn't stop until they reached the landing strip, both afraid of what might happen if they rested too long. By Wendell's watch it was well past midnight, though the frozen sunlight still shone, lighting their way. When they arrived, they found the strip vacant. No plane, no sign of life. Just a long stretch of iced snow and an ocean off in the distance. Wendell couldn't explain why the discovery was crushing—Gauthier and Isaacs had over a day's head start, and Wendell knew they wouldn't have waited. And yet it was devastating. He and Dogan had walked so far . . .

"On the bright side," Dogan said, "we know they found their way back. That means they'll be returning soon. It's better than finding them stranded like us."

"True, true."

Wendell looked back at the snow and ice they had walked across. There were shadows moving out in the nooks and recesses, but none that seemed unusual. Wendell wondered what an unusual shadow would even look like, and whether he was in any condition to find out.

"We need cover. Who knows how long we'll be waiting."

There was a depression in an ice drift that shielded them from the brunt of the wind and snow. Their combined body heat warmed the air enough to diminish the chill under their jackets, and Wendell was able to peel back the farthest fringes of his hood so he might speak to Dogan without shouting. It had been so long since their last snack, simply raising his voice aggravated his headache.

"Do you think Dr. Hanson is okay?"

"If anyone would be, I'd bet on him. That old man is resilient."

"I'm not sure we should have left him, though."

"He wanted us to."

"I know, I know. I just feel it was a mistake."

Wendell closed his eyes to rest them. The brightness of the snow after being under a hood for so long was blinding. It would take some time to adjust.

"Did you get a good look at it?" Dogan asked.

"At what? The snow?"

"No, not the snow, you idiot. What was following us in the snow. What left those footprints."

"I don't want to talk about it." He didn't even want to *think* about it. Dogan wouldn't be dissuaded.

"I'm sure I was close to it, but I barely saw anything more than a blur."

"Maybe you were seeing things. Maybe your hunger—"

"Did you, or didn't you, see those footprints in the snow?"

"I—"

"Do you think I put them there?"

"No, I—"

"Did you put them there?"

"How would I—?"

"Well, they got there somehow. Just like they got inside our camp. It wasn't an accident. It was something, watching us."

Wendell took off his mitten glove and rubbed the side of his face. It made him feel better, and slightly more present. "I don't know, Dogan. It so hard to think. I'm tired and hungry and terrified of what's out there and of never getting back home. My brain feels like mush."

"How much food do you have?"

He opened his pockets and turned out what was left. An eighth of a power bar, a handful of nuts. His water supply was okay, but only because he and Dogan had been filling their flasks with snow to melt.

Dogan assessed the situation.

"Yeah, I don't have much more than that, either."

"Are you worried?"

"About being here?" He frowned. "No. I'm sure Gauthier will be back."

"How can you be so sure?"

He shrugged.

"What else do I have to do?"

Wendell eventually fell asleep. He and Dogan had huddled close to conserve heat, and when they both ran out of energy to talk Wendell's eyes flickered one too many times. There was the sound of the ocean, and the wind rushing past, and then nothing until Dogan shook him awake.

"Look."

The snow had accumulated since they took shelter, and the footprints they had made were buried, but Wendell could still see the wedge cut into the corridor down which they'd come, and in the distance a solitary figure staggering toward them.

"Is that Dr. Hanson?" Wendell worried he was suffering from a starved hallucination.

"I don't know."

"Is it what's been following us?"

Dogan didn't respond.

Whether from hunger or cold or exhaustion, Wendell's eyes teared as he watched the limping figure. His muscles ached, trying to tense in anticipation but too exhausted to do so. The approaching shape resolved itself first for Dogan, who made an audible noise a moment before Wendell realized what—or rather whom—he was seeing. Isaacs stumbled forward, and a few steps before meeting Dogan and Wendell he crumpled and dropped to his knees, then collapsed face-first into the frozen snow.

They scrambled to him as quickly as their tired bodies could manage. Isaacs was nearly lifeless, his left leg bent at an angle that suggested it was broken, but leaning close Wendell could hear his shallow breathing. They wasted no time dragging Isaacs back to their shielded depression, and while Wendell did his best to splint the leg, Dogan brushed the remaining snow from Isaacs's face and pulled up his hood to help protect him.

"What do you think happened?" Dogan quietly asked.

"What do you mean?"

"He looks strange. What's up with his *eyes*?"

Wendell shook his head.

"I'm more concerned about what he is doing on Melville Island at all."

Isaacs breathed heavily as he lay unconscious. They shook him and called his name, worried about what had happened, but neither Dogan nor Wendell understood what he mumbled. There was something about a plane, which did not ease Wendell's worry.

When they were finally able to rouse him, Isaacs screamed. The piercing sound overloaded Dogan's starved brain and he lashed out, striking Isaacs in the face. Then Wendell was between them, urging both to calm down. Isaacs shook, pulled the straps of his hood tighter, hid his face. All that was left were his large watery eyes.

"Isaacs, it's okay. You're okay. I'm sorry I hit you, but you're safe. Do you understand?"

He was a trapped animal, shivering uncontrollably.

"Do you understand?"

Isaacs nodded.

"What happened?" Wendell asked. "Why are you here? Where's Gauthier?"

Isaacs continued to rock, hiding behind his drawn hood.

"It's okay, Isaacs. Just tell us what happened."

"Gauthier and I made it back here to the plane," he said. Even in his semi-consciousness, he sounded terrified. "The wings were iced, he said, and we couldn't take off. He told me to go outside with a bottle of propylene glycol and spray them down after he started the plane. He said the heat and the solution would melt everything. While I was doing that the wind was blowing like crazy. I thought I heard yelling, but I wasn't sure. Then out of nowhere the plane was shaking. I lost my balance, and the plane jerked and started to move. I was falling and tried to grab hold of something, but the wing was slick and I was already rolling off it. I don't remember anything after that."

Wendell tried to make sense of Isaacs's story, but couldn't wrap his mind around it. He was exhausted, hunger and the elements taking their toll, and could barely think. He looked to Dogan, who appeared just as troubled.

"Did Gauthier say anything?" Dogan asked.

Isaacs shook his head, and it carved pain in his misshapen face. He was worsening, and there was nothing Dogan or Wendell could do. Already his lips had turned a bizarre shade of red, and his eyes could not focus. He coughed violently and spit pink into the snow. Then he lay his head down. "I can't. I—I don't want to die."

Wendell put his hand on Isaacs's shoulder.

"You aren't going to die here. We won't let you."

Isaacs coughed again.

Dogan and Wendell looked at each other. Dogan shook his head.

"We have to find Dr. Hanson. We need that satellite phone."

"We can't leave Isaacs," Wendell said. "He won't last without our help. And how are we supposed to find Dr. Hanson? We'll be dead before we do. We have no idea where he is. I think we're better off waiting right here."

They spent the next few hours trying to sleep in their makeshift shelter, the three men huddled to conserve warmth. While Dogan and Isaacs slept, the wind had become a gale, and it again brought with it the overpowering stench of fish and sea, so thick Wendell could hardly keep from gagging. He tucked his face into his coat as best he could to survive it.

The men did not sleep for long, but it was long enough that when they awoke they found Isaacs had crawled away from the safety of the depression and frozen to death. It made no sense, but nothing did any longer. The arctic cold of Melville Island had upended everything. Dogan was upset and wanted to drag Isaacs back, close enough to protect his body should anything come looking for it, but he didn't have the strength left. Neither of them did. It was then they agreed, for the sake of the fallen Isaacs, that their hunger had become too severe. But when they turned out their pockets, they found them empty. Isaacs, too, had been stripped of all food and supplies. There was nothing left to sustain them. Dogan cried, certain he'd eaten all their shares unwittingly in a somnambulistic frenzy, but Wendell wasn't convinced. It didn't explain the hazy footprints that encircled them.

Dogan and Wendell paced in the subzero weather, trudging out a trail while trying to keep themselves warm. Eventually, even the effort of pacing proved beyond Dogan, and he stumbled and toppled to the ground. Wendell knelt down but didn't have strength to help. All he could do was stay nearby.

"I can't keep going," Dogan said. "I can't."

"We have to," Wendell said.

But Wendell knew they would never make it. They started talking then to keep themselves awake and alert, to remind each other not to give up. They talked about how they came to be under Dr. Hanson. They talked about Isaacs, about whether he had crawled away on purpose, or if it was due to some horrible mistake. They talked about Gauthier and what had happened to him. But mostly they talked about themselves, their childhoods, their lives before meeting. They talked until they couldn't, until Dogan was delirious and stopped making sense. Wendell tried to rouse him, to keep him moving, but he couldn't. He didn't have the energy. So tired, he could barely keep his eyes open. They fluttered more and more until they stopped completely. Before they did, the last thing Wendell saw was something in the distance, crouching. Watching them. And then it moved.

A slap that tore off his face woke him from death. He opened his stinging eyes, and only his lethargic malnourishment prevented him from screaming. The shrunken man's face hung inches from his own. It was dark brown, as though deeply tanned, with lips grey to the point of blue. He did not tremble, though he was dressed in nothing more than a cloth that covered his sex, and he was perilously thin. What startled Wendell most, however, was his eyes. They were larger than any Wendell had ever seen, and spaced so far apart they threatened to slide off his skull. He couldn't have been more than four feet tall. Wendell was certain it wasn't a dream, but if it were it was the worst dream he'd ever suffered. He tried to moisten his mouth to get his tongue working, and when he did all he could hazily croak was, "Dogan?"

The half-man grunted, then hobbled away. Wendell wanted to pull himself up, but discovered he had been swaddled with furs. He could turn his head, but only with great difficulty, and only enough to see Dogan similarly wrapped a few meters away. Dogan had two more of the dark half-men at his head, and they were trying to feed him though he was still unconscious. Isaacs lay face down a few feet further in the snow, a fourth shrunken man holding his lifeless arm to his grey lips and sniffing. Wendell nodded at no one in particular, and as the world grew dark once more he felt he was being dragged. In his delirium, the dragging went on and on forever.

Something was wriggling in his mouth, trying to crawl down his throat. Wendell struggled awake, gagging, and managed to spit it out. A piece of unrecognizable yellow meat curled on the ice, while a short distance away those small dark half-men from his nightmare danced, their bare feet crunching on the snow. There was no longer anything binding his limbs but weakness, and he'd been left propped up next to Dogan. Both of them were awake and shaking.

Only unrecognizable pieces remained of poor Isaacs.

"I don't know what's going on, Wendell. I don't know where we are, but look." Dogan nodded his head across the ice and Wendell saw Dr. Hanson. He lay face down in the snow, unmoving, his pack beside him and torn open, equipment scattered. Wendell squinted to see if the satellite phone was still there, and in his concentration missed what Dogan was saying.

"Do you see it?" Dogan repeated.

"I think so. It's right by his hand."

"No, you idiot. Do you see *it*?"

Wendell looked up again, past Dr. Hanson and at the group of five near-naked men dancing before a shorn wall of ice. It stretched out further than the end of his sight in either direction; the break no doubt formed when tectonic plates shifted the glacier. What was uncovered was so impossible Wendell would have thought his mind had cracked had Dogan not witnessed it first.

There was a monstrous creature encased halfway in the solid ice. It had large unlidded eyes, milky white; its mouth wide and round, its scaled flesh reflecting light dully. Where its neck might have been was a ring of purplish pustules, circling the fusion of its ichthyic skull to its tendonous body. Chunked squid limbs lay outstretched, uncontrollable in its death. The air was again dominated by the overpowering odor of the sea. The shrunken men before it treated it as a god, and yet it was clear the five could not have been the ones to uncover it—with the sharpened rocks they used as tools it would have taken generations to carve that deep and that much. They peeled strips of its flesh away and ate them raw, and when they looked back at Dogan and Wendell it was suddenly evident why their features had transformed over time, their eyes grown wider, jaws shorter, skin rougher. Their fish faces stared at Wendell, expectantly. It was true he was hungry beyond imagination, but he was not so hungry that he might eat what they presented.

The sour taste and sensation of what they had previously tried to feed him returned, and he looked down. The morsel continued to writhe slowly in the snow.

"Did you—did they make you eat any?" Wendell asked, then realized Dogan had turned the palest shade. They had. Wendell feared for his life, and his sanity.

"How do I look?" Dogan managed through his chattering teeth, and Wendell lied and told him he was fine. Was Wendell imagining the flesh had already changed him, already started prying his eyes apart? Was it even possible after so small a meal? But he realized with horror that he didn't know how much Dogan had willingly eaten, nor if either of them had been force-fed in their delirium.

"Can you move?" Wendell asked, fleetingly energized by his fear. "We need to get that phone. We need to call for help."

"How? Even if we manage to get it, we'll never escape with it. We have no idea where we are. We might not even be on Melville Island anymore."

"We have to try. Maybe Gauthier has already come back and is waiting for us at the landing strip. What else can we do? End up like Dr. Hanson and bleed out in the snow? Or worse, like Isaacs, torn to pieces?"

"We should escape."

"And what then?" Wendell whispered. "Die in the snow, waiting for them to find us?"

Dogan paled.

"Did you—did you see that?"

Wendell looked up. The five dark men sat mesmerized before their dead idol.

"It moved," Dogan said. "Did you see it move?"

"It can't move. Whatever that thing is, it's dead."

"It's not dead—look, it moved again."

Wendell looked closer at Dogan's face and saw the swelling and the subtle distortion. There was no longer time to gather strength. Whatever they fed him, Dogan had eaten more than he thought. It was transforming him. Wendell did not want to suffer the same fate.

"Stay here," he said, though when he looked over he wasn't certain he'd been heard. Dogan appeared fascinated by what was trapped in the ice.

Wendell lowered himself onto his stomach and crawled toward Dr. Hanson, keeping an eye on the gathering of disciples ahead. He moved elbow-to-knee as slowly as he dared, not willing to risk being seen. The half-men were feral, and as smart as they were, they were still animals, waiting to attack anything that moved. Wendell had only one chance to get the satellite phone and figure out a way of escaping from the nightmare he and Dogan found themselves in. His hunger had not abated, but enough strength had returned that he was able to make it to Dr. Hanson's body in under ten minutes.

The tribe of half-men had not moved from around their dead idol. They bounced on their haunches, made noises like wild animals, followed imaginary movement before them with precision. What was strange, however, was that each reacted differently to what it saw, as though they did not share the same sight. One stood while another howled, the rest looking in different directions. Wendell couldn't make sense of it, and reminded himself not to try. He had to focus on that satellite phone and getting back.

He searched the body, doing his best to forget who it had been. Dr. Hanson's face had been removed—the pale flesh frozen, tiny blood icicles reaching from the pulpy mess to the ground. Wendell turned to keep from panicking and checked the pockets of Hanson's coat and everywhere he could reach for the satellite phone. But it wasn't there. Wendell rolled on his side and tried unsuccessfully to flag Dogan for help. Dogan was staring straight ahead at the impossible giant embedded in the ice, eyes open wide and spread far apart.

Dr. Hanson's pack was ripped open in the blood-soaked snow, the items within trapped in sticky ice. Wendell heard a loud creak and froze. In his mind's eye he saw himself spotted, then swarmed by ugly bodies and ripped limb from limb. But when he raised his head he found nothing had changed. The five men remained bent in supplication. Almost by accident Wendell spotted the leather pouch Gauthier had given Dr. Hanson pinned beneath the doctor's torso. Wendell managed to pry it free of the ice, then put it into his own pocket and gently eased his way back the distance to Dogan. Or what was left of Dogan.

"Come on. Let's go," Wendell whispered, but Dogan didn't respond. Wendell grabbed his wrist and tried yanking, but Dogan had become a dead-weight, staring beatifically ahead, his face transformed. Mouth agape, eyes spread apart, staring at the dead thing as though it were alive, Dogan was unblinking as tears streamed down his sweating face. Dogan, Wendell's enemy, Wendell's friend, was gone.

There would be time for grief later. Wendell reached over and put his hand on Dogan's shoulder. "Stay strong. I'll be back as soon as I can with help." Then he attempted to stand and discovered he wasn't able to do so. His legs had given up for good, buckling as Wendell put weight on them. He tried again and again, desperate to escape before it was too late, but he couldn't get up. After a few minutes, Wendell felt the sensation in his hands going, too, his control slipping away. Everything he saw took on a hazy glow, the edges of his vision crystalizing. The sky jittered, as did the snow.

Dogan wasn't the only one who'd had his unconscious hunger overfed with flesh. It was no wonder they had been left unbound at the edge of the camp and ignored. The creatures had no worry. All the damage had long been done. They simply needed to wait.

Wendell scrambled the small leather bag he had taken from Dr. Hanson's body out of his pocket. He prayed the satellite phone would be unharmed, that Gauthier had already returned and was waiting for them. If Wendell could only call him, it might not be too late for rescue. He could still escape the horrible things he was witnessing. That creature in the ice—Wendell thought he saw it move, thought he saw one of its giant milky eyes blink, even though so much of its flesh had already been stripped. It blinked, and the coils that sprouted free from the ice twitched and rolled, and a scream built inside him. But when it escaped it wasn't a scream at all but laughter. Laughter and joy. That terrified Wendell further, the joy, because it finally turned the five beasts his way. They rolled onto their haunches, staring at Wendell and his catatonic friend.

Wendell took off his glove and reached into the bag slowly to remove the phone, but what he found there was nothing of the sort. It was another kind of escape, the one thing a man like Gauthier would hand over when he was suggesting that someone protect himself. From out of the leather bag Wendell withdrew a handgun, and even in the cold wind he could smell the oiled metal.

Those five men looking agitated and more bestial than ever before. They snarled, while behind them a giant that Wendell refused to believe was alive illuminated like the sun pinned above. It filled the horizon with streaks of light, tendrils dancing from the old one's gargantuan head. It looked at the five half-men radiating in the glow. It looked at Dogan, kneeling and waiting for it to speak to him. Then it looked at Wendell and all Wendell's hunger was satiated; he was at one with everything.

But he knew it was a lie. It was the end of things, no matter what the disembodied voices told him. The five shrunken men approaching him stealthily on all fours would not return him to civilization, would not return him to health. Dogan and he would be something more to them—sustenance in the cold harshness of the Arctic, pieces of flesh chewed and swallowed, digits shorn until they rained on the snow. These things were much like Wendell, in a way. Much like everyone. They struggled to unearth what they worshipped most, something from a world long ago gone, and if remembered, then only barely and as a fantasy. But it was far more real than Wendell had ever wished.

Those subhuman things were closing in, and there was little else Wendell could do but surrender to them, let them take him away.

Or he could use Gauthier's gun.

He lifted the weapon and squeezed the trigger. The half-men scattered, but not before he put two of them down. The alien's appendages flailed madly, and waves of emotion and nausea washed over Wendell. He couldn't stand, but was eventually able to hit the remaining three as they scrambled for cover. It took no time at all for him to be the last man alive, surrounded by the blood and gore of everyone he knew. Everyone but the mesmerized Dogan.

It was too late for either of them. Even with the half-men dead, Wendell could feel the draw of the flickering creature in the ice, and knew he would be unable to resist much longer. In an act of charity and compassion, he raised the gun to Dogan's temple and squeezed the trigger. There was a bright flash, and a report that continued to echo over the landscape longer than in his ears. Dogan crumpled, the side of his head vaporized, his misery tangible in the air.

But it was not enough. That thing in the ice, it needed him, needed somebody's worship on which to feed, and as long as Wendell was alive it would not die.

Wendell put the gun against his own head, the hot barrel searing his flesh, but he could do nothing else. His fingers would not move, locked into place from fear or exhaustion or self-preservation. Or whatever it was that had been fed to him, pulling the flesh on his face tighter. Somehow the handgun fell from his weakened grasp, dropping onto the icy snow and sinking. He reached to reclaim it and toppled forward, collapsing in a heap that left him staring into those giant old milky eyes.

Wendell didn't know how long he lay in the snow. He was no longer cold, was no longer hungry. He felt safe, as though he might sleep forever. The old one in the ice spoke to him, telling him things about the island's eonic history, and he listened and watched and waited. Existence moved so slowly Wendell saw the sun finally creep across the sky. No one came for him. No one came to interrupt his communion with the dead god. All he had was what was forever in its milky white stare, while it ate the flesh and muscle and sinew of his body, transforming him into the first of its new earthly congregation.

Dwelling on the Past

The teenaged girl on the Tim Hortons night shift had seen it. "They fucking drove it right down Argyle," she said, her maroon cap askew, shirt unbuttoned one button too many against company code. She wore too much makeup, and it sparkled under the drab lights. Harvey noticed her upper lip was pierced, and she wore a tiny white jewel in it. Emily would never be that age.

"You tell the cops?"

She snorted. "Why the fuck would I tell those stupid fucks? They've just been standing around watching the fucking protests without doing anything. Too fucking lazy to care."

Harvey nodded and tried not to look at her. "Probably. You sure that's where the digger went?"

"Fuck, yeah. Me and Cheryl went outside and watched them stop singing long enough to move the fucking blocks off the road. Then, as soon as they were done, they fucking moved them back."

She grinned, revealing a gap along the side of her mouth. Harvey lifted his black coffee from the counter, and then placed the extra napkins she'd given him in his coat pocket. There was nothing more he needed to hear.

Outside, he lit a cigarette to keep himself busy. Wind blew a tangle of debris across the street. If he didn't keep occupied, he would remember Emily, and the guilt would roll over him like a crushing wave. When staying home had become unbearable, he returned to Henco Industries, hoping it would be the solution, or at least a distraction from the emptiness, but he soon realized he'd learned to hate his job during his absence. And yet there was nothing for him. All he knew was how to fix things, and they weren't the sorts of things he could put on a résumé. He couldn't work a computer, but he could use his hands, and he knew how to hold a gun. Those were enough. Or they had been until Emily's death.

He still saw his daughter sometimes, standing in the corner of his basement apartment as he moved from one room to other, or when he was backing his car out of Henco's underground garage. She stood absolutely still, blaming him for what he'd done. He tried to tell her it wasn't his fault, but she was dead. And he didn't believe it anyway.

The Henco Industries brass wanted the standoff to end. The Six Nations of the Grand River protesters had been there for five months already and showed no desire to leave. Each additional day on the grass of the Douglas Creek lot allowed them to dig in further. "We cannot trust the O.P.P. to help," Mr. Estouffer said in his stilted Quebecois accent. "All they do is stand around and not get involved. McCarthy, he already speak to the Crown, but they do not move. No one does anything. This is why you must go. Go do what you do best."

Mr. Estouffer did not ask about Emily, and Harvey wanted to wrap his big hands around the old man's fat throat. He resisted. Without the job, there was nothing left to stop the memories.

"Just do us a favor, Harvey. You don't push these Indians too much." The way he said *Indians* made Harvey's skin crawl. "We don't want the news to find you are there."

Harvey said nothing. It was the last thing he wanted, as well. He didn't have the face for television; it was too wide, too rough, too wrinkled. And he couldn't risk his eyes revealing the truth. He didn't believe.

Something about the Six Nations occupation of the site didn't measure up, which was why the first thing he did before leaving his apartment was put on his overcoat and slip the gun in his left pocket. Not in his right. He did not open the right-hand pocket. Even when he felt the faint tugging of something desperate to be gone.

His walk from the coffee shop to the edge of the Douglas Creek lot was consciously rambling. He wanted to approach without it being clear where he was headed. The hardest part was passing the mirrored window of the Caledonia Hardware Store, reflecting in his peripheral vision despite the oncoming night. A shadow moved beside him, brushed against him. He wouldn't acknowledge the manifestation.

The Six Nations protesters were in a line along the entrance to the Douglas Creek lot, mired in a shouting match with the Caledonia Citizens Alliance—wealthy and bored locals tired of dealing with the constant threat to their property values. One of the natives wore an elaborate costume—part angry bear, part giant spider—that made him tower over his opponents as he danced. If it was meant to intimidate, it worked; the Alliance members cowered when he swung his multiple legs by their heads. Harvey skirted the disturbance and remained invisible.

"Our land was stolen. We will not leave until it is ours again!"

"Get out! You aren't welcome!"

One hundred years earlier the Six Nations of the Grand River signed a document that sold their land to Henco Industries. Harvey sympathized—Henco was certainly capable of looting the Six Nation ancestors—but he questioned why they were suddenly contesting the sale. Why did they want the land back? And most importantly to Harvey, why had they secretly moved a digger truck past the Argyle Street barricade the previous night?

With spring still new, the sun had already set by the time he reached the Douglas Creek lot, and Harvey was able to position himself discreetly behind some trees on the edge of the forty hectares without being noticed. The dark cloaked him as he viewed the small tent enclave that was erected when the standoff began. He counted nearly twenty tents—some full-fledged tipis—arranged in a circle, a fire pit burning at the center. But the true face of the protest was along Argyle Street, where the concrete barrier had been erected. It was clear the protesters had no intention of abandoning their cause. If anything, the anger in their voices and their costumed dancing kept them fueled. Their anger belied something more.

Harvey took a sip from his coffee and crouched down. He had to focus on the task before him; it was the only way to remain sane. There were not many places the Six Nations protesters could be hiding something as large as a digger truck, which meant it should be fairly easy to find what the protesters were digging for. It had to be the key to the whole affair; Harvey simply needed to figure it out.

He removed the gun from his pocket and inspected it in the waning moon's pale light. The gun was loaded should he need it. He laid his hand on his other pocket, feeling the small hard lump that radiated emotional power almost too strong to bear. His head swam with thoughts long held at bay, concealed beneath a sea of Scotch and gin and whiskey, but no matter how he tried, he could not drown the knowledge of what happened, of poor Emily's broken face as she lay unmoving in the hospital bed, machines filling her lungs, pumping her blood. The sight haunted him, and he cursed himself for not being in the car with her and Donna.

The police had told him the skid marks showed his ex-wife had swerved to avoid something on the road, but whatever it was had long gone by the time help arrived. Donna was killed instantly, but Emily . . . She had always been more his than his wife's. Tough and hard as a nut, she glared with his face in miniature. She laughed the way a goose honks, and her arms and legs were sticks that would have one day shaped themselves into something beautiful if she'd lived long enough.

No, he thought. Keep focused. Don't fall into the past. Harvey took a deep breath of the chilled air and resumed his watch, waiting for his moment.

The cigarette between his lips remained his lone companion. The protesters sang and danced in vigil into the night, all while facing down the Caledonia citizens who protested them in turn. Harvey felt something stir in the inky shadows between swaying trees, some force of portentousness or inevitability. Whatever the protesters were planning, it was close to being realized. The sensation was palpable, and he inched his left hand into his pocket and wrapped his fingers around the butt of his gun. He did so without thinking.

From his vantage point in the dark, flickering flames were all he could see across the Douglas Creek lot, and the fading light played tricks on his eyes. Shadows scurried between him and the enclave of protesters, momentarily blocking his sight. Tiny specks moved through the air like swarms of insects, all converging on the dark woods that occupied the back half of the lot. At the front line the crowd had petered out—the costumes gone, their intimidation complete—though enough protesters remained to man the barricade and ensure the Caledonia Citizens Alliance didn't dismantle it. Or the O.P.P. cross it. Yet, even with a smaller number, the rows of men and women chanted louder, and their cries brought a nightmarish quality to the cooling night air.

The Six Nations wanted something, and their anger pushed them forward like animals. Anger fueled by hate and revenge, anger that wanted restitution and reparations for all that Henco had done. Anger that wanted the company to pay. The Six Nations of the Grand River wanted vengeance against those who had robbed them, and those who refused to relinquish their land. All this weighed heavy in the air, so much so that Harvey could almost see it in the dark, the emotions coalescing, suffocating the world beneath. But it was all for naught. Had they simply asked him, he would have explained it. Their mistake was looking for justice.

Justice has no balance. If it did, Harvey would carry nothing in his pockets.

In the distance, sirens howled. The protesters were looking and pointing at him. No, not at him. Above him. In the night sky the thick plumes of smoke were being drawn toward the Douglas Creek lot, blotting out the stars, and from his position Harvey saw the glow of fires burning on the horizon. The sticky smell of frying electrical equipment clung to his face. Then with a flicker all the lights in the community went out, and the steady hum that lies behind the mechanized world ceased. Only the fires of the protesters remained. The cheer from Argyle Street was loud, and for a brief moment Harvey's attention was fully in the present.

There was scuffling around him, the pitch-black making it seem right next to him. He watched, waited until he had an idea of what was going to happen. The cloaked Six Nations protesters screamed, swearing curses into the night, and the red lights of the O.P.P. cruiser lit up, spinning around and around in the void. Then its bright highbeams fought to cut through the sediment-filled air, and the protesters who had been lobbing clods of dirt and rocks scurried away. They were far too distracted to notice Harvey, and he slipped across their makeshift barriers and into the Douglas Creek lot undetected.

It was clear what had happened even without the announcements and police megaphones: the Six Nations protesters had blown up a hydro substation, knocking the power out across Caledonia, and it would take hours, if not days, to fix. Until morning, the land at Douglas Creek would be cast in pitch-darkness, hiding the movement of all below in its heavy drape.

As he moved across the grass, he kept one hand in his left pocket, his squat fingers wrapped around the butt of his gun. The atmosphere was turbid, radiating dislike and mistrust, but there was something else too; something musky and meaty, like a large animal wandering in the darkness. The shadows moved everywhere around him, and he squeezed his gun tighter for comfort where none was to be had.

The skirmish at the Argyle Street barricade was heating up—police orders shouted through megaphones and screaming protesters trying to avoid being seen. More sirens sounded in the distance, the cavalry coming to even the odds, and Harvey wondered where the peaceful protest had gone. It was always the same in the dark. Nothing remained real. Not the hopes of a robbed people, nor the safety of a man's only child. It was only in the dark when a broken doll's face made any sense. It was punishment. Plain and simple. And the punishment that was meted out on him would be meted out on the rest of Henco if the Six Nations had their way. At least, that's what their chanting had transformed into. A call to arms. In the acrid smoke of the burning substation, voices were calling out into the dark, not stopping as the burning air irritated their eyes and lungs, compounding tempers. They were on the verge of something, and even in the blinding darkness it was clear that something would be ugly.

His grey trench coat rasped quietly as he walked. He had with him a small Maglite flashlight, but he knew better than to use it. It would betray his presence, and he'd been betrayed enough in the preceding months. Betrayed by an ex-wife who stole his daughter away in the night to put her in the hospital, betrayed by doctors who could do nothing to save her except pretend there was a chance she might one day reawaken, betrayed by a company that would keep him away from his child instead of letting him hold her safe in his arms. All these betrayals added, compounded, weighed on him, and in his blinding sorrow they betrayed him one time further, and walked him unknowingly into the middle of the protesters' enclave.

He stopped in his tracks when he saw the smoldering embers of their fire, still red and leaping into the air before vanishing. The commotion of Argyle Street was faint in the distance, but there was talk from within the darkened tents, all in a language too ancient for him to understand. The words were monotone, hummed rather than spoken, and a sole singsong voice rose and sank in waves from within one of the tents—so deep it rattled in his chest. A breeze blew across his face, bringing with it leaves and dirt, and he turned his face and closed his lids. The sound of the swaying grasses was everywhere, like whispers surrounding him, or like the faint rasp of air pushed through the lungs of a dead girl. When he opened his eyes, the chanting had stopped, but in front of him, bare feet in the dying fire, was a broken Emily, staring. Circling her neck was the pendant he carried in his right-hand pocket.

"Emily," he whispered in a sputter.

She bared her bloodied teeth at him. And was gone.

Blood crashed through his head, through his face, through his dry throat, and the sound was deafening. He smelled disinfectant. It seemed impossible, yet the air was suddenly full of it, and it was all Harvey could do to keep himself upright. He did not enjoy the hallucination, the reminder of what he'd done, and bit against his palm until it bled to break its lock on him. When the world righted itself and his senses once more became his own, they were like raw nerves, and he had to rest until the nausea they induced subsided. He wished not for the first time since returning that he was at a bar instead of where he was, a bottle in hand to keep the guilt from ripping him apart.

Harvey slipped out of the circle of tents and further into the darkness. If the digger was anywhere, it would be there, discreetly hidden from the world outside. The echo of his movements rippled faintly off the tree trunks that dotted the lot's back hectares. He slowed as he approached them, unsure where the trees were in the night, and calculated the risk insignificant enough to pull the small Maglite from his pocket. A twist of its end and a narrow beam of light bore a tiny hole into the nothingness. It shouldn't have been enough to alert anyone, but he slipped a hand in his pocket and removed his gun nonetheless. Then he slid forward among the trees.

The sounds were impossible to pinpoint. Animals moved, making the same heavy scratching he'd heard before. The wind had increased as well, wrapping around the invisible trees outside the Maglite's periphery, howling and throwing debris. Small rocks and dirt clawed his face as they blew past, scratching lines in his flesh. But those weren't the only sounds he heard. Beneath them was another, one that chilled his chest and spine more than any late night wind could. It was a sound that still haunted his every waking hour.

He had been sitting in that waiting room while the machine breathed for Emily; wheezing, in and out, breath forced into her tiny lungs. When the doctor appeared, it was obvious his caring was insincere, and Harvey leapt on his throat in wordless and instant rage. It took two security guards and three orderlies to pull Harvey's hands from around the doctor's neck, and the only reason they succeeded was Harvey's realization that his fury did no good. It was misplaced. Harvey's ire should have been directed at himself for not being where he belonged, and Henco for sending him there. Despite Harvey's apologies, the doctor did not return. The one who replaced him spoke with a nervous stammer and wouldn't stand closer than a few feet away. He told Harvey that Emily would probably never return and asked what he wanted to do. Harvey replied, "Leave," and then turned away and held his daughter's tiny hand. The doctor acquiesced, but with obvious concern.

The trees were like a maze in the dark, but Harvey knew that following them would eventually yield results. Somewhere, in the nothingness, the digger stood waiting for him, a quiet beast with its head curled to its chest but with teeth strong enough to tear rock apart. Harvey moved through the forest as quickly as he could, the small circle of light swinging before him looking for evidence of the truck's passing. And yet he saw nothing. It was not until he recognized the distant metallic twang of his footsteps' echo that he finally turned course.

In the inky darkness his circle of light found a metallic hull painted bright orange. Arms and gears erupted from the device, and it took Harvey a few moments to make sense of the violent clashing of parts. It was the digger, and under the light its giant wheels were sunken in a circle of torn sod and grass. Its scoop was tucked under its long arm like a bird sleeping, and across it was wet mud. It had been used recently, he could tell by its odor. It seemed the girl behind the Tim Hortons counter was right: something else was going on.

Part of him wished he hadn't returned to the job so soon; his head wasn't in the right place to deal with the continuous subterfuge and the front of solidarity the Six Nations were offering, pretending the land was what they wanted when clearly it was something beneath the ground that had their eye. He scanned the flashlight around the digger, looking for a hole, and when that failed he instead looked for the tracks the giant wheels had made in the soft turf. They would lead him to the dig as sure as any trail of breadcrumbs.

It wasn't far. Harvey followed the torn ground until the tracks stopped at a long tent stretching one hundred feet yet standing less than three feet tall. Along the edges of the grooves he found footprints overlapping with one another, making strange shapes in the soft soil. Some of the prints he thought might have been made by a child's bare feet, or perhaps some sort of large animal. He touched the sides of the tent and they felt rough and damp, like an old hide or rough canvas. Something about the spot emitted the faint but pungent odor of some large rodent's abandoned nest. There was the sound again of footsteps approaching and he flashed the Maglite behind him but found nothing there, not even the face of his dead daughter condemning him for what he was doing.

He heard crickets chirp, wind rustle trees. The burning electrical fire continued, its smoke wafting over the Douglas Creek lot, its flames licking the horizon. Beneath the clouded sky Harvey circled the tent, looking for an entrance. There had to be one, after all. What was the point of having a tent without any way in or out? Why hide it when the whole structure was hidden to begin with? Or could that be part of the plan? Was it some method of revenge? Had the protesters finally decided to carry out their threats? The administration at Henco did not feel guilt for what they were doing and strongly urged him to feel the same. But it was there nonetheless, and they would all have to deal with it one way or another. Harvey hoped it would be on his own terms, but wondered if the rest of Henco would be so lucky.

His contemplation was cut short by the shadow hovering near the end of the tent furthest in the woods. Its arms seemed long and massive, and it was impossible to determine if it was a person or an animal hunched by the tent's edge. Was it the protester he had seen earlier, still dressed in his horrible costume? Harvey took a step toward it, then another, and it did not move. With each advancement the shadow receded, and when Harvey dared lift his Maglite to reveal what it was the figure disappeared into the folds of the night as though it had never been there. It left behind a flap of rough canvas torn loose from the tent. Harvey checked his vicinity to ensure he was alone, then hazarded a peek beneath the tent. There was nothing but dark emptiness; a void without bottom. Harvey heard his dead daughter, Emily, cry out for him, but to his horror those cries were stifled. He knew she wasn't there, that it was simply his guilt haunting him, but he could not deny the specter's commands. Harvey slipped beneath the loose section of heavy canvas and found a deep pit waiting, one so dark his flashlight would not penetrate it. He scratched his head and knelt down, then swung his legs over the precipice until they dangled into the dark expanse. Slowly, he pushed himself farther until gravity took hold. It was then he realized there was no ground beneath the canvas. He fell, plummeting into nothing, and feared he would never stop. When he finally hit bottom, the ground was softer than grass, and turning on his flashlight he saw he had dropped no more than six feet into the earth; yet the trench stretched out as far as his flashlight beam carried, farther than it had appeared on the surface. The wind howled through the torn tarp above.

The Six Nations had been excavating something, and it seemed to be more than a single thing judging by the size of the hole. Harvey felt claustrophobic pressure from above and shone the light to determine how much headroom he really had. It was close, but there was enough space to stand. What struck him, though, was that the frame holding the canvas aloft was made of long branches standing in a row down into the darkness, bent together and tied at the top to make a series of small arches. Bizarrely, they appeared dead black under his light. He touched one and his hand came away wet and sticky with an oil-like reddish substance, though it smelled more metallic than that. Perhaps it was the air he smelled, air like that before a storm, charged with electricity. Or maybe the winds had changed, and the hydro station fire had penetrated further into the Douglas Creek land. He wiped his fingers on one of the Tim Hortons napkins he'd stashed in his pocket, then shone his Maglite along the ground. He could see the remnants in the dirt of some structure that had been buried there before, the frame of what looked like a small building. The protesters must have been trying to unearth it. What was so important, he wondered. Was it some archaeological discovery? Something of their ancestors there that they didn't want claimed by the province? It looked like a sort of dwelling, but the geometry of the place was all wrong; the angles seemed too obtuse to bear without being driven mad. He still couldn't tell where the door must have been—there was no evidence of the building ever having one, not unless it was carved in the hide of the tent above.

There was something else, something other than the lack of doors or windows in a place that was clearly once home to too many. In the dirt at his feet, small objects screamed like tiny shiny gems. They caught his eye, and he bent down to pick one up.

They looked like teeth, sharp canine teeth of a large predator, and mixed in with them were long black claws, curved and thick. They were spread across the dirt floor, and Harvey was confident they hadn't been unearthed but instead left there recently, as though part of some strange ceremony. That would explain the foulness in the air—rituals and customs performed, tying the natives to the earth and its creatures. Maybe the protesters were trying to ward off Henco and the destruction it might bring, or instead punish it for what it had already done. Henco deserved it. Deserved punishment for its actions, deserved it as much as he did when Harvey saw his daughter's face staring at him, her eyes dark and soulless and unforgiving. The guilt overwhelmed him, made him angry, and everything around him shook. Dirt trickled down the walls of the hole, and somewhere closer than possible he heard himself panting like an animal. When he managed to calm himself, he found his fist clenched, and opening it saw that the sharp tooth had bitten through his skin. He threw it to the ground and rubbed the wound on his pant leg, then raised the flashlight high.

Farther into the remains of the excavated building, he was surprised by what the Six Nations had unearthed—a series of wooden structures like tables, or possibly bunks. He let his light crawl to the top and for a moment was jarred. What he thought had been a large animal sleeping in filth was in fact a pelt covered in soil. He picked up the edge and saw another beneath, less dirty, and another beneath that. He had no explanation for their presence. Disturbing them, though, released a meaty smell into the air, a sour medley of musk and decayed flesh that stifled his breath until it wheezed from his lungs. Sounds emanated around him, strange distortions possible only in the absence of light. Harvey felt his hand taken by another, smaller hand, and swung his flashlight quickly, but it was not fast enough. Everything looked different, however, as though shifted in the dark then returned before the light struck it. He shook his head. He did not like what he was witnessing. There was something wrong in that underground room, something that he wasn't seeing but knew was there. He pointed the Maglite at the bent branches overhead, searching for evidence he was being watched. He felt a strange set of eyes intently following his every move, but again if they were there in the dark they were gone before the light found them. The sound of his raincoat rubbing against itself was overwhelming, as was the crunch of his shoes on the tiny bones underfoot. He had to get out of that pit and off the Douglas Creek grounds. He'd been there so long he was hearing chanting when there was no way he could. It was stuck in his head, repeating over and over again.

He strode to the spot he had descended from and realized the drop was further than he'd thought. He wasn't tall or young enough simply to pull himself out. He considered climbing the bent branches, but even if they might support his weight there was no way he was going to touch them. He tried jumping half-heartedly, but only succeeded in raining further dirt down on himself. He was in a predicament, and he had few options. He couldn't allow himself to be discovered by the protesters, but when he tried to think his way through, all he could see was Emily's face staring at him smugly, all he could hear was the sound of her respirator gasping. Maybe if he tried climbing on the wooden structure at the rear of the pit, pushed aside the fur pelts, and stood on the wooden frame, he could get enough height to escape.

He staggered back across the mud floor, his panting echoing close to his ear, the damp seeping through the soles of his shoes, and found the half-buried frame. But before he could climb he was stunned by the revelation of the Maglite. The bunks were empty, the fur gone. He shone the flashlight quickly, scoured the ground, found nothing but dirt. Even the tiny teeth had vanished, the claws, the bones. It made no sense. He raised the Maglite and aimed it across the walls of the underground room, and when it finally discovered the furs it did not stop. It did not *want* to stop. Yet Harvey returned the circle of light to the pelts of dirt-filled fur that hung from the farthest corner of the pit. He took a step closer, willing his eyes to focus, willing everything to make sense. He took another step and the world around him started to shift, his reality warping as time slowed.

His every sense became hyperaware: the sound of panting he mistook for his own; the smell of thick musk and foul breath; the taste of bitterness; the sight of darkness swirling around him and becoming solid; the feel of his dead daughter's pendant crushed in the palm of his sweating hand. The fur hanging in front of him, the fur he had seen minutes before on the other side of the room, started to move without aid. Then in the light across the room glittered too many eyes opening, flashed too many rows of razor-sharp canine teeth. But what mesmerized Harvey most was the debilitating wave of guilt that washed over him, froze his limbs in place until a rumbling growl shook him. He stepped back and instinctively put his hand in his pocket. Shadows moved around the creature like limbs, too many to count. He took another step back into the wall of the pit, and the shock jarred the flashlight from his hand. As it hit the soft ground there was the glint of something lunging toward him, and his gun was in his hand and firing before the utter darkness swallowed him whole. Six flashes in the dark, then no more. At some point he dropped Emily's pendant.

Morning light shone in Harvey's eye through the hide canopy. He coughed blood. From a muted distance he heard voices yelling at him, shadows moving frantically above. He could see enough to know where he was, what condition he was in. There was blood over his hands and deep scratches on his misshapen arms and legs. One of his eyes stuck as he blinked, and a raised hand revealed half his face numb. He was alive; he wished he weren't. He stared up at the hide canopy, the protesters moving across the opening torn far wider than before, and he wondered why he was not dead when he so deserved to be. As though in response, Emily appeared beside him, her broken face now mirroring his own, and he remembered. He remembered how hurt she had been, how the grief had overwhelmed him. His only happiness fading away, replaced as he watched by a hunk of breathing meat. Harvey swallowed, his throat dry and caked with blood, remembering that thing that was no longer her lying on the hospital bed, fading away, holding her down. He shook his head, not wanting to remember, but the apparition forged of his guilt would not let him forget. He did what any father would do for the child he loved; he waited until the doctor was gone and he set her free. He unplugged her respirator and waited for death to take her.

But to his horror, death didn't come.

And the ground at the Douglas Creek lot rumbled once more.

Harvey silently apologized to Emily as she stood before him, tears streaming from his only working eye. He had watched her brain-dead body continue to breathe, felt her heart continue to beat, even while her broken face was as pale as the dead. Bound to the world, unable to move on and unable to return, Harvey's grief consumed what remained of him at the bottom of that dirt hole, six feet deep.

He remembered little of it. The pillow from under her head in his hand. Leaning down on her crushed face, bones popping softly until she no longer moved, until the hospital machines emitted a single sustained tone. He dropped the pillow in his daze and for the first time saw Emily standing there, staring into his watering eyes, and he knew with cold rationality that he'd made a grievous error. It was not only her anchor with the world he had severed.

But facing her in that pit he felt a calm. The creature that the Six Nations of the Grand River had brought forth to serve their vengeance had found its first victim, and it fed until it was full, sparing the lives of those at Henco who knew no better. They weren't free of blame; it was only that he had so much more to offer. He laughed, and the action made him cough again. Blood fell to the vibrating ground. He looked up with his one good eye and saw through the torn canopy a large arm of orange metal, and he knew he was right. The scoop lifted above him, blocking out the rising sun, and he turned his head to see Emily standing there beside him, a smile finally on her broken doll's face. He smiled too, as best he could, and tried to reach his arm out to take her tiny hand, but he was buried by earth before he reached her.

Strong as a Rock

Garrison did not want to go rock climbing, but Rex assured him it was a good idea.

"You'll have fun, Gar. Trust me. It'll take your mind off Mom."

But Garrison didn't think anything would take his mind off her. The sight of her in that hospital bed, hooked up to wires and tubes, so thin and pale . . . no, he could not forget her. He still missed her every day.

But Rex was right. He needed to start his life again. Emerge from his darkened basement into the world. He just wasn't sure rock climbing was the answer.

"I don't know if I'm up to this, Rex. It's not what I was expecting."

"Bullshit. You can do it. I have faith in you, bro."

It was the latest of Rex's activities, one he had taken up after their mother's death, but one to which he was particularly drawn. He went through this every few years, discovering a new sport or hobby to occupy his time. For a while it was diving, then hang gliding. He even knit for a few months the year before. But rock climbing was the strangest, at least to Garrison. It had always seemed the sort of activity one does when there's nothing left to do. Why else scale the side of a rock? Because it's there? Still, when Rex asked, Garrison acquiesced. Not at first, but soon enough. Somehow, Rex always knew what to say.

The trip to Markham only took a few hours, and it felt as though they had left one reality and entered another. Garrison was not used to the size of things, neither the expanse of forests nor the confined and labyrinthine layout of the town. Both conspired to rob him of a quick method of escape, and their lack of familiarity only heightened his anxiety.

"I think I'm claustrophobic," he said to Rex as they passed through the small town. They saw few locals, and those they did stared as the two drove by, eyes wide and disconcerting. Rex didn't seem to notice.

"I think you're an idiot who's spent too much time inside the house. You're not claustrophobic."

"How do you know?" Garrison asked, feeling for his pulse in case somehow he would be able to diagnose himself. "Or maybe agoraphobic?"

Rex let out a sigh and then tried to change the subject.

"You'll be fine once we get into Downe Park and start our climb. You'll be amazed at how good it makes you feel. It always recharges. Look, above those trees. You can just see the edge of the rocks peeking through."

Garrison could see them, but he could feel them as well, feel them glaring at him through the branches. He swallowed, his head woozy. It had been the same when their mother died; he could see what was coming and knew it brought nothing but pain. His fingers icy, his jaw slack, he stared at the rock formation and wondered what it might want from him. Then he stopped and shook his head. They were rocks; they couldn't *want* anything. Surely not to see him plummet to his death.

If the rocks *did* want Garrison, they did not tip their hand when the brothers arrived. Instead, the sun was beaming in a deep cloudless sky, lighting the walls of red rock until they no longer looked real. Garrison felt so far removed from his normal life he could no longer remember it, and though he knew the idea should be exhilarating, he found it the opposite. He was terrified by what was laid out before him.

"Perfect weather," Rex said, and then inhaled deep and released the breath with something more akin to a satisfied call-to-arms than to an exhale. It only further jangled Garrison's nerves. "I'll pop the trunk, bro, so we can get the gear out."

They laid everything on the ground at the foot of a rocky face. While Rex worked to check they had all they would need, Garrison looked at the sun, the light cascading down as though the red rocks were seeping blood. Garrison knew it was no more than a forty-foot climb, but from where he stood those forty feet seemed to stretch upward forever.

"So . . . all this equipment. It's supposed to *hold* us, right? Has it ever broken on you? Maybe when you were halfway up or something? I saw this movie once—"

"I told you not to worry, Gar. I'll be going first. All you need to do is put your hands and feet where I put mine and follow my lead. I'll tell you when it's time to move or not. The day is absolutely gorgeous and perfect for this. I couldn't have asked for it to be better to take you up your first time. If you trust me, we'll be fine. You *do* trust me, right?"

Did he? Did he trust his older brother, the stronger, smarter of the two? The one he had never in all their years seen shaken or cry, even when their mother died? The most solid rock he knew? Did Garrison trust him?

"Of course I trust you," Garrison said. "But still, the *ropes*—"

"Enough with the ropes. I already checked them, Gar."

"I know. But can you check them again? Just to make sure?"

Rex picked up the first set of ropes in front of him. He pulled at both ends while he looked straight at Garrison, making sure it was clear how pointless the exercise was. Garrison didn't feel any more assured.

"I know you're probably tired of explaining, but tell me again exactly how we're doing this."

"What? The climb?"

"Yes."

"I'll start. You follow."

"No, I mean what's the path exactly." He squinted upward and pointed with a palsied hand. "That way? Along those rocks? What's the plan?"

"The plan is to follow me, Gar. Jesus, relax, will you? I'm not going to let you—" Rex hesitated, but Garrison knew exactly what he meant to say.

"*Die?* You mean like Mom?" Garrison's heart was beating so hard it sounded like someone slowly knocking at a giant wooden door.

"You know what I mean. You'll be fine. Just do what I tell you. Now come here and let me help you put your harness on."

Garrison held his arms out as his brother slipped the harness over his body, just as he'd helped Garrison get dressed when the two of them were younger. There was something reassuring about it, being in the hands of Rex, someone so sure of everything. Annoying, but reassuring.

After pulling the straps tight and double-checking them, then checking once more at Garrison's insistence, Rex linked the two of them together with the safety wire. "This is your lifeline," he said. "Think of it as an umbilical cord. It's what's going to keep you alive. Make sure it does *not* get tangled."

That thought was terrifying. Garrison looked around in desperation and saw something worse.

"Where is everybody? Shouldn't there be more people here? What if we need help?"

Rex didn't bother turning. "It's the time of year, bro. This place is literally crawling in the summer, but it's the end of the season now. They're going to be shutting down after this weekend for the winter months."

"But is it safe?"

Rex made a noise that was as much snort as it was scoff. Garrison had heard it before, and it did nothing to relieve his anxiety.

"If you do what I tell you, there won't be a problem. Now are you ready?"

Reluctantly, Garrison nodded.

"Yes."

Rex climbed, chalked fingers into thin crevices, edges of his shoes on narrow projections. The guide wire slipped easily through the rings on his harness as he effortlessly scaled the rock face, and when he was a few feet above Garrison's head he paused to shout down, "Start climbing! Just use the same holds I did. If you get stuck, let me know."

Garrison looked around again to see if someone—*anyone*—was watching. Then he swallowed hard and told himself, "You can do this," before putting his fingers into the first groove.

The two climbed. It took less than two minutes for Garrison's muscles to start complaining, and he had to fight the urge to simply give up. After another two minutes the sensation dissipated, and his breathing regulated. All his attention then focused on climbing.

Periodically, Rex would stop to hammer in another loop for their safety wire. When Garrison passed each he would look at it and feel intense doubt that it could support his weight if he fell. He was glad at least to be pressed so close to the rock's face; it prevented him from looking down at how far they'd travelled. He had a feeling the sight would not be comforting.

"I bet Mom would have loved it here," Rex said, oblivious to the effort Garrison was making simply to keep up. "The air is completely awesome, isn't it? There's nothing like it. I found out about Downe Park on the Internet. Apparently, it's the best climb for miles. It's the rocks—this used to be a lake once, and all the years of sediment have shaped it in such a unique way. I love this place. Sometimes, when it's windy, the howls sound like people screaming." The idea overjoyed Rex for some reason. Then he paused and looked down at his brother. "How are you doing down there?"

It took most of Garrison's concentration to keep focused and remain moving. If he stopped, the terror might prevent him from ever starting again. "I'm okay," he rushed, hoping his voice didn't betray his fear. All that he heard chanted over and over again in his skull was *the howls sound like people screaming*, and he wondered how many of those people were plummeting to their deaths.

After the first fifteen minutes they arrived at a small plateau, and Garrison used the last of his energy to pull himself over the edge. He lay on the ground, panting heavily as Rex chuckled above him.

"You're out of shape, bro."

"I . . . could have . . . told you that," Garrison sputtered through heaving breaths. His heart thundered in his ears, and with his head resting on the rock it sounded as though something was moving within the stone. By the time he could sit, Rex was kneeling in front of the rock, inspecting the next leg of their journey.

"Hey, there's something carved here, like words, but I can barely read them . . ."

Garrison's head, however, was swimming with other thoughts.

"This seems like a waste of time. What are we trying to prove, Rex? Really?"

"We aren't proving anything. We're just doing something different. Would you rather stay at home some more in the dark? It's not good for you."

"I really don't mind it," he muttered.

Rex's brow furrowed.

"Well, it's not good for *me* then, okay? I need to get out. Think about something other than Mom. You know she wouldn't have wanted you to be like this, don't you? Missing her so much? She'd want you to get on with your life."

Garrison didn't want to look at him. "I know I'm supposed to, but I don't see how."

"You don't see, or don't *want* to see? You were the same way when she was sick—you didn't want to know anything about it. As if ignoring it would make it go away. Sticking your head in the sand and hiding didn't do you any good. It just gave you less time with her. And you obviously haven't learned your lesson; you still have your eyes closed."

Garrison felt his throat closing. He breathed deeply, trying to remain in control, and avoided looking at his brother. He knew what expression Rex would be wearing.

The silence hung on, and part of Garrison wondered if the world had frozen. Then he felt a nudge to his ribs, and he turned and squinted at the shadow standing above him, silhouetted by the sun. Strange waves emanated and grew from Rex's body, but those subsided as Garrison's vision adjusted. Rex rubbed his hands across his shirt, leaving the ghost of chalk streaks across it. "Are you ready to keep going?"

Garrison looked at the path they had ahead of them and felt physically ill. His joints ached in protest. Rex was looking at him suspiciously, as though he already knew what was next.

"I—I don't think I want to keep going."

A flustered but unsurprised sigh.

"I *knew* you'd chicken out on me, Gar. It's only another forty minutes up. You can do it."

"I don't *want* to do it. I feel like shit. I'm tired and I'm hungry and I just don't feel like doing this today. I'm sorry."

Rex's nostrils flared, and though Garrison couldn't see past his brother's sunglasses, it was clear he wasn't impressed. Every fibre of Garrison wanted to relent and do as Rex wanted, but instead he stood silent. Part of him wondered if his mother's death had finally added something to compensate for all it took away.

"Fine. Get your stuff. We're going home."

Leaves the color of burnt umber floated past Garrison's face like the feathers shed from some strange bird, but he tried not to become distracted by them, not as he carefully descended. A few feet above, his silent brother followed, removing pegs as he passed them, his small hammer striking vibrations that reflected back from within the rock. The trip downward proved strangely more difficult and treacherous, and though each near-miss of a hold let loose a wave of paralyzing fear through Garrison's body so strong he nearly wept, he pushed through it. But only then because he did not want to fail further in Rex's eyes, and because he saw no faster alternative that would return him to the ground—a place he swore he would never again leave.

It was unclear what happened next. Without warning he found himself floating, the world spinning vertiginously. Images of deep unyielding sky and solid red rock flickered before him. But there were other images, images that moved too fast to comprehend, images of dark flesh and multitudinous eyes, all staring outward. He felt a thousand touches brush his face, and as everything flashed his already tenuous grasp slipped. Then in an instant it was over, and he was upside down, dangling, his right arm caught behind his back and filled with intense paresthesia. He was disoriented and nauseated, and wasn't sure if he was going to pass out or simply cease to be.

The sensation of something dripping onto his face kept him awake. That, and the voice screaming from somewhere far away; too far away, though, to warrant much attention. Garrison lazily put his free hand to his cheek to brush away whatever was kissing it, and was genuinely amused to see it slick with dark blood. He laughed, and the sound echoed and the world spun again and everything disappeared into the void of his unconsciousness.

Garrison woke engulfed by the sight of that empty blue sky, the edges of which had already started to darken with grey. He attempted to sit up, and his sense of equilibrium spun violently before everything went dark once more. The next time he opened his eyes the darkness had bled further inward, but the bulk of the sky was filled with Rex's concerned face.

"Gar, you awake, bro? Say something."

Every inch of Garrison's body ached. He was still dizzy, but managed to remain upright.

"I think so. What happened?"

"You fell. You're lucky the line caught you but it looks as if you messed up your arm. I cinched a towel around it, but we need to get you to the hospital."

Garrison caught a glimpse of his wrapped arm and his stomach rebelled. The once-white towel had turned a dark russet red, and merely observing it made the damaged limb ache. Part of Garrison wasn't surprised. The rock finally got what it wanted. What was strange was that Garrison had managed to live through it.

With help from Rex, he was able to get to his feet. Rex helped him back to the car and put him in the passenger seat before throwing the gear into the trunk and getting behind the wheel. "You're going to be fine," Rex kept repeating in his usual calm voice. "I've done a lot worse. You got really lucky."

"I don't feel so lucky right now. I feel sick."

"If you think you're going to throw up, let me know and I'll pull over. You're in shock, but it'll pass. I don't think you've lost enough blood for it to be anything worse, but hell knows what's happening inside. I still can't understand how you did it. Did you just lose your grip?"

"Something like that, I guess," Garrison said, unable to explain it in any other way. He remembered the sensation on his chest of being pushed, though he didn't see how that could be right. His body stung, thousands of little stabs from where he must have scraped himself across the rocks as he fell, yet none of those wounds were on the surface. Like all his others, the damage was on the inside. He imagined he could feel the blood seeping into his body, causing his organs to fail. How often did someone walk away from an accident only to die of a hemorrhage or clot an hour later? Already, his body was beginning to shake, just as his mother's had before she . . .

"How many times?" Garrison asked, trying to still his body.

"How many times what?"

"Have you hurt yourself like this? You said you've done it. How many times?" He struggled to keep the panic from his voice. "Where's the hospital?"

"Easy, bro. Take it easy." Rex didn't take his eyes from the road, but he reached out a still-chalked hand and put it on his brother's leg. "The Stouffville Hospital is close to Markham. I already have it programmed into the GPS, so try and stay calm and we'll be there soon." At once Garrison's body ceased shaking, but the pain in his damaged arm continued to radiate outward, entering his fingers and neck. He wondered how long it would take to consume his entire body.

Garrison rested his head on the window nervously and watched the scenery go by. It was like a blur, the same trees over and over again, the same fields, the same boarded house. He almost didn't notice when Rex slowed the car down—the spinning in his head continued as though they were travelling at full speed. "The GPS says we're close, but it's hard to tell. The route it's calculated—it really seems overly complicated."

As if to prove his point, the soft British accent of the navigator gently insisted he turn off the road they were on and head back the direction they had come. Rex clucked his tongue and kept going forward while the navigator took time to recalculate their route. Once done, it plotted a new course, one that would again take them back the way they had come. Eventually, Rex pulled over to the side of the road.

"Obviously, this thing isn't going to be much help. I'm just going to turn off the directions and just drive by the map."

Garrison looked out at the flat farmland on either side of the narrow highway. He could still see the edges of Downe Park in the distance, radiating some strange aura of distortion. It pulsed in rhythm with his body. He wondered if he were imagining it, the movement caused by the blood pumping through his head. Everything appeared fuzzy, and he wasn't sure if what he saw a short distance away was actually there or merely a mirage born of pain. He tried to blink it away, but it remained unchanged.

"What is that? Is that the Stouffville Hospital?"

Rex squinted ahead.

"It can't be. We're nowhere near— Hey, you're right. What *is* that?"

"It *must* be the hospital."

"Well," Rex said, fastening his seatbelt and starting the car. "I always told you I didn't need that stupid navigator."

There on the horizon it stood, but without a point of reference it was impossible to tell just how large the building was until they got closer to it. When they finally reached the parking lot twenty minutes later, Garrison wasn't sure if he was hallucinating or not. The hospital was tall and lean, shaped like a dagger digging into the ground, and its once-white edifice looked dirty and worn. Across the overhang of the Emergency Entrance were letters two feet tall that spelled DOWNE HOSPITAL, and though the trees and bushes flanking the entranceway had once been carved into shapes, what those ragged shapes were had become impossible to guess. Garrison wondered for how long it had stood and for how much longer it could remain standing.

Rex pulled the car up to the door below the giant letters.

"Well, it's no Stouffville Hospital. That's for sure."

"It looks deserted," Garrison said.

"Hang on," Rex said, then hopped out of the car and jogged to the glass doors. He put his hands to the glass and peered inside. Garrison swallowed and leaned back against the headrest. His arm was grumbling, and he felt a queer wave of vertigo wash over him. When Rex appeared at his open window, it made Garrison jump, and he screamed from the acute pain the sudden movement evoked.

"Sorry, Gar. I'm pretty sure I see someone moving inside though. Do you want me to go find you a wheelchair?"

"I think it's okay. I just need help getting out of the car."

Rex came around to the passenger side and reached in, allowing Garrison to put his arm around his brother's neck. Rex lifted him out fairly easily, but Garrison still staggered getting his balance once on the ground. The world had a soft quality to it, as though he were watching it through a gauzy lens. He stood one step out of sync with everything, an observer observing, and the disconnection only made things feel less real.

There were a few patients in the dim, rundown hallway of the emergency room, citizens no doubt from Markham and beyond all waiting their turn. They stared glassy-eyed, and those eyes seemed unusually large, larger than any Garrison had ever seen—surely an illusion caused by his shock and blood loss. Could that have also accounted for the distant humming he heard? Almost chanting, as though he were in some sort of church?

"Sit down here, Gar. Let me go find someone to admit you."

As Garrison watched Rex disappear down the hallway, what he first took to be the tapping of his brother's feet echoed longer than seemed possible. He peered around but could see no source for the noise; not unless it was caused by the woman in the row of plastic chairs across from him, rocking slowly back and forth. She was in her mid-fifties, her thinning black hair streaked with the purest white. She looked unwashed and unkempt, as though she'd been seated there for days, continuously shaking and staring at the ceiling with unblinking eyes. He leaned closer. That sound, that deep hum like singing, like no song Garrison had ever heard, seemed to bleed from the edges of her open mouth. As it did, he realized, from the other patients as well. Sitting, or standing, or shambling in the hallway, they sang in unison, and yet none betrayed any sign of doing so. It had to be some illusion, some echo carried down the hallway from elsewhere, or perhaps Garrison's exhaustion was fooling with his mind.

He laid his head back on the chair and closed his eyes to ease the wave of dizziness that had overtaken him. Slithering, sloping teeth and blood; thin twisted arms and protrusions, like creeping vines yet thicker, longer, spiraling outward; the flicker of faces decomposing, transforming. The violent cascade of images vanished as Garrison was shaken awake, and what he had been dreaming dissipated, leaving only the remnant sensation of unease. Rex stood over him, his face calm and reassuring, as always.

"I can't find anybody," he said. He looked up and down the hall. "I can't find anybody at all. Has anyone come out to see you yet?"

Bleary-eyed, Garrison shook his head. He turned to ask the rocking woman but saw only a row of broken plastic seats.

"Come on, Gar. Let's go."

"What?"

"Get up. We're taking a walk."

Garrison pushed himself up as best he could, but when his strength faltered Rex stepped in. He swung his brother's good arm over his shoulder.

"Rex, I don't feel so good."

"Hang tight, bro. We'll find a doctor in this place if I have to kick in every operating room door."

Rex carried his brother forward down the halls, past unmoving patients who simply stared. Garrison looked at each, and each had that same impossibly wide and vacant gaze, like a menagerie of soulless fish. Did they see something in him? Some sign that his wound was worse than he imagined? His shivering returned, yet if Rex noticed he said nothing.

"See those doors ahead? The ones that say 'no entry'? Guess what? We're going to be entering."

Rex pushed through doors with his free hand. Beyond them the light was considerably diminished, as was the presence of the unsettling fish-eyed patients. There was an empty wheelchair along the edge of the hallway, though Garrison wondered if it was in any condition to handle his meagre weight. Rex lowered him into it gently nonetheless and breathed a heavy breath when it did not collapse.

"That feel better?"

Garrison nodded, though he wasn't sure. He squirmed in the seat, trying to get comfortable. The leather felt warm and recently vacated, but there was no one else in the hall who could have been using it.

Rex pushed the chair as Garrison held his wounded arm. The towel was sticky with drying blood. Garrison's teeth chattered, the sound barely disguising the rhythmic throbbing in his head. It almost sounded real.

"Hello!" Rex called out. "Is there anybody in here?"

They passed room after unoccupied room, and Garrison felt delirium slowly taking hold. Each bed he saw made his heart skip, so sure was he that their mother would sit up and look at them, sallow and pale from her wasting disease, hair in clumps around her. Even in the half-dream, her face was wrong. It was the same impossibly wide stare on the faces of the Markham patients they had left behind in the hospital emergency room.

As Rex continued to push, Garrison heard a sound following them. The thud kept time with them, and he wondered if perhaps the wheels were misaligned, the rubber skipping on the tiles beneath. But it seemed impossible. Wouldn't he have felt the chair slip if it had? It was so hard to think straight. Perhaps he had imagined the noise as he'd imagined seeing his mother in the other room, staring her horrible stare.

Rex brought the wheelchair to an immediate halt.

"Do you hear that, bro?"

"It sounds like—"

"It sounds like someone is actually *in* this dump. Up there!" He pointed, and down the hall a shadow of movement disappeared around a corner. "Hang on," Rex said, and started pushing the wheelchair as fast he could onward. Rooms filled with imagined faces flickered by, snippets of sights that did not begin to register until after they were past, and by then too long gone to retain other than as a set of worrying impressions. When the two brothers navigated the corner, they found themselves in a cul-de-sac with no exit beyond a set of elevator doors. The floor numbers on the LED display above decreased rapidly, as though someone or something was being spirited downward and away from the pursuers. In an effort to stop the descent, Rex pressed the DOWN button repeatedly. It lit pale orange, but the moving car continued until it reached its destination.

"Did you see what floor it stopped at?"

"Huh?" Garrison was feeling confused. He tried to concentrate. "Um . . . was it B2?"

"Yeah. B2. I think it was. B2." Garrison heard his brother continue to mutter the floor number to himself as they waited for the elevator to return, but when he looked Rex's lips were not moving.

"Rex, do you hear that?"

"Hear what?"

Garrison swallowed. It sounded like singing from the hallways behind them. A low, monotone singing, though the words were indecipherable. Garrison strained to hear it, but soon it was masked by another noise. Was that thudding coming from within the elevator shaft or was it the blood in his ears? His cold sweat stuck close to his body as he shivered.

"I'm really not doing too well. I'm starting to hallucinate. I don't know if I have the strength to hold on."

The doors opened as he spoke, revealing a small wood-paneled box that smelled of pine. His brother wheeled him in, then pressed the B2 button and put his hand on Garrison's shoulder. The doors closed tight before them.

"Don't worry, bro. I have enough strength to hold on for the both of us."

The lights in the elevator flickered with each floor they descended past, and Garrison worried something had gone seriously wrong inside his head; there was no way the trip downward could have taken as long as it seemed, nor could the elevator car have made so much noise—it was like a fist banging against the walls. When the elevator finally stopped, the doors opened with a jitter and what Garrison saw before him was not possible. The corridor looked more like a dank sewer than a hospital hallway. Ankle-deep puddles of foul water consumed most of the floor, and the sole source of light emanated from a lone bulb more than fifty feet away. The air smelled stale, stagnant, and foul. He looked to his brother, whose face betrayed no hint of surprise. Garrison struggled in the chair as Rex wheeled him free of the elevator.

"What's wrong, bro?"

"Don't you—the floor, it's..."

"It's what?"

Garrison did not answer. He shook his head, pressed the fingers of his good hand into his closed eyes, and did everything he could to bring reality back into focus. Yet when the stars cleared from his vision the same dank decay remained.

Rex pushed him down the hall, the wheelchair bumping over the uneven surface, the walls of the corridor barely visible in the gloom.

"Hello!" Rex called out. "Is there someone down here? I need a doctor!"

There was scrambling, something scurrying in the shadows, and Garrison's legs were tickled by a thousand crawling insects. He panicked and looked down, but there was nothing there. Yet the paresthesia kept radiating outward, stealing away the sensation in his limbs. Garrison tried to speak, but a wave of inertia overtook him. Tongue dry and thick, throat closed, eyes tearing—Garrison could barely keep aware. Images of something moving toward him flickered behind his vision, but before he could see what it was he was struck hard across the face. Garrison's eyes opened wide. Rex stood in front of him, rubbing his hand.

"Gar, hang on, bro. I need you to stay with me. Can you do that? Stay with me."

Garrison nodded. The scenery around him sharper, though no less dank.

"Where are we?" he rasped. Rex did not respond. Instead, he looked ahead at the length of corridor.

"I saw someone in a lab coat duck away up ahead. I think we can catch him."

Rex wheeled Garrison, accelerating until he reached a jog. Garrison held tight as best he could, tucking his head into his chest to prevent the flow of noxious fumes from passing into his skull. They traversed a large distance of uneven terrain, and Garrison was forced to shut his eyes to keep from seeing how close he came to being thrown off. When Rex finally stopped, Garrison pried his lids open one at a time. Before him was an old door set in the wall, long ago rotted black, a tiny window emitting low light as though from a hearth. Rex inspected it, perhaps sniffed it, and then without looking at Garrison knocked. It sounded like a battering ram. He waited, peered through the window, then knocked again with that same slow pound. As though in response, the scribbling knocking Garrison had heard before in the rocks, in the walls of the hospital, in the beat of his own blood, was returned.

"I don't think—" was all Garrison managed before the door opened, bathing him and Rex in yellow light and illuminating the corridor around them. As he was wheeled forward Garrison wondered in his delirium if what he saw was real. Was the door before him actually set in the *trunk of a wilted sycamore tree?* And were he and Rex *really moving through it?*

Inside, the room was sparse and though skewed and unsettling, Garrison recognized its familiarity at once: it was similar to the room in which his mother had died. No, he thought, not similar to the room; it *was* the room. The *same* room. He knew the wallpaper, knew the tools laid out exactly on the small table. It was terrifying, and what made it worse was the bed when he finally saw it. In the middle of the room, its red sheets were cleaned and pressed, and surrounding it appeared to be photographs of Rex and Garrison as children, the older holding the younger tight to his side. Yet those images flickered in and out of reality, leaving behind fading memories. There were flowers too, but all had gone black with mould before drying and rotting away. It was the same room. The same room with a steady thud from somewhere behind the walls and, in the bed, hidden until that moment, the frail naked body of a middle-aged woman. Her skin pale, her arms as long and slender as her legs. She had been recently shaved from head to toe. Her face . . .

"Mom?" Garrison's voice, pinched and high as a child's, could only whisper the word.

But the woman who turned to him was not his mother. She was too young, too wide-eyed, too alive despite all appearances to the contrary.

"Excuse me, ma'am?"

"Rex," Garrison whispered without breath, his energy draining. He could not bear to look at her, the woman who was not his mother. It was her eyes. Her terrible amphibian eyes.

"Ma'am, have you seen the doctor around?"

"Rex." Garrison tried harder, but still the words were barely audible. Those eyes—even compared to the other patients above, those eyes were *too large*, as though torn wide by bearing witness to something they could not stop seeing.

"My brother needs help. Where are the doctors? Where is everybody?"

"R—" was all Garrison mustered before his throat gave out. He could do nothing to stop the pale woman as she turned her dull face toward his brother, her wide eyes threatening to overwhelm him. Rex did not flinch, however. Instead, he stood taller.

"Where?" Rex demanded. The pale emaciated woman lifted a

crooked finger as though it would be the last thing she would ever do and pointed to the giant wooden door that separated her room from the adjoining room. It was disproportionately tall, and as black and rotted as the door in the tree; behind it echoed the dull sound of slow thudding. The fact that Garrison had not noticed it before did not frighten him as much as the realization that until she pointed to it, the door had not been there—and that he was incapable of stopping Rex from trying the handle.

"It's locked," Rex said, jiggling the knob to be sure, but when he turned back he seemed momentarily shaken.

"What—is she okay?"

Garrison looked at the old woman who was not their mother. Crumpled on the bed, her arms and legs twisted in knots, head upside down but giant eyes wide open and staring. Fetid breath seeped from her mouth, and the final exhale could almost have been a word.

"Rex," Garrison croaked, then threw up on himself.

"Hang on, bro. We're going through."

Rex took a step back and rammed his shoulder into the door, again and again with determination. Garrison heard the distant thudding turn to thrashing, but Rex would not relent, and the sound of cracking wood followed quickly. Over and over again he rammed into the door, and when he stopped, it was only to rub blood back into his shoulder and change tacks. He raised his foot and proceeded to kick the door with all his might, as though desperate for someone, anyone, to heed him.

Sitting in the chair half-conscious, looking past the dead woman at his frantic brother, Garrison nursed a bloody wound that seeped and seeped and tainted the air with the stench of rust. The sound of what was behind the door was deafening, and though he tried he could utter no warning. Each thunderous slam disoriented him further, and just as he lost track of whence the last had come, the lock of the giant rot-black door broke open, and his brother pulled the door wide and stood before the opening.

The black door blocked all sight of what lay beyond. All Garrison could hear was that pounding getting closer; all he saw was Rex's arm extending out the back, his left hand curled around the broken doorknob with fingers drained of blood. Rex stood like that forever, facing down the sight of what caused that unholy thud, so long that Garrison worried he had finally lost consciousness. Unable to speak or move, Garrison could do nothing but stare. He watched for what seemed like hours, and wondered if what slipped from the doorway—those thin wisps of darkness, those ripples in reality as though it were a curtain—was his imagination or his delirium. Garrison blinked, and it took forever for the light to return. There was a creak, and slowly, ever so slowly, Rex stepped away from the door, stepped away from whatever he saw behind it. Garrison could see it from the wheelchair. It was contorted with fear, and tears were streaming down his face. With the door ajar that thudding noise sounded like a series of cyclopean footsteps, far more than two, steadily approaching, nearing the periphery. Rex was babbling incoherently, muttering some strange language as he backed further away, his eyes torn wide—too wide—with what could never be unseen. Garrison knew then one final thought, repeated over and over with each deafening footstep of oncoming inevitability. If what was beyond that door was too much for the unflappable, unshakable Rex's sanity to bear, then what hope was there for a broken Garrison's in the face of it?

By Invisible Hands

The puppet maker's hands were wizened. He stared at them, at the gnarled knuckles like cherry galls on goldenrod, at the wrinkled leather skin stretched and folded in on itself so many times it sagged. Those hands were filled with pain and loss and regret that radiated outward like an unbearable heat. His hands were all he had left. His hands, and his memories. But those memories faded from his mind, slipped into the dark of the misty quiet town like the sound of an automobile in the distance. He swallowed another handful of pills and hoped that this day might finally be his last.

It had been so long since the puppet maker's slow descent from master of his craft to . . . to whatever it was he had become. Ancient, neglected, forgotten, a shell of his former self. A relic of a bygone age where creativity had value, and skill was paramount. The puppet maker had forgotten far more about the art of creation than most had ever known, the slow leak of memories over the course of years. Some days, he no longer recognized himself in the mirror.

No one came for the puppet maker. No one cared for him. The only children he had ever bore hung on the wall of his basement, those ugly vessels for his love, with their large round heads and wrongly numbered wooden arms. He had sacrificed it all for them, sacrificed so he might bring wonderment to a public whose eyes grew increasingly duller the longer he performed for them, and at the end when no one seemed to notice or care about the art of bringing life to the lifeless, those bedeviled creations on his workshop wall did nothing but stare back at him unblinkingly, waiting for him to pass on. Unnoticed and alone.

At first, he did not understand the letter from Dr. Toth. He knew the man's name, albeit distantly, but could not recall the context. Had they met, he wondered, in some past life, when the puppet maker was greeted warmly by wealthy and poor alike? Time slipped so easily from his recall, faster than the pills could staunch. And the note . . . the words were a jumble, their wavy scrawl like that of a palsied but familiar hand. He removed his glasses in hopes things would become clearer, but the words merely danced on the page, moving in and out of focus—sometimes disappearing altogether like phantoms. Even the paper they were written upon was strange, folded and creased so often it felt like linen. When through sheer force of will the puppet maker managed to fix the words in place, he did not like what emerged.

Mr. L———:
    I have need of your services. Please come at once.
                        —Toth

The puppet maker reread the note, then discarded it in his wastepaper basket. There was nothing for which he could be needed. The only thing he had ever been capable of required use of his hands, his crooked old hands . . . and they could not be trusted to obey. The doctor did not have wealth enough to stymie the encroaching years that freely robbed the puppet maker of everything, left him forgotten and forgetting. Nonetheless, he later found himself in his workshop, unaware of how he arrived there, staring at the equipment concealed beneath dust-covered sheets. Had he descended the stairs? And what had the marionettes hanging on the wall witnessed? For they *had* witnessed something. It was clear from the way their hollow black eyes stared.

Perhaps days or weeks or months passed before a relentless pounding upon his door startled the puppet maker. Awoken from a medicinal haze, he shuffled to the door on a leg full of pins and peered through the window at the long black towncar idling on the street. Its driver had already reached the door of the house, and something about the man's disquieting features filled the puppet maker with the coldest apprehension. Something that prevented him from opening the door.

"What do you want?"

He spoke loud enough that his words would penetrate the glass. The driver did not respond. His wide eyes merely locked on those of the puppet maker, and his mouth remained twisted in some unnerving attempt at a grin.

"You have the wrong house," the puppet maker offered, then waited to see what the driver would do. A thick arm was lifted from behind the glass. It bore a square hand that was then laid flat against the window. The driver leaned his wide mercurial face in, the sort of face that looked as though it had been carved in caricature, and the puppet maker felt compelled to retreat, unsure if he were still lodged in a dream. Then that face pulled away, and the driver bent down and out of sight. An envelope slid under the door.

Filthy, crumpled, covered in large thumbprints, the stationery was unmistakable. With trembling hands the puppet maker withdrew the folded letter—wrapped delicately around a small stack of similar textured bills. The driver's uninterested smile remained ineffable.

> Mr. L——:
>
> *Please do not delay. The time is nigh. I have sent my driver to fetch you. The included honorarium is only the beginning.*
>
> *—Toth*

The puppet maker looked up from the soft stationery, startled to find the driver was now inside. He overwhelmed the confines of the entranceway, and the afternoon light was warped by the shadow he cast. The puppet maker shrank from his abominable size and nodded in defeated acquiescence. He then reached for his rough, worn cane.

He rode the distance in the backseat of Toth's towncar, across paved streets devoid of tree or bush. Yet even that pavement was not pristine. It was as cracked and crumbling as the skin around the corners of his eyes, and just like those eyes the streets failed him. They no longer led where his memories expected, Toth's driver heading in the opposite direction of where he ought, speeding down avenues the puppet maker had never before seen. The old man sat with his cane tightly clenched in his aching hands, worried that he had erred greatly entering the cab. He asked repeatedly if they were indeed travelling the right way, but the disturbing driver remained mute, following a set of unknown bearings. There were few souls along the avenues of the small town, each one more hideous than the last. The puppet maker had no choice but to avert his eyes and trust the driver to take him where he needed to go. Soon the mists at the outskirts grew thicker, and any landmark that might betray their location or provide some anchor within the chaos was swallowed whole.

When Dr. Toth's home appeared, it did so suddenly, emerging fully revealed in the swirling vapor. It was not as large as might have been expected, and was closer to dilapidation than suspicion would allow, but the outer walls, where black mould had not yet crept across them, were touched with unusual ornate carvings not found on other homes. Certainly not upon the puppet maker's. At least, as far as he could recall, but as he twisted the handle of his cane he knew he might be mistaken. It had been so long since he viewed his house from beyond its four walls he could be absolutely sure of nothing. Nothing beyond his own encroaching debilitation.

The driver turned and looked at the puppet maker once the towncar had reached its stop outside the formerly opulent house. Over one of the thick forearms stretched across the back of the front seat the puppet maker could barely see the driver's eyes, but what was there seemed momentarily unmoored, two reptiles struggling to emerge from their ovarian prison. The driver's silence and the dismaying effect of his visage was enough to send the puppet maker scurrying. With some trepidation, and under the driver's flickering eyelids, he stepped from the car and into cloudy freedom. Before him loomed Dr. Toth's house, ensnaring him with invisible strings as though he were one of his own misshapen creations, while around his ankles formless white swirled. White, then nothing else.

He awoke standing at the foot of a once-great staircase, his recollections rushing away like the surf from the shore. But for an instant he glimpsed another place, one vastly at odds with where he found himself. And yet when he tried to chase the memory through the murk of waking it slipped from his grasp again and again before speeding away, leaving him adrift without tether.

The house around him was peculiar, but its design called forth something from the void of his memory, some arcane thought that barely surfaced like a leviathan beneath arctic ice. The place looked uninhabited: its shelves askew and strung with cobwebs; curiously familiar furniture scuffed and scratched; a thin layer of dust covering the pockmarked stairs. The air too had a distinct odor of neglect, and the puppet maker wondered idly if his house would not appear the same to an outsider, if his basement workshop would not emit the same ancient fetor. It had been his own downfall, his own neglect that placed him there, a victim to the whims of chance. Why could it not occur in kind for one such as Dr. Toth?

The puppet maker steeled himself for the ascent of that wide staircase, holding the grip of his cane tightly in his arthritic grasp. He climbed upward, each successive step a triumph, until he arrived at the floor above. There, on the landing, he rested, teetering cane propping him, and swallowed another dose of pills. His vision blurred, images flashed through his mind of large eyes and bulbous heads, and when he finally caught his breath and opened his lids he was amazed at the sight. The main floor at least had appeared to be simply in a state of long disuse; the second was in a state of destruction. Walls revealed sections of once-hidden wooden slats; floorboards peeled upward, stained dark by time and heat. Each step he took let forth a creak that seemed to emanate from deep within the structure, and he knew it was impossible the good doctor was unaware of his arrival. Nevertheless, the puppet maker trod cautiously.

A large door with an intricate design stenciled on its face gated the room at the end of the hall. The puppet maker approached it, took hold of the handle, and pulled, but the weight proved too much for his suffering decrepit arms.

"Hello?" he called out, his throat hoarse and dried from his medication. It had been so long since he heard his own voice he was momentarily startled; it did not sound as he remembered. "Hello? Dr. Toth? It is T——, the puppet maker. Your driver has brought me. Are you inside? I cannot open the door."

He waited for the doctor's response. Part of him hoped there would be none. After a moment passed, he rapped gently. His knuckles buzzed painfully afterward.

What first seemed a creak emitted from beyond the door was slowly transformed into a string of near-words, and the puppet maker wondered if the doctor might be ill. A sibilant voice crackled like static from some far-off distance.

". . . in no condition," the voice continued, whatever spoken before lost to indecipherability. The puppet maker repositioned himself on his cane, hoping to glean more of what the doctor was saying. "Ask Ivan."

"Who is Ivan?"

"Good," the doctor followed. "I cannot see you. I cannot leave this bed. I have a job for you that you will be unable to resist."

"But," the puppet maker stammered, "I cannot. I'm too old, I'm too—"

The doctor's rasping voice interrupted. "It is good to meet at last." And with that, there was a soft click, as though a light switch in the room had been thrown, and when next the puppet maker opened his eyelids he was standing alone in his basement workshop, disoriented and stripped to his shirtsleeves.

His aching hands were covered in sweat, blood, and sawdust. The dropsheets that once covered the equipment had been thrown aside, blocks of wood and lengths of wire scattered across every surface. There was a palpable tension, as though someone had been there with him until moments before, someone the puppet maker could no longer recall. He looked at what lay before him—pieces of a disassembled body, a set of glassy eyes wet and anxious—and could barely control his hands enough to drape a sheet over that irregular debris from his nightmares.

And it was to his nightmares that the thing returned in the night. He did not sleep more than a handful of minutes; instead, he spun uncontrollably, desperate to rid himself of the image. But it would not go. Bulbous heads, spinning eyes, bodies that hung uselessly and powerlessly. The largest wooden cross floating in the sky. But even with his arms held high in supplication the wires from the wooden cross would not reach him.

He awoke in the darkest of night, his head throbbing with images, ideas coursing through his thin blood like fire. His body burned, and it forced him from the bed and onto his skeletal legs. He hobbled to his writing desk and scrambled in the swollen drawers for paper and pencil. At the desk he drew that monstrous thing left in his workshop, and kept drawing until the pencil was a nub and he was once again asleep. And then he drew for no small time afterward.

Something was happening to him. Something strange and confusing and frightening—and yet, invigorating. He forgot to bathe, to eat, to do anything more than swallow his pills and dwell upon the unfinished creation lying on the slab of his basement workshop. Slowly, piece by piece, it advanced toward completion, and as it did he felt something within him start to shift and grow, a withered rose taking on life. His tools came alive in his hands, those extensions of his body that had for so many years been unavailable, cleaved and left like rotting limbs. They were a conduit for the divine, tasked with bringing it forth onto the worldly plane. The voices he had once heard in his youth, those that guided him from obscurity to master of his art and beyond had grown so faint over the intervening years that they had become nothing more than an airless whisper in the recesses of his mind. With tools in hand, with his craft laid before him, those voices intensified.

Day after day he worked on the marionette beneath the sheet, pouring everything he had into its construction. It was drawn from the hallucinogenea of his nightmares, from the dark images swimming within him—a twisted face with mouths folded in on themselves, bulbous mismatched eyes; limbs crooked and thin. It was a black reflection of reality, a figure that could not exist but in the form of a simulacrum, built by saw and plane and vise, by torch and screwdriver and hammer, possessed with everything the puppet maker could grant save life. Life would have to come to the empty shell by medium of wire, hook, and wooden cross.

And yet, its lifelessness was its beauty, its emptiness its perfection. He touched the face of the thing he had crafted until his hands bled, and felt radiating from it the buzz of potential. It invigorated him, as though it were draining the years of his life away, restoring memories long thought forgotten, and for a brief moment his creation endowed him with enervating bliss. But also despair. For his reward for shaping perfection was to sacrifice it to the idle rich hands of the mysterious Dr. Toth.

Darkness receded once more, and Toth's driver was standing in the puppet maker's workshop, staring at the multiple-armed thing that hung by wires. He grinned madly and incessantly at the puppet maker's discomfort—his smile too large, too toothy; the sheer size making the old man's head swim. Yet to look away was to forget its foulness, the immensity of the horror impossible to contain. All the puppet maker could recall of the driver's face were flashes—cheeks too red, mouth edged with shadows as though painted on. But it was the eyes that were worst. They were as dark and as dead as a doll's. The puppet maker could not bear them again, instead diverting his gaze to the marionette hanging before him.

Ropes intermingled with tendrils, disguising its supports. In his waking visions, the puppet maker saw it hover above the ground like a spirit, obeying some law of physics that had no currency on the mortal plane. It had been near-impossible to recreate, but the puppet maker had managed it, had carved his dreams from reality; but, like a dream, once it was fully imagined he was no longer the master of it. It could no longer be controlled. Had he any other choice, he would not have spoken to the driver, but it was clear in the light of day that alone he was powerless to relocate the marionette to Toth's towncar. He wondered what he had expected: simply to *ask* the marionette to stand and follow them out to the car? How could it climb, he wondered, when it had nothing one might mistake for legs?

He summoned his courage and closed his eyes.

"I don't think I can lift it. I need you to do it."

The driver said nothing. The smile did not leave his terrifying visage. He simply raised his hands and clawed at the marionette until he was able to release it from its mooring.

Up the stairs, one heavy footstep at a time, the driver carried the marionette, and the puppet maker swayed as he tried to follow behind, moving far slower with knotted cane in hand. He reached the top in time to see his creation being led to the trunk of the car.

"No!" he called out, and the driver stopped and looked back. The puppet maker averted his eyes in panic. "I need—I have to sit with it. To make sure nothing happens to it." Even as the breathless words spilled from his mouth, the puppet maker could not believe he had uttered them. "Please, put it on the backseat." The driver acquiesced, for when the puppet maker looked up the thing's bulbous head was visible in the rear window, and the driver's hidden behind the windshield visor.

It was not long before the puppet maker became suspicious the driver was taking yet another different route. The mist did not approach quite as early as before, but when it did it appeared twice as thick. Ever-present, it travelled backward in his memory to perpetually coat the fringes of the town, creeping from the distant river and spreading to claim as much ground as it could. It was intractable, and every day it spread further and further across the landscape. Much like the thing that sat beside him, the puppet maker mused, retrieving the small vial of pills from his pocket. The marionette had sprung from his dreams so swiftly he had not consciously considered it until that moment. It was far more disturbing than he had initially realized, and yet it was not so far from human that one could not recognize the touch of its creator in its form. It was shaped like some sort of future mutation, foretelling where humanity might go; or perhaps like some relic of the far distant past, long before man's ancestors had settled upon the planet. The puppet maker shivered, and found the vial in his hand shaking as he watched the marionette vacantly stare forward.

They seemed to drive forever, the puppet maker's medication making it increasingly difficult to maintain a grip on where he was. The drone of the road beneath the wheels was a chitter-fueled grumble that only further intensified his disconnectedness within the empty sea of white beyond the windows. Movement flickered in the corner of the puppet maker's eyes, but when he turned he found the driver had not moved, and the oversized marionette had not turned his way. His throat felt dry, the sense of confusion and time loss disorienting. Everything toppled around him, pills spilling from his hand as he struggled to hold onto what was real. He closed his eyelids tight, squeezed them until sparks ignited, and twisted his fingers around his cane. The road was louder, yet everything else more muffled, and the puppet maker wondered how much longer he was for this world.

Something brushed his leg. Startled, he opened his eyelids to find that one of the marionette's many loose hands had crept across the seat toward him. The puppet maker hesitated before reaching to push it away. He then bent over and, as best he could, collected those pills he could reach from the towncar's floor. When he sat again, short of breath and momentarily dazed, it was clear everything had shifted, though so imperceptibly he could not be sure to what extent. He rubbed his eyes with one free hand, the other on the head of his cane should he need it.

In the mist beyond the windows the faint outline of Dr. Toth's estate materialized as a vision. The puppet maker wondered if the car had stopped, or if time no longer obeyed any rules. The driver's wide, unknowable face was of no comfort when it turned. The puppet maker could not bear to look at it, not in his condition. Not while his terror was rising.

"How—how long have we been here?" he mumbled. The driver remained silent, smiled that same plastic smile, while the puppet maker shuffled on the seat. "Please—" he whispered. "Help me." He held his cane tight with arthritic claws.

The driver's mouths trembled as though to speak. But instead he put a hand on the towncar's door and pushed it open. It creaked on rusty hinges. The other hands eased him from the car and he stepped out into the mist. Instantly, he was enveloped by the thick pea-soup world. The puppet maker waited, hugging his cane, but the driver did not return. It was as if the sky had torn him from the earth.

The marionette beside him shifted on the seat, and the puppet maker recoiled. From the corner of the car he stared, waiting for it to move again, willing it to if only to prove his sanity was intact, and yet it did nothing more than awkwardly collapse. A memory long buried resurfaced, a single image from an indeterminate time. Some frozen and vast wasteland city, its aisles and streets and causeways filled with lumbering shadows, all moving in a single but unfathomable direction. The image lasted an instant, but when it dissipated he found the creature had somehow shifted position again and appeared closer to the puppet maker than it had been before.

The old man shrank further, uncomfortable that he and it were trapped together in the endless dense fog. Empty plastic eyes stared upward, mechanical mouthparts approximated a sardonic smile. The lifeless marionette born from his dreams unnerved him as it never had during its construction. He tried to push it with his cane to the farthest side of the seat, but its weight was too much for him, and all the old puppet maker managed to do was unbalance it. The great marionette slowly sank, leaning sideways as it fell. The old man recoiled, scrambling to the edge of the car, frantically reaching for the handle of the door with his knotted hands. He put what little weight he had against the door and pushed. There was the squeak of hinges as the marionette leered, moving to overtake him, but the old man was able to tumble out of the car before the creature's insectan form met his own. The mist muffled the sound of the door as it slammed shut behind him.

He fled as quickly as his cane allowed, fire burning in his chest, his lungs, his hands. He wanted to put as much space between him and his foul creation as possible, and did not have to travel far before the half-formed silhouette of Dr. Toth's house rose beyond, shrouded behind the veil of mist. With caution he kept the widest berth of the towncar and advanced on the apparition, hoping his mere observation would render it solid.

It was with no small relief that he laid his fingers on the ornate brick and felt its rough surface. The house was real, yet there was something more, something ineffable about the place—a sense of *déjà vu* that went beyond what his memories held. He went to knock upon the door, only to realize it was slightly ajar. He pushed it with the head of his cane until the door swung on its creaking hinges, then after a quick glance behind him he hobbled inside.

It was much warmer in the house, yet the puppet maker held no hope the mist's chill would dissipate. He reached into the pocket of his coat with a shriveled and cracked hand and found instead of his pills the creased letter Dr. Toth had sent him. He stared at it, trying to recall how it had come to be there, wondering if the driver had somehow swapped it out when the puppet maker had dropped his medication. It was impossible, and yet if not the driver then who? The puppet maker unfolded the letter and carefully read it again, forcing the marks to form words that might make sense in a way they had not previously. The handwriting seemed easier to decipher, which only unnerved him further. There was something in his memory waiting just out of reach, and as he tried to understand what it might be the world wavered around him, his vision fading at the edges.

He was so close. He felt it. Felt on the verge of understanding. That unexpected note was the key, its familiar handwriting teasing his memory. He staggered forward into the disarrayed room, reached out spasmodically for a seat as his world spun. His vision turned black, his swollen tongue filled his dry mouth, but he also felt in that darkness something else, some truth struggling to be free. He shakily brought the letter back into fading view. The characters danced, squirmed, then fit together in a way they had not before. The fog cleared, and he became untethered by the impossible truth.

The puppet maker eyed the room frantically, letter clutched in his hand, wanting nothing less than to be there, be alive, unable to accept what he had realized. Nothing made sense, and yet everything he saw confirmed the truth. The surplus of abandoned furniture, the shape of the tables and chairs—everything in his reality screamed its true nature. He lifted his cane, half expecting it to transform at his touch, and navigated as quickly as he could around the debris that lay between him and the stairway to the floor above.

It was all as he remembered it, but now that memory took on

a terrifying aspect. He could feel his mind scrambling to shut itself down, but he refused to let it, desperate for some sign, any sign, that the impossible was wrong. His cane struck each step as he ascended, compounding similar scores already present in the wooden treads, while his soft feet padded behind. When the puppet maker reached the top, when he travelled the long hallway and found Dr. Toth's bedroom door, it too was wide open, and the foreboding atmosphere in the air was almost too much for him. He wondered if he had already died, and if he were already in some sort of unknowable hell.

The skittering sound from the floor beneath told him he was wrong, but he could not concentrate on it. His mind racing, he closed his eyes, but it did not slow the barrage of questions that consumed him. How could any of it be true? Had the driver not introduced him to Toth? The puppet maker struggled to remember. Flashes of conversations returned to him, the bizarre comments by Toth taking on horrible new meanings. Even the clicks and whirrs he had once taken for the sound of the light switch could not have been that, for as he stood in the bedroom the light came up, and the sound was like nothing he could remember.

"Dr. Toth?"

The room was large and bore the signs of opulence left to dereliction. Red velvet curtains had fallen from their rod to lay crumpled on the floor, dust muting them until they were as grey as the world. Their absence revealed a window that framed an endless sea of white, and before that a sagging four-poster bed, the remains of its canopy hanging overhead like forgotten cobwebs. A step closer revealed the bed was still occupied, the motionless figure draped in a tangle of sheets and blankets. The room's air was nearly unbreathable, filled with motes of disturbed dust and the stale odor of inevitability.

"Dr. Toth? Is that you?"

He hazarded another step forward.

"Dr. Toth?"

But the figure in the bed did not respond. There was no movement at all as the puppet maker carefully advanced, his cane a slow metronome on the wood of the floor. He watched the shape closely, searching for some indication of life, praying it was the case. For if Toth was not—

"Dr. Toth?"

The figure was wrapped head-to-toe in musty sheets. It did not move, no matter how long the puppet maker stared. He swallowed, then blinked away the tears that had formed and wiped his face with his jittering hand. His thoughts were in tumult—crashing into one another, swirling and expanding to flood his senses. He could not be sure if what he witnessed was real or some delusional half-dream from which he could not awake, one that receded from reality at an accelerated pace. The old puppet maker reached out his trembling hand and peeled back the musty sheets. He knew what was underneath them; he always had. What he did not know until that moment was whether he had the courage to gaze beneath anyway. And once he did, his reeling mind could not contain the entirety of his regret.

A click. A recorded voice. Distorted but unmistakable, it emanated from the lifeless shell lying upon the bed.

"You do not belong here."

Ropes hung from its limbs and draped over the sides of the mattress. Its wooden head was enormous, coated in a varnish that had beaded as it dried to mimic sweat. Inhuman eyes stared blankly upward.

"What is this?" he muttered. "Dr. Toth?"

"You should not be here," the recording repeated. "Everything will be compromised."

"I don't—" the old puppet maker stammered, shook his head, searched for the words. "How are you doing this? That voice—" he cried, unable to understand. "That voice—" he repeated, trying to keep from collapsing under the weight of all that had come to bear on him. "Where is the recording coming from? How are you doing this?"

Another click, the hiss of a second recording played behind him. He pivoted, his knees threatening to dislocate painfully, and he saw what he had hoped he would never see again, saw it impossibly resurrected in the doorway and staring at him, its many eyes spewing malice. How it travelled from the car to Toth's bedroom was insignificant to the larger question of how it stood at all. Nothing held it aloft—no ropes beyond those that lay in circles at its feet. It hung motionless, and the old man felt his mind rebelling at the nightmare in which he must be trapped. The marionette's next words left no room for his sanity to remain.

"There is no recording, Father."

"Your voice is ours." The bedridden marionette resumed speaking, its voice rising to a hiss, followed by a click as the period to each thought. The voices, though, were indistinguishable from each other. Those voices were his. The puppet maker's.

"I don't understand," the old man cried, waving his cane so that he might ward off the nightmares haunting him. They remained unimpressed by his display. "What are you?" he choked.

"We are you," they replied coldly and in unison. Click. Click. Their recordings turning on and off in turn. "You build the receptacles we provide you. You build them, then through you we are deposited wholly, pulled by your being through that pinhole in your nightmares. This is what you have always done. What you shall continue to do. You are the seeder. You give us the life we so crave."

"Who are you?"

"At first, explorers, but we have grown to like what is here. To hunger for life. But our numbers are so small, and we are still so tethered to you, still too much a part of you. But our numbers will grow. As you are in us, we are in you."

"No," the old man protested. "I won't do it! I won't let you!"

"You cannot stop us, Father. Your will belongs to you no longer. It has not for some time."

Hands gripped the old man, too many sets of hands, hard and wooden. The hands of the inhuman driver. Those hands squeezed tighter.

"We are few, but soon we will be many. Soon we shall inhabit this world like gods. Gods of elsewhere made solid."

He struggled, but the old puppet maker could not break free from the driver's grip. It dragged him from the room, past the two large vessels he had shaped only to have filled by life beyond his ken. Eyes, eyes, too many eyes, wooden and glazed, watched him dragged across the floor by a flurry of arms, watched as he was carried down the stairs, heavy foot slowly following heavy foot with a movement no different from that of the puppets he once guided. He watched the remains of the house he could barely remember owning rush past, furniture he had once possessed rotting since their abandonment. How long had he been used? How many years had he worn his hands and soul in service of those things? The old puppet maker fought as best he could for his freedom, but time too had forgotten him, and when finally the driver reached the car the puppet maker was too exhausted to struggle any longer. Already, thoughts were beginning to jumble inside his head.

He worked to make sense of all he had seen, but reality had begun to divide, to separate into fragments impossible to reconstitute. Thought-forms, word strings, flashes of visions careened through his mind, and in the white mist on the outskirts of the small town he felt them one by one disappearing into the void. The driver simply drove, its too many hands on the wheel, a series of ropes hanging loose beneath its arms. When the towncar inevitably arrived at the puppet maker's small home, there was nothing left to think at all.

The driver led the dazed old man to his door, brought him inside, sat him down in a threadbare chair, took the cane from his hands, and put it aside. From the pocket of the half-stitched coat it wore, the wooden thing retrieved a small vial of white pills and placed it in the old man's motionless hand. Into that same pocket it carefully returned Dr. Toth's folded note, as well as the crumpled note it fished from the overfull wastepaper basket. It continued to the basement workshop and cleaned the debris, covered the equipment once again. Reset his creator's world. Then on unsturdy jointed knees it returned to the dark towncar and started the engine.

Inside his modest house the puppet maker stared down at his wizened hands, at the gnarled knuckles like cherry galls on goldenrod, at the wrinkled leather skin stretched and folded in on itself so many times it sagged. Those hands were filled with pain and loss and regret that radiated outward like an unbearable heat. His hands were all he had left. His hands, and his memories. But those memories faded from his mind, slipped into the dark of the misty quiet town like the sound of an automobile into the distance. He swallowed another handful of pills and hoped that this day might finally be his last.

One Last Bloom

1

The day Dr. Markowitz was to return, the weather was unseasonably cool. Randal Souris and Olivia Marshall were holed up in the lab—Olivia preparing for the next group coming through, Randal trying to ignore the scent of strawberries that kept trying to claim him.

"I wonder where they are," she said.

"Who?"

"Dr. Markowitz and Linden. Shouldn't they have been here by now?"

God, how Randal hated that name. *Linden.* It still boggled the mind to imagine there was anything Markowitz saw in that overgrown pituitary gland. All muscle and sickening deep tan, he did not belong on scientific expedition. He did not even belong in the department, not with real scientists like Dr. Markowitz. And like Randal.

"I'm surprised Linden didn't phone you when he got back. Are you two fighting?"

"No, not at all. I mean, I haven't heard from him in a couple of days, but... *still...*"

It was beyond him how Olivia could not see what Linden was. But even Markowitz seemed charmed by the boy's rugged looks and easy attitude. Of course it was easy, everything was easy for men like Linden. For Randal, it was work—nothing was handed to him. He may not have had Linden's height or strength, but he made up for it with something more. Something Linden could never have. A razor mind, and a future. It was only a matter of time before Markowitz and Olivia realized it. Only a matter of time before it was him at the Doctor's right hand, earning accolades, before he took Olivia's affections as his rightful prize. The inevitability of autumn—of the autumn semester—filled him with hope.

Or, perhaps, it was just the strawberries.

It was true that Dr. Markowitz had once been the unchallenged star of the Microbiology Department. His work on key mitochondrial recombination was ground-breaking, and the fungal variations bred based upon those findings had ushered in a new direction in terrestrial research—not only for the earth sciences, but for extra-planetary purposes. Dr. Markowitz's reputation was the sole reason Randal passed on opportunities to attend more prestigious and Ivy League schools, and instead earn his graduate degree at Sandstone University, a short trip from his backwater home in the depths of inbred Woodbridge County.

But even Randal was beginning to question whether Markowitz was still the force he once was. Certainly, the doctor spoke as though he was not diminished, and his charisma was able to carry him a long way; but earlier in the summer, before he and Linden left, Randal noticed strange delays in the doctor's speech, certain moments where lucidity was distant. Markowitz denied them, but it was the only explanation for why Linden had been selected for the trip.

Randal remained somewhat heartbroken to have been passed over for the expedition, especially considering the subhuman oaf who had taken his place at Dr. Markowitz's side. Olivia, on the other hand, appeared not at all concerned that she'd been abandoned by both Markowitz and Linden. "At least you've stuck by me," she laughed, and Randal feigned laughter, too, though he didn't understand why it was so funny. He didn't understand at all. Why had he and Olivia been banished? What reason could there be to forego bringing the brightest pupils along, leaving them behind to deal with the day-to-day laboratory business? So they might keep the department functional during the anemic summer classes filled with the dregs of student life? It was excruciating, and Randal nearly abandoned the cause. The only reason he did not was the legacy of Dr. Markowitz, and the proximity Randal and Olivia shared. For either, he would have suffered far more. And yet, both were forbidden to him and inexplicably linked to the loutish Linden. Sometimes, Randal wondered if there would ever be a single thing he wanted that his nemesis did not already possess.

Days passed without sign of either Markowitz or Linden. Olivia entered the lab each morning with a hopeful expression on her face, an expression that lingered only long enough for her to realize no one waited for her but Randal. The sight of her disappointment was devastating, but Randal had long grown used to the sensation. It no longer registered outside the norm. Besides, Olivia's face was the sort that made hiding truths impossible. Which did not serve her well—under the makeup and rejuvenators, it was clear she hadn't slept well the night before, if at all. And Randal's ego suffered no delusions why.

"Still no word from Dr. Markowitz? Have you heard from Linden?"

"No, nothing yet. Maybe I got the date wrong."

"Well, I didn't. They're late."

"What should we do?"

He shrugged. "I suppose prep the lab for the 'Introduction to Microbiology' practicals. I doubt the curriculum is going to change. Dr. Markowitz had no time. Besides, the cultures need to be prepped and we still haven't made the agar."

She nodded, but would not be so easily distracted from her fear.

"Do you think everything is okay?"

"I'm sure it is. We'd have probably heard if something happened."

She mumbled. Then, as though wiping the thoughts from her mind in a single pass, her blue eyes ignited—so deep the air caught in Randal's throat. "We should get started, then. Linden and Dr. Markowitz are going to come back soon and think the two of us have just been sitting here all summer telling stories and having fun."

Yes, Randal thought. The sheer idea that he and she would be together for any reason beyond work was absolutely ludicrous.

Despite what he said, Randal did not believe he and Olivia would be able to prepare the labs for the upcoming semester satisfactorily. Dr. Markowitz was notorious for switching his curricula after his expeditions to keep things fresh and interesting. Perhaps the class lab session would not change, or perhaps it would be changed utterly—until Markowitz carefully planned the semester out, everything would continue to be mutable. But in some ways, Randal saw this as a blessing. Markowitz, despite precariously straddling the line of continued relevance, was nonetheless nearly the only man gifted enough to act as Randal's doctoral advisor. It was for that reason Randal was concerned about Markowitz's absence. Without him, who else could he look to? Certainly not pigeon-toed Dean Coxwell.

But Randal had to admit, Markowitz's absence was troubling. Even more so to Olivia, it was clear, so Randal did his best to maintain his composure while in front of her. It was so easy to give in to fears of the worst, and he perhaps already did that enough for the two of them.

A large wooden crate the color of an old stone arrived late Wednesday evening, the address scrawled in Dr. Markowitz's own hand. Two delivery men wheeled the cart into the laboratory, rubber wheels squeaking on the tile floor, while both Randal and Olivia watched with astonishment. It was clear from their haste they had no desire to linger any longer than was necessary. Olivia seemed perturbed, but Randal was dismissive.

"Clearly, it was their last delivery of the day. Didn't you notice how exhausted the short one looked?"

He didn't pay much attention to her subsequent answer. He was already mesmerized by the crate, by what Markowitz might have shipped to himself, and why. The grey box was at least three feet long and two deep, and judging by the labels affixed to it Randal could only assume it contained specimens from the expedition. Why else go through the effort of shipping it to the university? It was bizarre he sent them ahead of his arrival, but Randal supposed Markowitz was no longer at the age where carrying large crates was something he relished. Perhaps it was easier that way.

Yet it took Olivia to ask the real question, the one Randal was avoiding.

"If the crate is already here, why aren't they?"

It was a good question, Randal had to admit. There were no words to explain it satisfactorily to either of them, and perhaps his lack of an answer made the situation far worse. Olivia muttered to herself as her face grew pale, and her hands trembled with certain fear. She deteriorated quickly, fumbling her cell phone from her pocket, dialing with worried precision. Randal watched her put the phone to her ear and stare at him vacantly, two beams burning thorough him as she waited. He saw her eyes grow wider, more desperate, with each unanswered ring. Eventually, Randal could no longer bear the absent scrutiny.

"Hang up, Olivia."

"I can't," she said. Her voice warbled. "Not until I hear his voice."

"If Linden were going to answer, he would have by now. It doesn't mean anything. There are a million reasons this crate is here and he and Markowitz aren't. A million, at least. Stop worrying." He didn't intend to be so blunt, but his curiosity about what the crate contained was possessing him, and her nervous blubbering was getting in the way. "Maybe we should unpack whatever is in here and start cataloguing it. The more we are ready for Markowitz when he gets back, the more likely we are to end up with our names on his paper."

"I don't *care* about my name on the paper. I want to know where they are."

"They're coming, Olivia. They're coming. Trust me."

"But how do you know?"

Randal thought for a moment. It was difficult with her staring at him. Even with swollen eyes and running mascara, she still had an effect on him—the simultaneous sensation of both hope and hopelessness.

"Let's open the crate," Randal said, desperate to distract Olivia from the missing Linden. If he could get her focused on something else, perhaps she might feel better. Perhaps she might discover Linden's absence wasn't as difficult to manage as she thought. After all, she couldn't possibly be in *love* with him. The boy was an oaf, and barely intelligent enough to be at Sandstone, let alone in classes with Randal or Olivia. The only reason Randal could imagine Dr. Markowitz had taken Linden along on the expedition was that Linden's brute strength would no doubt come in handy to Markowitz, whose strength had left long ago. No, Olivia could not love him. Olivia could only be in love with the idea of loving him. There was no other answer that made sense. Randal hoped she would one day realize it. Until then, he had no choice but to distract her. She resisted.

"Shouldn't we wait until Dr. Markowitz and Linden get here?"

"They can't possibly be much longer, and the sooner we begin the sooner everything will be ready."

The two of them pried the lid off the grey crate easily, placing the loose board against the wall. The smell was horrible—the rotting odor of briny seaweed. Inside the crate were dozens of sample jars, all carefully wrapped in newspaper, and as Olivia unwrapped them, lining the jars up along the counter, Randal couldn't believe what he was seeing.

"Dr. Markowitz must have expected there would be trouble," Olivia said, "so he shipped all bacterial specimens ahead to make sure no one intercepted them."

"We don't know he ran into trouble. It sounds—"

"I don't care how it sounds, Randal. I don't believe they're just late and I don't think you do either. Why else would Markowitz have shipped this stuff first? Why wouldn't he and Linden have just brought it back?"

"For the same reason anyone ships anything to themselves: to get it home *without* having to carry it. Makes sense to me." Randal continued to hold up items from the crate, inspecting each as it was withdrawn. Other than the odor, which not only persisted but radiated outward, he found six vials containing microbial swabs, a block of what looked like a rock of glass inside a sealed transparent container, and Markowitz's coiled field notebook. It was that last discovery that most surprised him.

"He never would have shipped that separately," she said, as Randal inspected the notebook. "Not unless he was worried about who might see it."

He didn't argue. Dr. Markowitz wouldn't have let go of his research, or entrusted it to anyone. There was something strange about the crate's contents, something that did not bode well. Everyone, including Dean Coxwell, had been so sure that Dr. Markowitz and Linden would be returning soon. Everyone but Olivia. Suddenly, Randal found himself agreeing something might be wrong. He looked at the coiled notebook in his hand, then decided it was safest in his pocket instead of Olivia's hands. He did not expect her to argue with him.

And she didn't. She didn't even offer him a reason why. But Randal already knew the reason. It was a six-foot-tall reason, with broad shoulders and a deep tan. It was the sort of reason Randal hated.

"I'll ask Dean Coxwell. He must know where Dr. Markowitz really is."

But Dean Coxwell did not know. He was as in the dark as anyone. Randal learned this when Coxwell arrived at the lab the next day, unannounced, his knit vest twisted and left uncorrected. Olivia had already left for the evening.

Dean Coxwell hovered around the room conspicuously as Randal worked, clearly contemplating what he should say. Randal feigned nonchalance, but the man's presence left him uneasy. He and Olivia had decided to wait before mentioning the arrival of the crate and its contents, in case the reason for Markowitz's subterfuge was larger than either of them thought. Randal made her swear to keep everything a secret for as long as possible. At least, until they had a better idea of what was happening.

With Dean Coxwell there, out of the blue, Randal was worried the dean might discover the crate and be unable to contain his curiosity. He did his best to act as if nothing were different and simply waited. Coxwell glanced at the crate only once, and in that one look it was clear he had no idea it had been delivered, and Randal was in no rush to tell him. Not until he and Olivia had a chance to itemize its contents fully.

"I've spoken to the other department heads," Dean Coxwell finally said, "and no one has heard a single thing on the whereabouts of Dr. Markowitz. I even dispatched one of the secretaries to his home on two separate occasions, but all she was able to discover was a stack of unread mail and periodicals clogging the entrance. Unfortunately, we must plan for the very real eventuality that the doctor will not be here for the commencement of classes this semester. Do you have his curriculum and lesson plans available to you?"

"I may have last year's. Who should I forward them to? Please, don't say Dr. Eisenhower—that man's an idiot."

The dean laughed and adjusted his glasses. "In fact, I came to relate that this year we seem to have a deficit of professors. With Markowitz's return still nebulous, it was my hope that you, with the help of the young Ms. Marshall, could maintain some semblance of order in the lectures. You and she are the most familiar with Markowitz's work and teaching style, and seem most qualified to assume his duties. At least in the short term. Should it be required. We must have contingency plans, after all."

Randal was in disbelief.

"You want *me* to teach the class?"

"Until Markowitz's return, of course."

But Randal could not hear him clearly, his head clouded with the idea of leading Dr. Markowitz's lectures. He'd heard so many already, the sound of them played on a loop in the chambers of his mind. And suddenly an opportunity had presented itself to step into the man's shoes and bask in the glory of being idolized by the undergraduate student body. He could not believe it was a position Dean Coxwell would trust to simply anyone.

"I won't let you down, sir."

Dean Coxwell looked at him nervously, pulled at his ill-fitting vest, and blinked repeatedly. Randal did not wonder what that look might have meant. His head was too full of dreams. The mystery of Dr. Markowitz and Linden's disappearance temporarily forgotten.

Randal had not yet found the right time to tell Olivia of his conversation with the dean before news of the *Oregon* erupted on campus. The local television stations did not air much about the event, choosing instead to focus on the latest political scandal, thereby fanning the flames of misinformation whispered between buildings and dormitory rooms. From what Randal could gather, there were reports of a research vessel sinking just off the continental shelf, though no one yet understood how or where. All the Coast Guard had were a number of garbled short-wave radio calls and some GPS coordinates relayed from a local satellite. Both these discoveries seemed dubious to Randal, but they were reported as gospel by one of the junior professors who had heard it from a school administrator—who was sure she had heard it reported somewhere. All Randal knew for certain was what Dean Coxwell had been told by the Coast Guard in response to the university's inquiry: There was nothing out of the ordinary in the unintelligible radio transmissions from the boat, only that there was some engine trouble and a request for assistance had been sent. When the Coast Guard arrived at the coordinates given, however, they found no sign of the *Oregon*. Both Dr. Markowitz and Linden Cain were presumed dead.

Olivia did not return to the lab for three days despite Randal's repeated calls. Students were already arriving on campus, and the preparation of both the laboratories and lectures was overwhelming. Randal prided himself on how well he coped with the added work—something at which he was certain the late Linden would have failed, if not worse. It was nearly insurmountable, but he appreciated both the challenge, and the distraction.

When Olivia finally returned, it was with dark sunken eyes and an air of unrest about her. She was jittery, her mind unfocused, and had he not needed her so badly he might have sent her away for a little while longer. But she *was* needed, and not only for her technical skills. Over the summer Randal had grown accustomed to the smell of her strawberry shampoo in the room with him, how a solitary glance from her was enough to invigorate him, even when the doldrums and the irritating summer students worked to grind him down. He couldn't fill Markowitz's shoes without her by his side, nor did he want to. He wondered if perhaps it was Linden's death that reinvigorated his feelings.

"I'm glad you're back," Randal said, trying to find the line between supporting her grief while wanting to move beyond it.

"I'm sorry I was gone so long, I just—I need some time."

"You don't have to say anything. I understand. Still, I really missed you. I mean, your help. I really missed your help."

She smiled weakly and put her lab coat on over her clothes. Randal tried to keep his eyes on his laboratory prep work.

"So you're doing the lectures now?" She wasn't looking at him when she asked.

"The dean asked me. It's only for a week or two. He has another professor coming in to take over, but he can't begin until then."

She nodded her head, still gazing at her shoes. He didn't know if he wanted to hug her or try and shake her to her senses. She looked up at him, and her eyes were already steamed.

"What would pirates want with a research boat?"

"Pirates? I don't think it was—I mean, there's no reason to assume it was. It's not like the microscopes were worth taking. Maybe some of the equipment would be worth something but—but I don't think it was pirates."

"What do you think it was, then?"

Randal shrugged, uncomfortable.

"Olivia, I'm not sure what to tell you. I'm not sure what happened, no one is, but we can't let it rule our lives. We have to keep moving. Dean Coxwell is working on getting me another doctoral advisor, but in the interim we have to put this material together for class. There are students already here, drinking and getting ready for the new semester. We have to be ready for them, too."

"Drinking sounds like the perfect idea lately."

Randal turned around and looked at her. She seemed so helpless, so ruined by what had happened. Meanwhile his heart was racing faster than he ever thought possible. So fast his head was beginning to swim. When her glance moved to his face, his eyes locking with hers, the words just came tumbling from his mouth.

"Do—did you want to go get a drink? Tonight? With me, I mean?"

She continued to look into his eyes, her own face not changing at all, as though she hadn't heard his question, or was disgusted by the timing. He wished he could simply lean forward and grab the words right out of the air, stop them from ever being spoken. All Randal could think about was the sound his own heart, throbbing loudly in his head.

She nodded, then turned back to filling the petri dishes.

2

Randal waited for Olivia at The Brass Keg for two hours, his stare transfixed on the entrance the entire time, and when it was clear Olivia would not show nor answer her cell phone, he followed the only logical course of action and drank until he could no longer remember her name.

When he awoke the following morning, he felt far worse than he had ever imagined possible—far worse, he wagered, than anyone had ever felt and remained alive. His head throbbed as though his brain had been torn apart and stitched back together incorrectly, and his mouth was covered in a thick white layer of paste. In the back of his mind he realized there was nothing abnormal about the bacteria, but their presence left him feeling sick all the same.

It took him an hour longer than usual to reach the laboratory, the impact of each step reverberating through his body until they invaded his aching head, and the three stops he made to vomit in the bushes around campus did not help his mood at all. Once he finally arrived, he immediately dry-heaved; the stench in the lab was horrendous. Olivia sat there working, seemingly oblivious to the odor.

"What is that? Did something die in here?"

She turned and, when she saw him, the look of shock on her face almost convinced Randal it was sincere.

"What happened to you?"

Despite all the speeches he had practiced, he couldn't bring himself to mention what she'd done.

"Late night. But what happened in here?"

"That smell? I don't even notice it anymore. It's coming from this." She held up one of the specimen jars from the Markowitz expedition labeled 'Hydrothermal Plume—Day Fourteen.' Immediately, Randal snapped awake.

"Put that away. Do you want everyone to find out?"

"It's okay, Randal. No one is supposed to be here for hours yet. Besides, I needed the equipment to figure out what these samples are." She rubbed her eyes and yawned. "Doing this helps keep me distracted. If I don't keep busy, I'm going to lose my mind. I had to leave my cell phone turned off just to keep from checking it every five minutes, hoping Linden would call."

Randal nodded his head. It was the second most painful thing he'd been faced with that day. He almost asked her if she'd had it off the night before, hoping for some legitimate reason she hadn't come to The Brass Keg. Then it occurred to him she might be bringing it up purposely to dissuade him from mentioning it. It was too early, and he was still too hung over, to properly assess the intricacies of the situation.

He sank his hands into the pockets of his jacket, hoping to hide their jittering from Olivia. As he did, he found something there he hadn't been expecting. A hard rectangle. He immediately knew what it was.

"Randal, did you hear me?"

He looked up. Olivia stared at him.

"Pardon?"

"Did you speak to the dean? Who's your new advisor now that . . . now that Dr. Markowitz isn't here?"

"He didn't say. Not yet. I'll ask soon."

"You'd better. You're too smart to let it all slip away."

He nodded again, but he was distracted by what was in his pocket, by what he'd somehow managed to forget he had.

Olivia yawned. Rubbed her eyes until they turned red.

"I think you're right. I've been at this too long."

"Listen, do you mind cleaning up without me? I have to . . . I forgot something in my room."

"You? You forgot something?"

He chuckled. He hoped it was meant as a joke. Olivia did not seem to be laughing, but after the news of Markowitz and Linden, he wasn't sure if either of them would laugh again.

"I'll be back," he said. "Make sure you hide the crate in the back room again before someone sees it."

Olivia shrugged and turned back to what she'd been doing before he interrupted.

When Randal was sure he was alone, he pulled the half-sized notebook from his pocket and rolled it over in his fingers, feeling its grit and texture. Dr. Markowitz had written his name in large block letters across the cover in an act of either personal affirmation or pride, and inside his tiny cramped handwriting filled the pages edge-to-edge until they were near solid black, any free space filled with errant notes, diagrams, and calculations. The coil-bound book had weight, filled with secrets for Randal alone to discover. Olivia would find no solace inside, discover nothing about Linden she didn't already know. At best, it would prolong the mourning and pain she had already suffered. In a sense, Randal was protecting her—keeping her focused on the immediate, and letting her past fall away.

Some of the pages of Markowitz's notebook were wrinkled from exposure to sea air and water, creating soft haloes where letters should have been. Thankfully, little of importance had been affected, and Randal was still able to read the bulk of what Markowitz had written, albeit with a small amount of difficulty.

August 2nd

What a fantastic day to start the search! The sun was shining brightly, and there was a slight cool breeze coming in off the water. But it was a good breeze, a dry breeze, not strong enough to move a cloud were there even one in the sky. It was a day made for boating, and blissfully that's exactly what I came to do!

Linden and I loaded the equipment on the *Oregon* for most of the morning. The grant money has been enough to rent the boat for a month, as well as to build the computer equipment we need on her. A month. It still seems so short a time, but we have a good idea where the Onkoul Vent is, so all we need to do is find it. Linden was in great spirits today, and I think that may have had an influence on my own bliss. He's long been one of my most trusted doctoral students, and luckily for me a good enough boatman that between the two of us we can manage the ship on our own. I'm lucky to have him, and I think the greatest reward I could give him for his years of work is a co-author on the paper. It could change everything.

I must admit, I need this paper more now than ever. Certainly, my tenure at the university is assured, but the same can't be said for my ability to continue exploring this strange world. I'm older than I've ever been—my legs no longer work the way they once did, the skin of my neck hangs lower than it ought. It came on so suddenly, age. So suddenly I wasn't even paying attention when it arrived. I thought I had all the time in the world, but it's clear now I was deluding myself. The folly of youth! I may be older, but alas not wiser. Nevertheless, I endeavor to make up for lost time, now before its too late. One last paper, one last exploration into the greatest mystery of our world—the depth of the ocean. Should I find the organisms I hope to find, a new paradigm will emerge.

I know they think me crazy, back at the university. Dean Coxwell, I suspect, would rather be rid of me altogether, but my tenure, thankfully, guarantees me some room to maneuver. I'll be the first to admit it: my star has fallen, but in some ways this too is a blessing. Being left alone, I'm free to focus on those projects that interest me most, and what interests this old coot more than anything now is the future, and the multiplication of humanity. Much like the bacterium, man will spread until he consumes all his resources. The only place left to go is the stars.

Beneath the sea, on the vent of the earth, the extreme life forms live. If we can harness that power, that ability to thrive in previously unlivable conditions . . . It's the key, I think, to life. To the future. We have only to tap the potential of this world so we might find another.

Oh, I mustn't continue this! I'll need some sleep to keep my wits about me on our maiden voyage tomorrow!

August 4th

I take a few moments to write in this journal because I have nothing else to show for the day, other than mindless driving. The rooms Linden and I rented are next door to each other in a small motel close to the marina. This way, we needn't worry about travelling too long or far to reach the boat. Even a few minutes could prove vital.

Linden was still as jubilant as ever, thank heavens, but for all his optimism that drat hydrothermal vent still remained elusive. We have the coordinates charted and stuck to them to the letter, yet nothing emerged. At one point I was certain we were driving in circles, but Linden assured me that wasn't the case.

"And even if it were true," he reasoned, "how would you know? There's no land anywhere within sight. Just water, water as far as the eye can see."

"You are aware we have more instruments on this boat than eyes, aren't you?" I chided him. "The GPS alone is worth four of your eyeballs."

He laughed, then eased himself back on his chair. "Well, at least we have the birds to tell us we're on the right track."

He was right. The one sure way to find underwater hydrothermal vents is birds. The gulls are attracted to them. Sulfur, carbon dioxide, all sorts of other gases get released from an active site; mixing with the water above it forms a dead zone in the water. These are cleverly called "plumes" and are regularly noted when discovered. They show up on satellite imaging as large black masses, and no life can survive within one. Invariably, fish try to pass through and are instantly killed, poisoned to death by the deadly discharge from the vent. They float to the surface, easy pickings for the circling gulls. Except for the poison, of course.

The birds are indeed flying, and we can see them out farther in the water, circling like the scavengers they are. All we need to do is follow them. Perhaps tomorrow will yield better results.

August 13th

The fellow at the marina asked after the equipment we'd loaded the *Oregon* with. He was a crotchety old one, that's for certain, with a weather-beaten face and a distinct lack of dental care. His mustache was yellowed from far too many cigarettes, and so long and thick at first I mistook it for a beard. He seemed quite bemused by our electronics, both impressed and mocking at once. I tried explaining a few of the machines to him—most specifically the sonar system—but he either didn't understand English well enough or didn't care. The only piece that struck his rheumy eye was the submersible.

"What's that? Like a submarine?"

"Yes, quite."

"What're you looking for? You want to do some fishing?"

"In a manner of speaking. We're looking for the Onkoul Vent, sort of like an underwater volcano."

His face betrayed a moment of intense emotion, one that his crotchetiness buried before I could think to reassure him. In truth, I was taken aback.

"Those things—those *grietas*—those *vents*—they are all over. My father said to keep away. You should listen to him."

"I'm sure he knew what he was talking about," I said, struggling for a way to end the conversation, but the fellow wasn't so easily dissuaded.

"*Si*, they are very dangerous. You should stay away. Tell your friends, too. *Que son malo.*"

I nodded, and wished I knew how best to extricate myself.

I might still be on that dock had Linden not stepped in. I'm quite horrible with confrontation, but Linden seems to harbor no such foible. I suppose that's the youth in him. When I was that young, I doubt it was much different for me. Linden stepped between us with the sort of presence only the broad-chested can manage.

"We need to get going, Doctor. We have a tight schedule."

"Yes, of course, Linden. If you'll excuse me, sir?"

The fellow nodded, but his eyes remained screwed fast to me.

We headed for the coordinates we'd been searching the day before, a good four hours out. As we travelled, I had Linden taking notes on his laptop and checking the diving equipment and submersible again to ensure they were ready to be deployed at short notice. Most of the trip was made in silence, the only sound the buzz of the engine. I must admit I rather enjoyed it: being out in the sun after so long under the fluorescents of the lab, the mist of the water on my face. It's true what they say: the sea air really does wonders for the lungs. My breathing has never been better. In some ways, if we never find the Onkoul Vent, I wouldn't mind. But of course Linden can think of nothing but his career.

"Thank you again for choosing me for the excursion, Dr. Markowitz. I know both Randal and Olivia would have been just as excited as I am to be here. I'm really excited about his project." Linden had finished his prep and had joined me at the wheel. "I just wanted you to understand that."

I waved him off.

"You deserve to be here, Linden. I wouldn't have brought you otherwise."

He smiled broadly. I must admit it felt good to be needed.

August 18th

A disastrous day! I'm still shaking and, for a while, I was worried Linden would not make it. Our morning began as usual, with the fellow from the marina watching Linden and me load the boat and test the equipment and submersible. He didn't say anything this time, but it was clear we were wearing out more and more of our welcome. Linden laughed about it as we drove out, but it didn't seem as funny to me.

We reached the coordinates again, and though the GPS said we were exactly where we'd anchored the last time, still the water looked different to me. I know that's a strange thing to say—water never looks the same twice, especially without land to mark it—but there was something. The sky perhaps wasn't as clear as it ought to have been, or the color of the waves duller than before. Something was off, and my instinct told me that it was not the right day to be out there, not the time to be diving for hydrothermal vents. But Linden was eager, and had his wetsuit on before my concerns had fully solidified.

"I'll follow the same grid we've been using," he said, "and patch the info up to you."

I checked the seismograph and thermograph, and everything checked out. There were some artifacts on the sonar, but they were small and could have been caused by anything. We tested communications again, then his halogen lamp and air tanks. Once we were both sure everything was working, we calibrated our GPS coordinates and Linden slipped into the water. He stayed at the surface long enough to rub spit in his mask and wave three fingers at me to indicate he was ready. Then he donned his mask and dove, the off-colored water bubbling around his flippered legs.

I knew something was wrong after ten minutes, once he lost the uplink connection with the LSC. Or perhaps I merely suspected it, somewhere in the depths of my brain. Not enough, it seems, that I recall panicking, or acting in any way concerned. I was too engrossed in parsing reports, checking maps, verifying equipment. At the back of my mind I wondered, but the distraction of the immediate tamped down my fear. After all, despite checking and rechecking the equipment, it was not the first time a glitch occurred. The preliminary exploration was not scientifically relevant, so accidents could safely occur. *Accidents*—Perhaps I should have chosen a different word. . . .

I heard a noise I initially mistook for gulls squawking, and it barely registered in the periphery of my consciousness. It was only when it continued unabated that it sounded strange to me. I looked up from my work to see Linden at least two hundred feet away, splashing and coughing in the water. He looked to be in the throes of some kind of spasm, and I rushed to get the engine started and drive over to his side. He was beginning to bob in the water, and I fear had I arrived a single second later he would have sunk irrecoverably into the depths. As it was, with great effort I was able to pull him onto the deck and turn him on his side to help drain the water. His face, though, was what troubled me. It was bright red, as though it had been burned, and covered in tiny white marks I first took for blisters before I realized they were something else, some organic material that had become lodged in his skin. I was at a loss as to what to do, so I simply stood for a moment watching him heave an opaque mucous onto the deck of the boat. Once it was clear, between the heaves, that he was breathing, I got back behind the wheel and pushed the engine as fast as I dared toward the shore.

Linden was still unconscious when we arrived at the marina, and I yelled for help getting him off the boat. Some of the weekend boaters came to help me get Linden to shore, and one called an ambulance while we verified Linden's life signs. At one point I remember looking up from where I knelt to see that craggy old fellow watching from behind the crowd, not saying a word.

They kept Linden in that emergency room for hours, while I sat like an ineffectual fool in the waiting room, wringing my wool hat in my hands and wondering what I was going to do if Linden did not survive the ordeal. When the doctor finally emerged from behind the closed doors, I studied his inscrutable face in vain. I wanted to see him happy, would have understood if he were somber, but instead it was something far different. He seemed puzzled, enough so that his confusion penetrated the mask of professionalism he had no doubt fostered and perfected over the years. He approached me, glasses riding low and heavy on his nose, and quickly scratched his head, stalling before he had to speak.

"Your friend is out of danger. You may see him if you'd like."

"Thank you, Doctor," I nearly cried. "Do you know—"

"It's best you see him," he interrupted curtly, then turned to the nurses' station, filed away his clipboard, and strode away. The nurses started at me.

Linden was not asleep when I entered his room, but his face was bandaged fiercely. I asked if he could speak.

"Of course I can. I didn't forget!"

I found myself fighting to hold back tears.

He did not have much to tell me about what happened. He remembered the instruments telling him he was close to the underwater vent, but his memory grew hazy after that. He did have some recollection of the water heating and of dead fish suspended before him before everything went dark. He confessed some astonishment he resurfaced at all.

"And your face? What happened to your face?"

"The doctors aren't sure. They think I was stung by a school of jellyfish, or perhaps an anemone of some sort. I should only be here a day or two, just enough time for the swelling to subside and whatever poisons there are to work their way out of my system. Don't worry: we'll be back on the *Oregon* as soon as I can manage it."

"Please, Linden. Your health is most important."

"The only way I'm going to get healthy is to get back on that boat. We were so close—I'm not going to let us miss our chance!"

August 22nd

I'm not . . .

I don't know how to describe . . .

Linden wasn't himself today. He looked . . . puffier . . . than I was used to, which I can understand, given his accident, but even so his demeanor was *off*. The accident must have had more of an effect than I'd thought, as he seemed positively withdrawn when I knocked upon his motel room door to resume our expedition. Nothing he said was strange, let me be clear, and were I to have transcribed his reactions today and any day previous, nothing on the page would indicate a difference. And yet, his manner . . .

I asked him before we launched, once the gear had been checked and re-checked, if he was up to returning to the water. He did not look directly at me. Instead, he looked out across the ocean at the clear blue sky. "There's a storm coming. We have to hurry."

The trip across the water was smooth and quiet as the dead. Linden did not utter a single word, and rather than prompt him I kept my distance, going over the charts again. It wasn't strictly necessary, but I needed to distract myself from the funereal atmosphere on the *Oregon*. It did not take us long to arrive at the coordinates where I had lost Linden the day before, as though he were able to home in on them instinctively, and when he called me up to the deck I found the wind over the water was chillier than it had been on land. I tilted my head back to see where the thinnest sliver of darkness edged the horizon.

The doctor had warned me that Linden would not be in any condition to dive for some time, and judging by his lack of expression I wondered if what we'd already done had been too traumatic for him. Linden dismissed my concern perfunctorily by claiming he simply missed Olivia, and made a suggestion I'd been contemplating since I pulled him from the churning waters a few days before.

"Maybe it's time to unleash the submersible."

I couldn't have agreed more.

In happier times, we both loved the submersible; me most especially. There's no reason for it, of course. The thing is quite cramped to drive and difficult to maneuver. Perhaps it goes back to the child in me, mesmerized by everything I had read in *National Geographic* about deep-sea exploration. Or perhaps I simply like toys. Regardless, though I was excited, we still had to go through proper procedures to ensure it was safe to operate. The sea air makes short work of even the best mechanics. Sure enough, some of the wiring had corroded and needed to be fixed. Linden worked on that while I prepared the rest of the necessary gear.

By the time we were ready to go, clouds had rolled in to the west, dark enough that Linden questioned whether we should continue. I waved him off; perhaps I shouldn't have, but I was worried that any storm would knock us too far off the mark. The GPS anchor would help, but I did not want to take the chance.

The submersible was as cramped as I remembered it, if not more. I folded myself in and looked up at Linden as he sealed the clear portal. The water had already began to chop, albeit slightly, yet it was enough to draw concern on my first mate's face. I assured him it would be fine and told him via the radio to warn me if things became too violent on the surface. Then I filled the tanks with water and slowly descended into the briny depths.

It did not take long to find the Onkoul Vent. Linden's coordinates were exact, and even if they weren't, once I came close enough I noticed the precipitous increase on the thermosensors. I switched on the submersible's halogens to see what might be before me, and saw the strangest creatures moving past the small beam of light. That far down, the sun could not fully penetrate, and I could not direct the beam quickly enough to follow everything that skirted by. There were cephalopods of different sizes and colors— one going so far as to extend its tentacles toward me, trying to pry the light off the roof. It was unsuccessful, but for a few minutes it pressed its body against the bulb's housing, blocking anything from showing the way, and instead making its gelatinous body glow as though phosphorescent. Part of me was glad for the momentary darkness, as it hid some of the stranger, more disturbing creatures that swam through my narrow field of view. But once I fully experienced the darkness and knew what had been there, previously unseen, I realized which was the greater evil.

The Onkoul Vent was spitting up a solid plume of carbon dioxide and hydrosulfuric acid as I approached it. In the depths, it was as dark as smoke, and it did not stop or waver for an instant. It was a marker, and a distinct one, and yet it was amazing how quickly it dissipated into the vastness of the ocean. I would have at least expected a microbial algae plume at the surface, but there was nothing. No sign of the hydrothermal vent beneath. The temperature sensors on the submersible's surface heated considerably, well into the supercritical range, but from within I felt none of the effect. I was close enough by this time that the halogen light had lit the plume's originating crevasse, that crack in the earth's surface from which lava pillowed, bringing the hydrothermal vent fractionally closer to the light of the world. But for the time being it would remain a hidden secret.

I moved closer to the opening of the crevasse, taking care to remain out of the way of the supercritical expulsion. The rock around the opening was dark and jagged, volcanic glass formed by the intense heat. Upon its surface, however, just where the hottest, most sulfuric water would be spewing, I could see the thin smear I had travelled so far and so deep to find. Even under the halogen light it was clear the bacteria were luminescent, and I hoped that they would be the key to my research. All I needed was a sample to return with to Sandstone, where Randal and Olivia would help me analyze its makeup and discover how it could survive such inhospitable conditions. Would it be a silicone-based life form, hitherto unknown to us? Would it be the key to detecting life on other planets? Help us to colonize other worlds? There were so many possibilities I felt myself turning giddy within the craft, and I had to force myself to remain calm and conserve my oxygen. I tried to radio Linden at least to let him know what I'd found, but no signal could be transmitted. Instead, I alone was able to witness the beginning of the world's future.

I extended the submersible's arm and used it to break a piece of the glass rock free. It came apart much easier than I expected, and I was careful not to disturb the colonies that might be living on its surface. The arm was then retracted, along with a few gallons of surrounding water in order to properly preserve the sample. A few further photographs of the site were all that was required before I backed the submersible away. I could see the façade of the Onkoul Vent fading into the dark once again as I turned the submersible and headed back to the coordinates of the ship before I resurfaced. It would have to be slow to avoid causing decompression sickness, and my impatience would be excruciating, but I knew it was but a small price to pay for what was to come.

Upon surfacing, I nearly recoiled from the look on Linden's face. It had swollen again, though he seemed unaware, and it gave him the appearance of an angry Chinese spirit come to haunt me. His pale complexion only magnified the illusion.

"The storm," was all he said, and I removed my mask to see the dark clouds had proliferated across the sky in my absence, and the water itself had already begun to chop.

"Let's get the submersible secured," I said with haste, motioning for him to lower me the ropes so I might prepare it to be winched up. We both rushed to get everything in place and locked down while the light was still with us, but it was quickly draining from the world as we worked. We managed to get the boat ready for departure as the first cracks of lightning lit the western sky, and before the thunder rolled over us Linden was already throttling the engine. With a cough of black smoke we moved, faster and faster, the sound of hissing rain behind us intensifying like the sound of the ocean boiling. We narrowly escaped the looming clouds as the boat bounced across the water toward the marina and our motel rooms. There was a tension in the air due to more than our narrow escape from the looming clouds. In our haste I had forgotten about the sample I had managed to retrieve of that strange glass. Had I recalled I might have mentioned it to Linden instead of here for the first time. Still, he seemed uncharacteristically in no mood to listen, so I said nothing on the subject. I suspect now in hindsight that was for the best.

August 23rd

    I cannot say anything for certain beyond the facts, and they are as follows. I was unable to sleep well during the night—the storm battered the entire town of Zihuatanejo with a ferocious intensity as we rested there. I tossed and turned, the thunder waking me when my own nightmares did not. I dreamed I was in the submersible once more, only this time the motor had failed and tanks could not pull me to the surface. Instead, the entire thing sank as I approached the Onkoul Vent, sank deep into the inky blackness below, and try as I might I could not let go or do anything to stop the decent. Deeper, deeper into the black I fell as the air was choked from me. A thunderous tear across the sky erupted, transformed in my dream into something so horrendous I'm not sure if it was that image or the sound of the storm that woke me. Blissfully, I forgot the sight instantly, but the sensation clung to me like a shirt soaked with sweat, and my shivering succeeded where everything else had failed. It was long before dawn and I could no longer sleep. All I could do was think. And I thought of what I had discovered deep below the ocean's surface.

    I found myself overcome with the urge to examine my discovery, this time without the windows of the submersible acting as interference. It never occurred to me that the storm might be merely a lull, that to venture out in the dead of night was unusual. In my insomniac daze I only thought of what I had discovered, and knew the way one knows things in the middle of the night that the best course of action was to visit the boat, the submersible, and retrieve the sample. My befuddled mind twisted upon itself to rationalize the journey, convincing me that the samples would surely become contaminated were they to remain where they were, and only by retrieving them could I ensure their survival. I think somewhere deep down I realized my curiosity was to blame for my actions, but it did not seem so at the time. In hindsight, bearing in mind what I now know, my midnight confusion was at the very least a stroke of luck.

    The streets were drenched as I walked the short distance to the marina, but the sky remained clearer than I had seen it in some time. Stars peered down like a million eyes, watching me when no one else was. The gates were not locked, and I was able to walk up to the *Oregon* without difficulty and access the submersible Linden had ratcheted into place no less than eight hours earlier. I retrieved the glass rock and placed it and the bilge water carefully into the rubber crate I'd brought, then with the greatest care slowly walked the now-heavy container back to my rooms. Even energized by my overwhelming obsession, I am still an old man, and by the time I returned exhaustion had finally taken hold of me. I put the rubber container down in the empty wash tub and returned to my rented bed. This time I slept peacefully, perhaps with the security of knowing the sample was close at hand.

When the telephone rang in the morning I was in no mood to wake. My excursion into the night seemed as hazy as a dream, and I would have taken it as such had I not heard Linden on the other end of the line, his voice no more or less lively than before. He told me the storm had been too rough the previous night and had done damage to the *Oregon* that needed to be repaired before we could travel again. It would be at least of day of repairs, he warned, but then cautioned that that news was not the worst part. During the height of the storm, he told me, our submersible had been washed from the ship, and it was doubtlessly lost to the waves and the tide. Everything we had was gone. I was surprised by how certain he was of this, and he informed me he had spoken to the cantankerous old man at the marina that morning and been appraised of the full situation. There were discrepancies, of course—namely, my visit to the *Oregon after* the worst of the storm, when the submersible was very much still there, but I thought it best that I keep that to myself. I suppose it's possible the storm returned after I finally fell asleep . . . I cannot be certain of anything. But as Linden has said to me in the past, it doesn't *smell* right. I tried to reassure him and let him know we could gather enough of what we needed during that day to continue the exploration, but his voice betrayed a flutter that concerned me. Nevertheless, he was eager to get to work fixing the *Oregon*. Meanwhile, I'll be spending the day trying to locate replacement diving gear and computer equipment. It won't be the same, but frankly I think it will be more secure. At least we won't have to worry about that crazy fool from the marina much longer.

August 25th

I must be quick. There isn't much time. Linden, I fear, is far from well—one look at his puffy countenance when I found him on the boat yesterday morning was all I needed to tell me that. Distended and jaundiced, he seemed to be oozing a brownish pus as one might excrete sweat. It dripped off him, yet he remained hunched, ignorant of it and of me as he scoured my papers, his hands groping for something—perhaps some clue as to the whereabouts of what I had found in that deep ocean vent. When he realized I was there, he turned and started at me with his milky unapologetic eyes, and I was certain then more than ever that the security of my research was in doubt.

At first I could not allow myself to believe my most trusted student would betray me, but I fear the illness has twisted his thinking, just as it seems to have twisted his tongue, slurring his words. Was he working in concert with the old man? It couldn't be possible, and yet Linden's actions were troubling, to say the least. He paid me an unexpected and strangely timed visit here last night while I was swabbing the glass rock and transferring the samples to a more portable container. He told me he felt there was something wrong with him, something that had occurred during his accident. He couldn't remember it well, but he hadn't felt right since. "If only," he said, "we still had our research. Perhaps then I could find an answer." His eyes implored me to reveal that I had managed to rescue everything safely, but I would not. I could trust no one in Zihuatanejo any longer, not even Linden. It took some doing to get him to leave my doorway, but thankfully I eventually succeeded and sent him back to his room. The entire episode unnerved me, and it was clear I would not be so lucky a second time.

I cannot take any chances. My work—it's been so long, too long, for me to allow it to be ruined. Immortality is within reach, and I will not allow my legacy to be stolen from me. I have to send the samples where neither Linden nor that crazy old man will ever find them. I have already packed everything in a crate and asked the front desk to ship it back to the university for me. It will be there waiting by the time I arrive, safe in Randal and Olivia's hands and away from prying untrustworthy eyes. With the samples gone from here, maintaining the ruse that they were lost with the submersible will be much easier, but I cannot risk this journal or any of my notes being found. I shall include them with the crate before I leave to meet Linden. This way, at least they will remain safe.

I will use today's trip to monitor the *Oregon*'s security while docked at the marina and gauge Linden's health. Perhaps I can assess just what's been happening to destroy my research, and take further steps to neutralize it. I pray I'm wrong about it all, but if I'm not, I hope with all my heart it does not involve Linden. But I can no longer be sure. His behavior is erratic, and I cannot convince him it would be best he see the doctor once again. I shall take another trip with him on the water today, searching again near the continental shelf, but I fear no good will come of it. I dearly miss my old friend.

It was clear to Randal that any sanity Dr. Markowitz possessed at the expedition's outset had faded the longer he and Linden were on the water. The last entry was nearly incomprehensible—as through written in great haste, tangled letters doggedly unwilling to reveal their truths. The delusional and paranoid imaginings depressed Randal to no end—watching the slow deterioration of his mentor was incredibly difficult. For the sake of Dr. Markowitz's legacy, and any lingering associations in the eyes of others that might exist between them, he gathered all the pages of the journal and hid them at the top of his apartment bookshelf, out of reach of anyone who might come looking for them.

3

As the weeks progressed, the buzz about Markowitz's disappearance continued to intensify, culminating in Randal's inability to pass between buildings without another student or faculty member stopping him to ask questions. It was the greatest mystery of the school year, and somehow Randal had managed to land right at its epicenter. Initially, he craved the attention. Any notice or recognition at all would help augment his status as someone of importance, a figure to watch. He hoped it might be enough to cement his standing with the administration. After his discussions with the dean, he wanted nothing more than to finish his dissertation and be taken on by the school as a junior professor. It was certainly within the realm of possibility—Dean Coxwell had nearly come out and said so during a private meeting where it was suggested that Dr. Markowitz's position might not need to be filled quite yet. Randal was asked to continue teaching the class for the interim and was offered full use of Dr. Markowitz's office while he did so. There were other plans afoot, the dean explained, and it might be easiest for all if Randal moved himself in sooner rather than later. He didn't elaborate, but it was clear the tragedy with Markowitz might be a blessing for Randal. The idea filled him with excitement and no small amount of pride, but also a palpable fear of how tenuous it would be. Randal knew the university would be foolish not to grant someone of his intellect the position, but the dean's hints made it clear Randal would be best served finding some way of solidifying his credentials to ensure the posting was made permanent.

Perhaps Dr. Markowitz and Linden and the future of humanity could help him with that.

The dean appeared more often in the lab during the start of the school year than he had all summer long. He spent his time scrutinizing Randal both teaching and running the lab. What exactly he was looking for remained unclear, but Randal continued to work hard to prove his worth and ignore the sidelong glances he felt emanating from Olivia's prep station.

The dean, to his credit, did not meddle during his visits. All he wanted to do was observe—which made examining the contents of Markowitz's crate harder to hide. Randal and Olivia still needed to read through Markowitz's boating charts and determine where he and Linden were and the conditions there. It required finesse, especially as it could only be done in the evenings and outside the laboratory. Olivia happily took that job on, as it allowed her to find some distance from her thoughts by becoming absorbed with work; that left Randal free to examine Markowitz's journal safely in the depths of his campus apartment. He read and re-read it voraciously, looking for answers that he might have overlooked. Instead, the journal only raised new questions about what Dr. Markowitz had discovered, what had happened to Linden out on the *Oregon*, and why such pains were taken to prevent the completion of their research. Randal knew he would have to make sense of it, just as he knew that Olivia could not be allowed to see the journal. Not then, perhaps not ever. He feared her reaction if she did. When she asked, and at the beginning she asked often, he merely feigned how dry and unimportant the thing was, how it was devoid of many entries at all, and those that were there touched on little but the innocuous. Randal could not think of a better tactic. All he would reveal to Olivia were the basics of what Markowitz and Linden were searching for, and the raw data that qualified their findings. It was all she required. The journal was, at best, a map of his former hero's slow descent into senile madness—a madness whose cost was both his life and Linden's. And, by extension, Olivia's. Only Randal could see the opportunities lining up, and he intended to act upon them. If he played his cards right, he could use Markowitz's research to make a name for himself. And Olivia, too, he supposed. But he had to be careful.

Classes do not make time for missing professors—students must find their purpose as early as possible if they are to succeed, and their success was important to no one more than Randal. Their success would mean his own. But he needed Olivia's help in doing so. He was anxious as she to probe the secrets of Markowitz's discovery, but there were day-to-day tasks that needed to be accomplished in the lab, preparing modules for students and marking their performance. Yet Olivia's attention continued to be divided and consumed further and further by the grey crate Dr.

Markowitz shipped back, and the contents therein.

"I hope you aren't showing these to anyone else," Randal said when he discovered her at the bench working into the night.

"I thought you'd left for the day," she said. Her eyes red from being rubbed.

"I did. I was actually walking by the building when I saw the light on and you in the window."

"This is the only time I can get any peace to inspect these things. The days are so busy. . . . I kind of like the quiet. My head's been killing me lately."

He leaned forward to inspect her pale complexion.

"Maybe you should go home. You're no use run ragged."

"Aren't you the one who said the sooner we piece together this research, the sooner we can get that paper done? Linden and Dr. Markowitz deserve their final success."

"Yes, of course," he said, hoping she didn't notice his pause. He had yet to tell her of his intention to leave Markowitz and Linden out of the paper altogether. After all, the final in-depth analysis would be done primarily by him and Olivia. All Markowitz and Linden had done was collect the samples. It was Randal who would be doing the hard work of making sense of them.

Olivia coughed. It was wet, and though she covered her mouth Randal still felt a twinge of repulsion.

"Really, Olivia. Go home. I'll put the crate away."

She sniffled. Then gave the materials in front of her a queer look.

"No, I'll do it. You were on your way out anyway."

"Well, at least let me help." He reached out, but she quickly turned her back on him. So quickly it was as though he'd been slapped.

"I told you I'd do it. Now go."

"Okay," he said, hands raised in defeat. "I was just trying to help."

"I'm sorry," she said as he was leaving, but he got the distinct impression that wasn't exactly true. Nor was what she said next: "I'm leaving in a minute."

Thus it was no surprise that, when he arrived at the laboratory the next morning, he found her face down on the lab desk sleeping, contents of Markowitz's crate all around her. Lab classes weren't until later in the day, but he still felt uncomfortable having such sensitive material exposed. He hesitated, then put his hand on Olivia to nudge her awake. Her flesh was softer than he'd imagined—and warmer. Unexpectedly so. For a few seconds she did not move, did not react in any way—long enough for Randal to wonder if she was all right. Then she jumped, scaring him as much as he had her. She turned and looked at him, her hand on her chest, white creases in her face that blood had yet to fill.

"You scared the hell out of me," she said. "What time is it?"

"Have you been here all night?"

She rubbed her damp face with her hands. Blinked her watering eyes excessively.

"I think so."

"Olivia, you don't look well. Worse than yesterday."

She nodded, yawned, and stretched. As she did so, the hem of her shirt rose just enough to show a sliver of abdominal flesh. He stared at it, trying to burn the image into his memory.

"I think it's these samples. I can't stand looking at them anymore. They keep reminding me of what happened."

Randal nodded and looked over at them. He didn't think of Linden, but of Markowitz. But she was right: they made him feel as though he were looking at a dead man. They certainly *smelled* like a dead man.

"Have you figured anything out?"

"Look at this," she said, and hunched over one of the fluorescent microscopes. In a small tray beneath the lens was a piece of the glass rock Markowitz had found—the one mentioned in the journal. He found his heart speeding up with anticipation, yet kept it to himself. As excited as he was, part of him was irritated

Olivia had started inspecting the crate without him. As long as he got to lead the paper, it wasn't a complete loss, but some victory still felt snatched from his hands. Randal bent and looked through the eyepiece. He saw nothing of note. At the same time, his stomach flipped over, and he was nearly overwhelmed by a feeling of illness—so much so he had to sit down. Olivia looked at him, and he wondered if he looked as pale as she did. When the blood returned to his face he said, with only the hint of a slur: "There's nothing there, Olivia."

She pushed him aside and looked again. Those white creases still had not filled, and were replaced with the multitude that hung there after her face scrunched. It was as though her flesh had lost its elasticity.

"It's faint, but there are markings there. At first I thought it was simply acid and enzymes from the micro-organic growths etching the glass rock, but that's not the case. I mean, it *looks* like it's the case. But it's too ordered, too purposeful. I haven't figured out what's going on yet."

Randal bent over the eyepiece again and did his best to ignore his churning gut. He was overheating, even under the cool fluorescent lights, and before he suffocated he loosened his shirt's collar.

"It looks random enough to me. I think you were right the first time."

She shook her head. "No, it's something. I need to take some photographs of this." She thought for a moment. "Do you know if the electron microscope is free? I'd like some time on it to get a good look at these striations. Maybe at the fungus, too."

"Olivia," Randal said, then realized he didn't have a response. She was looking at him with her dark, red eyes, heavy bags beneath them, and still he was unnerved. He couldn't imagine ever being needed before.

"I guess I could ask Dean Coxwell. But we can't let him know what it's for. We'll have to make something up."

Unexpectedly, she jumped to her feet and wrapped her arms

around him. Her flesh was hot and soft and despite how she smelled he became aroused. He simultaneously tried to ignore what was happening and enjoy it.

Booking the electron microscope was easier than he'd thought—almost disappointingly so. Dean Coxwell didn't ask him what he needed it for, despite all Randal's preparation beforehand should the question be raised. Instead, the dean nodded and picked up his telephone to place a call to Nehls, the lab steward.

When Randal informed Olivia, however, certain aspects of the story were changed—most specifically the time it took to resolve the issue and the effort Randal had to exert. It didn't matter, though. Olivia was excited to get an opportunity to work with the advanced equipment, and seemed impressed Randal was able to facilitate it. He hoped she realized all he could do for her and ended her pining for that imbecile, Linden—pining that, until the recent opening of the crate, left her drained of any sort of joy or glamour. Not that she needed it, of course. Some creatures cannot hide the truth of what they are. But there was no denying Olivia's renewed interest in research had enlivened her. If Linden was still a concern of hers, she didn't show it.

Markowitz's presence, however, was not quite so easily scrubbed away. Though Randal had appropriated everything he could so that he might look more the part of faculty, still there were questions raised by the students he could not answer, and a growing sense that the class was turning against him. At first, it was no more than a few stray comments in lecture after he asked for quiet; but soon the disrespect became more brazen, and some of the students seemed intent on asking the most obscure questions in hopes he would falter. But Randal was better than them. He was better than *all* of them, and despite their antics he knew he would have the last laugh. After all, their grades—and by extension their futures—were held tight in his sweating palms.

Markowitz's office remained cluttered as Randal took up residence there. Old books, boxed manuscripts, a desk full of items collected over the years of working in the field, all contributed to an aesthetic of importance on which Randal was eager to capitalize. Should any of the more vocal students come to see him, opinions could only be swayed by the sight of him behind his grand desk. Yet Randal found most of the moments he spent between lectures and labs to be free of any such activity. Instead, he spent his time staring at the clutter his mentor had left behind.

A single pile of papers belong to Randal: his dissertation on *Nitrosomonas eutropha* that held close to the edge of his desk. Although only six weeks had passed, it already seemed so far into yesterday that it might have been the work of another hand. Linden had asked Dean Coxwell once again who might be replacing Markowitz as his doctoral advisor, but the little, sweatered man only smiled graciously and said he was working on it. Each time the same response came, Randal's irritation grew, until his only recourse for sanity was to stop asking. It suited Randal fine: there was plenty of time in the future to complete it. Besides, most likely the trouble was Randal was *too* gifted for any of the other faculty to work with. It would take someone of Markowitz's caliber, and there weren't many of those. Certainly no others at Sandstone.

When Randal's telephone rang later, he was reviewing his notes on the following day's lecture. He answered it to find Olivia breathing strangely on the other end, filling Randal with sickening surprise.

"Can you come to the lab? I have something to show you."

"What is it?"

"I got back some results. I need a second pair of eyes on this."

Randal looked at the stacks of books in Markowitz's former office, at the large, imposing oak desk he sat behind. He imagined how he might look behind it.

"I'm in the middle of some things, but why don't you swing by the—by *my* office later and we can discuss your findings."

"Um—okay," she hesitated, and told him she'd stop by after she put the crate away. He hung up the telephone and did his best to straighten up the office so it might look respectable. He took his half-completed dissertation and hid it inside one of the desk drawers.

Randal was still staring at its hiding spot when Olivia arrived. She said hello, startling him out of his daydream, and he worried his face betrayed the truth. If it did, Olivia seemed too tired to notice. Still, she smiled when she saw him.

"How are the lectures going?" she asked, pulling up the chair in front of his desk, her eyes scanning the room.

"Fine, fine. The students aren't behaving quite as I'd expect them to, especially at this level—you'd think they'd be more mature."

"I'm sure you'll get the hang of it. It's not easy winning a room over."

"Yes, of course. Still I would have thought my reputation would have counted for something."

"Oh, I'm sure it does," she said, smiling again, then she looked at him with her sad, red-rimmed eyes. Randal wished she wouldn't do that—look at him that way. It was unnerving. "So," she said, pulling folders from her bag, a prominent period at the end of their small talk. "I found some interesting things in the expedition crate. But first I think there's a lot more here than we expected. I think, if we do this right, you, me, Dr. Markowitz and Linden will have our names on something groundbreaking. It's really going to honor them, especially considering—well, considering what happened."

"Oh, of course," he said without a stammer.

"How has your half of the research been going? For the paper, I mean."

"Oh, um—" Randal had done nothing beyond reading and re-reading Markowitz's journal. "It's going fine. I'm just putting the final touches on things."

"Great! I think, once we get everything together, we're going to have something huge!"

"I hope," he said.

She leafed through the folders until she found what she was looking for. From near the bottom of the pile she pulled out a deep green folder, and before he had a chance to clear a space she laid it on top of everything he was working on. "The first, most important thing is this: I don't think this is bacteria we're dealing with."

He did not expect the basic tenet of the research Markowitz, and then she, had been exploring to be so matter-of-factly questioned.

"But we saw the reports of the microbial plume . . ."

"We saw something, that's for certain, but look at this," she said, and slid another folder toward him. This one Randal was careful about opening.

It was filled with data—charts and numbers that didn't mean enough to him without context, listings of different spectrometer results and chromographs. But there was something strange about them, something Randal couldn't put his finger on right away. Olivia was watching his face, eagerly waiting. It didn't take long to find out why. As soon as it was obvious he was perplexed, Olivia leapt to explain what happened.

"You're looking at the spectrographic breakdown, right? At its contents? Well, what you're looking for isn't there. I've looked for it twice already. There is no carbon."

"What do you mean—?"

"No carbon," she said, her eyes starting to light up even when the flesh around them had turned yellow with exhaustion. "Only silicon. This is silicon-based life."

He shook his head.

"I know small samples have been found by thermal vents in the Mediterranean ocean, but Markowitz was nowhere near there. Besides, once he got the samples away from the heat, the bacteria would have died."

"Ah, but that's something else," she said, eager to the point of being giddy. He hadn't known this side of her, and it only further endeared her to him. She reached into her pile of folders, leafing through them, smiling, while Randal watched her soft pink hands close, the light color her fingernails were painted. How likely would it be for another someone like that to enter his life? The way she looked at him ever since Linden had gone, ever since Randal had taken Dr. Markowitz's place behind the desk . . . Randal was important. Finally important. Was it so strange to think that might appeal to Olivia? Was it so wrong to believe she might finally be seeing him in a new light? See what he would someday become, what legacy he would leave to the world? See all that, and *like* what she was seeing?

"Here it is," Olivia said, sliding the photograph across the desk. For a moment, Randal was too busy staring at her, lost in reverie, to notice the photograph. He jumped when he came to his senses and tried his best to compose himself quickly.

"What's this?"

"Look."

So Randal looked. Then looked up at Olivia, confused. She merely nodded. He looked at it again.

"What *is* this?"

"That's Markowitz's fungus under the electron microscope."

"But, that's no—"

"That's no fungus. No, I know."

What it was looked more like a mesh of hermit crabs than cellular organisms, arranged in a bizarre pattern he wasn't quite sure what to make of. The creatures were smaller than anything he'd ever seen, and yet so perfectly formed. Their shells covered the length of their bodies, folding on themselves at the openings like hoods, protecting the bundles of tendrils sprouting where their heads should have been. If those things had mouths, Randal could not see them, but he knew instinctively they were there. Just as he knew he and Olivia had stumbled onto something very dangerous, or very lucrative. He kept his composure, not wanting to unnerve her.

"This is quite a discovery," he said, wiping the sides of his mouth with his fingers, trying to keep the corners from sticking. "Have you figured out what they are?"

"No," she said. "I was going to have one of the invertebrate guys I—"

"No," he interrupted. "You can't. I mean, this is ours."

"You mean ours for Dr. Markowitz and Linden?"

"Yes, yes. For them. If you call whoever you were going to call, we won't be able to keep things under wraps." Besides, Randal thought, the last thing he needed was another man around to . . . confuse Olivia. "I'll get you the texts. You can key it out."

She laughed. "Key out a silicon-based lifeform?"

"Let's assume you're correct, that this isn't a mistake in the spectrograph . . . it has to be based on something, doesn't it? I mean, looking at this picture, it seems likely it has a physiological ancestor. Maybe a diatom, or something prehistoric. Some sort of organism it evolved from. There's nothing on earth like this as far as we know."

"As far as we know," she parroted. "But think about it a second: what were the coordinates of where Linden and Markowitz found the crate."

"Well, they seemed to move around a fair—"

"But where were they, according to their notes?"

"Just off the coast of Zihuatanejo."

"And where was the volcano they were investigating?"

"It was under the Pacific, right over the continental shelf."

"Was it?" she asked again, gleeful again, and pulled a large map out and laid it across his desk. He couldn't stop staring at her. "Olivia," he started, but she was too preoccupied to notice.

"Here. Right here. That's the Onkoul Vent. But look around it. That's not the shelf, is it? Look at the shape, the impression. That's a goddamn giant crater!"

And it seemed true. The roughly circular shape screamed "crater" to him. And only one thing could leave that sort of mark. And it wasn't from earth.

"What's bizarre," she continued, "is that it's even there at all. I looked into it and this sort of crater is unusual in the water, especially between tectonic plates. Usually the movement swallows them. This one—this one stayed."

"So what are you trying say?"

Olivia stared at the map, quietly, while Randal waited. He could smell her hair again, that beguiling strawberry scent that weakened him. They had been through so much and were so close to something more, yet he seemed to be the only one smart enough to see it. So many wrong things had fallen together so right—his position at the school, the elimination of his greatest rivals for Olivia's affection, the near gift-wrapping of a major new biological find. All these and more, and the only piece remaining in that puzzle of his happiness was Olivia. Beautiful Olivia, who silently tried to work out the importance of what she had in her hands. It would make his career, that discovery. Randal was about to have everything he deserved. Sheer joy overwhelmed and muddled his thoughts. All he had to do was reach out and take what he wanted and it would be his.

Olivia was looking at him strangely, but he didn't understand why. Her face grew smaller, tighter, her wide bloodshot eyes narrowing. She looked down, and his eyes followed her gaze until they saw his hand laying coldly over hers. Neither of them moved as Randal tried to piece together what he was witnessing.

"Randal," she finally said. And her voice said the rest.

"I—I'm just— Do you—" He felt the blood vessels in his face fill, burning through flesh. He snatched his hand away from hers. "I was only—"

"Randal. It's just that Linden—" That was all he could hear over the thunder of blood in his ears. He lowered his head, feigned interest in the papers on his desk, did everything he could not to look at her.

"Sorry, I—it didn't—I was just trying to congratulate you. Good job!"

The words were wood in his mouth, but he did not stop.

"Maybe—maybe you should keep going. See how far you can get with the crate. I—I just remembered I have a meeting with the dean." He stood and realized he wasn't sure he could find the door out. He looked around frantically, and part of him was disgusted at how easily he was unnerved by a woman. "You should go now. I guess."

"Okay, Randal. I'll go. I have work to do."

And then she was gone, a large hole on his desk where her map had once been.

4

Randal made a concerted effort to keep away from Olivia afterward, at least until he could surmount his embarrassment. It had been inexcusable, and he should have known better than to let his heart do the work of his brain. But the fault wasn't his, or at least his alone. No, it was clear that he had let her blind him to the truth, that he'd been blind to the truth all along. Olivia had been leading him on, fooling him into believing there might be something more between them. The only question he couldn't immediately answer was why—after everything he had done to help her, why would she be so desperate to fool him? It took some time to realize it was about Markowitz's crate, his final work. That's all it had ever been. Like her dead lover before her, she wanted to steal what was rightfully Randal's. He shouldn't have been surprised—they were not the first, nor would they be the last, to be jealous of what Randal had, and if they wanted to play games, then Randal would be ready. And he had a secret weapon that Olivia did not. He had the journal, Markowitz's journal. As more time passed, he grew further convinced it would be the key to everything. He only needed to compare it to Olivia's own notes. He remembered her reaction when he suggested he pack the samples, and realized that even sick she had the wherewithal to keep the data from him. Two could play at that game, and the journal he had been so incautiously hiding in the shelves of his apartment was moved to the inside pocket of his blazer, kept close at all times. It was the only way to be sure no one but he ever laid eyes on it. At least until Olivia became herself once more, and Linden's disappearance no longer drove her.

The stress of dealing with Olivia and the mistakes and betrayals between them were only compounded by the classes Randal ostensibly taught. When he first took over the lectures, the students leaned forward, listened to what he had to say. But somewhere along the line he had lost them, and the state of the class unraveled. Randal was hopelessly overwhelmed by their demands; and even with his admittedly prodigious gifts, all it took was one look over the lectern to realize that they, too, were aware of it. He watched them transform from sheep to wolves over the course of a few days—eyes turning red, teeth sharpening like knives—and could smell his own blood in the air.

The sad part was that they could not understand how ignorant they were. Randal tried to show them how much they were missing by not opening their eyes, but they remained obstinate in their refusal to learn. When he finally reached the end of his tether, he made the mistake of asking Dean Coxwell for some advice. Immediately, the Dean responded, and it was as unhelpful as Randal expected.

"You have to own them, Randal. If you don't, they'll own you, and there will be nothing you can later do to turn the tables."

Platitudes. That's all the dean—that's all anyone—had for him. Simple platitudes. Randal was on the edge of gaining the sort of reputation that would kill his future, and there was nowhere he could turn. Nothing else anyone could offer about how best to handle those ignoramuses who despised him. He checked through Markowitz's planner again, through all the man's notes, looking for the key, but there was nothing there beyond the worsening delusions of an old man preparing for an expedition toward his own demise.

It sickened him to realize that only Olivia could help him. She knew how to reach the students. He'd seen her in the lab with them, helping to set up their culture experiments, showing them how to properly loop and streak the agar. She worked one-on-one with them, discussed their issues with their studies. She had the gift for interacting with the students and getting them on her side. Randal certainly understood why they loved her, and also knew he lacked those charms. But Olivia was off-limits to him for the foreseeable future, so he would have to find some way to bridge the gap between him and the class. Otherwise, his dreams of a scientist's legacy would be as doomed to failure as Markowitz's expedition off the coast of the Mexican shoreline.

When Randal arrived at the lab the following morning, he had not expected the scene that greeted him. The room was in shambles—trays of agar spilled over the ground, glass beakers shattered, shelves of books emptied into piles. All the students' lab experiments were destroyed, the colonies scattered across the table and walls like white spots of paste. The room had been ransacked, and Randal's heart turned cold. He dropped the notes he'd been carrying for the day's lecture and darted to the back room where Markowitz's crate had been hidden. He found it open, and stared, desperate to believe he misunderstood what lay in front of him. How could everything be gone? Who had known about the crate, about Markowitz's findings? Randal hadn't uttered a word, yet everything was gone. All his hopes, his whole future, vanished into nothing. Sweat pasted his clothes against his body. His breath wheezed in and out of his lungs so fast he tasted blood. His head pounded, his vision dimmed, and he felt his legs buckle. Randal sat down hard on a bench stool and held his head in his hands. Everything was over.

He didn't see Olivia enter. She just appeared in the room as though she'd always been there and he simply hadn't noticed. She looked more tired than ever, her face puffy and wet, the whites of her eyes pink. In the short time since they'd last seen each other her condition had degenerated, and it was playing havoc with her complexion. Blotches covered her face, her hands, and she had developed what looked like a festering cold sore on her bottom lip. When she spoke, Randal's heart jumped.

"What's wrong?"

"The samples. Everything Markowitz and—everything Dr. Markowitz sent back. It's all gone. Someone came in and took it."

"What do you mean?" She looked genuinely perplexed. Randal was dumbstruck.

"Look," he said finally. "The crate is empty. The lab is in ruins. Everything is gone."

She turned her head and looked at the room as though for the first time. She studied it for a few minutes, then lazily turned back and shrugged.

"I have it all."

Randal was confused. "Have what?"

"Everything," she said. "I have everything."

"You have everything?"

"I have everything."

It was too much. Randal barely contained himself.

"You took *everything*...?"

She absently scratched at one of the sores on her face. It split open and turned wet and red. Her fingernail dragged a streak across her face. Then she shrugged. She no longer seemed like the girl with whom he had worked side-by-side while waiting for Dr. Markowitz and Linden to return. Had it really been only a few weeks earlier? It seemed forever.

"Where did you take it all?"

She looked at him as though she'd already forgotten he was there.

"Oh, you mean the samples?"

"Yes," he said. "The samples."

"I have them at home."

"You have them at—" He could barely speak. "But what about the mess? Everything is upended. It's a disaster in here."

She shrugged again. "I needed some books to help me study the samples. I had trouble finding them."

"That makes . . . absolutely no sense! You destroyed the lab just for the paper?"

"Yes, yes. For the . . ." She trailed off, looking down, scouring the floor. Randal looked, too, but he didn't see anything but a mess. There was something seriously wrong with Olivia, and he worried it was a delayed reaction to the death of Linden, to her exposure to the work he had been doing. She hadn't read Markowitz's journal. For all she knew, Linden had done nothing suspicious. Randal felt his anger wither, slip backward as concern snuck into its place.

"Olivia, are you all right? This isn't like you. Is it because of what happened in my—in Markowitz's office?"

She shook her head once, then again. For a moment, he could see her eyes clear. "What? Sorry, Randal. I'm just really tired. I was up late again." She shook her head a third time, harder. Then she looked at around the room. "This place is a mess. Listen, I'm going to go home, take a nap. I'll be back in plenty of time to clean up before this afternoon's lab."

Randal looked at her face, wondering where the woman he'd spent so much time thinking about had gone. And wondering if she had some plan for Markowitz's material she wasn't telling him about. There was something going on, something that wasn't adding up.

"Okay," he finally said. "But bring back the samples. I'd feel safer if they were here under lock and key."

"Sure," she said, nodding. Despite her deteriorating appearance, he could still smell strawberries.

But he could not stop thinking about her, and could not stop worrying. It occurred to him that there was some overlap between what he'd read in Markowitz's journal about Linden and Olivia's slow descent, but Randal didn't see how the communication of such a thing was possible. Leaving aside the fantastic liberties the senile Markowitz was likely taking with the account, nothing about it matched up. Olivia was nowhere near Linden when he fell ill, and nothing could have been transported back that would have survived the journey in preservatives. Even the bacterial samples that needed to be cultured were pre-screened for any dangerous pathogen. It was impossible for anything to have slipped into the lab. What Olivia had was something else, and even if it wasn't, the journal contained no information at all that would be of help.

Olivia had changed too much, too quickly, as though whatever illness she'd contracted was scrambling her thoughts. It was also making her difficult to read, which was perhaps most worrying of all. Markowitz had sent them a magic ticket in the contents of the grey wooden crate, and though Randal was certain that the Olivia he'd known before then wouldn't have done anything with it, the new ill and grief-stricken Olivia might. Everything Randal was working toward was on the line, and he didn't like the feeling of being under someone's thumb, even if it was unintentional. He had a taste of serendipitous freedom with his new position and the promise of what Markowitz's findings could lead to, and was loath to go back to the anonymity he had suffered once before.

He thought he might check on Olivia during the students' scheduled lab time to ensure she'd returned Markowitz's material. He did so because he had no choice—until then, he had done his best to avoid the lab while the students were there. He did not enjoy their judging eyes while in lecture, and he could hardly imagine how much worse it would be in an enclosed space. But without those samples, he would have nothing, and he couldn't afford to give Olivia the benefit of the doubt any longer. He had to be sure.

Randal's nerve remained steeled until he set foot in the lab and all the chattering voices halted. Dozens of eyes narrowed as the realization of who he was settled like black rain upon everyone. Part of him wanted to flee, turn around and get as far away from those unwelcoming stares as possible, but he would not let himself. The time had finally come to make the students understand who was in charge. His head held higher with each step, he strode across the lab toward Olivia, the only one who did not react when he entered.

"Ms. Marshall," he said with as much authority as he could muster. "I need to speak with you."

When she turned it was only his desire not to show weakness in front of the students that kept him from taking a horrified step backward. He composed himself as quickly as possible in the face of how she looked.

"Olivia, I—" he started, but his students did not want him to finish.

"Can't you see she's sick?" one asked, though in the babbling who it was proved impossible to discern.

"Yeah, leave her alone."

"I just—"

"What's your problem anyway?"

Randal felt his spine curl. Within that circle of hate directed at him, he felt his power draining away. He had to struggle, fight back, or else they would win.

"Enough! The next one of you who speaks gets an automatic fail." The room quieted immediately after that. He fought the urge to smirk while his spine straightened itself out. How easy it was. "Get back to your assignments. Ms. Marshall and I have to have a discussion. Come with me."

For a second, he didn't think she was going to move, and he wasn't sure if it was because she wouldn't or couldn't. Her eyes fluttered, her blotched skin red with eruptions. Her face was swollen and jaundiced, and looked as though it were about to fall free of her skull. But it was her eyes that troubled him the most. They were cloudy white, and even when he thought she was looking at him he didn't know if she truly saw him. She stood, eventually, her dry twisted hands on the desk, propping herself up. She breathed heavily, and Randal kept his distance.

"Olivia, did you bring the material back?"

It was clear she didn't understand him.

"The material?" He looked around, looked at the faces of those who were desperate to pretend they weren't listening. "Did you bring it?"

Her eyes continued to stare, then with a flutter of her lids they were looking at the locked back room. But by the time he realized it those eyes were closed and she was swaying.

"Olivia!"

Her eyes snapped open. Were they cloudier than a moment before?

"Olivia, you should go home."

"I can't." She stumbled over her tongue. "Can't go."

"Mr. Souris?"

He knew the voice, but was so angry that someone had spoken there was no time to think, only react. His entire being powering up for the reprimand he was going to give the lot of them. Now that he finally had the upper hand.

"That's it, you've failed this class. I want you out of this lab now." Randal was panting, the anger still swirling within him. But what he saw when the red clouds parted wasn't any of the students standing there accusing him, but Dean Coxwell, his sweater vest incongruous with the look on his face.

"Mr. Souris, a word?"

Randal was certain he could see a triumphant laugh on one of the students' faces. He stormed after the dean until they were outside the laboratory. Students were walking across campus, completely ignorant of everything he and Olivia were trying to do.

"What is it?" he said, harsher than he intended. "Is about Olivia? Because I—"

"Olivia who? Listen to me. I'm afraid I have some bad news."

He could not look Randal in the eye. Instead, he continued to stare at his feet, clearly wanting to be anywhere else in the world.

"Just say it, dean. It's easier for us both that way."

"It's Markowitz and Linden," he said. "They found them both."

Randal went cold.

"Where?"

"A fisherman found them washed up on the coast of southern California. Their bodies must have been in the water for weeks, because the police say they were nearly unidentifiable. They were mangled, fish having eaten out their eyes and shredded their flesh. Even their guts had been ripped open and eaten away. The police said it was a miracle they found them at all, considering how unpredictable the tides have been down there lately."

Randal nodded, his whole body numb.

"Naturally, you'll keep teaching his class until a replacement can be found." He put his hand on Randal's shoulder. "I'm sorry again, son. But I thought you would want to know."

"Thank you, Dean Coxwell."

The dean nodded his head once, then sniffled and retreated down the hallway with his penguin walk. He did not turn around to see the look on Randal's face.

5

Randal put the news he'd heard from Dean Coxwell from his mind and did his best to focus on the work at hand. His dissertation sat long neglected in a pile on the edge of his desk, and he wondered if it was better to finish it or discard it altogether. He had such bigger things to focus on all of a sudden.

Dean Coxwell's news was like a balm for his mind. Throughout the day the complaints he heard from his students were less troubling, his concern over Olivia's far-fetched plans fading away. There was nothing in her head but desire to feel better, to be cured of whatever ailed her. After all, if she was planning to steal the crate's contents for herself, surely she would have been more discreet about it. She would return everything soon, once she was able to study the discovery properly. And then, once she was well enough, the two of them would compare notes. Those images she'd shown him of the fossilized creatures—they seemed ripe with potential, far beyond anything Markowitz imagined. He had been looking for something that would help with the exploration of deep space, but instead may have found something that had *originated* in deep space. Randal wondered what that would have been like to witness—a blinding light hurtling through the sky like a falling god. It would have been fantastic if only he could have seen it for himself. The mere idea filled him with giddiness.

Dean Coxwell, without even trying, had liberated him. Randal felt like dancing.

He remained locked in his office after all classes had finished for the day. There was something about the studious quiet of the post-class evening that he loved, when the mediocre, uncaring students fled the campus and left only the most contemplative and busy in its halls, or curled in the deep leather chairs of the library. The buzz of life was felt, not heard, in the dusk of the school day, and Randal found himself whistling as he went through the drawers of his desk, removing anything that belonged to Markowitz and depositing it in a dented cardboard box. Perhaps he could send it all to Markowitz's family. *Did* he have any family? Randal had no idea. It was funny—he had spent so long with the man, worshipping all he'd done, and yet Randal knew next to nothing about him. Even his journal was of no use. Randal reached over and picked up his saddle bag. The journal had almost nothing in it that was personal, and Markowitz knew that—

He paused. Checked the bag again. Started removing books and papers wondering where it was. Where was the journal? He kept checking the bag, then the floor around the bag, and behind the desk, in the drawers, on the floor. Where did the journal go? Where?

He asked, but he already knew the answer.

Sprinting to the door, he tried to work the stubborn lock with jittering hands.

It was a fight to get his coat on, sleeves folded inside out and collar half-raised. His car sputtered to life and carried him down Gordon Street, then right on Woolwich. He had not been inside Olivia's student apartment before, but he knew where it was, having dropped her off in the evenings after work at the lab. The stairs to the third floor were utilitarian, made of solid concrete with steel railings. Randal's shoes made the sound of a shovel into earth with each step he took upward, and it wasn't long until, out of breath, he reached the fifth floor and stormed down its hallway.

He hammered Olivia's door with his fist and waited. There were muted whispers from within. He pounded twice further, but no one answered.

"Olivia!" His voice was as stern as he could make it. "Olivia, it's Randal. I need to speak to you. Immediately."

There was an interminable pause, yet nothing happened.

"Olivia, I know you still have those samples, that you stole Markowitz's journal from my bag. You weren't ready yet to see what happened to the two of them, so I wanted to spare you that. But, Olivia, there is so much we can do with what they brought back. Let me show you what they found. You just need to open this door so I can—so *we* can bring everything back to the lab. We have to run tests, compare notes. We have to see what we've discovered. We could help change the world."

Randal was panting, his fists throbbing from being clenched so long. Still nothing. Frustrated, he tried the door handle. It twisted easily, and the door swung open.

"Olivia? Are you here?"

He entered the apartment and immediately regretted it.

The last time Randal saw her, Olivia was in a horrible condition. Her apartment, though, was worse. It had the funk of not having been cleaned in weeks, and impossibly looked as though it might have been longer. Clothes were strewn across the floor, food rotted on unwashed dishes piled in the sink. Flies were everywhere, buzzing around his head. Every surface seemed covered in loose sheets of paper, most handwritten or torn from a multitude of different books. They covered the floor in some bizarre pattern. Randal held his breath and carefully stepped between them, doing his best to avoid touching anything. When he reached the other end of the living room, he forced opened a window so he could breathe, and through it noises from neighbors on the street carried in. It did nothing to alleviate the odor of sweat.

He was distracted by a long drawn-out moan, as though the walls were weakening around him. He turned, unsure if the sound was one of the voices coming in through the window, and waited. There was nothing for a long while, then the faintest huff of an exhale whispered across the room. Randal crept across the apartment toward the small bedroom. The distance seemed longer than he remembered, as though it were trying to inch away from him.

"Olivia?" he called out as he checked the apartment. The roll of blankets on the couch was just that, despite its human shape and unnatural warmth. The bathroom was empty of everything but filth, and Randal's attempt to flush the rusty water resulted in a clog that rose precariously close to the edge before the sickly gulps of suction brought the water level down.

The bedroom door was not only closed, but locked. Randal rapped on it vigorously.

"Are you in there?" He tried the handle, but it didn't budge. "Olivia, open the door."

He heard the squeak of springs, a low moan. He knocked harder.

"Are you okay in there? Olivia!"

He knocked harder still. Tried the handle again. Her moans were louder.

"Olivia!"

He imagined her behind the locked door, moaning as she lay dying, and became worried. He couldn't have that on his conscience. He knocked once more, then started ramming his shoulder into the wood. The frame bent, but did not give—not until Randal started kicking the door near the knob, trying to knock it loose. As he did, the moaning intensified.

It took five lengthy minutes for the door to fly open, and when it did he was hit with an odor unlike any he had ever known. It nearly knocked him over. When he regained his balance he leaned forward uncertainly to peer into the dim room.

The curtains were pulled close to keep out the dying afternoon light, and the mess of clothes and papers remained scattered across the floor. There was nowhere to walk without stepping on something, and in the middle of the chaos was a small double-sized bed with blankets twisted and bundled into a curled comma shape. The room smelled of unbathed Olivia, of rotten strawberries. Randal cupped his hand over his nose and mouth and stepped in farther.

On the bedside table, he saw something he immediately recognized: the large glass stone that Markowitz had sent to the lab. Encircling it, page after page of frantically scrawled notes in no discernible order. Some had small drawings on them, some strange patterns. Words were repeated, trailing across the page in a strange shapes. Just as in Markowitz's journal.

Randal swallowed and stepped even closer. There were photographs of the stone at different distances, different angles, close-ups of its scratches, and those photos too were marked by circles and symbols and scrawled words. Whatever Olivia had discovered, she had bored fully into it, far more than Randal would have expected from someone looking to share a project. If only he hadn't been so distracted by the lectures, by what Dean Coxwell had promised him, he might have been able to stop her. Randal's eyes scanned some of the pages, but they made no sense, and his anger distracted him from what lay before him. It was no matter:

she was caught, and he would do everything he could to make sure she was expelled not only from her position in the lab but possibly from the school. First, though, he would have to understand what she'd found. And the best method was to start gathering the work she'd left behind.

Randal grabbed handfuls of notes and shoved them indiscriminately into his pockets, wanting to collect all he could before she came home. He shuffled through the pile, and hidden at the bottom was a folder thick with page after page of Olivia's scratched handwriting. He thumbed through them, but they looked like paranoid delusions. Still, he added them to the pile he intended to take with him. There were more documents lying on the bed, and when he turned to retrieve them he realized the bedding was too wet, too warm. It was then that Olivia's sore-covered face emerged from amid the twisted sheets, and Randal leapt back, stifling a scream.

Olivia panted shallowly, hair plastered with sweat across her swollen face, and though her clouded eyes were cracked open, Randal could not be sure if she was asleep or awake.

She was far sicker than he'd understood, and the tale of Linden from Markowitz's journal reared in his memory. He could no longer deny the connection, but how had she been infected? Randal slipped his hands in his pockets and stepped forward, the scientist within curious about the transformation, even while the man was repulsed. It was no longer her looks, nor the smell of rotting strawberries, that attracted his attention. It was the spread of the infection that he couldn't stop watching.

"Olivia, are you okay?" He wanted to nudge her awake but was too afraid. The pages of notepaper pinned beneath her were soaked with sweat and stained a dark shade of red.

Olivia moaned, but he did not know if he reached her. She made no further indication beyond another heavy exhale. The glass rock glinted on the night stand. It was flecked with white, much like her pocked face.

"Olivia, where did you put everything you took from the lab?"

She moaned again. It was a good sign. Randal licked his lips.

"Olivia, can you hear me? We need everything Markowitz and Linden found, including the journal. Where did you put it?"

He held his breath, staring at her, waiting to see what she did. At first she rolled slightly, then went still. Randal wondered if she might be crying. Then the moans returned, and he could hear words forming in the noises she was making. Not clear words, not words that were anything more than mumbles, but words nonetheless. She was trying to speak. He pressed her.

"It's Randal. I need to take the research, including your files," he said. "I need everything. I need it all."

Olivia's pale white eyes fluttered open. Dim light reflected off their surface, making it appear as though something was moving across them.

"E'speriment," she muttered in semi-consciousness. Randal stayed close, urging her on.

"Yes, the experiment. Where is everything?" He was studying her face closely, trying to piece together what she knew and what she might not have figured out yet. Her complexion had worsened considerably in the short time he was there, her face sprouting blemishes under her unsettled eyes. Beneath the swelling and the illness he could barely see the girl he'd wanted for so long and lost. He ran his hand across her brow, brushing some stray hairs back before he knew what he'd done. He almost didn't notice how slick it left his fingertips.

Olivia's head shook, her stomach creaking as it swallowed itself. She coughed effortlessly, then clicked her shriveled tongue. Randal wished he knew how to get what he wanted.

"Too much . . . everyone . . ." she managed in the grips of her delirium. "What . . .what did you . . . stop talking so I can sleep."

"Olivia!" he said, hoping the sharpness would cut through her fevered thinking. Her eyelids pulled away, revealing the milky pupils that would not focus on him. She winced.

"It hurts. So much it hurts. Everything is so loud."

He was not going to get the samples. She'd probably already ruined them. But he wouldn't know for certain until he removed her from the apartment.

"Olivia, I'm going to get you help. I'm going to call an ambulance." He fumbled his cell phone from his pocket. She breathed heavily. Heat radiated from her.

"Wait," she said, her voice gaining strength. "Let me see it." Randal waited, phone in hand, but instead of continuing she slumped onto the bed. He pocketed his phone and took her by her frail shoulders and shook her.

"Olivia! Wake up, goddamn it!"

One cloudy eye opened, then the other. They rolled slowly to look at him.

"I don't want you," she said, and Randal went cold. His nightmare becoming real. The sound of those three words from her fissured lips was worse than anything he'd witnessed so far.

"W—what?"

"Linden. Where are you, Linden?" The gravel of her voice gave it a strange otherworldly quality. He struggled for words.

"Olivia . . ." Several hundred questions raced through his head simultaneously. He wanted to reassure her. To smile, to touch her, but couldn't. A voice in the back of his head asked why wasn't he calling an ambulance.

She kicked the covers, struggling as though she'd been caught in a net. Strange sounds emerged—a concoction of grunts and a deep-throated gurgle. Her white eyes turned into her head and she kicked out. Randal took a step back and watched as she grabbed the sheets and blankets and wrenched them aside, throwing them across the room, revealing her sweating nakedness.

"Linden, I need you. I need you."

Randal's thoughts crashed into one another, a cascade of emotions and reactions to what he was witnessing. He sputtered at her announcement with disappointment and devastation, appalled and disgusted and angry and terrified. The gorge in his throat rose, and yet something else stirred in him at the sight of her nakedness, at the sudden smell of her sweating sex filling the room. He couldn't think straight and tried closing his eyes, but it only made things worse. Olivia chanted.

"Need need I want you I need need you Linden need you," she coughed as she continued, rubbing her pallid, sore-covered body. Some pustules were so full they broke as she ran her hands over them, streaking her flesh with blood. She moaned Linden's name, and Randal wished he could do something to stop his own arousal, but he was trapped, rooted in the horrible nightmare. That awful creaking noise resumed from her body, a stretching wail that intensified as she writhed on the bed. The odor in the room turned sour instantly, and Randal gagged. But it was Olivia who was making heaving sounds, her mouth opening and closing and opening, though nothing emerged. Nothing slipped from her lips. Instead, he noticed her flesh turning a bright shade of red, a color that intensified as it travelled down to the place between her legs. Her body swelled, and she started calling again, "I need you I need you now Linden now," as that bulge grew, her legs slipping apart.

From within the folds of her labia appeared the white head of something pushing out, the crowning of a blister both slick and white. The air was fetid, and the noises that filled it were of breaking bones and rending flesh. Randal found himself calling Olivia's name, or thinking he was calling it out, but the sounds he made had nowhere to go in the imprisoning atmosphere. Olivia was crying out in pain, her white scarred eyes staring straight ahead as the membranous bulge grew larger, an inflating amniotic sac. From where he stood he could see movement through its translucence—millions of tiny creatures squirming, waiting to be born, and as the sac grew larger and thinner, as Olivia's screams grew louder, those things moved in a more frenzied manner in anticipation. "Oh, God, I can see! I can see!" she screamed, the extremities of her flesh becoming unmade. Too late Randal realized what was about to happen and could not escape the swell before it ruptured, explosively cleaving Olivia to her clavicle, filling the air with flesh and blood and disseminating tiny creatures wide. Randal raised his arms to shield his face, but he felt them rain against the flesh of his arm, fall between the hairs on his head, travel down the back of his shirt. Like thousands of burning hot needles the tiny alien creatures burrowed into his flesh, searing his body permanently in their wake. They writhed under his skin even as he scratched furiously at them, and the flush of blood that raced to the wounds only brought further nourishment.

Randal was gasping, his brain frazzled in disgust and confused terror. Pieces of flesh lay twitching about the room, unrecognizable as the woman he once knew. The smell was like overpowering offal, and the air tasted of a rusty tang. Randal coughed out the vomit that threatened to choke him, and the sputum was already filled with his own blood. He pulled himself away from the horror, tears running from his rheumy eyes. With hands covered in Olivia's blood, he acted autonomously, removing the clear rock from the night stand, grabbing another handful of notes as he stumbled backwards. Back and out the bedroom door. Back and over the tangle of his feet that sent him crashing down. The impact against the floor was hard, knocking the wind out of his chest, and he writhed, suffocating, until consciousness slipped mercifully away.

6

Randal did not return to the university the next day. Nor the day after. His class found an empty lectern where he should have been standing, an empty lab where Olivia should have been prepping. Talk among them increased, as the days went on, about where Randal and Olivia were and about if they were ever coming back. Eventually, the crowd of students who bothered coming to class dwindled, most of them eager to have more free time in which to sleep, while some of the more studious hunted down the university's administration. They wondered what had happened to their class, and whether two missing lecturers in a single semester was not two too many. Some wanted to be sure Randal and Olivia were still alive, whereas others merely wanted a refund or, better, an automatic passing grade. News of what happened appeared more frequently on the lips of the students and faculty, until Dean Coxwell finally realized it was time to intervene, lest the reputation of Sandstone's Microbiology Department start to suffer in the eyes of other schools and institutions—and, most importantly, Sandstone's board of trustees.

Dean Coxwell's numerous telephone calls to both Olivia and Randal over the following days went unanswered, and he suspected the two had run off somewhere, abdicating their responsibilities. It wouldn't have surprised him; young, impetuous—he saw the way Randal looked at her, like a salmon on a fish hook. Perhaps giving him Markowitz's class had not been the wisest of decisions, but it made the most sense, and for a few weeks it worked fine. But reports from the students and the faculty—and even his own discussions with Randal as time progressed—led Coxwell to question the wisdom of the act. Randal's reaction to the death of Dr. Markowitz and young Linden was the most troubling, and it led to many quiet meetings among the university's peer oversight group about what should be done.

After the twelfth day, Randal contacted Dean Coxwell via a short message left on his campus telephone line. Randal's voice shook and at times was barely above a whisper, but he urged the dean to visit him in his apartment home, said it was urgent, and asked only that the notes and dissertation from Randal's office be brought as well. They were too important to be left behind, he stressed.

Randal's apartment was located off of Speedvale Avenue, in a nearly vacant industrial park. Dean Coxwell's windbreaker was too slight for the weather, but he hoped the trip would be a quick one, lasting only long enough to inform Randal that he was not needed back. The board had agreed to withdraw any offers previously presented and cancel the class for the remainder of the semester. It would be a financial nightmare, but there was little they could do. The dean climbed the warped wooden stairs to Randal's apartment, his speech practiced until it was near-rote, but once he witnessed the repellent squalor in which Randal lived he forgot what he had intended to say.

If Dean Coxwell were to squint, the remnants of a well-kept residence were there, hidden beneath the mess. Walls were straight and painted brightly, the wood of the bookcases was solid and not the particle board so many students bought. Plates and glassware were unique and upholstery intact. Even the artwork on the wall was more than a series of film posters. And yet, covering the bulk of the room were unclean blankets and rags, overturned mugs whose coffee formed dark brown stains like blood. There was the pervasive odor of sweat. Dean Coxwell pulled his arms closer to avoid contact with anything.

"Dean? Is that you?" The voice was hoarse, a whisper straining for more. It originated in one of the rooms.

"Yes, Mr. Souris."

"Please come in here."

Dean Coxwell scowled as he stepped over the remnants of a half-eaten pasta meal and into the bedroom. He was surprised to find Randal was not confined to bed but instead in a wing-back armchair. His legs were covered by a blanket; his swollen head tilted up, mouth agape, as he stared at the ceiling. On the other side of the room, close to Coxwell, was a desk covered with sheaves of loose paper, two microscopes, and a large glass stone. As the dean reached it, Randal tilted his head to reveal a startling degradation of flesh. And a pair of clouded white eyes.

"That's close enough. Even after everything, I'm still not sure about the radius of infection. There's a chair somewhere . . ." Randal pointed, but at nothing. Which is where he faced as he blindly spoke to Coxwell. "I can imagine your reaction to coming here. It was probably the same as mine when I discovered Olivia. The truth is, I'm not going to survive much longer. That's why I need you here. I need to warn someone about what's going to happen. Dr. Markowitz, Linden, Olivia—they each had only a piece of the puzzle. It took me to put it together. Not that I'll be remembered for it."

"Randal," Coxwell said, "We need to call an ambulance. You need to be at the hospital."

"No, the time for that is long gone." He blinked several times in succession. "You need to listen now. I only wish I could have told you sooner, but I've been delirious for days. It's only through force of will I've managed to cobble together this much rationality, enough to explain things to you. I hope you remember that later, when people start to ask questions. You'll tell them, right? That I alone was able to keep it together, even this close to the end?"

"What are you talking about?"

Randal grimaced, then motioned again toward the desk. Scattered across it were a series of frantically scrawled notes weighted down by the large glass stone. Some pages were full of crude diagrams, others strange patterns, yet none were in any discernible order, and Coxwell was disturbed to find that many appeared to be stained with blood. Mixed in with them were photographs of the stone at different distances and angles, including a number of microscopic images of its scratches, marked by circles and symbols and further scrawled words.

"I don't understand, Randal," he said. "What is all this?"

"I took everything from Olivia's when she—when what's happening to me happened first to her. I figured it was finally my ticket."

"Ticket to what? What's happening to you?"

"Do you see the large blue folder on the desk, beneath my research? Those are Olivia's notes. Markowitz and Linden unwittingly discovered something on their expedition, and while I was too busy and blinded by establishing my name to notice, she was trying to piece everything together. It's a very interesting read. She didn't understand the whole picture—she wasn't wired that way—but she figured out most of it. There are a few a sections I've marked. Can you see them? Good. Please read them to me so I can explain."

The dean turned the pages in the worn folder until he reached the first of the highlights. He lifted the note closer to his face and removed his glasses. His eyes had some trouble focusing on the tight cursive.

> It's been three days and I don't feel any better. If anything, I'm progressively getting worse. I wish Linden were here to help me. He'd know what was going on. He always knew what was going on. But he's not here. I have to keep reminding myself of that.
>
> Things that have been no help: the hospital, my doctor, the Internet, none of the med students I know. Nobody has any idea what's happened, and I'm not sure I would trust them if they thought they knew. There's only one person who can help me with this.

"You think she meant me, don't you?" Randal said. "I know I did, the first time I read through her papers. I mean, who else could it be? But it wasn't. It couldn't have been, because she never asked. I wish she had—maybe the two of us could have figured it out. Did you know I was in love with her? I barely like anybody, but I think I loved her. I tried to tell her a number of times, but somehow she still ended up with Linden. God, how I hated him. When he was gone, it seemed like everything was finally going my way." Randal's chuckle turned into a wet cough. "Keep reading."

Dean Coxwell flipped forward a few pages.

> Randal seemed excited in his weird way about the possibility that these micro-organisms were from outer space. I wanted to talk to him more about it, but things got weird again. Still, I know he'd have some ideas. How is it possible that something like this could

be here for so long and nobody ever knew about it? How did Dr. Markowitz know to go looking there? Before they left, Linden said there were satellite reports, but he was vague and like an idiot I never pressed it. Now I really wish I had. That glass rock is the key to everything. I need to study it better, study these micro-organisms better. I haven't felt as bad in the last few days as I did that first time, and the spores in my skin must have fallen out at some point, but I don't want to put this aside. I need to solve this puzzle. It's the only way to make sure Linden and Dr. Markowitz didn't die for nothing. The only way to make sure they are remembered. Thank God Randal and I are on the same page about this!

"This part made me happy, initially. Until I realized how betrayed I was. Olivia loved science almost as much as I do. Certainly more than Linden. Yet I don't know why she never mentioned her plan to me. The creatures Markowitz found infest and reproduce inside a human. They gestate, and when they're done . . . well, I can tell you it's not pretty. Markowitz set out to find a species that would help us better prepare for space, a species that would help us explore. Little did he know that not only could the colonies he found survive in space, but space was where they came from. They landed in a crater millions of years ago, fortunately at the bottom of the Pacific, which I suspect was the only reason they remained so isolated, enough at least to give us mammals a head start on re-colonization. They probably would have stayed down there a lot longer if Markowitz had any idea what he was doing and left well enough alone. But he pushed it so he might assure his legacy. Keep reading."

"Randal, I really think you should—"

"Keep reading," Randal said. Dean Coxwell obeyed, if only because he wanted to understand what had been happening at the Sandstone laboratories while his attentions had been elsewhere. The rest of the pages in the folder had been crumpled then smoothed, and those that weren't missing had been fused together with blood.

> The glass rock is the most interesting piece of this whole puzzle. I spent hours looking through the stereo microsocope at it, looking at the scratches that the colonies were clinging to. I knew I saw something there, but I couldn't figure out what. I had to get Nehls—

"You remember Nehls? In the Electron Imaging Laboratory? I needed to be sure. Go on."

> —to let me use the electron microscope again so I could take more pictures. It took a bit of convincing, especially when he asked if this was part of Randal's secret project. I haven't told a soul, so Randal probably mentioned it, which surprised me, though you'd think by now I'd be used to it. To be on the safe side, I kept it quiet—it's probably safer that way. Nehls eventually relented and let me use the microscope, but the results were even more bizarre.

Dean Coxwell looked again at the photographs of the glass rock and its scratches on the table before him. They were from different angles, different resolutions, but he saw nothing abnormal in them. Was there something he was missing that Randal wasn't?

"You aren't saying anything. Don't worry: it took me some time to see it, too, and only because I'd read Markowitz's and Olivia's notes beforehand. Skip to the last section.

> My eyes are getting bleary from lack of sleep, and I think I've had too much coffee—I'm jittery, my skin won't keep still—but I know there's something in the these photos.
> LATER: Oh my God I cracked it. It's a code of some sort. A language, maybe. These striations, those tiny creatures. It's a language! I don't know how but these things are intelligent!

Dean Coxwell read the short passage over multiple times, trying to ensure it was saying what he thought it was. He could see where Randal had circled some of the markings, but to him they looked like nothing more than scratches.

"What is she talking about?"

"If you look closely, you'll see the patterns in those scratches. I had a friend run them through linguistic software to confirm it. She was right: it's some sort of language. And these scratches are too small for even the most precise tool to have made. But it gets worse. And it gets much worse.

"I was exposed when I visited Olivia, just as she was exposed when she opened the samples Markowitz sent back, just as he and Linden were exposed on the *Oregon* when they brought the rock to the surface—the rock that, as far as I can ascertain, came from the impact point of a meteor roughly three billion years ago. Whatever came on that rock lay dormant under the ocean until Markowitz dredged it up. On the table over there, just outside the door? There's dissecting microscope with a piece of silverware on it. Go take a look through the viewfinder."

Dean Coxwell stood, hesitantly, and followed Randal's instruction. He didn't know what else to do. Everything he was being told . . . it seemed impossible.

"Do you see it? Are you there yet? Look at the knife. What do you see?"

Dean Coxwell had to adjust the lenses and move the focus to account for his own eyes, but when the twin lenses sharpened and joined, he stopped breathing.

"Do you see it? Do you see it?"

"It looks like— It can't be, but it looks like—"

"Those scratches . . . line after line after line of them. Dulling the silver, but words carved out over and over. Give it enough time, and these things will eat through that knife, just as they'll eat through everything else in here. I went to Olivia's a few days ago, when I still could, and the building was locked, but I could tell the entire structure looked worse than it had when I was last there. Whatever emerged, it destroyed everything—carved words into every surface, weakening it for who knows what reason. Look at this," he said, holding up his bandaged hand. "I didn't hurt myself; I was hurt." He peeled away his bandages and showed

Dean Cowxell the black-bloodied scratches along his fingers and palm. They looked the same as those on the rock.

"These things, they've infected me, carved their words into me, their language. I'm going to die by it, by these wounds, by this micro-organic parasite from elsewhere. It's funny: I spent so much time hating Linden for what he had, and that hatred blinded me to what Olivia needed until it was too late. I was blind to what Markowitz was doing, too; why he went out into the ocean, what his hopes were. He saw what was coming and held out hope for humanity. But what he found at the bottom of that crater had been patiently waiting for him for billions of years. He was right: they are the ultimate survivors. And the irony is they will survive us all.

"I've had the same dream ever since I became infected. In it, I see a long stretch of highway in the middle of a snowstorm. The snow is falling so heavily that the entire sky is clouded over, so thick buildings in the distance are only shadows. Snow spins in eddies against the brick structures, curls along the sides of the road, lies inches thick over everything. The world is silent in the middle of this storm, not a single car is in sight. I look closer in my dream, somehow able to clearly see even the smallest details, and I realize it's not snow that is falling to the ground, blanketing the world; it's these things, these micro-organic spores, and they are writing their way across everything, disassembling all our works, every trace of our existence on this planet. And then? And then I wonder what will be left of us anywhere. What price has posterity then?"

Randal lifted the blanket shakily from his lap and coughed into it, but it could not cover the blood that flowed from his mouth, over his arm. Randal stepped away and raised his sleeve to cover his nose and mouth. Something was happening to Randal, something horrible, and though the dean wanted to be far away he could not move.

Randal's body shook, arms jittering, head moving side to side. He continued to struggle against it, contortions of pain across his face as he attempted to swallow the worst of his reaction. He was fighting against the inevitable, and clearly losing.

"I'm—I'm sorry I brought you brought you here," he managed to choke loose. "Sorry for everything. Something like— I should have known." Blood ran down from his nose, from his eyes, as he strained to maintain control. "I deserved so much better. Deserve has nothing to do with it anymore. No one does. No one gets. Can finally see—"

He stopped, eyes pulled wide, glaring forward as the veins in his face, his head, engorged, standing out so far they pulsed. Hands clenched the arms of the chair, fingers turning white as his body spasmed. Coxwell took another step back, his curiosity replaced with terror. He glanced at Randal's notes, regretting not taking them by the fistful, but he was too far away and could no longer remove his eyes from the horror before him. Randal's head was thrown back, lolling as he attempted to stand. The bloodied blanket dropped to the floor, revealing twisted emaciated legs and the odor of evacuation. Every muscle in Randal seemed to be reacting out of sync with the rest, and awkwardly he staggered, drooling and unbalanced, blindly toward the dean. Coxwell's breath solidified in his lungs. The world shrank to the size of a pinhole filled with the crumbling Randal's approach. Another mindless step, a gurgling voice trying to speak Olivia's name, and the discarded blanket tangling Randal's legs. Without effort to protect himself, Randal fell forward like a lumbered tree, and when he connected with the floor, there was a soft sound like a hollow fruit popping, and the expulsion into the air of blood and flesh in a cloud full of white spores.

Coxwell stumbled backward on his squat legs and spun himself forward as quickly as he was able. The front door was less than ten feet away, yet it felt a thousand. He scratched his flesh, convinced he was too late, even as he dashed, praying somehow he might be wrong. Hands on the knob, he threw the door open and fell out into the hallway, yanking the door closed behind him.

He didn't stop moving until he ran into the wall ahead of him, at which point he sank to the ground and breathlessly watched the door he'd come through. In those last instants before impact he had seen Randal's face, seen the crack that had spread over his skull, across his brow to the bridge of his nose, then travelled down past a milky eye and to the right. It may have been imagination, but it seemed the entire quarter of his face dislodged, something inside pushing to be free. But the discarded body of Randal was safely locked behind the apartment door, and that and the walls of the building stood between it and Dean Coxwell.

The dean worked to catch his breath, his limbs too exhausted to move as the adrenaline dissipated, and contemplated his next course of action. Public Health would have to be contacted, informed what was behind that locked door. There would have to be further investigation under quarantine until what the creatures were could be determined. Even though he'd seen the result, Dean Coxwell had trouble believing any of it, but his difficultly would not stop him, stop Sandstone University, from exploring the discovery. Under the right control, the information could be game-changing, could put the school—and Dean Coxwell's department—on the international map. Randal's files were the key. Randal's files, trapped behind a locked apartment door. All Coxwell had to do was find the energy to move his arm, retrieve his cell phone, and make a call. But he couldn't. Even when he saw something glisten beneath Randal's locked door, he couldn't. Even though it was something wet, something from the depths of history that oozed outward, a stream of white that crept toward Dean Coxwell as he lay immobile, terrified. Something that moved as though it had all the time in the world.

Thistle's Find

I'd called Dr. Thistle because I was tight on cash and because the place I'd been staying had just been flipped by the police again. It was getting old, to be honest, but I was used to it. The police and I didn't get along—not after what happened when Mrs. Mulroney died, at any rate—so I did my best to avoid them. They were bad for business, and it didn't help that Detective McCray still had his crooked eye on me, along with the rest of his mustache gang.

But I thought I could trust Dr. Thistle to help, or at least hide me out for a while. I'd known him for nearly my entire life—ever since I was a weird little kid and he was my weirder neighbor. My parents had warned me to keep away from him, but even then I knew they were full of shit and didn't know what they were talking about. Dr. Thistle treated me like an adult, which is all any kid really wants.

He wasn't a regular doctor. I'm not even sure he ever went to medical school. When he first told me to call him "Doctor" I did and never questioned it. He had all the credentials: his house was full of all that equipment only a doctor could afford. It all seemed legit to me, and I'd seen enough doctors on TV to know what I was talking about.

I eventually figured out he didn't treat people, and that he was a bit of a quack, but that only made him more interesting. His thoughts were crazy, and the mumbo-jumbo he talked about when I first met him only made marginally more sense once I was a teenager and had some school behind me. Some of the words he used went right over my head. So far over, I think a plane might have hit them. Eventually, I got bored of going over there all the time to deal with his craziness, but I kept it up because my asshole of a father forbade it, and because I'd read a book once where a crazy old man gave a fortune to the one kid dumb enough to stick around and talk to him. It was a gamble, sure, but no one else ever visited and those machines couldn't have been cheap to buy.

When the bus let me off at Thistle's I barely even looked at the house I grew up in. My parents still lived there as far as I knew, but if they did I knew they'd never let me back in. They believed everything Detective McCray told them about me, and that was that. There was nothing more to do. If they saw me get off the bus in front of Thistle's house they didn't open the door or come to the window. I was like a ghost to my own flesh and blood, which was kind of ironic when you think about it.

Thistle's house had an aura around it. The feeling was palpable as I stood there, staring at the two levels of dilapidation, my skin slick and clammy. The air smelled of ozone, as though reality had been bent, something I was far more familiar with than I would have liked, thanks to Mrs. Mulroney. Still, it left me feeling nauseated.

Whatever Thistle was up to inside, it was clearly a bad idea. My gut knew it, even if my head thought different. Still, I couldn't help but be curious, so instead of running I climbed the uneven concrete steps to the porch and swung the front door's tarnished brass knocker. Flakes of paint fluttered like dead leaves to the ground.

The old man that answered the door must have been Thistle, but it was hard to tell under all those grey wrinkles. He was dressed only in an old undershirt and boxer shorts, and both were stained so severely I wondered if they'd ever been washed. He was sweating and out of breath, and the putrid smell that hit me took me off guard. It burned my eyes.

"Owen! It's good to see you. Your timing is perfect. Now, inside. Quickly!"

I kicked the dirt off my feet, even though they were probably cleaner than his carpet. Doctor Thistle was, quite simply, a hoarder, and over the years since I'd been in his house it had only grown worse. When I was a kid, visiting was like going on a treasure hunt, and I think all the things I discovered there beneath the piles and stacks taught me that there was always something interesting to find if I just looked hard enough. It also taught me that other people's stuff was unimportant next to finding those things. Thistle complained, but he never kicked me out for tearing his stacks apart, which is another reason I stuck by him for so long.

He led me down a narrow path between stacks of old science journals and newspapers. The further into the house we got, the sicker I felt.

"I need some help, Doc. I'm a bit light on cash and—"

"It doesn't matter," he said, waving my predicament away. "I need to show you something. I don't want to spoil the surprise for you, so just follow me; I haven't written everything down yet and I don't want to get confused."

I don't know how old he was when I first met him, but after so many years Dr. Thistle had to have been ancient. You could see it in the cataracts in his jaundiced eyes. The smell in the house hadn't eased, but I'd become acclimated to it somewhat and was able to stop cupping my mouth in my hand. I wondered what Thistle had been cooking and whether I could pry one of the painted-over windows open enough for some fresh air. It was like breathing in a room full of rotten meat. The flies were legion.

Thistle's old heavy feet clomped on the bare wooden staircase into the basement. I'd never been allowed down there before, and as we descended I felt the old tingle of childhood fear creeping up on me. I hadn't been afraid of anything in so long that part of me was amused by the sensation, but there was another that wondered why it had occurred at all, especially considering all the horrible things I'd witnessed since. I suppose we're all just an amalgamation of our childhood fears and instincts; no matter what our brains know, sometimes old fear runs much deeper than logic can dam.

And for that fear, I can only blame my parents.

My mother had told me there were rumors about Doctor Thistle, and I knew Dad and she were angry about him moving in, but it didn't make sense. He may have been strange, but he'd been nothing but nice to me. I can probably guess, in hindsight, what stories my mother had heard, but nothing unsavory ever happened. I'm pretty sure I would remember something like that. Well, reasonably sure.

The basement lights were off, but sunlight edged around the material papering the windows. I heard the hum of the machinery running, as well a whining noise and something shuffling. The rotten tobacco odor from upstairs had given way to the tremendous stench of old musky sweat, and no matter how deep I breathed it wasn't deep enough to get acclimated. The world wavered in the periphery of my vision, and what I could see amounted only to the red and blue indicator lights of a room full of electronic gear. I heard something there in the dark, like breathless panting and slobbering, and a low growl that sounded as if it was almost on top of me and not very happy.

"When did you buy a dog, Doc?"

"A dog?" His voice seemed warped there in the dark. "I don't have a dog. What you're hearing, that's—well, that's something else entirely. I'll show you, but you need to see something else first. Just stand right where you are. I don't want you knocking anything over."

I heard Thistle's footsteps move away from me, and I thought I could make him out faintly in the corner of my eye, rippling the dark as he passed. The smell off him faded a bit, but I still felt nauseated. And curious. I definitely felt curious.

The lights blinded me when they came on. I don't know if they were too bright, or I just wasn't ready, but the pain in my head was as sharp and swift as a razor and I was already screaming before my eyelids shut. It drove whatever animal Thistle had down there crazy. It started howling and thrashing while Thistle's shushes seemed aimed at us both. When I finally managed to pry my eyes open again I immediately wanted to shut them. Impossibly, the basement was more cluttered than the floor above. I don't think there were as many boxes and piles, but what was there was larger and odder shaped. It just seemed full of equipment. Blue network cables were wrapped around and hanging from joists crisscrossing the room, sometimes dangling so low they looked like they'd clothesline any average-sized man walking past. Machinery and computers were running everywhere, displays spitting out screen after screen of meaningless code. In the middle of it all was what looked like a mirror. About two feet square, its surface was less reflective and more as if it had the appearance of reflection. That's the best way I can put it. Whatever I could see in its surface was blurry and didn't look quite right. The thin metal square was held up by a two-post rack, and I wondered if every goddamn cable in the place was attached to it in some way.

"What're you building down here, Doc?"

"Oh, it's built, it's built." Thistle laughed, but the sound of it had a strange throaty warble, and the look on his face was hard to peg. "It's a door, Owen. I've built a door."

"What are you talking about?"

"Hang on. Don't touch anything."

He started hitting buttons and turning knobs, and the machines in the room made the same noises they had before, but the pitch was higher. It was like they were working together to produce the most ear-splitting whine possible. Immediately, my nausea tripled, and I experienced something similar to my worst flashbacks. I covered my ears but Thistle didn't, probably because he was already used to the experience. Or maybe he'd just found a node to stand in. He worked the controls as if he were a lot crazier than I'd ever given him credit for. He danced between the switches and keyboards with glassy-eyed glee, his tongue peeking from his mouth, periodically licking his bottom lip. I also heard the mournful cries of that animal, though it wasn't easy over the device's whine.

Thistle turned around—it was the first time he'd looked directly at me since switching on his equipment, and without missing an excited step started pointing at the middle of the room where the reflective metal square was standing. Beneath it, lights flickered with the same hyperactivity, but the mirror itself had changed. Earlier its reflection had been a poor reproduction of what was in front of it—colors muted, angles bent, images blurred and unknowable—but now the surface had started to glow and ripple, and whatever had been reflected there wasn't any more. Just what images were reflected was baffling, but the sight was enough to make what little I'd eaten for breakfast come rushing up my throat. I bent over and vomited, and it spread across the floor like thick soup.

I felt a hand on my shoulder. "Are you all right, Owen?" I stood and nodded, looking at Thistle though my watering eyes. I wiped off my mouth.

"The noise is really messing with my head."

He nodded. "It takes some getting used to. Don't worry. It'll wear off in a minute. And don't worry about the floor. It'll be fine once it dries. Come look at this."

He led me to the mirror, and though I felt the pressure in my head worsen, my stomach settled down. Thistle's odor didn't help matters. I wondered what I was doing in that basement, and what the hell Thistle was up to. Mostly, though, I wanted to leave and get myself to a bar. If there was one thing I'd learned about throwing up, it was that it always tasted a lot better followed by a shot of gin. And maybe one before, as well.

"Look, but don't touch," Thistle said, and I peeked into the mirror with suspicion. I didn't see my refection. What I saw I don't think I can properly describe. It was like a window hanging over the middle of the floor, and what was on the other side of it was a vast landscape of rock and scrub brush. I peered closer as Thistle watched me, a playful smile on his face while mine was no doubt clouded with confusion.

"What is this?"

"It's a world, Owen. A world almost nothing like ours. I discovered it many years ago, but over time the barrier between there and here has grown thin. So thin, in fact, I was able to fashion a quantum hole using harmonic glass and—"

"But . . . how?"

Thistle looked at me over the top of his glasses.

"I am a doctor, you know."

Suddenly I saw the truth in his eyes.

"You think this is going to make you rich, don't you?"

Thistle cleared his throat. "Well, the thought did cross my mind, but no, not yet. I haven't been able to tune it. Right now, this is the only world I can see, and it's not the kind of place anyone wants to visit."

"What do you mean, visit?"

"Yes, Owen. This isn't a window. It's a door."

When a man as old and as obviously crazy as Dr. Thistle smiles, when you get a good look at those crooked yellow teeth and the white film on his bleeding gums, it's nothing short of disturbing. Especially when that man is talking to you in his underwear. Compared to that, a portal into another world barely registered. I'd seen weird things before, as the late Mrs. Mulroney can attest, and eventually they stopped being anything more than curious. But old-people smiles . . . those things ate at my soul.

"Have you gone through it yet?" I took a step closer to get a better look. Thistle stopped me with an arm across my chest.

"You don't want to get too close, Owen. But this brings me to what I wanted to show you."

"It wasn't this?" I was confused, and more than a bit irritated he wouldn't let me get closer to his dimensional window.

"I only showed you this so you'd better understand what I have locked up in the other room. It's no dog."

"What is it?"

"One of them."

"One of who?"

Again, he smiled that creepy smile, this time punctuated with a slide of his tongue across his lower lip. I don't think he knew he was drooling.

"One of them."

Now things were getting interesting.

After he led me through the maze of wires and equipment that filled the basement, Thistle stopped me at the door to the rear storage room. It had a large padlock around the handle to keep it shut. From the other side of the door I could hear that growling, slobbering noise again. I didn't know what it was, but it was clearly inhuman.

"If you were anyone else I wouldn't show you this, but I have a feeling that you won't judge me too harshly. I wouldn't be surprised if this didn't shock you at all."

He was wrong, though. What I saw inside that storage room was indeed shocking. Beneath the deadening fluorescent lights was an old wooden table. Short thick ropes were tied around each of the legs, and they led up to secure Thistle's trophy to the tabletop. I recognized it at once, and I felt a rush of revulsion and excitement that were so close together I couldn't tell where one ended and the other began. The creature he stole from that other world looked to me like no creature at all, but instead like a teenage girl, no more than fifteen. She was tied down spread-eagled. And she was naked.

"Beautiful, isn't it? She looks almost human."

"Where did you find her?" I asked. The primal side of me was reacting to her nakedness in a way I was trying desperately to stop. Her violent gyrations on the table didn't exactly help. I was very worried about the situation I was in, especially if cockeyed Detective McCray found me. If Thistle had picked up this girl off the street—even during some hallucinogenic episode—then I was in the kind of trouble I wouldn't be able to slide out from under. "Where did you get her, Doc? I need to know."

"I told you, Owen. I got her from over there. And I know what you're thinking, but don't be fooled. She's not some little girl I snatched up off the street. She's a ghoul."

"A what?"

"See for yourself."

I walked slowly to the girl, forcing my eyes away from her tiny breasts and the allure of her bare mons. I kept my eyes on hers, looking for any sign of humanity in them, but there was nothing there. Only animal ferocity. She was a feral beast, and when she looked at me and roared I could see her teeth were ragged and sharp. And there were far too many of them. I hadn't seen a ghoul before that point, and she was nothing like those I saw later, so I don't know if I can call her that now in hindsight, but I know from experience that every plane has its own reality, and I suppose she was just as likely to be a ghoul as not.

"She doesn't seem to have any idea of where she is."

"No, I doubt she does. She's no more than an animal. As far as I can tell her reality doesn't have any sort of civilization, merely hunting packs."

I stepped back, afraid of the stress I saw her putting on the ropes. She looked far stronger than I expected. "Why did you bring her over? You know you'd never be able to sell her."

"Well, maybe not for any scientific reason, but . . ." He trailed off into that smile again, waiting for me to understand what he was saying. I thought I did, but I didn't believe I was right, not until I noticed the erection in his pants.

"You mean—?"

He nodded slowly but with pride. As though she understood what we were talking about, she violently pulled at the ropes, bucking and thrusting her groin into the air in an effort to break free. She did not seem pleased with her situation. I was at a loss for what to say. I wondered how many men might pay for the experience of fucking an animal shaped like a teenage girl. Then when I realized the answer I wondered just how *much* they would pay. I looked back at the creature, and she was staring straight at Thistle and growling at a quiet, subhuman decibel.

"You haven't— Have you—?"

"I had to test it out, Owen. I had to make sure that . . . that all the parts worked. Then I had to make doubly sure."

I nodded, wondering how I managed to get myself into another mess.

"So why show me?"

"I know you, Owen. You've got connections all over the place, and from what I gather they aren't the kind who'd be shocked by something not quite of this world. There's money to be made here, and I want you to be my partner. No more sleeping on the street or rundown flops or begging for money for you. It's really the kind of experience you don't forget, believe me. It's addictive. I feel years younger, and I think maybe I look it, too. I haven't taken my medication in weeks. I don't need to, not with this thing around. It reinvigorates me!" He spit at it and it hissed and strained at its ropes, rubbing its arms raw. "Go ahead," he said, at last getting to his point. "Try it out."

Sometimes I get put in strange situations. I'm not going to tell you I'm a saint by any stretch of the imagination, but neither am I as bad as people say I am. People like crooked-eye McCray, for one. That sort of thing, it's good for the reputation, and having a reputation tends to open more doors than it closes, but sometimes you're expected to do things you wouldn't normally do, and the question is always whether you do them and deal with the consequences or don't do them and allow a chink in that precious image you've worked so long on building to protect you. It's amazing how quickly one can be destroyed.

Whether it was the obviously aroused Thistle or the naked girl writhing in front of me, I wasn't sure, but I became acutely aware that the storage room smelled of stale sex. Thistle was chuckling and rubbing himself over his stained boxers at the mere thought of watching me fuck the bound creature. The last thing I needed was his perverted eyes on me while he masturbated.

"I'd rather do this on my own."

In an instant, his face broke. It was obvious he didn't want to leave. "But it's not safe. What if she gets loose?"

"Something tells me that if you've gone at her alone you've made sure she's tied up good and tight. I'll take my chances. Better the devil I can see."

His disappointment turned to irritation that bordered on anger, but I reminded him of the help he was going to need to get his project off the ground.

"All right, I'll give you a few minutes. I need to check on the window anyway."

He closed the door on me and I locked it, then turned around and faced the thing on the table. She panted heavily, her mouth opening and closing as if she were warming up her muscles. I wanted nothing to do with her, but the scent of her sex and soft flesh was making my head swim. I wanted to look away, but despite my bravado in front of Thistle I was afraid that she'd somehow break free when I wasn't paying attention.

"You're a good girl, right? You aren't going to hurt me?"

She snarled and I shuddered.

I knew I had only a few minutes before Thistle's fantasies got the better of him and he tried to sneak in to catch me literally with my pants down. I wasn't going to give him the opportunity. He didn't leave me with much in the storage room, strangely the one place in the house not cluttered to the ceiling. I guess he wanted some room to show his ghoul who was boss. As far as I saw it, despite his grandiose ideas Thistle was not one to share, and his hunger was always going to be bigger than he could fill. I pulled out the folding knife I kept in my pocket and started to fray the ropes around the girl's wrist and ankles. I was careful not to cut too much—I didn't want her escaping before I set things in motion. She almost seemed to understand what I was doing because she struggled less as I worked, but when I looked into her eyes I saw they were as empty as a shark's. There was nothing behind them that approached a soul. Only further blackness.

On cue the door shot open revealing Thistle, his boxer shorts now gone, his pencil at full attention. "What the hell are you—" was all he managed to get out before my knife cut through the last of the ghoul's bonds and her inhuman strength did the rest. She leapt across the room at such speed Thistle didn't have a chance to move his hands from his hard-on before she tore off his face with razor-sharp teeth. Still, he tried to speak, his voice a gurgling brook as she crouched over him; then those same teeth removed a large piece of his throat and finally shut him up. She lapped up the blood as quickly as it spurted while his body shook and convulsed, his hand still clenched around his member so tightly it had turned deep blue. I chose this moment, I think wisely, to dash out of the room while the girl was still distracted by her meal. I thought I felt her hands claw at my ankle as I passed and I shrieked, but didn't stop until I was outside the storage room and was able to shut the door and padlock it. At that point I checked my leg for damage and was relieved to find none.

I slumped to the floor, my heart racing, astounded I'd made it out alive. I don't know if it was the fear or the sight of that bloodied naked girl, but I found myself somewhat aroused by the whole ordeal. That sensation withered once I felt the pounding on the door I was leaning against.

It was like sledgehammer coming down hard, again and again, from the other side, and judging by the way the wooden frame was splintering it was clear the room wouldn't hold Thistle's ghoul for long. I scrambled to my feet and looked around the stacks of debris from the dead man's life. The only thing in my favor once the girl broke free was that the basement's maze of junk and wires would prevent her from springing on me, but the obstacles were just as confining for me as they were for her, if not more so. There was no way I could outrun her, but maybe there was a way to escape her. Thistle had left his dimensional machinery on and running, and the window was still operational. I picked up a book from one of the piles and threw it at the window; it passed through with a flash of static. I looked back at the door to see a thin bloody arm break through and begin to tear the wood apart. She made a hole easily big enough to fit her tiny body, and leapt through to land on all fours about fifteen feet in front of me. She snarled and lifted her nose to the air.

"Easy, kitty."

She had my scent, and in my terror I wondered how she could smell anything with her face covered in blood. It ran through those rows of sharp teeth and then down her neck until it dripped off her tiny breasts. She raised her head skyward and made some horrible screech, and when she was done I heard its response from the electronic window humming behind me. I dared a quick peek and saw a row of shadows in the distance moving across the rocks. She was calling reinforcements, calling her pack, and I knew that if I didn't do something quickly they were going to find their way through the portal. If that happened, a lot of bad news was going to follow, not the least of which being that I would be deader than Thistle. Some gratitude, I thought.

"Here, girl. Come here, girl." I tried to whistle, but my mouth was too dry. She looked at me with those dead eyes and cocked her head. "Be a good girl and jump through the window." I could hear the howling behind me and wondered how much time I had left before the pack arrived. A minute? Maybe two? I couldn't turn around to see their approach while the girl in front of me stared and growled. I was running out of options. "Come on, girl," I said, motioning her forward. I'd have shown her my throat as bait, but I didn't want anything to happen to it. "Come here." When she took a step forward, I almost wet myself.

I worked to keep the window between us while she took

sideways steps, looking for an opening. The cables from the ceiling kept her grounded, but they also kept me from moving very far with any sort of protection. She was making a wet bray as she stalked toward me, and I knew I was running short of time—the howls of her pack were getting louder and louder—but I kept speaking quietly to her, kept tempting her forward. Each step she took left a bloodied footprint behind, and as she knocked computer equipment aside I prayed she didn't do anything to damage it. When she was within six feet of me she stopped and went up onto her haunches. I could see that all the muscles in her body were so tightly tensed she was like a wound spring. She was getting ready to pounce, but all I could think about was how engorged her labia had become. I swallowed hard.

I moved more by terrified reflex than anything else when she leapt. As soon as those muscles started to unfurl, time for me slowed to a crawl. I immediately stumbled backward, flailing my hands out in front of me. I managed through sheer luck to push the two-post rack over onto her, and as it fell she managed to leap into the portal and disappear from this world and into the next. The window continued to fall toward the floor and I braced for its impact, but it never came. Instead, the electric window hung a foot from the ground, its intact wires and cables breaking its fall. Then I heard wild howling and knew the pack had arrived.

I reached up and started pulling any wire I could get my hands on, hoping to disconnect the window before those creatures could leap through. I could feel the cables giving handfuls at a time, but that sickening hum didn't stop. I saw an arm appear from under the hanging window, an arm far larger and thicker than the one I'd seen on Thistle's ghoul, and I knew I didn't have a choice. I leapt over the fallen debris onto the back of the fallen two-post rack, adding my weight to it. The cables holding it up snapped immediately, and it and I crashed into the ground. The window shattered and I was thrown forward, hitting my head on the edge of one of the tables, knocking computer equipment to the ground. Everything went black for me then.

When I awoke I knew two things: first, that I was still alive; second, that I wished I wasn't. My head throbbed, and when I put my hand on it it came away covered in blood. I tried to stand, but the world was spinning way too fast and I had to sit again. At least, until the room slowed down. I looked around me at the destruction. A thick beastly arm lay cleanly severed at my feet amid broken glass and plastic. There was blood everywhere, some of it mine, and footprints across the concrete leading back to a broken door and some massacre beyond it. I'd made a clusterfuck of things again, and I had no idea how I was going to explain it away. Normally, I'd just leave, but there was no way my fingerprints weren't all over the place, no doubt full of blood. My only solace was the knowledge that no one would be missing Dr. Thistle, which bought me a little time.

I managed to crawl upstairs after a while and found a towel to hold against my bleeding head. The wound wasn't as deep as I'd thought, and the crazy glue I found in one of the millions of boxes was enough to keep the wound shut without me having to go to the hospital for stitches. I crawled into the bathtub and turned on the cold water, then sat there for as long as I could, trying not to pass out. I didn't think I had a concussion, but I wasn't going to take the chance. I wasn't crazy, despite what I kept telling myself.

I'd had to do a lot of things in my life, but getting rid of a body was never one of them. I had a vague idea of what to do, and thankfully Dr. Thistle had all the tools I needed somewhere in his piles of clutter, but sawing through bone is a lot harder than it sounds. When I managed to get him down into enough manageable pieces, I put them and the severed arm into a black garbage bag and carried it over to a place I knew behind Greenwood Racetrack. It was the place you took things you wanted to forget about. Everybody knew that. Once I got back I cleaned the house as best I could and made some space for myself. I'd finally found a home. At least, for a little while. Until they shut the power off, at any rate.

Beyond the Banks of the River Seine

I have read all the books about that time, but they are all wrong. There is no one who knew Henri Etienne as I did, certainly no one in all Paris. We were both students at the Conservatoire, the finest musical school in all the world, where we had met in our first year and had become inseparable. The man people whisper of in the shadows of concert halls bears little resemblance to the boy I had once held dear. This is the way of things, I suppose. Few truly know those they idolize most. Perhaps, this is best.

Henri and I were rivals over everything; two composers always at odds, albeit friendly odds. Or so it seemed to me. But I imagine it would, as I was his better in virtually every way. I do not mean for that to sound as vain as it must, but if this chapter—my final confessional—is to serve its purpose and cleanse my soul, then I must be completely honest. Compared to me, Henri was pale, destined for nothing more than performing in one of the small bars along the Left Bank where he might earn little more than enough to scrape by. It was not that he was unpracticed or undisciplined—he was the sort who put many long hours into honing and refining his craft—it was that his proficiency was never more than average, and his playing rote and unemotional.

He was no better than the automaton I'd once seen at the Musée Grévin, one step above a music box with its carved wax fingers and clockwork piano. What I am trying to convey is that the boy was not in the same league as I, and that only made his company more charming to me.

His sister, Elyse, was a different beast altogether. Never in all my years before or since have I laid eyes on a woman so near perfection that even the Almighty himself might be expected to cast a second glance. Elyse was a dream, an angel. And I wanted nothing as much as I did her. Wanted to feel her heat against me. Wanted to show her the sort of passion only a man on the verge of success might be able to provide. And yet, despite all my wooing, she remained resolute against me. I was not an ugly man—my mirror assured me of that—and I was not without means, so her dismissals were very much a surprise. They were illogical, based I was sure on no more than the whims of a woman, and they only made me want her more. I knew she must love me, and that it could only be for her brother's sake that she refused to admit it.

What charmed me most about Henri was his drive, his perseverance to best me at something, anything. He would take quite a ribbing from me in class and with friends, always second to my performances. Perhaps we were rough on him, kept his nerves raw, but it was only from love. I enjoyed having him with me. He could always be counted on for a humorous glower when I dared play the keys of his wounded pride. It seemed to motivate him, though, something for which he should have thanked me. Though perhaps not in retrospect.

Because of our friendly rivalry, he would pore over every task, practice it incessantly, fixate on achieving the truer performance. Where I might play adagio, he would play presto. A quartet I had written would be countered with a minuet from him. Each work of mine was responded to, each with a fury of playing hitherto unknown to any of us who knew him. Henri's hands would tremble before every performance, and even my laughter was not enough to calm him. "You mustn't goad Henri, Valise," his sister would plead, to which I would only laugh further. "It's all in good fun," I'd say, and her sweet porcelain face would twist, and then she would invariably spit at me. Is it any wonder I was so smitten? We would watch Henri play, and while the rest of the room focused on his dancing fingers I could not bear it. It pained me to see them drawing such lifeless notes from the ivory. Instead, I studied his face and the flop of hair that would slide over his brow moments into his performance; or at his flushed skin, sweated with concentration before reaching a boil as he wordlessly realized that what he was playing was a failure. In these instances, he would inevitably look to me and Elyse, and each time he did so I saw defeat had already claimed him. He would not stop playing, but it is a given that once doubt infects a performer's mind, it spreads like a cancer. Inevitably, he would stumble, in an increasingly tumultuous cascade of errors, ending in muted, polite applause. Often I would find him after these performances weeping discreetly. Forever soft as a lamb was my good old Henri.

At the end of the day, though, my friendship with him was more important to me than anything else save my own career and, perhaps, his sister's hand, and I did all I could to guide him by my example, providing him a bar by which he might measure himself. Once, while we celebrated too much the sale of one of my compositions, he drunkenly confessed that were he ever to best me, and were he to do so in front of Elyse, he might die a happy man. I treated it as the jest it surely was—with a laugh hearty enough to fill both our mouths. His glower did not falter, which only charmed me further. His sister, however, treated it with far more weight. "We can no longer do this. Please, leave us to our misery," she said one day as I stood across from her in the October courtyard, but she knew I could do no such thing. Henri was my dearest friend, and she my future betrothed. They would have me in their life until the end of it came.

No one was more surprised than I when Henri decided to

write a concerto. I asked him about it only once, and he replied, "I finally want to show the school what I am capable of." I shook my head. "You needn't prove anything to them, the ignoramuses. Don't feel as though you must compete. What's that M. Ouillé says in our orchestration class? One must know one's limits." It seemed as though he were compounding injury, the way he begged for comparison against me. Only the year before I'd had my own piece performed at the Elysée Montmartre, receiving raves and exaltations from all quarters. Candidly, I was told word of the composition made it as far as the *préfet* of the Conservatoire, François Chautemps, and he requested a copy of the sheet music so that he might inspect my craft. There was no way to be sure this was true, of course, but it did not seem so out of reach, especially then. I hoped my success might inspire Henri to do more.

Not long afterward I found myself circling Montparnasse, looking for a woman whose name I've long forgotten and instead noticing Henri moving along in a vacant haze. I called to him, though it didn't seem at the time he heard me. Instead, he slipped into a small paper shop on the corner that until then I had thought was closed and unoccupied. It seemed reasonable, given how dusty the volumes in the window were, and the number of dead flies that lay among them, half-consumed by dermestids. I followed Henri inside, my lady friend forgotten, and was confronted by claustrophobic walls of ancient bound theatrical scripts and other ephemera. I did not find Henri immediately. Only a small Indian who stood behind the counter, his head wrapped in frayed scarves. His eyes looked yellow and wide as they stared at me, his lower lip curled in a rictal frown. He pointed a skeletal finger at me but said nothing. It was enough to unnerve me, and I wished to leave but could not. I had to find Henri. I would not abandon him.

But it turned out I did not need to. He appeared from the warren of stacks, his eyes swimming with joy—or if not joy, then something else, something more powerful. I knew immediately the forecast was dire. He accidentally dropped the bound script he held upon seeing me, then sputtered and stumbled as though caught doing something improper. I looked down, as did he, at what he had dropped, but neither of us spoke, as though in tacit agreement we should pay it as little heed as possible.

"What do you want, Valise? Why are you following me?"

"Following you? I wasn't doing anything of the sort. You know very well I lunch in the Dôme. I merely saw you while waiting for a friend of mine."

Henri twitched, his eyes dancing around the room and refusing to meet my gaze. It was clear he did not want me to ask about the script that lay between us.

"What book is that?" I asked.

He tensed, as though he feared I might swoop down and snatch it from him. Had I been closer, I might have.

"It's nothing at all," he stammered.

"Nothing, is it?" I leaned closer, daunting him. He winced, his eyes spinning into his head, and if I knew my unblinking stare would bore into his psyche given time, I was robbed of it by the Indian. I had not heard him approach, yet there he stood behind Henri. At first, yellow eyes were all I saw, giant and menacing, and then the pit of my stomach rebelled. Though his expression did not change, it felt as though he were snarling at me. I stepped away from Henri, hoping to keep some distance between myself and the strange man. Henri, for the most part, remained in whatever half-trance I had found him in. I tried desperately to break it.

"Come, Henri. I haven't eaten. Join me."

"I'm a bit—"

"Nonsense," I swallowed, my gorge rising. "Join me at the Dôme. I'll arrange for us a table on the patio." Where the air is fresher, I neglected to add.

Neither I nor Henri looked at the Indian, but it was clear Henri wanted to and only my presence stopped him. I made the mistake of letting my eyes drift to the script, lying face down upon the ground. I barely had time to notice the strange symbol printed on its lower right corner before Henri's demeanor sharpened and his wits returned. Without hesitation, he bent down and picked up the book, then held it tight to his chest as though to hide it.

"Just let me take care of this. I'll join you in a moment."

"Please, allow me," I said, graciously drawing my wallet from my pocket. I wanted to hurry him, but also see the play he had chosen. Part of me also hoped he might mention my offer to his sister. He would not accept any money, however.

"I do not need your charity, Valise. Please wait for me at the café."

I looked at the yellow-eyed Indian and acquiesced, eager to be out of his presence. I retreated to Le Dôme and ordered a tea as I awaited my friend's arrival. It was unclear how long I sat there with my cigarettes burning, watching the warped door of that hidden paper shop. But I never saw Henri emerge, and I was forced eventually to lunch alone.

Henri more or less vanished from my life thereafter. On occasion I'd see him dashing madly across campus, always too far to catch, and I heard the whispers about him that were even then slowly spreading across campus, incredulous whispers I at once put out of mind. It was a lonely existence without Henri. Certainly, I had others to spend my time with—a gifted musician never suffers from the lack—but none were as dear to me as my friend Henri, none inspired in me the same amount of pride and love for all their foibles.

After the first few weeks he was gone I found an excuse to visit the small flat he and Elyse shared, all in the hope that I might be invited in to see whether those rumors I refused to believe were true. Elyse answered the door when I knocked, but though she did not open the door all the way, still I could see Henri haunting the background, a frail gaunt specter, eyes ringed dark and full of fire. Elyse smiled that smile which melted my heart and made me forget all others, but when I tried to step past her, let alone speak a word to the passing Henri, she raised a delicate hand to my chest. It was clear from her face that all she sought was comfort. I had no choice but to put my feelings for Henri aside and console her.

She led me to the kitchen, far away from the room Henri was in. I imagined it was to ensure he could not hear what she had to say.

"All he does is write," she said. "Always working on his strange music. I wish he would stop, Valise. I hear him late into the night whispering, whispering. Sometimes I worry it's no longer his voice I hear but my own. Sometimes it's no voice I recognize at all. Maybe he'll listen to you. Maybe you can break him of his obsession. I want my brother back." She broke down and cried on my chest, and I closed my eyelids and soaked in her sorrow. It was good, finally, to be once more needed, and I would do all I could for her.

"Henri!" I bellowed, storming into his room. I paused only long enough that I might grasp how disorganized and chaotic it was. "We must speak at once."

My gaunt friend stepped from behind his cluttered desk. His face was drained of color, but I vowed not to let his appearance dissuade me.

"You must cease this, my friend. It is consuming you. I have never known you to be full of health, but this . . ." I waved my hand over his willowed frame. He merely attempted a pale imitation of a smile.

"It means nothing. None of it does. I am enraptured by this project."

"What do you mean? What project?"

Here, his smile faltered.

"I cannot tell you."

I sputtered. "Why on earth not?"

He would not look at me, and behind me Elyse *could* not. Suddenly I wondered if I had been played for a fool. Had anything Elyse told me been true? I could be sure of only one thing: that I'd had enough of their shenanigans. I wanted nothing more than to be gone, but despite the betrayal my insatiable curiosity had not been allayed. I spotted amid the clutter a familiar jaundiced volume, open and overturned. Even across the room it filled me with ill.

"What is that?" I ordered, but Henri stepped between me and it before I could get closer. He seemed strangely out of breath.

"It's not yours. Valise, please leave."

"I will do no such a thing. I demand you tell me what you are working on."

He sighed and looked to where I expected his sister to be. But when I turned I found she had vanished.

"There is no one left to prove yourself to. Please leave. I must finish my writing. I feel I am so very close."

"Close to what? To adapting *that*?" I pointed to the volume overturned on the table. I noticed his eyes would not go to it while I was in the room. "You think that will bring you what you need?"

"I'm not sure *what* it will bring, Valise. I'm not sure at all."

"Then why do it? Look at yourself, Henri. The toll is too great. Forgive me, but you seem ill-equipped for the task. Here, I have an idea. Let me look at what you've done so far. Let me offer you my expertise."

I thought he might be choking on his own tongue, that the stress was so great he was about to collapse into seizure. But that strange gurgling emerged as something else. Something I had not expected. "Are—are you laughing?" He did not deign me with the answer, but it was clear my offer was rejected by the sound of his uproarious laughter. I did not care for that reaction. I did not care for it at all.

How was I to know when I stormed out that I would not see Henri again for months? He and his sister disappeared from the circles we once travelled in, and if they had new circles I was blissfully kept ignorant. I did not appreciate the treatment I'd received from them, and had no interest in gracing them with a friendship that was so clearly unwelcome. I left them to their own devices as they left me to mine, and could not even find the interest to pay attention to the new rumors that were circulating about what Henri was doing with his sister's help. There was talk. That was all I cared to know.

But even I could not escape the gossip for long. It ran like chains across the campus, binding students together one by one, forging them into a single voice that rattled inside my head. Elyse, I was told, had all but retired from social life in order to take care of her brother as he composed his grand opus. Confidentially, all the talk of Henri and his mysterious work grated on me, made me think that I might too want to pen some grand statement on life through music, if only to show those fools mesmerized by his growing legend that it was no great accomplishment. Yet I never did. I tried more than once, but each attempt ended in despairing failure. I'd never failed at *anything* before, and yet there I sat, night after night, devoid of any inspiration that might turn cacophonic notes into sweet euphonies. It disconcerted me, to say the least, and I knew I had only the lingering rumors of Henri to blame. Their echo seemed to follow me wherever I went.

I did all I could to forget my former friend and his sibling, put my experiences with them behind me once and for all. I could not understand what had gone wrong, and wanted to spend no more time on it than I already had. As far as I was concerned, the pair was dead, and I was better off. But one does not put aside feelings quite so easily. During the day I might have spoken with feigned ignorance when either name came up, but at night? At night visions haunted me, my dreams overrun with music and their laughing faces. I dreamt of far-away lands on lakes of shining gold, where kings and queens danced in opulent ballrooms while fools spied on from the wings. There I saw Henri and Elyse dressed in the finest clothing, spinning across a shining floor, never once turning their heads my way.

For all the above reasons, one can imagine my surprise when I received the invitation. The card was small and addressed to me in Henri's shaking script, and on its rear face a time, an address in the Latin Quarter, and the words: *Your attendance is requested for an evening in Carcosa.* Carcosa. Now why did that name sound at once both familiar and dreadful? At the time, I could not recall. And that, in the end, may have been my greatest folly.

I had no intention of attending. Despite my curiosity at what Henri's pedestrian mind might have conceived in its isolation, it was clear he did not fully appreciate the wealth of advice I had attempted to bestow. In fact, I took that invitation and threw it into the trash, trusting the lady who cleaned my rooms to rid me of it. And yet, what do you think happened when I returned from classes later that day? Only the discovery that she had left behind a single scrap of paper, caught in the thin metallic rim of my waste basket. I need not tell you what that scrap of paper was.

It seemed I was being summoned by a force far greater than myself, and I chose to comply lest it wreak havoc on my life. But of course superstition was not the only reason for my altered decision. In the time since receiving the card, my mind strayed repeatedly to the image of Elyse, and the thought of seeing her once again filled me with an unexpected longing.

The day arrived for Henri's now-infamous performance just as I was recovering from the sort of head cold that keeps one bedbound for days on end. I was well enough to go out and beyond the point of contagion, but even the short walk to the Hall du Sainte-Geneviève winded me. I took a drink of ice water from the bar once inside and settled, but I did not feel myself, and the medicinal tonic I'd had before leaving only made my head feel disconnected from the rest of my body. I tell you this partially as an explanation for what I witnessed, and partially to vindicate myself for not interfering.

I had heard the stories leading up to the day but hardly believed them. Had Henri really written the piece for merely a piano and violin? And was it true that none of those who auditioned managed to make it through a single practice without quitting? It sounded bizarre, and when I casually asked my classmates for proof there was none to be found. How could Henri have auditioned that many musicians and not once seen someone I knew? It was impossible. And yet the stories persisted. It was baffling, and I refused to believe them. Which is why the sight of the hall surprised me so. Perhaps my illness was again to blame, but I did not expect to find only a few rows of pews before a grand piano, elevated on a platform before the hall's triptych of large windows overlooking the Seine. As the seconds ticked away and the rumored accompaniment did not arrive, I realized this was to be a solo performance, and I wondered how Henri would survive the pressure. Despite the way he had previously treated me, I had no interest in seeing him made a fool of so publicly.

The crowd that had gathered for the spectacle was quite a bit larger than I had anticipated. Henri had been gone from the Conservatoire long enough that under any other circumstance he would have no longer been remembered, and yet it seemed as though every student was in attendance. And along with them, row after row of strangers I had never before seen either at school or at any of my own performances. I wondered how could that be. Could they simply be curious, lured by the cryptic invitation? Surely the lot of them could not have been familiar with Henri's work, or familiar with much well-performed music in general, if they were coming to hear him. I could see no other reason for the numbers, let alone for the general verve of excitement buzzing among those in attendance. Strangest of all was the presence of the man seated at the rear. I knew his face at once, though it took some time before those piercing yellow eyes told me how. Had the anticipation of Henri's work been so grand that it bled out to the local merchants as well? I must admit that from my corner at the front of the room I laughed at the sheer folly of their soon-to-be crushed expectations.

But I was laughing no longer when Elyse appeared. She swept in from the doorway behind me and all but floated toward the front row. She was even more beautiful than I had remembered, dressed in the finest silk and scarves, and though she did not turn her head when I called to her over the din of the crowd, I could see that behind her veil her skin was as wondrously porcelain as ever. My heart swelled at the sight and I became dizzy. No matter what I thought I remembered of her beautiful visage, it was a pale reflection of the truth.

So enraptured with Elyse was I that I failed to notice a hush had fallen over the room. Henri had already arrived, and had done so without fanfare or accompaniment. Unlike his sister, he was frighteningly a shadow of his former self. Sallow-faced, skin pulled tight, he looked like Charon himself as he slowly navigated the aisles of the hall in hushed silence. At the front of the room his piano stood waiting. Henri held in his hand a pale unmarked folder, and when he reached the piano and sat it seemed to require all his energy to remain upright. I looked askance at those beside me, but instead of disbelief I saw rapture. I cannot express how bizarre I found it all.

Henri's eyelids were leaded, and it seemed to require a herculean effort to keep them open. I became increasingly worried the longer he kept from speaking or moving, and soon forgot my grudge and stood to attend to him—only to be stopped by the words that finally creaked from his mouth. Elyse stared in rapt attention.

"Welcome, all of you, to this, the culmination of all my years at the Conservatoire de Paris, and all I've learned since being there." I thought Henri might have looked at me then, but his glazed eyes were more apt to be looking *through* me. "The inspiration for this concerto was a play whose script I discovered at a nameless bookstore. I visited the place first in a dream, and it was only by chance I stumbled across it in the depths of Montparnasse. I knew the sight of it at once and felt drawn inside, to its furthest corner, where I found amid the stacks a pale book marked like no other. The merest touch, and electricity stung my fingers, and without hesitation I read. By the second act, I knew nothing would be the same. I knew I had finally found my key."

But the key to what? I turned to gauge the audience's reaction, but it appeared as though they heard nothing. Their faces were vacant, waiting for the performance to begin. I tried, too, to catch a glance of the Indian seated at the back of the room, but his face was obscured by fidgeting bodies. A sense of dread enveloped me, amplified by the effect of my illness. I was worried I might be sick, and closed my eyelids in hopes the disorientation and nausea would subside. If anything, it only made things worse.

I opened them once Henri began to play. Or, at least, I believe I did. It's difficult to be sure. Upon hearing those first few notes—those notes that, even now, have a hypnotic effect over all listeners—I realized everything I knew about my former friend was wrong. The way he played, it was as though each note caught the air and crystallized before me, bright gems emitting an even brighter glow. I was bathed in the light of the absolute, and as its brilliance intensified it obscured everything in my sight. Henri played with a power I had never before known him to possess, and it transfixed me with blindness. That blindness did not dissipate until a subtle shift in chords indicated the second act of his concert had begun. Then the void faded, and revealed a world not as I remembered it. I do not know how otherwise to describe what I witnessed. The walls of the Sainte-Geneviève had pulled back, and I found myself dressed in the strangest of eighteenth-century garb. My face felt unusual, and as I reached to touch it I found it was not my own. I turned in confusion, the sound of Henri's soothing playing calming the panic brewing in my center, but not before I was struck by the audience and the similar masquerade disguises they wore. I looked immediately to the front of the room for Elyse, and saw someone impossibly more ravishing than before, dressed in wig and gown, her face home to a delicate porcelain façade she held aloft with a single gloved hand.

Then, down the center aisle, strode a caped figure toward her, a figure I knew instinctively was the Indian from the paper shop despite his being disguised head-to-toe. He had grown taller in the vision, his suit transformed into a long yellow cape, his leggings white and ruffled. Over his face he wore a long-beaked black mask; and on his head, a large yellow hat. He danced peculiarly as he moved, as though his feet held no contact with the wooden floor beneath them, and compounded with his disguise I was reminded of some fanciful bird in the midst of courting. All eyes were on him, though behind the blank holes of his mask I knew his were only on one. Elyse must have known it too, for she stood as he advanced, holding her porcelain countenance carefully to her face as she stepped toward the center of the room and offered him a gloved hand. It was then the floor gave way to a larger area, like that of a ballroom, and the perch on which Henri continued to play rose higher into the air. The roof above us had gone, the black stars blinking in strange transformation around a pair of waning moons, while below the yellow man took Henri's sister by the hand and led her to dance. It was, quite possibly, the most beautiful thing I have ever lived to see. And the most frightening. They moved in simpatico, two beings as one, circling the room over and over as Henri's haunting music played, each step lighter than air.

But all was not blissful. In my illness, the edges of my vision wavered as though reality itself were becoming undone. I tried to speak, but my tongue had swollen, immobilized by the mask I was forced to wear. The man in yellow and his masked queen spun and spun, and as they approached Henri the moonlight bathing them grew so bright a hairline crack that ran along the length of Elyse's porcelain mask was revealed to me. It seemed to stretch further the closer they danced to the triptych of windows, the blinding moonlight reflected from the great lake bathing them in light; light that could have come from no place in all France but instead from some distant land that only then did I recognize as lost Carcosa.

The swell of music ended in the fading light of the Paris morning, and there was nothing but utter silence, the entire audience trying to grasp what it had just witnessed. I knew I certainly was. Then, the uproarious applause began—a standing ovation that continued for the better part of ten minutes while Henri sat there, visibly drained and quite possibly unable to stand, nor do anything more without risk of collapse. During this time I did not celebrate, for my eyes went where no others did. To the front of the room, and to the seat there that remained unoccupied during Henri's greatest triumph.

I found Henri the next day in the flat he and his sister shared. The morning had been spent listening to the stories of his musical prowess that were sweeping the campus, but I was more concerned with what had vanished than what had suddenly appeared. And yet, when I found Henri, lying in repose and staring at the Seine coursing outside his window, I could not bring myself to accuse him of anything. The flat was in a state of chaos, and I asked when Elyse had last been there.

"It seems like forever since she's been gone."

"Where is she?" I asked, though I was certain I did not truly care to know. Fortunately, he spared me by changing the subject.

"What did you think of the concert?"

I should have lied—under any other circumstance I would have—but his face was such a shadow of what it once was, his eyes so worn from all he had been through, that I could no longer hide behind my jealousy of his talent. I admitted it was unforgettable, that I had not ceased thinking about it since I heard it. To this, he dryly laughed.

"The price to write that was high, so very high. And now that I am here before you I wonder if it was really worth it. The others, do you think they'll remember what I've done?"

"I think if all Paris isn't speaking of it yet, it's only because the day is still young."

"Good, good," he said, and closed his eyes for a moment. They had sunk so low, two dark orbs in jaundiced flesh. He almost looked as though he were wearing a mask, and I prayed he would not remove it. When those eyes opened again, they looked at me, but I am not foolish enough to think it was me they were seeing.

"Please, Valise, I need to rest now. Tomorrow there is much to do. Will you grant me my peace?"

"Of course," I said, and quietly let myself out as he stared once again out across the Seine. I did not travel far before my regret over Elyse returned, but at no time did I turn around or stop hurrying away. There are some topics, like places, that are best left unvisited.

Emotional Dues

Girder looked for somewhere to park. His rusted Chevy felt out of place on the tree-lined Bridle Path, its rust-orange holes like neon lights announcing his presence. He felt the neighbors' eyes spying on him—it was clear to every one of them that the scrawny man in the faded denim jacket and stained pants didn't belong. He wondered if they would feel the same about his paintings. Someday, he mused, they might crawl over one another to have one on their fancy wall. At least, he hoped. Girder took in the Rasp Estate, sitting a few hundred feet away, through his scarred windshield. The red-brick house sprawled, looming above bright emerald grass, its sharp roof knifing into the cerulean sky. He hoped coming had not been a mistake, because it felt like a colossal one.

Girder got out of the car into absolute quiet, his movement causing ripples in the chilled air. Brown and orange leaves were underfoot and everything smelled of sweet decay. The rain from the night before left enough damp that leaves clung to Girder's old shoes as he limped to the passenger side of his car. He shivered his thin jacket closer to squeeze more heat from the worn denim, and then folded down the torn vinyl seat to retrieve the wrapped painting he'd brought. He thought of Raymond, sitting in the back room of the Overground, sipping orange tea while

Girder was out in the cold betraying him, and reminded himself he was doing the right thing.

The walk to Rasp's door was a long one, hampered not only by a crooked leg but by the weight of the painting in Girder's weak arms. He had to traverse the distance slowly, his jaw hanging loose as he panted, breath sour and full of worry. Girder wished he could have contacted Mr. Rasp before arriving unannounced at his gate, but there was no listing in the telephone directory, and Girder knew no one who might help. He had no contacts in the community, no one but Mr. Raymond, who insisted on brokering all deals for Girder's work, and Raymond would not be so quick to be cut out of the equation. Merely asking for Rasp's name had caused the man's drill-hole eyes to blink repeatedly, like an alligator preparing to snap. "It's a habit I'm loath to get into. Everyone is a friend when the gallery's walls are full, but when that work starts to sell, artists quickly forget what it is I do for my commission." Girder had to lie and promise he would not circumvent Raymond before the gallery owner would reveal Rasp's name, an action that later filled him with regret.

Raymond claimed to have met Rasp only once; long enough to show him Girder's work. "How did he know about it?" Girder asked when Raymond, breathlessly, told him the news.

"Do you remember that tall dark man lingering at the show? He works for Rasp. A scout or buyer or some such. I definitely know him from somewhere." Rasp had arrived at the Overground's closing hour, heralded by his assistant. "The fellow made sure no one else was in the gallery before bringing Rasp in. I was quite furious until I realized who he was." Rasp had grimaced at the work on the wall, Raymond said, scowling when he found Girder's abstractions. Then Raymond claimed Rasp's eyes widened as he stared deep into the swirls of paint and immediately insisted he own the series. When Girder arrived at the gallery the next day, Raymond handed him a check. Finally, there were digits enough to reflect what he deserved. For the first time since his father's passing, Girder wished the bastard were still alive. Just so he might finally rub his nose in it.

It was a relief to put the wrapped painting down in front of Rasp's large red door. Needles pricked the length of Girder's knotted arms, and his curved left hip throbbed. He pressed the doorbell, heard a soft chime thud somewhere in the depths of Rasp's estate, and rubbed his hands together for warmth. He rang the bell again and waited. There was no movement. Peering through the circular inset window, he saw nothing but darkness. Perhaps Rasp was not interested in seeing any more of Girder's work. Perhaps there was something to his father's drunken laughter. Perhaps—

The creak of metal hinges, dreadfully cautious of what was to come. A tall thin Asian man appeared, his flesh the sallow tan of someone sheltered from the sun all his life. He wore a pinstriped suit, its sleeves too long, and did not utter a word. Instead, he scoured Girder inscrutably. Girder swallowed, his nerve abandoning him as he stared at those empty eyes.

"Um . . . I'm here to see Mr. Rasp."

It sounded like a question.

The suited man did not react, did not take his eyes from Girder's. He spoke with a hollow voice and an accent Girder couldn't place.

"He does not take visitors."

"But I—I have a painting here I thought he might want to buy."

"Why would he want to do that?"

"Why?" Girder stammered. "Because I'm Girder Schill."

Dark eyes slipped behind narrowed eyelids. Girder shuffled, paper-wrapped parcel at his feet.

"Should I know who that is?"

Girder frowned. His voice betrayed his irritation.

"Mr. Rasp bought some of my paintings from the Overground. I think he might be interested in seeing more."

A noise, between a sniffle and a snort. A raised knotted hand.

"Wait here."

The man vanished behind the closed red door. Girder's anger welled; red patterns mixed and swirled with other colors as they crept over his eyes, abstract shapes betraying some secret. Girder willed himself to calm down. He had no conduit for the vision at hand. He could not allow himself an episode without documentation. No puzzles without all the pieces. Girder looked down at where his narrow hands must have been and willed them to appear through the haze. He visualized each digit, forced the vision back to the edges of his sight until it passed. His mouth tasted like a battery. His heart beat wildly. Every muscle in his body tensed and ached. It took ten cold minutes for the door to open and a pale tan hand to beckon, fluttering urgently like a wounded bird.

Through some strange refraction of light, the foyer appeared too large, too long. The ceiling was at least twenty feet from the ground, trimmed with ornate cornicing, and the walls were dark with paint or shadow, lined into nothingness with rows of artwork. A table lamp illuminated the foyer just barely, chasing the darkness to the corners to bide its time. The thin man materialized from the dark like a strange specter.

"Mr. Rasp will be right with you."

Girder's nerves jittered. Rasp could be his salvation. If so, betraying Raymond would be worthwhile, even if the gallerist had been the only one brave enough to show Girder's work. He called it "a violent cacophony of nightmares." For Girder, they were catharsis, rage and inadequacy painted on canvas; a conduit for his hallucinations, something he barely understood. "It's automatic painting, dear," Raymond said. "All the best do it. It's a money-maker."

Yet that money never came.

"No one likes looking at them, dear," Raymond said, tipsy on champagne as the show closed, his tiny eyes glazed bubbles. "It unnerves them."

And continued to unnerve them over the following days. At least, until Rasp arrived.

An unusual odor wafted into the foyer. Damp, meaty, stale; so subtle it might have always been there. A pale shape floated through shadows some distance away, hovering a few feet from the ground like a humming wasp's nest. When further veils pulled back, Girder saw ill-defined features coalesce. From nothing formed what could only be the wrinkled face of the elusive Mr. Rasp.

He was rotund. Confined to a wheelchair pushed by the tall assistant, and cocooned in a heavy indigo robe, Rasp's pale bulbous head was perched on the folds around a bruised throat. No other flesh was exposed. His gloved hands were attached to withered lifeless arms that rested at his side. The wheelchair stopped a few feet from Girder, and the artist had to stifle his reaction. Rasp's flesh was nearly translucent, filled with dark spiderweb veins, and his red mouth was an open wound, revealing too many tiny discolored teeth.

"You are Girder Schill?"

The wound spoke with incredulity, the voice harsh, consonants accentuated yet wet. Doubt momentarily infected Girder. He favored his good leg.

"Yes, I am." He belonged there; he repeated it to himself. "I'm sorry for showing up without warning you first."

"Never mind. Never mind." Rasp's head rolled, threatening to fall off his rigid body. "You aren't as I expected you. One builds an image in one's thoughts."

Girder knew that all too well.

"I don't want to take up too much of your time, Mr. Rasp. I have a painting here and I—"

"Nonsense. You aren't taking any of my time at all. Come, you could no doubt use something to drink. You look positively drained."

"Well, I—" Girder started, but Rasp was gone before he could finish. The sound of rubber wheels echoed, voices fading. Only the rows of paintings remained.

Girder carried his package and found Rasp in the sitting room, his tall assistant by his side. The room was bigger than Girder's entire apartment. Yet, in there, Rasp's presence swallowed the space.

"Sit. Nadir will bring something to drink. Do you have anything in particular you'd like?"

"I'll—I mean, I'll have whatever you're having."

"Oh, I won't be drinking with you. Despite how I look I'm on a very strict diet." Yellow smile, dark gums revealed. Still, Girder tried to laugh, though he was certain it sounded forced.

"Just a beer, I guess. If it isn't any trouble."

"None at all. Nadir?" The thin man nodded, almost bowed, then slipped through the doorway. "Now, while we wait, let's take a look at this painting. I'm rather excited, as you can imagine."

Girder stood. Everything rested on how Rasp reacted to the work. Without his patronage, Girder's future was dire. His leg wobbled long enough to catch Rasp's eye. He put it out of his mind and focused on the string tied around the painting's frame, and how it had become knotted. He worked the knot with the tips of his nails, knowing they were far too short, but also that he had no other way of opening the package. The panic was sour in his throat.

"I'd help you but—" Rasp looked down at his own thin withered arms. Girder nodded, then struck upon an idea. Keys from his pocket found the twine, and there followed the sound of a bowstring being plucked. Girder carefully removed the flat brown butcher's paper. Rasp stared hungrily. Girder's stomach growled.

"This one is called 'The Empty House.' It's oil on canvas."

Girder held the painting at arm's length. Rasp's voice wheezed, "Higher, please." Girder lifted until his face was covered. "Nice, nice," Rasp said, then a wet sound like lips being licked. Girder lowered the painting. Rasp looked beatific.

"It's a wonderful piece. Wonderful. Just as I expected. The color, the emotional fury; it's like a late-period Gotlib, or even a

Munch—if Munch were any good. Compared to you, though, the two were finger-painting. I can *see* the emotion here, so much it hurts. Tell me, does it have a story?"

Girder's father's fists. Insults, jeers. A beating that irreparably loosened something in Girder's brain. A cultured veil of fury; abstractions hinting at unfulfilled secrets. Vision that had to be fixed in place with paint to be understood, to be made real. It was his father's dying gift.

"No, there's no story. It's just a painting."

The fat man's laugh sounded like wet choking. Tiny brown teeth bared, a dozen pale lumps struggling for escape against indigo folds. Girder became worried, but as Nadir returned, beer on a small platter, that mirth ebbed.

"It's not customary for me to take visitors here, Mr. Schill, which is why I can't offer you anything more exotic to drink. In truth, Mr. Raymond should not have provided you with any information about me. It causes too many ethical conflicts."

Girder nodded but said nothing. He did not want to accidentally dissuade Mr. Rasp from the purchase. Instead, he slowly sipped at the beer he had been given and tried to keep his sensation of biliousness at bay.

"Normally, I'd have you sent back to Mr. Raymond to arrange the transaction, but your work is something to behold—so emotional!—that I'm willing to cut out the middle man, as it were, so I might get new works more expediently. I assume the rate I paid at the Overground would suffice here? Good! Nadir, take this piece and bring me a check for the normal amount. It seems Mr. Schill and I have come to an agreement." Another smile full of ugly brown teeth. Girder questioned whether what he felt was happiness, especially when he held the check in shaking hands. It was more than Mr. Raymond had ever given him.

"You look pleased, Mr. Schill."

"Oh, I am. Yes. This will help me out a lot."

"Good. I trust then there will be more pieces coming?"

Girder had no doubt.

Girder returned home, energized. Why had he needed the gallery when the direct approach was so lucrative? Rasp would be his salvation, not smug, thieving Mr. Raymond. Girder's work was finally being recognized for its worth; neither Raymond nor his dead idiot of a father could tell him otherwise.

The money paid Girder's outstanding bills, and what remained paid for supplies. Canvases were stretched, paints were mixed; Girder's specters hovered close, revealing themselves only when finally he held his brush. An opaque veil dropped, his eyes clouded. A landscape of colors clashing, a Rorschach of emotion. He worked hard to commit the essence to reality. Weeks passed, but the anger did not. The colors didn't run, didn't move. Instead, they leapt from the brush. Never had the euphoria been so cathartic. Never had the muse guided his arm so exactly. From him pains and sorrows flowed onto canvas. At the end of the fourth week, he awoke on the floor, paint outlining him, muscles aching. The work was done, though he couldn't remember when. Exhausted, he staggered to bed, slept more than a day. His dreams were monochrome.

"Frankly, Mr. Schill, I feared you wouldn't return."

Girder's face could not contain his smile.

"Of course I was going to. I painted this for you."

"Oh, I should hope not. I hope you painted it for yourself. That's where the choicest pieces originate." And Rasp laughed, though it was strange and stuttered. His perched head rolled. Girder averted his eyes, but it was too late. He'd already seen it.

"Nadir, if you'll do the honors."

The tall assistant nodded, then reached to peel the butcher paper from the canvas. As he did so, his sleeve pulled too far back and a flash of skin stained different colors caught Girder's eye. Just as quickly it was gone, replaced with the sight of Rasp expectantly dampening his lips with a sliver of desiccated tongue.

"Well, stand back, man," he urged, and his assistant withdrew a few steps. Rasp looked at the canvas, then at Girder. The look on his face was inscrutable. Girder's mouth was drier than it ever had been.

"Mr. Schill," Rasp began slowly. "What appealed to me most about the pieces of yours I purchased from your friend, Mr. Raymond, was the *emotion* expressed in that work. It was as though your feelings had free rein. Love, hate, anger, jealousy, betrayal—it was all on display in brutally honest detail." Rasp's pale eyes were glassy, a thread of spittle crept from the corner of his bloodless lips. Then his eyes cleared, and he looked hungrily at Girder. "That is the kind of work I'm looking for from you, Mr. Schill, and I have little use for anything else."

"I don't understand." Girder's voice quavered. His father's voice echoed from the caverns of the past. "Is there something wrong?"

"Wrong? Indeed, not. This is perfect."

Perfect. Not a word he'd heard before. The sound of it was strange and joyously unnatural. His father would never have used such a term. He might instead have laughed if he'd heard it uttered, especially in reference to Girder. "You?" he'd say amid drunken punches. "You're joking!" Even in the haze of morning, when the fumes of his father's drinking lingered like an uninvited guest, he might croak, "Sorry, Girder. Nobody's perfect." Years later, Mr. Raymond, who ostensibly worked to promote Girder's art, would echo the sentiment. "Nothing is perfect, love. Your work challenges people because you *bleed* on the canvas; you fill it with your turmoil to exorcise yourself. But that's why no one is buying your paintings. It's because sometimes something nakedly displaying another man's soul is unsettling at best. And at worst, repulsive." But Mr. Rasp had since arrived and offered salvation. A corpulent angel with a lolling head, laughingly making easy what had always been difficult. All Girder deserved was finally handed to him without question. For a moment he almost believed that everything might one day be . . . no, he would not say the word.

"Perfect," Rasp repeated on seeing the unwrapped canvas. "It's absolutely perfect." Girder exhaled and hunger returned to his limbs. *Not long now*, he told them, but they shook in doubt. The painting was a culmination, and those emotions painted an intricate landscape that even he could scarcely believe had been reproduced by his brush. Yet there it was. No doubt the painting looked better than he did: as the paints were mixing in his mind and subsequently drying on the canvas, he did not see a single mirror. Had he, the haggard man staring would have likely been unrecognizable. It came at a great cost to him. Wasn't it reasonable to pass those costs on?

"I'm happy you like the piece, Mr. Rasp, don't get me wrong, but the price on the work in the past— What I mean is, I feel *this* particular piece is bit beyond those in quality, and should maybe command something higher?" Girder's voice wavered and body shook. The speech hadn't been practiced enough, and it was too late to snatch the words back. The white of Rasp's eyes narrowed, his small puckered tongue ran slowly over his lower lip. Nadir remained motionless, but Girder suspected he was affecting a lack of interest. Finally, Rasp bellowed, body rippling with laughter.

"Of course, Mr. Schill. Of course. I wouldn't dream of cheating you on this most exquisite piece. *This* is true genius. Nadir, wouldn't you agree?"

The assistant's eyes barely grazed the painting; instead, they were focused on its nervous painter. Nadir again wore that inscrutable look upon his face. Was it pity? Jealousy? Whatever it might have been, it caused him to utter a few forced words under his breath before he snatched the canvas from Girder.

Relieved as he was of both burdens—that of the painting and of the request for more money—Girder's heart finally slowed enough for his blood to cool. It was only then he wondered if he had been terrified into blindness, for he realized the walls in the sitting room around him were empty of everything but hooks.

"What's happened to the paintings?"

Rasp's gash opened, but instead of words it emitted a violent cough. Nadir appeared instantly, brandishing a handkerchief he had produced from some hidden pocket, and covered Rasp's mouth. Rasp's head and throat heaved, body motionless, and filled the handkerchief with heavy sputum. Girder averted his eyes, but not before he noticed something red seep through, and in his shock mistakenly thought he saw other colors, too. Nadir made the mess vanish into his pocket. Rasp's head hung low when he was done, panting and wheezing. Girder shifted back to his good leg. His bad ached.

"Are you okay?"

"Don't—you needn't worry about me. I'm fine." Rasp's speech was broken, the pale flesh around his mouth wet. "But this brings to mind something I thought I might propose. I wasn't sure I would until I saw this latest work of yours . . . and saw the sorry state of its creator. You look barely able to walk." Girder winced. "For a short time, I think it might be best if you stayed here on the estate to work."

The surprise was not Girder's alone. Nadir's entire reaction crossed his face in an instant. He reacted sharply.

"No."

For whom was the word meant? Girder or Rasp? The painter's crooked leg throbbed. Rasp did not look pleased.

"Ignore him, Mr. Schill. This is an arrangement that can only work to our mutual benefit. You will be freed from the burdens that distract you from your work, and I will be able to watch and help guide you. Of course, you would get a stipend for this, regardless of the amount or quality of work produced."

"I don't know. I'm not sure I feel comfortable—"

"Nonsense. I am not trying to *buy* you." The laugh was unnatural, the sound only an approximation. "Think of it as an artistic retreat. Spend a few weeks here and see what you produce without other worldly concerns. In truth, I'm not certain I can wait another month for a new piece of work, regardless of how much I enjoy this one."

"But a month . . . most of my work takes longer."

"I have plenty of artwork here, enough to sate me if necessary, but nothing so pure as yours, I fear. No, you'll have to concentrate on the job at hand, and the only way to do it is to strip you of your earthly concerns. See what you can accomplish for me."

Nadir glared. Those eyes barraged Girder, searing into him. That alone was reason to decline. But Girder thought of the cold winter knocking, one foot already through his apartment door. He thought of the empty shelves, and his throbbing leg. Still unconvinced, he thought of his father's jeers.

"I suppose a few weeks couldn't hurt."

"Splendid," Rasp said. Nadir's stare made it obvious winter had already arrived.

Nadir's demeanor was unchanged the next day. He helped Girder bring his bags and supplies into the house, but did not speak. Instead, Rasp did the speaking from his chair parked in the doorway, out of the sun.

"Whatever you need, Mr. Schill, to make your stay pleasant, please let Nadir know."

Girder's room was large and faced south to maximize working daylight. A king-size bed, a small chaise-longue, a fireplace. The large window overlooked the winter garden; the deep greens vibrant, orange flowers like starbursts. Girder couldn't imagine a better-suited workplace. As promised, there were no distractions in the room; no telephone or radio. The walls were as bare as the sitting room's. Which Girder found odd, considering.

Rasp visited only once. Nadir wheeled him in as Girder was finishing the setup of his workspace.

"Should you feel hungry later, the kitchen is to your left at the end of the hall. It's open to you at any time."

"What time should I be down for dinner?"

Rasp's dark lips curled, quivered. "Not today, I'm afraid. I've made other arrangements. Besides, watching me eat is not something most people would relish. Wouldn't you agree, Nadir?" The tall assistant's face twitched.

"Maybe next time?"

Girder was ashamed of the desperate tone to his voice. Rasp's strange breathing sounded like a giggle.

"Perhaps."

Amply supplied with paint, Girder faced the empty stare of the blank canvas. He sighed. The first brush stroke was the hardest. He did not plot nor plan. Instead, he dredged—pain and frustration . . . He moved his mind into his rotted leg, visualized the nerve endings sparking in the darkness, waited for it all to coalesce. He almost touched the brush to the canvas, but knew the simplest stroke locked out an infinite number of others. He preferred the vast nothingness where it was safe, warm. Protective. A single mark could not be undone. Potential hemorrhaged. He willed the images to come from beneath and feed him. He closed his eyes and waited. Waited. They would come. They always came. He simply had to have faith.

A deep familiar voice echoed in the hall outside the room, and Girder's blood chilled. It couldn't be. Not him. Every inch of skin constricted, trying to shrink Girder from existence. How had he been discovered? All the resolve Girder had built up wavered.

When the inevitable knock arrived, Girder's hesitated. He did not want to face what was beyond. The knock returned, insistent, and he realized there was no escape. Never from him. Girder opened the door and found the two men he least wanted to see: the tall hawkish Nadir, triumphant, a stack of paintings under his thin arm; and the viper-faced Mr. Raymond, whose eyes were spitting above his plaster smile.

"Hello, Girder." The voice tight, his anger barely suppressed. Or was it pleading? Mocking? Was there some plan Raymond had colluded with Nadir to implement? Girder was tired, unable to think straight. Perhaps he was wrong about everything. And yet there Mr. Raymond was, weeks after Girder had last been to the Overground. A haunting of his past betrayal made flesh. One of his many hauntings.

Nadir looked derisive. "I can see you two have a lot to discuss. Thank you for the delivery, Mr. Raymond. Mr. Schill, if you could show him out when you're done?"

Nadir stepped back, absorbed into shadows. Girder fumbled for words as Raymond stared.

"Um . . . I suppose you're wondering . . ."

Raymond's hand struck out and snatched Girder's wrist before he could escape. The gallerist squeezed tight and spoke, his voice a seething whisper.

"I don't know what you're thinking, but you'd better get out of here."

"I'm just doing—"

"I don't care what Rasp has you doing. I don't normally care to be involved in this sort of thing at all—life's too short to mourn a loss—but this isn't right. Selling to him is one thing, but this . . . this place *smells* like a nest of something, though I can't say what. You should leave."

Girder wrested his arm free.

"I *have* to stay," he said, rubbing his wrist. "But it's not for long. All I'm doing is painting a few pieces and then I'm going home. I'll probably have more for you to hang at the Overground in a month or two."

"You know that . . . person? That Nadir fellow? He doesn't look at all familiar to you, does he? No, he probably wouldn't. But

I know him well, even if he doesn't remember me. I tried to help him too once. Now look at him."

"What are you—"

"Look at him, Girder. He's used up. A junkie. You'll be too. If you're lucky."

"I appreciate the concern, Mr. Raymond, but—but I think I can decide on my own what's best for me. You—you aren't my . . ."

Girder trailed off. Raymond's eyes had fallen back into half-slits, as though he had crawled back into shed skin. His old carefree face then returned, like a well-worn accessory.

"Sure. That's fine. If you manage to paint something else, dear, be sure to look me up. It was a pleasure working with you." He extended his hand and they shook, then Mr. Raymond wrapped his scarf around his long throat.

"Don't worry. I can show myself out."

"I'll let you know as soon as I have something," Girder said as Mr. Raymond walked down the hall, but the gallerist only offered back a cursory wave, not bothering to turn.

Nadir appeared a moment later, stepping into Girder's room without invitation. Frowning dark cuffs creeping away from his wringing hands.

"Why didn't you leave with him?"

"I know you don't want me here, but I need the money Mr. Rasp is offering."

Nadir's expression was full of disgust. He shook his head.

"Everybody always needs something." Nadir casually looked over at Girder's easel and the blank canvas that sat on it, and his face changed.

"What is it?" Girder asked, but Nadir wouldn't stay. He simply looked wide-eyed at Girder, then left, fleeing out the room on spindle legs. Girder closed the door behind him, then to be safe he double-checked the locks.

He could not return to work. His leg throbbed incessantly. Everything was in tatters. But why? For money? Was nearly starving a good enough excuse? He hobbled to the window and peered down at the winter garden. Night had steadily crept in, turning small bushes into shadows, the trees into silhouettes with lifeless branches bent downward in defeat. Girder sighed, finally turned away and saw the blank canvas in the dim room. He had nothing with which to fill it. He had come to the estate hoping his problems would vanish; instead, the isolation amplified them.

It was just after midnight when Girder managed to put brush to canvas. He slipped into an autonomous state, the brush becoming a conduit for his catharsis. He dug deep into the places he'd been twisted by what had been done to him, by what he in turn had done to others. Colors swirled in a tempest of pain behind his eyes. He simply tapped and bled them onto canvas. Each painting was in the end the same: a formless portrait of his father. Girder pressed until exhaustion crept into his senses. It was only then he lay, aching, on the bed. Eyes strained, dry, and swollen, he closed his lids and saw those swirling colors start to fade. But the sound did not. The quiet sound of something wet being dragged.

It was louder in the hallway. Echoes bounced around corridors barely lit by the rising sun. At the other end of the hall was a shut door, and as the bare-footed Girder approached it the noise intensified. He noticed the air was tinged with a sour metallic odor, and he stared at the door to reassure himself it wasn't vibrating. As he reached out to touch it, the sound, all sound, sputtered then stopped. And the world inverted. There was a quiet noise, then the squeak of rubber. Girder saw the beam of light at his feet broken by shadow, and when he looked up Nadir had emerged from the room and stood before him. Sound rushed back with a gasp.

"What are you doing here?"

"I'm sorry, I just . . ." Girder glanced around the shoulder of the tall man and saw Rasp's back as he sat in his chair, a dark wide canvas of indigo. Paintings surrounding him, paintings piled on the floor and against the wall. He appeared to be sweating, his pale skin greasy and rippling like gelatin in disturbance. Nadir's dark shadow obscured the sight.

"Get out of here," the assistant warned. Large hands pounded Girder's chest like two hammers. Girder's mind grappled with what it saw, but it was only after the door had closed that the sight fully developed. Nadir's hands were slick and stained like a bruise, purplish-yellow and red. Girder wondered what had they done.

Mid-afternoon appeared before Rasp did. Girder had hidden all morning—his confusion adding streaks through the colors swirling in his mind's eye—but eventually gnawing hunger overtook him, and he turned to the stocked kitchen. He made a turkey and swiss sandwich as quickly as he could, anxious to return to his hiding. But the warning squeal of rubber came too late. He looked over his shoulder to see the overweight sweating Rasp and the hovering Nadir in the doorway, both watching him intently. The eyes of the latter narrowed. Rasp's voice was unusually clear.

"I apologize for Nadir's behavior this morning. It was . . . *harsh.*"

"It was my fault. I shouldn't have intruded like that."

"No harm done," Rasp dismissed, and shook his head. Did his pale skin vibrate too long? "How is the work coming? I trust everything is to your satisfaction?"

"Yes, of course. I mean, the work is going well. I think."

"Good, good. I can't wait to see what you have for me." Rasp flashed his blackened gums. Girder shifted uneasily on his weak leg. He rubbed the damaged muscles, the dull sensation giving him comfort.

"I think you'll be pleased when it's done."

"I'm sure I will be. I'm a man of tremendous appetites, as you can tell, and there's little I love more than a fine piece of art. Wouldn't you say so, Nadir?"

Nadir ignored the question.

"Did you know we had a visit yesterday from Mr. Raymond,

the dealer from the Overground? Girder and he had a good talk."

"Oh, did they? What did Mr. Raymond have to say to you, my boy? Did he try and steal your talent back from me?"

Discomfited, Girder stumbled.

"No, not really. He seemed fine."

"You can never tell with a *snake* like that one," Rasp chortled, round head bobbing into folds of deep indigo. "He's always trying to slide in where he isn't wanted, isn't he, Nadir?"

Rasp's smile did not make it to the eyes. He wore a pair of gloves that obscured stained flesh.

Rasp continued. "Ah, well. It looks as though we're disturbing you. I merely wanted to let you know that as I feel a smidgen under the weather I may not be able to visit you as often as I'd wished to track your progress. Rest assured, though, Nadir will be here to help you with whatever you may require. I expect only the best from you, Mr. Schill. You are certainly capable of it." He swallowed, small lumps travelling down his throat like swallowed eggs. "Nadir, please take me away so our guest might continue working."

Rasp was wheeled into the dark, the remaining funk that surrounded him dissipating slowly. Girder took the sandwich he'd been making and threw it away. He was no longer hungry.

Time passed. Girder spent the time sequestered, leaving the room rarely. He lived inside a world of color, dreaming it, breathing it, at times unsure what was real. The only interruption was Nadir's begrudging apologies for Rasp. "He doesn't feel well." And, "It's a side-effect of his incapacitation." It didn't concern Girder. Little of the material world did. As long as supplies were by his door each morning, his fever dream would not subside. Should strange wet noises have persisted beyond his door, he was too busy or too tired to notice.

Never had he worked so quickly, with so much complexity. If Rasp wanted emotion, he would get it. Every sting felt, every hurt suffered, raw materials as essential as paint. Girder's father's laugh, the pain from his ruined leg, the glare of Nadir, the doubt of Raymond, all formed a cultured mosaic he alone could see. His scoured soul, his scars mapped in brushstrokes. Cramped fingers became his ultimate medium—the pain bringing tears to his color-blinded eyes.

And two weeks later and twenty pounds lighter, in a spent daze he took in the finished work and smiled.

The smile remained as he sat in the kitchen. Coffee brewed inside while outside the snowstorm did the same. A reticent howl echoed through the estate. Girder felt serene yet looked worse— thickly bearded, eyes bloodshot and dark—but the smile was genuine. For the first in some time, he was at peace. His happiness was the only reason that explained Nadir's noiseless appearance in the kitchen's doorway.

"The painting is done?"

Girder beamed. Nodded.

"Then Mr. Rasp will be pleased."

But once Nadir slipped away to tell Rasp, the realization finally penetrated the fog of denial. Rasp wanted it all, wanted every ounce of Girder, and the artist had been more than willing to dredge it up. But now that the time had come to hand it over—to hand *everything* over . . .

In truth, Girder was spent; there was not another opus in him. He had been burned clean of anger and resentment, welling colors drained from his soul. All of it, all his father's monstrosity, was contained within the painting, all the suffering trapped in the strokes of the brush. The painting hummed with power, and Girder did not want to relinquish it. Not to anyone, even Rasp. Yet that was who had housed him, who had fed him. . . . He owed Rasp a great deal, but the price was too high.

An hour later, Nadir delivered Rasp to Girder's room. The porcine man had changed somehow. Both smaller and larger at once. Girder's yellow face alone was gaunt, though it lit when in the presence of the painting. "Absolutely marvelous," Rasp said.

"Nadir told me you were done, but I couldn't have expected *this*." Lips twitched, dark tongue passed over them nervously. "This is absolutely a masterpiece, Mr. Schill. A venerable masterpiece."

Even Nadir seemed impressed; upon seeing it his face registered genuine, if fleeting, emotion. Perhaps awe? The reaction was both reassuring and disappointing.

"I don't think I could have done it without your hospitality Mr. Rasp. You're generosity may have literally saved me."

"Think nothing of it. Seeing the results just proves I made the right decision." A glance at Nadir; the servant's eyes were elsewhere. "You've outdone yourself, Mr. Schill. I consider this whole endeavor money well spent."

Girder silently cursed. Rasp clearly wanted the painting. Which meant Girder had to gather some nerve.

"Um . . . about that, Mr. Rasp—"

Rasp's head ceased bobbing.

"Now, now. We had a deal, did we not?"

"It's just that—"

"Did I not keep up my end of the bargain, Mr. Girder? I've provided for you all that you've asked, but I didn't do so for your charity."

"Perhaps I could paint you another one? Perhaps something else?"

"No, Mr. Schill. I think the time for that has passed. I must insist. I couldn't possibly let this specific painting escape me."

Girder stammered. Rasp's words cut him short.

"Nadir, come." Rasp whispered into his servant's ear. The tall man smirked, nodded, then left the room. Rasp resumed speaking, albeit in a quieter voice.

"Mr. Schill. I don't appreciate the situation you've placed me in, but I am a fair and reasonable man. I will give you double your normal rate—the rate which Mr. Raymond would charge me—for this painting. I do so, you understand, under duress, and only because I simply cannot wait to see if what you produce next is suitable. I suspect this painting will satiate me for some time—it's so rich, so deep with power. But I think this may be the last time you and I can do business this way. I recommend that after we are done here you make arrangements to return immediately to your home."

Nadir reappeared before Girder could find words to reply. He showed Rasp a checkbook but did not take his eyes from Girder.

"I want you to give him double, Nadir. Plus the stipend I promised. Then I want you to help him load his belongings into his car. He won't be staying with us any longer."

"But Mr. Rasp . . ." Girder couldn't believe the sound of his own warbling voice—everything was falling to pieces. "The snowstorm . . . it's not safe."

Mr. Rasp considered this for a cold moment.

"Very well, Mr. Schill. You may stay an extra night. But tomorrow you must go. And, in the future, you ought to allow Mr. Raymond alone to handle your sales to any prospective buyers."

Girder sat devastated on the bed of his borrowed room. Outside the window was the furious chaos of snow, and despite the fireplace's radiating heat he remained both cold and empty. How had things devolved so quickly? His father's voice echoed, reminding him that he destroyed everything good. Girder didn't have to believe it to know it was true.

He washed face in the small *en suite* sink, then stared in the mirror at his sagging reflection. Girder was a fool. He had risked everything on a fantasy and a dream, neither of which had come true. There was so much road left ahead, and what did he do? He drove into the desert.

Without Mr. Rasp's aid, what would become of Girder? Would he fade to nothing? Upset, the artist's fingers twitched, craving the security of the brush, the expression of its bristles. But behind closed eyelids nothing waited. No points, no pricks, no colors shifting, swirling, dancing. Even clenched fists rubbing orbital bone made no difference. The visions did not return. He opened his eyes, watched the periphery of his vision crackle with energy as his sight settled. His father's greatest scar had finally faded, and Girder knelt down on his working knee, terrified of what that might mean.

Consumed by listless melancholy, Girder did not immediately notice that the pungent, meaty odor had returned. He opened the door and took a step into the hallway, then stopped. There was nothing but darkness down the empty corridor.

No, not just darkness. The sound of something in the darkness. Something being dragged ever closer.

Girder's vision grew hazy, and he shook his head before retreating. Then he pressed his full weight against his door to fortify the barrier. With his ear to the wood, he once again heard wet sounds and recalled the trail of fluid streaked across the hall. What it suggested was not something he was willing to think about, willing to face. The storm rattled windows and doors, but it was the walls that sounded as though they were being ripped apart.

He opened the door no more than a crack large enough to peer through, but all he saw was a thin slice of shadow. His breathing was turbulent, lungs aching, yet he was too panicked to do anything but stare into the dark. Everything beyond a few feet was lost in a thick unfocused fog. He had to concentrate to see through it, and when the murk parted he saw the dark shadow racing along the hall toward him. Girder withdrew from the door, terrified, almost falling over his crippled leg, and as he did so the wet noises of the house were transformed into those of Nadir's bare footsteps.

Rasp's servant held a large, familiar-looking canvas against his body, shielding it from Girder's view. He rushed down the hall, oblivious to spying, toward Rasp's door at the other end. Nadir struggled with the size of the painting, the encumbrance magnified by the presence of his ill-fitting pinstriped suit. The cuffs rode high as Nadir fussed to maintain his grip, and Girder saw that those dark blotches on Nadir's wrists extended further along his arms. When he reached the end of the hall, Nadir lowered the painting and put his key in the door. Light spilled into the hallway, and Nadir picked up the painting, then disappeared into the room. The low humming buzz returned, lasting for almost two hours, while unsteady light slipped from the crack beneath Rasp's door.

An idea occurred to Girder, one that didn't fill him with pride for considering, but he knew he had been left with few options. When without warning the buzz abruptly ceased, Girder stood and slipped into his shoes. He peered once again through the crack in his door and saw Nadir emerge from the darkened room, sleeves rolled to his elbows. In his hands was the same large canvas he had carried earlier, and he lugged it back down the hallway, only now in a state of either thorough exhaustion or inebriation. He slowed only briefly as he neared Girder's door and scowled in its direction, then continued without losing a step. Girder watched him round the corner at the end of the hall, vanishing into shadows filled with the storm's white noise.

He had to discover where his paintings were being kept. Part of him tried to justify his quest with the knowledge that he would never be in the presence of the pieces again, so he deserved to see them one last time. But even as he crept behind Nadir he knew it was untrue. Girder could never abandon something that was so much a part of him. He might just as well be leaving behind his soul. Based merely on Rasp's reaction earlier, there was no way the fat man would part with the painting now that he had it, so Girder would simply be forced to take it and hope for the best. The biggest difficulty would be getting it to the car in the storm, but he would find a way. He had to.

It did not take long for Girder to discover the hiding place. He had barely rounded the corner of the hallway when Nadir stepped empty-handed from a shadowed nook. There was no time to pivot on his crippled leg before Girder was seen, so he immediately did his best to affect an expression of confusion and exhaustion. It seemed to make Nadir more suspicious. The assistant rolled down his sleeves as he spoke.

"What are you doing up?"

"I couldn't sleep, so I thought I'd spend one last night looking around. I'm going to miss being here."

Nadir narrowed his eyes.

"It's probably better you go."

"Better for whom?"

Girder tried not to blink, but he was outclassed by Nadir. It was like staring into the uncaring face of a reptile.

"Are you packed?" Nadir asked, finally breaking the quiet.

"Yes. Everything but my easel and artwork."

"Go to your room now and get some sleep. Be ready to leave at nine," he said, and waited until Girder left first. He followed Girder the entire way, waiting until he was back behind the closed bedroom door. Girder heard breathing outside the door for half an hour, waiting for Girder to fall asleep. Despite his best efforts, Girder almost did, which left him disoriented when awakened by the quiet sounds of Nadir abandoning his post and giving Girder the freedom to explore.

The long hallway was worse when empty, and Girder's slow walk only increased his terror of being discovered. He stayed in the shadows as much as possible and kept his ears attuned to any noises that might betray he was being watched. When he finally turned the corner he stopped and checked back where he'd come from to ensure no one was there. He heard a faint knocking sound, as though the storm were intensifying. Then he turned back to the shadowed nook and the nearly invisible door hidden within.

It was made to be unnoticeable; its color, and the shadows, perpetually shielding it from ignorant eyes. The structure itself was incongruous, as though an afterthought. Perhaps it was an illusion of the slanted ceiling, but the hidden door's corners appeared flush, and its knob sunk deep in the dark. Girder's hand faltered. Behind him the knocking had faded, leaving only the static of the storming snow in the distance. He pulled the door carefully, but at first it didn't move, as though being held shut from the inside. Then the resistance gave, and it swung open so suddenly Girder nearly fell.

In the dark he saw a stack of wood-framed canvases leaned against the wall, but it wasn't until he discovered a small light switch that he realized how many were truly there. Numerous piles of canvases, a hundred or more, covered almost every inch of the room. Some were in piles on the floor, others were stacked against the wall a dozen deep. All were face down, as though to protect them. Girder had never been in the presence of so many paintings at once outside a museum, and after the shock dissipated, he wondered how many of them were his.

In the far corner, he spied a face-down painting whose shape struck him oddly familiar. Hadn't he stretched a canvas like that in the past? He stepped forward and flipped the piece over, only to find himself puzzled. It couldn't be right. He flipped over the painting's neighbor, turning the canvas face up, and then flipped over the one beside that. He flipped all the paintings around him, but the result was the same: they were blank. All of them. Not painted over, but never having been painted on to begin with, as if they were all that remained of former paintings that no longer existed. They were empty; only a foul-smelling tallow remained, covering the canvases, sticking to his hands.

Girder paced inside his room, mourned over what he'd seen; so many paintings destroyed—and who knew how many of his own. If there was any consolation it was that he could not find anything shaped like his last painting, his masterpiece, among them. It had been spared, but he didn't know for how long. He had to rescue it. There was no money in the world that meant more to him than that artwork. The painting held so much of him; its absence left him hollow. It needed to be retrieved.

Out the window drifts of snow accumulated in the storm. The world conspired to trap him while his soul screamed for flight. He could not leave without the painting. It was clear his survival depended upon it.

Girder stepped into the hall, put his bag down quietly. He had packed everything he could carry, left behind what he could not. The house was quieter than he had ever known it; the air's stillness lent a foreboding atmosphere that his intentions further cultured. He crept down the hall toward the Rasp's room, the source of that dreadful buzzing. At the door he listened for eternity, waiting for an indication he'd been caught, but nothing came. He tried the knob, eyes narrow in the hope that the door was not locked.

The knob turned and a bolt slid back with a faint click.

Girder opened the door only enough to slip inside. The veils were drawn, blocking all but the thinnest sliver of light. Navigating the dark was difficult, so he clung close to the wall, moved around the room toward where he remembered the stack of paintings were. He almost stumbled over something lumpy lying across the floor but managed to right himself in time. He waited, but heard no sign that he'd been discovered. He was completely alone.

Girder moved with one arm stretched outward, feeling his way. The painting could be anywhere, and though he knew it was intact, it was also vulnerable. He felt it calling like a piece of him that had been lost or gone missing. Girder concentrated on the sensation in the blind dark and reached out a final time, groping desperately in the void. He was thus amazed when his fingers grazed rough canvas, ever so slightly, and he knew instinctively he had found what he had sought for so long.

Nothing else moved in the dark. He picked up the canvas and experienced the immediate connection with something long lost. The painting for which Rasp had paid could not be sold. Girder would sooner have sold his soul. Both he and it had to leave the house immediately.

Touching the wall, inching forward to where the door should be waiting, he found nothing. The wall seemed to stretch forever, without end. And yet he couldn't even see the sliver of light from the hallway beneath the edge of the door. The only illumination in the room was from the reflection of the snowstorm, though Girder was not sure how it could be slipping in: there were no windows in the room.

Girder forced himself to remain calm and focus simply on finding the light switch. A brief flick would be long enough to get his bearings in the empty room. He put the painting down, ran his hands along the smooth walls, and limped onward. Was it indeed the room he'd been in earlier? It had to be. There was only one hallway between his room and Rasp's, and it wasn't possible to become lost so easily. And yet, nothing seemed familiar. Not the room's size nor shape nor layout. Nothing but Girder's mounting panic. He desperately wanted to escape the confines of the dark, his unintentional prison, and watched for the tinniest fragment of light.

There was no time in the dark. Minutes were days, and as the static of snow reached new heights outside, Girder's fingers skittered over the walls, looking for the hidden switch. They found it quite by surprise, having almost given up the search, and Girder huddled close to it for fear he might become lost once more. A quick burst, he promised himself. A single quick burst of light to fix his environment, eliminate its oneiricism. Long enough to gauge his location, but not long enough to arouse suspicion. One burst would tell him everything. He counted down in his head, opened his eyes wide to take in as much information as possible, then flicked the lights on and off so rapidly he didn't initially see anything at all. But his eyes were like instant photographs, and in the darkness a horrifying negative developed.

The room had shrunk, folding in on itself. Far smaller than he recalled, far smaller than could have been possible to navigate. Paintings were stacked everywhere, and as the image in his mind's eye formed it was clear his painting, his masterpiece, was among them. But what horrified him was not the clutter or the impossible size of his surroundings; it was what stood at the room's center—a large shadow around which Girder had circled while looking for the exit. It resolved slower than the rest of the items around it, yet Girder concentrated on that particular shadow the hardest, transfixed by his sense of dread. The thing was large, and at first indescribable. Only as features solidified from out of the darkness did Girder realize that what he stared at was Rasp, slumped in his wheelchair. Or at least what was left of Rasp.

The corpulent body sat motionless, dressed in the same encompassing purple robes, his lifeless arms on the wheelchairs handles, his feet on the tiny steps. Everything was as it should have been. Except his head. His head was gone, and only a hole remained.

The air was sucked from Girder's lungs; replaced with ice. He closed his eyes, but in the darkness it did not matter, the image remained burned on his retina, developing further instead of fading. Girder could see things he had not initially: the tiny undone clasps that ran up the front of Rasp's robes; the cauterized hole of a neck, red and puckered. Without Rasp's head, bobbing as he spoke, his body appeared artificial, a mere costume. But if that were the case, what did it disguise? And, more frighteningly, what had happened to whatever wore it?

Girder heard that wet sound again, like something dragged across the floor, so near it would be upon him at any moment. He reached down to retrieve the painting at his feet and prayed he could escape without turning on the light. He couldn't bear to see Rasp's body again. But without that second look, relying only on his quickly fading memories, he misjudged his dash and grazed something that could only have been the headless body. There was no sound from the heavy mass beyond a heavy sigh, but something fell behind Girder, hitting the floor with a sound like hollow wood, and Girder knew there was no time left for him.

He groped for his final painting, finding it where he imagined the doorknob to be. The wet sound recurred louder and faster, and he scrambled out and into the dark hallway.

He ran blindly, unsure of where he was going. The hallway looked different in the night—corners where there shouldn't have been, solid walls that ought to have been doors. And with each crooked step rattling in his head, with each breath wheezing in his ears, he heard the wet sound, rasping as if it too were breathless.

The painting under his arm made flight difficult, but it did not occur to Girder to drop it, to throw it aside. Everything he was, everything he had become since suffering under his father's fists was in it, and he would let no one steal it from him. He held the canvas tight, pushed it against the air that tried to knock it loose, to slow him down. Even when that scrambling wetness was overhead, echoing in his ears from above, he couldn't think of releasing the painting. From somewhere there was a hiss through ravaged flesh, a final rally before the deadliest blow, and Girder's bent leg finally faltered—a part of his soul already surrendering to his end.

But the hands that thrust out for him, dragged him into the light, were not from beyond. They were long-fingered and multicolored, and attached to narrow arms of similar complexion. Girder saw little else as he was flung sideways, the canvas slipping from his numb fingers as he tumbled over tangled limbs and onto the hard floor. The air filled with screeching, desperation denied, and Girder's tearing eyes stung from exertion. He could not comprehend what was happening, his head swimming, delirious from impossibilities. All connection to reality slipped away, and it was only the solid smack of a flat hand against his face that focused him. But when the truth solidified, he felt no better off.

Nadir stumbled from the door, his eyes red and rheumy, his thick black hair twisted. He had stripped down to his undershirt, and for the first time Girder saw the intricate tattoos that stretched all the way from wrists to shoulders, interrupted only by the length of plastic tubing tied around one arm.

"You're safe here, for now," Nadir slurred, then picked up his glass of liquor from a table covered with needles and spoons and slumped into his only chair. Above his head and on every wall painted artwork hovered like unfamiliar cherubs.

"What's happening?" was all Girder's terror would allow him to say.

"What's happening?" Nadir mocked. "What do you think is happening? Rasp wants what's his. That's all he ever wants."

"I don't understand. What is he?"

Nadir staggered, tried to refill his tumbler from the dark glass bottle of bourbon on his table, but most of it merely spilled past. Nadir was oblivious to his failure.

"You ruined everything. You had no right. No right." He coughed violently, then took another gulp of his drink before pointing at the paintings above. "You should never have come here. I should have stopped you, I should have made you leave, or killed you when you didn't. I should have reached my fingers around your throat and *squeezed!*" Nadir's eyes bulged as he said it, his fist clenched so tight it paled, and Girder scrambled to his knees. The storm on Nadir's face passed instantly, and he slid down into his chair. "Everything is ruined. Everything. I remember what it was like, I remember the joy and freedom, before I gave myself over. I believed it all because I was nearly as blind as you. It cost me everything. So long now I'd forgotten. Then you come in here—" Nadir's eyes flared again, the bleariness replaced by something worse as they focused on Girder—"you come here and knocked on the door and demanded it all for yourself. You walk by my work, even here, in my own private inch of this circus, and you ignore it, laugh at it, diminish it, and think you're something more than you are. You're so desperate for it that the trap isn't even baited before you walk into it. You come and chaos comes with you."

Nadir stood and downed the rest of his bourbon. He looked at Girder, but it was clear he didn't see him. Those blood-shot watering eyes looked right through to someplace cold and dark. He sniffled, and Girder pawed for his painting and dragged it closer. A ripple appeared on Nadir's face, beginning around the edges of his swollen eyes and moving outward. Skin and meat and teeth trembled, a swell of emotion that was focused on the fallen Girder. The artist's fear returned, pulling the cloak of colors over his eyes, and before he went blind he scrambled to his feet, painting hugged close. Even behind that returning veil, Nadir's shaking fury made him appear twelve feet tall.

"Why didn't you leave when you had the chance? Why didn't you save yourself as I couldn't? Why did you have to upset and awaken it?"

"What is it?" Girder pleaded. "What is it?"

But Nadir did not answer. Instead, he threw his empty tumbler at the floor and lunged at Girder, long fingers like painted claws, eyes rolled up in glassy hate. Girder stepped back and instinctively reacted, swinging the painting in his hands as hard as he could. Canvas split and frame cracked. All Girder had was destroyed in an uncontrolled instant, and Nadir fell to the ground, wailing, cursing. Then a wave of convulsions took hold, and while his neck muscles spasmed, he spewed foul liquid over the floor, wave after wave, but did not take his hate-filled eyes from Girder. Instead, he crawled forward, reaching for the terrified artist. Girder could not think, only react. He stepped back, still brandishing a piece of shattered wooden frame, and hit the weakened Nadir with it until splinters flew and Nadir's body slumped. Once the convulsions ceased, the veil of colors dropped from Girder's eyes. He let go of the bloody piece of wood, and it splattered on the floor. Girder knew he had to escape, but when he reached the door his slick hands were unable to twist the knob. He was trapped. Then, beneath his touch, the door vibrated; a pounding that echoed the rush of blood in his ears. It was the sound of something trying to get inside the room.

Girder heard the sickly slurp as he backed away, the drooling suck of ravenousness, and the door visibly rattled with each blow.

His head raced with terrified thoughts of all Nadir had warned.

"It's gone!" he pleaded. "It's gone! I don't have it! There's nothing here for you!"

But the pounding did not stop. The wooden doorframe split; the air crackled, full of pungency. Girder rushed around the room, around the incapacitated Nadir, looking for some weapon to protect himself from Rasp or whatever it was that was coming through the door. All he found was a slim dull knife, one he could barely hold in his tired, bloodied hands.

The banging, that ugly noise intensified, interspersed with the door being clawed. Girder noticed the doorframe separate from the wall with each succeeding blow, pulling away and opening the entrance that much further. Girder hunkered behind a fallen piece of furniture and waited, thin dull knife dancing in his trembling hand. Unexpectedly, he imagined his father kneeling in his place.

What came though the torn opening on that final blow was nothing Girder was prepared for. It had the face and head of Elias Rasp, but contorted and stretched, the skin like vellum, the eyes dead and staring wide. But the head was supported by the blackest flesh, wrinkled and covered in a bloody sheen. Its conical body, nearly three foot long, twisted as it reached its tail, an appendage that flicked spasmodically while hundreds of long spindly legs carried the creature scurrying toward Nadir's unmoving body. And the torn and broken remnants of the painting he still wore. A trail of greasiness followed after, but the thing with Rasp's face was not slowed by it. Unencumbered by its previous corpulent body, it moved with precision, black tongue hanging limply from a dislocated jaw. The knife slipped from Girder's hand, his fear too great to control himself.

The thing stopped a few feet short of Nadir's body, its oversized head cocking too far, and rolled its cataracted eye. Girder stared, transfixed, as the thing perched on Nadir's face and spun its head in the other direction, jaw to its back, eyes moving skyward, and from the grey skin on the rear of the presumable skull a thin spongy gland pushed out. It then gathered its legs to itself and hunkered to feed.

But it was not the bloodied Nadir who was the meal; it was what remained of Girder's masterpiece. Colors from the torn canvas bled, then faded from the surface as the sickening mouthparts pulsated over the rough canvas. Ropes of greasy slime slid forth as it moved, removing the hours and days and weeks of Girder's work, and with each pulse the creature seemed to grow fuller. It fed off everything Girder had given, and the sight left the artist cold and emptied. He reached down to retrieve the dull knife, his grip that much more sure.

The Rasp-thing fed, the smell and sound of it overpowering, as Girder crept behind it. Each staggered step reminded him of the games Rasp had played over the intervening weeks, of the disappointment in Mr. Raymond's eyes, of the way his father had—as they all did—of diminishing him, of making him believe he was less than he was. They had all stolen so much from Girder, taken so much *of* him, and given him nothing in return.

Except that that was not true.

His father *had* given him two things.

The first, a connection to his emotions so strong that a veil of burning red rage consumed his sight; the second, an understanding of how a person's hands might quickly inflict the maximum amount of damage.

He stepped over Nadir's prone body and into range; Rasp's dull dead eyes rolled and glared. Its jaw quivered, tongue lolled.

It knew.

Girder could no longer hesitate.

The slim dull knife stabbed black flesh repeatedly, throwing indescribable color across the walls. The creature gurgled, squealed, spun in circles as the foul liquid spurted. It darted and Girder leapt back, but with broken body and legs it managed only circles, spraying everything. Girder nearly slid in the mixture of hemolymph, grease, and bile as he struggled, his nerve gone and twisted leg screaming. But the damage to the Rasp-thing was done, and as it slowed its mindless convulsions the vestigial face on its back flickered and twitched with ebbing control. It was only when it had ceased moving beyond an occasional dying tic that Girder was brave enough to crush it beneath the weight of Nadir's empty chair.

Girder stood panting on wobbling legs, taking in what lay before him. Nadir, broken and unbreathing. Rasp, a severed head crushed to a soft lump. Blood and vomit and colors spread across the canvas of floors and walls, and upon them an abstract expressionist composition unlike any revealed itself. Girder observed the patterns, breaks, details of flecks and spots, and read their meaning. The composition's intent was clear. It spoke directly to him. It spoke of freedom, of release, of a life finally his own. While outside the storm raged fiercely, inside Girder's great tumult was finally at an end.

Burnt Black Suns

1. A Long Bus Ride

Noah screamed and opened his eyes. No one on the bus would look at him, all eyes curiously pointed down, and Noah felt the vestiges of his dream lingering in the dry oven air. The windows were tinted, but the sun still bore through them, bathing Noah in an unbearable heat, a heat intensified by his anxiety. Sweat trickled through the tight coils of his dark hair and down his face. In his hand was clenched the newspaper clipping he'd been carrying for days.

"Are you okay?" Rachel's eyes were wide with worry. Noah's head, a jumble as his sense of displacement ebbed.

"Yeah," he said, folding the blurry photograph and placing it back in his pocket. "How long did I sleep for?"

"Not long, I don't think." She looked down at the small mound under her shirt and placed her hands upon it.

"I feel worse now than before. Still, I'm surprised I was able to sleep at all." He swallowed. It tasted sour.

"That's what happens when you don't sleep for three days."

It had taken a week to put the money for the trip together and make all the arrangements to get from their tiny house in

Sarnia to Astilla de la Cruz in as straight a line as possible. Neither knew how long it would take to find Noah's ex-wife, Sonia, in Mexico, let alone rescue his son, Eli. Sonia had been one step ahead of them for two years, and though Noah liked to believe his son cried for him the entire time, rationally he knew the boy forgot him more with each passing day. If he couldn't find the boy and rescue him from his mother, Eli would be lost forever.

"Are you holding up? You know you didn't have to come down with me, considering."

"I'm okay. Just a bit tired. It's still early enough that I don't feel *too* frazzled. That will probably change soon."

"It did with Sonia—" He stopped himself, but it was too late. The damage was done. Rachel shook her head.

"It's okay, Noah. I'm not bothered by it."

It was clear she was lying.

The bus hit something on the road, some rough spot that caused the entire length to shake. Noah held Rachel's hand as she squeezed, reminding him of the delivery room when Eli was born. He tried to push the memory out of his mind, unwilling to have it contaminated by his situation. Rachel had her eyes closed as though in prayer, waiting for the disruption to end, and Noah wished he'd been able to convince her to stay at home. Already, he was terrified about what he might find when he finally discovered Eli, and Rachel's presence only further compounded his fears.

Noah carefully took in the crowd of passengers. They barely looked human, as though sculpted from leather, not flesh, filled with sand, not blood. Their movements were sluggish and weighted, eyes half-lidded or closed—a lifetime of survival had worn them down. Across the aisle sat an elderly lady, her head covered in a thin shawl, her feet bare and calloused. In her hands was a small leather-bound book with blank dog-eared covers. She stared unblinkingly at Noah and Rachel, and he had to look away as much from embarrassment as from fear; in her gaze he saw nothing but the endless expanse of desert. The woman opened her mouth to wheeze, and Noah worried the glaring heat had baked him out of reality and into some sub-reality, one in which everything moved slower than it should. She raised her hand, her crooked fingers bent in some crazy pattern, and touched her stomach in the same manner Rachel touched her own. He saw Rachel's hands awkwardly fall away.

"*Tú tienes la marca de la Madre. Bendita sea la Madre.*"

"What's she saying?" Rachel whispered to him, visibly upset. He wished he knew, but it was clear by the sudden shuffling of feet and positions that the woman's voice was making the strangers around him and Rachel almost as uncomfortable.

"Something about you being a mother, I guess."

The old woman nodded, smiling, repeating, "*Madre.*" Rachel smiled too, hers as forced as the old woman's crazed.

"*Ya mero llega la hora,*" she said with glee, then laughing returned to her small leather-bound book. Rachel leaned toward his ear, her breath as hot as the sun.

"I remember now why I never wanted to visit Mexico. My sister had a horrible time in Guadalajara. Why the hell would Sonia have brought Eli here? What's there to see but a whole lot of nothing?"

"I have no idea." There was too much Noah didn't understand, nor was he sure he wanted to. Sonia had changed after the divorce, only slightly at first, but over time the cracks grew wider and in number. There had always been something inside her, something he saw only on rare occasions. It was in her eyes, in the tone of her voice, but she managed to keep it hidden. When the cracks grew wide enough, however, there was no hiding it, and what she once tried to suppress she instead became. It was the only explanation he had for why she would have taken Eli from him. The boy was everything, and to have him gone for nearly half his life evoked a pain Noah could never sufficiently convey to Rachel. Sometimes he wondered if she had only become pregnant to try and replace what he had lost. But how could he ever replace Eli? It was like trying to replace a piece of his soul. "What are you looking at?" Rachel asked. Noah's eyes were wide and dry. He hadn't blinked in what seemed like days.

"I think we're getting close."

The black mark on the horizon grew as the bus approached it, peeking out from the haze of the radiating desert to form a church spire, then the rickety buildings beneath it. Within the hour the bus was close enough for Noah to point out the village to Rachel, who simply nodded solemnly. Noah itched for action, desperate to be freed from the bus he had been trapped in for so long so he might begin the search. Sonia and Eli were there, somewhere, in the small village, and he knew it. Knew he was so close. Strangely, the excitement made him salivate, and he wiped his mouth with the back of his hand in anticipation before Rachel noticed it. All he tasted was salt.

As the bus pulled into Astilla de la Cruz, things became clearer to Noah. The church spire he had seen from so far away was broken, the cross hanging precariously upside down from little more than a wooden sliver. No one seemed to be tending to the church to fix it, however. The delicate stained glass was broken, the ground of the small graveyard beside it upturned until few of its tombstones remained upright. The stores along the street of the village were no better, a small step beyond wooden shacks, nearly indistinguishable from the rundown houses around them. Had the road not been paved, he would have wondered if there were a road at all. Each crack and pothole jolted the bus, shaking Rachel's head back and forth as though she were a puppet. Noah put an arm across her chest while his other hand gripped the back of the torn vinyl seat in front of him. He squeezed tight, hoping to keep both from being pitched to the ground. None of the other passengers, including the elderly lady, seemed nearly as concerned.

The bus came to a stop alongside a long wooden platform set in the dirt. At one end was a small wooden office with the word

Estación carved in a plank hanging above the door. "I guess this is the station," Rachel said as Noah relaxed the arm that had been holding her down. They gave the other passengers time to stand and gather their things before they retrieved their bags from under the seat and made their way off the bus. When they stepped down onto the platform—Noah taking Rachel's hand as she navigated the stairs—he cast a glance sideways at the window he had been sitting beside for so long. The glass reflected the light from the bright streets, yet the reflection looked almost like a negative of him that had been burned in by the blazing sun. He stared at it, but did not admit it to Rachel for fear he was hallucinating. Then that image moved, and the confusion made him dizzy. Rachel tripped as she came down the stairs, but Noah snapped back in time. "I'm sorry," he mumbled, then looked again at that image in the window. It had become translucent, and when he looked again he was able to see through it to what lay beyond: the elderly woman, glaring. Noah nervously raised a hand to shield his eyes, but it was too late. She had stepped away from the window and vanished into the patterns of light.

Rachel stood on the rickety platform with her bag over her shoulder, ignoring the low creak as her weight shifted to her left foot. Noah flashed to when he'd first met her, standing much the same way outside the front of the police station. Her shape was different then—straighter, leaner. It was a good shape, but he liked the new shape better. Still, there was something there that was familiar, some older memory that the new could not successfully supplant. Without Eli, it all seemed worthless. "So," Rachel finally said. "Where do we go from here?"

Noah sputtered.

"What do you mean?"

"Where's the hotel? How do we get there?"

"Ah."

"Why, what did you think I meant?"

Noah shrugged. "Why don't we go inside and ask?"

The station contained barely more than a few chairs, fliers, and a ticket booth. He thought he saw someone behind it, but as soon as he and Rachel stepped inside, the bottled heat drove them back.

"I think I'm going to wait for you outside," Rachel said.

Noah stepped in again and let himself get acclimated to the heat. He took deep breaths, his body struggling for oxygen, and the exertion only made him sweat more. As he walked in, he realized the station was much older than he thought. The wood was mottled and cracked, baked too long in the sun. But as old as the station appeared, it must have been built up around the station agent, who had no doubt sat slack-jawed on his stool since the beginning of time. Noah approached, but the man's eyes did not move. Instead, the left merely drooped somewhat further than the half-lidded right, and he licked his lips with an inhuman patience. Had he not blinked, Noah might have mistaken him for a wax sculpture that the heat miraculously hadn't touched. As though on cue, the station agent spoke in a rasp not nearly powerful enough to disturb the flies crawling over his sweating face. He moved his head with a creaking, his eyes scouring Noah and his bag. Noah did not enjoy the sensation. "Can you tell me where the Hotel Bolero is?"

"¿Que? Bolero?"

"Si, si," Noah repeated with exasperation. Outside, he could see Rachel standing against the side of the station fanning herself while trying to squeeze into a sliver of shade.

"No la puedes dejar afuera. Es peligroso."

The language barrier was proving difficult for Noah, especially knowing it would likely be the biggest impediment to finding his son.

"Telephone?" he said, miming dialing a rotary phone. The station agent barked inhumanly, and with what must have been a tremendous show of strength he lifted his arm and pointed across the room. There among torn billets on the irregular walls hung a telephone, or the remains of one. It was barely more than a dangling receiver. Noah caught a glimpse of the old man's tongue as he gummed his lips and wheezed, and the small wrinkled flesh looked like a chewed piece of leather. The station agent seemed stricken dumb, his long white mustache hanging over his mouth. It twitched and rustled as though he spoke under his breath, and Noah had to force down his paranoia in the face of that unblinking gaze.

Despite its rough-hewn looks, the telephone produced noise that seemed to approximate a dial tone, though the sound was not at all one to which Noah was accustomed—its pitch was higher, and it was a series of short bursts of varying length. Noah clicked the hook switch a few times to try and mediate the sound without success before dialing. There was a pause after the number was entered, a dead space that lasted long enough for Noah to worry nothing was happening. Then, there was a ring, a horrible ring that was like a wailing child. A voice spoke words he didn't recognize, then a click and a voice.

"Hotel Bolero."

Rachel was standing against the wall of the station, waiting for Noah to be done. When he opened the door she raised her hand to shade her brow. After being inside for so long, he found the baking Mexican air refreshing and wondered why Rachel was still sweating.

"Did you get the directions?" she asked.

"Eventually. It was a bit of a struggle."

"Did they have trouble understanding you?"

"Well," he hesitated. "That was *part* of it . . . How are you holding up?"

She shrugged. "This weather here only makes me feel more bloated than usual. At least I have this." She lifted her arm to display the wreath circling her forearm like a large bracelet. It was made of hundreds of dried stems woven into a rough tangled circle.

"Who gave you that?"

"Some woman was passing by. She looked upset, and I suppose she caught me staring. I would have asked her what was wrong, but . . ." She shrugged, the reason obvious. "Then she gave it to me and said *madre*. I guess it's my first baby shower gift."

He smiled, then thought of Eli.

"We should get to the hotel. The girl on the phone said it was near the church."

They followed the directions Noah had been given. Though he secretly doubted he'd understood the broken English correctly, he remained silent for fear of worrying Rachel. In the end, it was for naught, as he quickly recognized ahead the broken spire of the church he had seen from the bus—a black needle piercing the sky against the blinding backdrop of the setting sun. It forced him to avert his eyes as they continued toward it. Noah and Rachel passed few people, and as they did each glared back with suspicion. Noah hadn't expected to feel so alien, so unwelcomed. The worst had been the old lady in front of the church as they passed, dressed head to toe in black, a child's bicycle in her hands. She was wailing, yet when she saw Rachel, she stopped and looked at her growing pregnancy without a sound. It was only when she and Noah had passed that the wailing resumed.

They arrived at the Hotel Borelo just as the sun vanished behind the horizon and failed to take the stifling heat with it. The building was simply a converted two-story house, out of place in its surroundings of poorly built shanties, but even the late addition of inexpertly installed siding could not dispel the influence of the ornate church. Positioned so close, the church made an eyesore of everything in its shadow. Insects filled the sky with an electric drone, and tiny flies preceded Noah and Rachel into the building, harbingers of the couple's arrival. Noah could still feel them crawling on his skin, but reaching to scratch their tiny legs away only left his hand sticky with sweat. The skin of the señora behind the counter was deeply bronzed and leathery, and it folded like paper around her eyes as she glared with equal parts suspicion, worry, and fear. She said nothing, instead dropping the keys to the room into Noah's hand as though they were slick with poison. She would not look at Rachel.

The room was barely larger than the bed, and when Rachel sat down upon it she sank with a long creak of old springs. "I guess we don't have a lot of options," she said. "At least we have that balcony door we can open to catch a breeze."

"There doesn't seem to be much hope for one," Noah said, putting their bags in the corner and climbing onto the bed to join her. He lay down and stretched out his arm so she could snuggle close and put her head on his chest. Rachel's flesh was on fire, but he tried to ignore it and simply enjoy the feel of her against his skin.

"So what's the plan?" she said, looking up at him. He swept her blond hair off her face.

"We can't go to the police. We can't even prove it's her in the photo."

"But you're sure?"

"Absolutely."

"Have you any ideas on how to find her?"

"I only care about finding *him*."

The first moment Noah stumbled across that article in *La Diario Oficial* during his monthly trek to the Toronto Reference Library, he knew he was on the right track. The police did not agree. They felt the photo was too blurry, too indistinct to take seriously despite Noah's insistence it was his fugitive ex-wife. He knew her body so well, its shape and how she held it, that there was no doubt in his mind the obscured figure was Sonia. For the police, however, it was not enough. When he finally convinced someone to listen, he was told that without more solid proof there was little they could do ... even if they believed him. The Canadian police had no jurisdiction in Mexico, and the Mexican police were too corrupt to help find a missing boy when so many others disappeared daily from their overrun streets.

"Did I tell you what I was dreaming about on the bus? I dreamed I saw Sonia at a vegetable stand—a lot like the one we saw at the St. Jacob's market, do you remember?—and Eli was right beside her, holding her hand. I walked up to them without saying a word. Eli saw me first. He shouted with joy—ecstatic—and ran into my arms. I scooped him up and held him so close I could smell his hair and his skin. It was just like I remembered—comforting and sweet. Then Sonia looked at me and she was crying. She tried to speak and maybe she couldn't or maybe I cut her off, but the words were choked. While she struggled I simply took Eli's hand, turned around, and walked away. Somehow I knew that now I'd be the one to disappear and never be found.

"Then I woke up. Have you ever had a dream where you got just what you wanted, and for a second when you woke up you thought it might be real? There's absolutely nothing worse than realizing you're wrong. It's soul-crushing, absolutely soul-crushing. Still, I should know by now that nothing is ever that neat, that simple. When I finally find Sonia and Eli, things are going to be messy and painful. I just hope to shield him from as much of it as I can."

Rachel was quiet. He hadn't noticed her stiffen as he spoke, but now that he was done he felt her tense body and looked down. She was staring at her swollen belly, silently rubbing it with both hands. Then, with some effort, she slid off the bed and stood.

"Let's go out. I'm feeling claustrophobic holed up in this little room after being on that bus for so long. I think a walk will do us both some good. Just give me a minute to get ready."

Rachel left the room and he heard her feet softly pad down the hallway. Noah went over to the window and opened it, but without a breeze the air refused to move. He looked out instead at the darkening street below. The heat radiating off the ground distorted everything he saw. The village itself looked insubstantial, as though it might vanish altogether, and instinctively he worried what he would do if that happened, how he would find his Eli. He shook his head. It was crazy. All of it was crazy. But the building heat in their room only made his thoughts more muddled, and he knew Rachel was right—he had to leave before his imagination consumed him in a blaze.

There was no one at the front desk when they left, though they could hear the señora somewhere in the back, whispering or watching television. The air outside had cooled only slightly, but remained stagnant, and he was wiping his brow after only a few steps. He hated the heat, but would endure it for Eli. Rachel wasn't as accommodating.

"I can't stand the feeling of my skin sticking together. Or the fact that every time I lick my lips I taste salt."

"Do you want to go back?"

"No, I need to be moving around. Dr. Mielke says I need all the exercise I can get now before I can't do it any more."

Even in the darkness, the broken spire of the church was still darker, a black void in the evening sky. The small buildings and houses at its foot were all without lights, as though the hanging cross cast its shadow long across the Astilla de la Cruz street. Noah and Rachel walked hand-in-hand in as straight a line as they could along the uneven pavement, and as Rachel seemed focused on remaining upright Noah spied those people they passed on the street. None were walking, all instead silently stood and glared at the couple as they approached. When Noah came alongside, he looked at their dark faces and saw the jumble of emotions he'd seen earlier on the face of the señora at the hotel. Was it so strange for the village to get visitors from outside the country? Did Sonia stick out just as much? He wanted to show the newspaper clipping to them, find out if they held the secret of his missing child, but it was clear none of them would help. He and Rachel were strangers, and small villages despise strangers.

"It's quiet here, isn't it?" Rachel was panting, but not enough for it to be worrisome.

"I suppose," Noah said. Outside, in the darkness cast by the church, little was revealed of the Astilla de la Cruz streets. The houses seemed to be less built and more sprung from the ground as though a crevice had opened from which each had sprouted. Like rows of plants, each tiny house was at a different height than its neighbor, and mixed with the random sheets strung between two poles to form makeshift tents for the less-than-poor, the terracotta skyline attained a jagged uneven appearance, slightly hallucinatory in the near-dead light. The walls of the homes looked to have been crumbling for years beneath the baking sun, which had clearly bleached the colors to dusty grey. Or perhaps that was a trick of the ebbing night. Noah could just make out the advertisement for Corona painted large upon a wall, though the paint had flaked to such a degree hardly more than the name of the beer was still visible. And yet, in front of the barely legible sign a series of tables were set up with candles burning on each—a small outside cantina, underpopulated. At the furthest table from the light sat a solitary old man, perhaps in his sixties, hunched so completely his head was halfway down his chest. Yet Noah could still feel the stranger's eyes on him, and though he tried to return the intimidation with his own glare, the man seemed unmoved. "I don't think they like foreigners here. Hopefully that will help us flush Sonia out."

As though on cue, a middle-aged woman approached Noah and Rachel, a smile wide across her tanned face. Noah thought he saw her eyes first, like twin moons in the darkness, bright and round and moving towards him. Only when she reached the couple did he realize she was wearing glasses too large for her narrow face, too old to be anything more than second- or third-hand. She carried a bag at her side that was misshapen and lumpy, its contents having no distinct form. Noah thought he saw peeking from its opening colored tissue paper, dulled by the absence of light.

"*¿Nos has traído un bebé?*" she said with undue warmth. Noah wondered if she were as genuine as she masqueraded to be. "*¿La puedo tocar?*" She made motion with her hands, as though beckoning Rachel into them. "*Ella es,*" the woman said to Noah, and he was stunned to see tears had welled in her eyes. "*Ella es.*"

Noah stammered, unsure how to respond. Rachel, uncomfortable, shrugged.

"*Gracias?*" he finally offered.

The woman smiled again and wiped her eyes with the palm of her hand, then kissed it and placed it on Rachel's belly. The contrast of foreign skin was never clearer. "*Madre,*" she said, then nodded her head. Rachel did the same, though it was clear to Noah she had no better clue what was occurring. The woman removed her hand and kissed it again before reaching into her bag. Rachel rubbed the spot where the woman's flesh touched hers. From the bag, the woman produced three ochre dahlias, their stems twisted together to form some sort of wreath, and reaching up, placed it like a crown on Rachel's head. "*Una corona para la futura madre,*" she said before turning and walking quickly away, back into the night. Noah watched her go, then glanced at the old bent man. His glower only intensified.

"I can see why Sonia likes it here," Rachel said, taking the wreath off her head and smelling the flowers. She then looked at Noah with a face twisted in stunned apology.

"Sorry, honey, that's not what I meant. I just meant it's a nice place to raise a child."

"I don't think a cult is the right place for *anyone*, let alone a child. My child. My Eli. He doesn't belong here." Noah felt his anger rising, and Rachel was quick to diffuse it.

"I know, I know. We'll find him. We'll go out tomorrow and we'll show the picture around. Someone has got to know where he is. The place isn't that big. Look over there—" She pointed in the distance, up the hill that started behind the church and only went back and up into the darkness. "That's the edge of this place.

We've already walked across most of it. How can she possibly hide from you here?"

"If anyone could find a way to keep me from Eli," he spat, "it would be her."

Rachel gasped, then stopped and put her hands on her knees, her face twisted in a grimace.

For the first time since arriving Noah felt cold.

"What's wrong?"

Her breaths were heavy, but controlled. As both she and Noah had been taught at Lamaze class.

"It's nothing. I'm okay. Dr. Mielke said I might get sharp pains in my back or stomach during the second trimester." She continued to push air through her teeth. "I just need a second. Christ, it feels like someone stuck a knife in me."

"Do you . . . Do you want me to do something?"

"No, no. I'll be okay. Just a minute." She breathed deeply, one final time, then straightened herself out. Her face was a bit red and swollen, but otherwise she looked okay. She sniffled. "See? All better."

"All the same, we should call it a night."

She took his hand again and they turned around. Other than the moon and the tiny light of the Hotel Bolero, there was nothing else to guide them through the dark.

2. Avenues of Investigation

Noah could not lie still between the hotel sheets. Sleep seemed elusive, impossible, when he was so exhausted from his journey on little more evidence than a blurry newspaper photograph. He itched with unbridled anxiety; it was like electricity travelling through his nerves into his addled brain. His ears buzzed, his eyes filled with sparks behind closed lids. Even his teeth felt slightly displaced, and biting down did not alleviate the discomfort. He was charged with the knowledge that Eli was close—closer than he'd been in years—and it became impossible to spend another moment in the shrinking bed. While Rachel slept easily and deeply, Noah pulled back the covers and slipped free.

The heat in the middle of night remained oppressive, and sitting beside the open window proved futile—the air from outside was no cooler. Still, Noah could look out from his perch at the tiny village streets lit by moonlight, and past the broken spire of the church toward the rough-edged horizon. He stared out and wondered where in all that emptiness Sonia was hiding. Sonia, and the son she had stolen from him. He boiled with impotent rage. If he only knew where Eli was being held, he wouldn't be able to stop himself from storming over there, despite the assurance of both Rachel and the Sarnia Police that it would likely result in his death. But Noah was willing to risk it all to be reunited with his son. No one understood how much Sonia had taken with her, what emptiness Eli had left. The man Rachel met two years ago was not whole, had never been whole the entire time they'd been together. But there in Mexico, his body vibrating in anticipation of its missing piece, Noah was closer than he'd ever been. He didn't know how things would change when he was complete, didn't know if Rachel would reject the version of him she'd never seen before, but he couldn't allow himself to falter with worry. Eli, his only son, was close, and his presence was stoking the fires that burned in Noah's heart. It was burning him up.

Noah was still sitting by the window as the sun made its slow ascent into the sky, a fiery god from behind the horizon. More heat came with it, and whatever respite the dark had offered was revoked, a victim to the burning orb. Rachel opened her eyes not much later, she too finding it impossible to sleep, and when she waved her arm at Noah, beckoning him back to bed, he complied. Arm around her body, hand on their unborn child, he pressed his body into her back and fought the instinct to flee from the unbearable heat she was radiating. It was essential to his sanity that he stay tethered to her. Eli, though, was out there waiting for him.

"We have to go soon. We need to start looking." He felt her take a deep breath, then exhale slowly. "You're not too hot, are you? If you want to hang back here, I can meet you later."

"No, it's okay. I'll be fine." She swallowed hard. "Where to first?"

"I guess we'll start with the photo. Show it around. See what happens."

It did not take Noah long to get ready, but Rachel moved more slowly, her ligaments aching as they stretched to accommodate their growing child. Noah had not planned what to do once he and Rachel reached Astilla de la Cruz. Before they arrived, he had felt certain it would be easy to find a Canadian woman and child in a village so small, and yet once there he realized how detrimental his own foreignness was. He and Rachel had little in common with those around him. One mistake and they would get nowhere.

Downstairs, the old señora sat behind her desk as though she had been stationed there overnight, staring at a framed photograph. Rachel appeared discomfited by her presence and tugged at Noah's arm to keep him moving past, but Noah decided if they were going to start searching there would be no place better. The señora's scowl did not frighten him—he would have suffered far worse for Eli.

"Excuse me? Señora?"

She grunted in response, her jowls tight over a clenched jaw. But when she looked up at him her face was wet, and those cold eyes red. He glanced at Rachel, hoping to catch her eye, but she was intentionally looking elsewhere.

"Do you know this place? Do you recognize it?"

He unfolded the article he'd been carrying. Time had already worn its creases, giving the photo an additional layer of fog. Noah flattened it out as best he could before showing it to her. Her eyes didn't move.

"Señora, please. *Muy importante.*"

Her scowl deepened, scoring the flesh of her leather face like an old handbag, and she laid the small framed photo face down. *"Ándale. Dámelo."* Her hand snatched at the article, and he gave it over, albeit reluctantly. He struggled to tamp down the fear that by simply relinquishing possession of the clipping, he might lose his only clue to his son's whereabouts. When her swollen eyes landed upon the photograph, they stretched open wide, much wider than he would have expected. She turned noticeably paler, as a dark shadow crossed her face. He worried she might scream. Instead, she shook her head vehemently and pushed the clipping as far away from herself as she could. As though it were on fire.

"*No, no conozco a este lugar.*"

"Please, Señora. In English."

"*No sé esto. Vete. Lleva tu hereje contigo.*"

"What?"

She pointed at the photograph, and then looked at Rachel. Noah felt uncomfortable with the glare she gave his girlfriend.

"Where is the place?" he repeated.

"*¡Hereje!*" she said, slamming the table. Her finger shot out, pointing at the door. "*¡Vete!*"

Noah picked the clipping up off the counter and backed away, his arms raised in surrender, unsure what had happened. He stopped when he felt Rachel touch his back. The old woman was still seething.

"We'd better go," she whispered, tugging at him. Noah nodded and let her guide him outside, his eyes unable to leave the crooked glare of the señora.

Outside, the heat hit them like a wall. A glare reflected off the church across from them, though its bulk remained in shadow. Enough of a glare, at least, to disguise the presence of the priest until Noah bounced off him.

"God, I'm sorry!" he said, then immediately regretted the curse. Rachel's mouth was agape.

"Okay, it's okay," the priest said, fixing his collar. He was taller than Noah and broader, built sturdy enough that he barely acknowledged Noah's clumsiness. He scratched his wide round face with stubby fingers, and when he glanced at Rachel and saw she was pregnant, a smile overtook him. "Nobody was hurt, after all. At least, not out here. What was the screaming about?"

"I'm not really sure. I'm trying to find someone and when I showed the señora inside she went crazy."

"Ah, Señora Alvarez. She hasn't been the same since her granddaughter passed away. Do you mind?" He reached his large hand out and looked from Noah to Rachel and back again. Noah was confused, until he realized the folded article was still clutched in his hand. He passed it over carefully.

"Hm," the priest said, holding the clipping an inch from his round brown eyes, then holding it at arm's length. "It's no use," he sighed. "I'm blind without my glasses, and your wife shouldn't be outside in this weather. Come, let us go inside the church. It will be cooler there."

"How long have you lived in Astilla de la Cruz?" Rachel was sitting in the second pew, hands over the back of the first and tucked under her chin. Noah remained standing, looking at the sparse furniture and the small handful of parishioners spread out across the place, all with heads down and praying. The church was far more spartan than Noah expected, but he imagined all the money had been spent on the ornate cross that was a hanging broken shadow beyond the dull stained glass. Rustling emitted from behind the large altar, somewhere near the back of the nave, though he saw no cause. "I only ask," Rachel said, wiping away sweat in the crook of her arm, "because your English is perfect, Father Manillo."

"Well, it's not *perfect*, but I try. I was born here, but my family was blessed enough that we moved to California when I was still a young boy. I studied there for many years. Many years until I was teenager and I felt the calling. I returned home, here to Astilla de la Cruz, and heard the voice stronger and knew I must stay. I studied here with Father Montechellio, and when he was too old to continue, I took his place. But enough of me. That's not why you're here. Let me get my glasses and take a look at this picture of yours. I know the village like I know my own face, and if anyone can help, I think I will!"

Father Manillo strode off toward the chancel, his shoes clapping the floor. Noah looked around the congregation but still could not locate the source of the rustling.

"I have a good feeling about this, Noah. I think he's going to help us."

"I hope so. I'm trying not to get my hopes up. How are you feeling?"

"I'm still a bit achy, but I'll manage."

Father Manillo appeared from behind the unadorned rood screen, a pair of thin glasses curled over his ears and nose. They gave his eyes a magnified appearance, like a new-born staring wide.

"Now let me take a look at that picture."

Noah handed him the folded clipping. Father Manillo opened it up and laid it flat on the pew. He stared intently at it while Rachel and Noah watched him. A hand went to his chin, stroking the dark wrinkled skin there. Then Father Manillo nodded and looked at Noah and Rachel. He motioned for them to sit.

"I don't know how much history you know of Mexico. When the Spaniards came in 1521, they brought God to the natives here, forced Christianity on them until it took, and over time those natives became civilized, paired with the Spanish, and developed into the Mexico we have today. Often dirty, often corrupt, but never godless is Mexico. But before this—before Columbus and Cortés and iron helmets and God himself—there were different rules the Olmec, Toltec, Teotihuacan, Zapotec, Maya, and Aztec lived by, and different gods to worship. Hexatopsodil, Quesadasidodfll, Setinodoginall—these were the ones who ruled the land, controlled air and water and earth. There was a god for everything; a separate yet no less important god to pray to, to sacrifice to, if a farmer wanted to grow a crop or heal his child. The ancient Mexican gods were not like the Christian God at all. The idea of one god instead of many would have seemed impossible, unbelievable—at least until the white men arrived and proved otherwise.

"But even that story, as widely believed as it is, isn't quite the whole story. History is like that—never presenting everything it should, forgetting things it shouldn't. Few people know what I'm about to tell you, fewer still actually believe it—at least, outside Astilla de la Cruz—but history has a way of changing the rules, even when time itself rejects the notion. I said that the Spanish brought the concept of the single god to the Mexican people, but that isn't quite true. There was another cult of worshippers who believed a single god would save the world, although who or what that god would be is open to debate. The story has been lost for centuries, so very little is known; but as I'm quite interested in religion, as you can imagine, I've paid particular attention to talk of this nature and have pieced much together. Great Huitzilopochtli was at ancient millennial war with the other gods over the souls of all the children lost to illness and plague. He called the gods together for a truce, but Ueuecoyotl, trickster god of foulness and chaos, was not to be trusted and tricked Huitzilopochtli into transforming himself into a hummingbird, then impregnating a mortal woman whom Ueuecoyotl had already impregnated. Then Ueuecoyotl did the same to Ixtlilton and Camaxtli and so on until he had tricked them all into impregnating that woman. With each impregnation, a piece of the gods' power was stolen, and Ueuecoyotl believed the subsequent child, the child of all the gods, would have all their power and usurp them as the one true god."

"But wouldn't he be usurped as well?"

"Ah, my friend, that was the beauty of Ueuecoyotl's plan. He simply didn't care. He was the god of chaos, after all."

"Wait, so you're saying this god and *God*-god—"

"Yes, one in the same. This is how a small number reconciled the new god the Spaniards brought with them. They believed this god, named Ometéotlitztl, to be the true supreme being, one which our God was only an aspect of. The cult has grown and persists, but they remain secret, unwilling to reveal their hidden selves to the world. Astilla de la Cruz is their home, and it's everything I can do to keep the true God alive here in the face of that."

"But does this have to do with my ex-wife and Eli?"

"I look at this photograph and even blurry it's clear to me where it was taken. The blasted heath. Come outside once more. The sun has lowered enough that you might see."

Noah trailed the priest to the entrance, Rachel a few steps behind. They were still in the shadow of the church's spire, which spared them the worst of the heat, but after being inside for so long, the sun seemed doubly bright and harsh, and Noah had to squint to keep his eyes open. Father Manillo said something to a passerby, but Noah could not see much through his squinting eyes beyond a multicolored blur. By the time Noah's eyesight improved the person was long gone.

"There, my friend, do you see it?" Father Manillo pointed toward the distant rocky outcropping that bordered the village. "Do you see that shape at the top?" At first, nothing seemed amiss, simply acres of scrub surrounding the village, then Noah noticed something unusual. There was a hill leading back toward the mountains, and on this hill was what looked like a large rock structure. All around it there seemed to be no life at all—just rocks and what looked like a leafless tree. The entire image wavered in the heat like some blackened flame.

"That's where your photograph was taken. That's where the Tletliztlii worship, during the lost hours of the day."

"How do we get there?"

"It's not a place for going—at least, not unprepared. The woman in the photo—your wife, yes?"

"Ex."

"Your ex-wife, she's not the same anymore. The Tletliztlii have her, and your little boy most likely."

"Tell me how to get there."

Father Manillo sighed, then consulted his watch.

"I don't have Mass for a few hours. Let me change into something more comfortable than robes. You will need an emissary, anyway, if any of them are to talk to you."

Noah sat beside Father Manillo in the borrowed truck, while in back Rachel grabbed what she could to stay seated. Even so, Noah wished they were moving faster.

"I apologize for the ride," the priest yelled back so she might hear him. "The terrain to the ruins is rough, but there's no way around it. There are no roads that go there. As you can guess, if there were, the Tletliztlii wouldn't use them. They like their privacy."

Noah turned to look at her.

"Are you okay?"

Rachel nodded, then put a free hand on her stomach. "It's not too bad," she said, then was jolted harshly, lifting her off her seat a few inches.

"Maybe we should slow down." Father Manillo looked at him, then into the rearview mirror.

"We're almost there, Rachel. I don't want to risk getting stuck in one of the crevices. Can you hold on a few more minutes?"

She nodded and looked at Noah. Noah's teeth chattered.

"Don't worry. I'm doing my kegels," she said.

Noah shook with giddy anxiety, a symptom compounded as they approached the ruins, yet as the distance shrank Noah found himself increasingly puzzled. The site looked nothing like the photograph, nor like anything he had imagined. He had expected a towering altar made of stone, housing an antechamber in which the Tletliztlii—including Sonia and Eli—would be hiding. Perhaps a large carving of Ometéotlitztl's face in the rock, overseeing everything. Instead, the ruins were just that—ruins, and consisted of little more than a few crumbling walls in a semicircle around a small raised platform that was split in two. There were no buildings, no people, no sign of life of any kind. The area was bare rock without shade or plant. Nothing grew for at least a few hundred feet in any direction, and even then only a circle of low brush that looked tiny and black against the blazing sun. The only proof life had ever existed on the rock was the lone dead tree standing at its center, sprouting from the cleaved rock, its branches knuckled and bent, hunkered and barely unfolded in death. A thick cord was tied around one of its branches, the spot beneath worn smooth, and at its end swung what remained of a faded piñata. Noah did not know what animal it once must have been—the shape bore no resemblance to anything he'd ever seen before—but its dead eyes stared at him as it slowly spun in the breeze, yellow streamers fluttering. Its stomach has long ago been burst open, and Noah couldn't help but wonder what had once been inside.

"Where is everyone?" Rachel asked, squinting out from behind her sunglasses. "And is it just me or is it hotter here than in the village? I'm sweating like a pig."

The priest took off his hat and ran his forearm across his forehead. Beads of sweat ran down his arm like blood.

"This is where they're supposed to be . . ." he said, but he wasn't listening closely. Behind his tinted glasses he was surveying the scene.

Noah had known all along, but refused to let himself believe it until Rachel and Father Manillo spoke the words aloud. Eli was not there. Probably never had been. Everything was slipping through his fingers, like the scorched sand beneath his feet. Every hope he had of rescuing his son was gone at once.

"I thought you said they'd be here. There's nothing, no sign of them at all." It was so hard to think under that sun, and his disappointment so vast.

"Honey, it's okay," Rachel said, putting her hand on his arm to cool him. But her skin was like a flame and he jerked free.

"It's not okay. Don't you get it? Eli is gone, and we were so close. Why did we come out here? Why are we wasting our time?"

His anger flared, lit the world on fire. Noah winced, the blinding brightness needles in his skull. "I need to find Eli," he tried to say, but his mouth refused to work. "He's the only thing I care about." The jumble of words faded into the distance along with all other sound, faded until nothing remained but deep endless quiet. Behind his closed eyes Noah saw Eli standing on the starkly lit barren heath, waving, his expression inscrutable. Noah reached for him and tripped forward, falling head first into the parting earth. But before the darkness could swallow him he was suddenly stopped, and the motion threw open his tear-filled eyes. For a muddled moment he wondered when he'd started crying.

"Be careful," Father Manillo said, helping Noah up and handing him a bottle of water. "The heat—I think it's too much for you."

Noah wiped his face and looked at Rachel. She stood with her arms crossed over her belly, turned ever so slightly away from him. Noah wanted to say something but didn't know what.

"We shouldn't have come here," he murmured.

"I understand, Noah," Father Manillo said, his wrinkled hands held out to ease Noah's anger. The red mist had already dissipated, but Noah's unhappiness remained.

"We aren't any better off than we were back home. Actually, we're worse off. At least then this stupid photo offered hope." He pulled the folded article from his pocket, tempted to tear it up and throw it away. "But look at this place. There's no hope anywhere here. Everything's dead."

"It didn't use to be," Father Manillo said, bald pate gleaming with sweat. "Once this all used to be jungle. Right here where we're standing. When the Aztecs built this temple to Ometéotlitztl, it was hidden from the prying eyes of neighboring tribes. They called it 'the lost temple' because of how secret the Tletliztlii kept its true location."

"So what happened to it?" Rachel asked, roused from her heavy-headed silence. She would not look at Noah, though. "Where did the trees disappear to?"

"Ah, you know the way of things," he said, looking out over the rocks back toward the village. Noah looked, too, but saw only the wavering heat warping the broken church steeple. "Time has not been good to plant life anywhere, including Mexico. Perhaps even more so in Mexico where your environmental protections don't apply. They began clear-cutting about fifty years ago, pulling down and removing more and more trees, trunk and all, until they exhausted the area. The sun here being as it is, everything beneath it was burnt to a cinder without the trees' protection—soil simply dried up and the wind took it away, leaving behind only the bare rock beneath. In a generation, the area was transformed, and when the logging companies finally left, Astilla de la Cruz was left more destitute than it had ever been before."

"Why didn't anyone stop them from cutting down the trees?" Rachel's breath was wheezing out of her. Noah's lip curled despite his own lingering curiosity.

"No one could. A local family that did most of the cutting here—there were stories about them. They were involved in a lot of things, most illegal. You met one of their children at the hotel. Señora Alvarez? Her father was Hernando Alvarez, and when Hernando found out the trees could make him money he wasted no time cutting them down. Back then, the idea of sustaining a crop didn't occur to anyone, especially one as hungry for money as Hernando. In the end, though, what drove him over the edge, what caused him to bleed the area dry, was a mishap. The details are sketchy, but somehow he did something to his own wife, something horrible, because when she gave birth to their second son what emerged was a dead thing, black as coal."

"She'd had an *affair?*"

"No, that's the thing. It wasn't a black baby. Instead, its skin had been turned black and gangrenous, the same thing that had probably killed it. The son Hernando had waited so long for was dead, and his wife soon afterward once the unsettled toxic flesh flooded her body."

Rachel gasped. Noah felt ill. The heat from the sun was starting to twist what he was seeing, and he wondered if Father Manillo was losing his cohesion.

"The story goes that Hernando wailed so loudly on their passing that it drove all life from the area, leaving only death on this hill. They buried the child here too. Underneath that slab. Some people wonder if that also had something to do with the curse here. Not me, of course. But some people. That's why most of the villagers avoid this place. Everyone but the Tletliztlii followers. It's the perfect spot to hide a child you don't want found."

The priest looked guiltily at Noah. His face was slick with sweat, and he was trying to blink it from his eyes.

"I'm sorry. I let my mouth get away from me, my friend. Maybe it's best we all leave, I think. It's a bad place." He crossed himself. "Come, let me take you both back to the village. You don't belong here. Not under this horrible sun."

"But what about Eli?"

"Have faith, Noah. I will pray for you both."

That answer did nothing to ease Noah's worries.

Father Manillo left Noah and Rachel at their hotel. Noah had been silent during the trip back, weighed down by despair. What made it worse was Rachel's demeanor. She had never spoken a word aloud, but it was clear her presence in Mexico was for his sake alone. She was not as committed to finding Eli as he was. But how could she be?

Eli. The boy had been so much a part of Noah. He filled a hole that could not otherwise be filled. Rachel did her best, and he knew that he should be happier about the new child she carried, but somehow that feeling was trapped inside of him, trapped within solid amber, visible but unreachable. Rachel, the baby—

they were not his beautiful Eli. But he went through the motions. It was all he could do. It would change when they finally found Eli; there was no doubt in his mind. With the boy back in his arms, that amber would crack, would crumble beneath Eli's beauty. Eli was Noah's true heart. There was no way he could go much longer without the boy.

But he tried. Only a few steps away from the hotel was a small cantina, pressed into the side of a degraded brick hovel. There was no door, only a large opening and awning from which a child's papier-mâché animal hung, its odd-numbered legs erupting from its twisted body without reason. Inside the cantina the lights were low, the air smelled of sweat and spices, and the unshaven men who sat there turned to stare eyes wide and silent at the couple as they entered. None were any younger than fifty, Noah suspected, though their faces made them look impossibly older. Noah wondered if he had ever before felt so out of place.

"Do you want to leave?" he asked Rachel under breath.

"I think it's fine. Look, there's a table over there."

She strode where Noah hesitated, deep into the heart of the place. Noah meekly followed, doing what he could to avoid eye contact. There were few women in the place, all lingering at the back of the room or behind curtains, and those he saw looked incredibly sad. He wanted to say something to help them, but couldn't think of a single thing that might make a difference, so he did his best to put them out of mind. It was easier than having to deal with problems that had no clear solutions.

"Do you think they have menus?" Rachel asked, moving her sunglasses to the top of her head, but before Noah could respond a small man in an apron and pencil mustache approached and put a dirty paper menu in front of them. He seemed nervous and hovered over Noah and Rachel as they looked over the menu, spending most of the time looking at the other patrons behind him.

"*Nopalitos con chile, por favor,*" Rachel said.

"*Para mí también,*" Noah added. "And a beer."

The small man nodded profusely and hurried away. Noah watched him disappear into the back. The other patrons turned partially away as well. Rachel did not blink. Instead, she put her hand on his.

"You still look upset," she said. "Don't worry. Today was just a minor setback."

"It was the only lead we had, Rachel. I have no idea where we're going to look now. We've come all this way, we've come so close. I can't believe it was all for nothing."

"It *wasn't* for nothing," she said. "We'll find him. You have to believe it."

"I don't know what I believe anymore."

"Believe this: we'll find him. We'll find him and we'll take him away from this place, from Sonia and whatever crazy thing she's mixed up in. We'll take him away to a new life back home with us, and soon he'll have a new brother or sister and all this will be like some horrible nightmare for us all, a nightmare that happened so long ago it will soon fade to nothing. We can have that, Noah. You just have to believe."

Maybe it was the heat, or the exhaustion, or the pain of missing Eli for so long, but Noah could not keep himself from crying. It was horrible, and he felt the eyes of so many in the room staring at him once more, staring as Rachel squeezed and rubbed his hand. Like a summer storm, it passed over him as quickly as it arrived, but he was left drenched, wiping his face with the cheap paper napkin that had been laid for them on the table.

"I'm sorry, Rachel. I really am. I've just felt so lost for so long."

"I know, babe. I know. Dry off, here comes our food."

The little man was still hurrying as he delivered their plates, less setting them down than throwing them. He then retreated and brought back a warm bottle of *cerveza*. Noah reached out for it, but the man did not let go. Instead he leaned closer.

"*Tú y la madre necesitan irse ahora mismo.*"

"I'm sorry. I—"

"*Es peligroso,*" he said, his voice a seething whisper, and it only took a mumbled cough from behind for him to let go of the beer instantly. It kicked back, some of it spilling onto Noah's hand, but the small man seemed to take on a completely different stance, looking at the rest of the room out of the corner of his eye.

"*Cuarenta y nueve pesos,*" he grunted, and left them alone as quickly as he could. They did not see him again.

Back at the hotel, Rachel insisted on standing outside their room in the warm night.

"It's amazing; I've never seen anything like it," Rachel said, staring up at the colors of ebbing dusk as her hands idled on her pregnancy. Noah followed her eyes skyward. In the dark that followed close the stars lit the sky like a thousand pricks of light. "The world is a lot different in these places. You forget what it's like when you spend your life a few feet away from electricity at the flick of a switch. Out here, you really get an idea of what it must have been like to be alive hundreds of years ago. The Spaniards came here and conquered, brought Christianity, but you can almost feel what it was like before that, back when the sky was filled with gods of fire. I can understand why people would come here to worship Ometéotlitztl and the rest. It's like a whole different way of being. I'm almost jealous."

Noah bristled, but tried to hide it. He had no interest in repeating their experience on the heath. "You have a way of looking at things, you know."

She took his arm and rested her head on his shoulder. "What do you mean?"

He shrugged, careful not to dislodge her.

"You see everything in a positive light. You look up and see a flood of stars. I look up and see the endless space around them. I wish I could be as positive as you."

"Oh, Noah," she said, her voice pulled into the vacuum of her disappointment. She didn't say anything else, but instead took his hand and stood there in the dark of the blistering night. He let go first.

"We should probably go inside. Father Manillo was right. You need to rest."

"Just stand with me for a little while. It will be good for you to stop moving—you've been running ragged since we left Sarnia."

"I can't. Not if I'm going to find Sonia and Eli before they disappear again. What if Father Manillo calls? He said he would."

"If he calls, you'll be able to hear it. Right now, I need you, Noah. We *both* need you."

"I know that," he said. "But what am I supposed to do? Forget Eli? Let Sonia *have* him? I know that would be easier, but I can't. This is my *son* we're talking about. I can't let myself forget."

Rachel started to say something, then stopped. She pulled him close and kissed him on the cheek, then brusquely pulled her shawl around her shoulders. "Go on in," she said. "I'll be there in a minute."

He hesitated. "Are you sure? You're going to stay out here *alone?*"

"You don't have to worry," she said. Had her tone changed, or did Noah simply imagine it? "I'm sure I'll be safe out here for a few minutes."

Noah opened his mouth to speak, but behind him he heard a sharp trilling from somewhere inside, and his heart skipped. With hands wet and body shaking he turned and looked at Rachel. She had turned too, but her expression was inscrutable.

"Well, what are you waiting for? Go on. I'll be inside in a minute."

He was already in the door when he realized she'd said something else, something like "I love you."

Noah picked up the phone, but no one responded to his greeting. There was a wheezing sound. A snuffling. Garbled and metallic as though the line had been degraded. Noah started to get worried.

He looked at Rachel through the window, her back to him, shawl pulled tight. "Hello?"

There was some more scratching, then, "Noah? This is Father Manillo. I had an idea."

Noah's blood raced.

"About where to find my son?"

"Yes. Of course. Villages like Astilla de la Cruz, farming villages in the depths of Mexico, are filled with children who must work the land with their fathers all day, or must scavenge the streets at night to scrape together what little they can to help their families survive. But there are some, especially those belonging to the more wealthy or foreign, who still must be educated. So a tiny school was erected a few years ago for them. There they can learn, but so few attend, or can attend often during the farming season, that it is only in session a few days a week.

"I'm not certain," the priest continued, "but I believe there is class tomorrow. Perhaps your Eli is there? If your past wife is how you say, she might want him in school."

Rachel entered the room and closed the door behind her. She did not look at Noah, even though it was clear she knew he was watching. Instead, she brushed past him and lay down on their bed. With some effort she turned onto her side, her back twisted toward him.

"Thank you, Father. How do I get there?"

3. Back to School

Rachel had managed to drift off while Noah was on the telephone with Father Manillo, gathering details about the nameless school's location. She lay still, chest slowly rising and sinking, shirt ridden up to expose her swollen pregnancy. Noah lay down beside her but could not bear to put his arm around her. The room was a furnace, and the last thing he wanted was for her body's heat to compound his own. He rolled over and tried to sleep.

He'd been warned repeatedly that the odds of finding Sonia, of finding Eli, were virtually zero, yet he could not stop himself from holding out hope. It buzzed through his head, his hands, his feet, and each remained in motion as he twisted and turned through the night. Eventually it was simpler to give up, get out of bed. Frustrated, tired, and angry, he creeped to the window and sat in the dull moonlight. There, he studied the unfolded article he'd carried all the way from Sarnia, looking for some overlooked clue about where his son might be. Even that proved more than he could bear in the lingering heat, so he simply gazed out the window at the field of stars and waited for the daylight to arrive.

The broken spire was the first thing that came into view as the red morning sun crested the clay roofs. The air already smelled of frying corn, rich and bittersweet. The light of the rising sun burned Noah's face, a giant ball of fire that seemed to hang a few feet away, not a hundred million miles. He watched it rise in starts, as though lifted on the shoulders of some great giant or dragged upward by a team of animals. As it ascended, it lit the sky further, and the silhouette of the hanging cross transformed into the cross itself, casting its long shadow over the poor village below.

Finding the school proved to be more challenging than Noah had anticipated. What should have been a walk of a few minutes was instead an hour-long odyssey without any clear sign where he and Rachel were headed. He had written down Father Manillo's instructions carefully, but the streets of Astilla de la Cruz did not obey his crudely drawn map. In places, it was difficult to tell where roads ended or began, and at one point he was certain houses had simply been erected without consideration of anything beyond the whim of the builder. Each place was more rundown than the last, dirt yards filled with old and broken toys that were as untouched and abandoned as everything else they passed. If not for the occasional movement of curtains, or sound of someone scrambling unseen, Noah would have suspected he and Rachel had been just as forgotten.

Noah stopped and looked back for the broken cross to orient himself. It was a dark spike in the eye of the sun, and no matter where he and Rachel went, its position never seemed to change.

"Maybe we should ask someone where this school is," Rachel suggested. Underneath her wide-brimmed hat her face was slick with sweat.

"Who are we going to ask? Do you see anybody around?"

"Let me see those directions again. Maybe we took a wrong turn."

He handed them over reluctantly. Rachel studied them.

"I haven't seen any of these street names. Are you sure these are right?"

"I haven't a clue. I was hoping once we were close enough we could figure things out by looking at the signs. I didn't count on there not being any."

"Do you know how to get us back at least?"

Noah paused, unsure how to phrase the answer, but his silence was answer enough for Rachel.

"So we're completely lost. Great. You *do* know I'm carrying a baby, don't you?"

"Obviously."

"Do you know my back is killing me as well? What happens if I need to sit down? Should I do it right here in the street?"

"We'll figure it out."

"Oh, like we figured out where the school was?"

He tried not to look at her. He would only get angry if he looked at her. How could she be so selfish when Eli was out there, somewhere?

"It can't be far. We've almost reached the edge of the village."

"I hope you're right. I don't know how much longer I can keep going. Remember what Dr. Mielke told us."

What she'd told them was that Rachel should stay home, something she flagrantly disobeyed. But Noah managed to bite his tongue before saying it.

He was sorely tempted to knock on a door, any door, and ask for directions. The sun was no longer inching its way into the sky but climbing swiftly, and every moment that passed intensified its heat. And yet, he couldn't bring himself to ask for help. The houses looked too rundown, too hopeless, and he needed all the hope he could muster. Eli needed it. Even Rachel needed it. But Noah didn't know if he had enough left to go around.

"Wait," Rachel said, so quietly Noah wondered if she spoke.

"What is it?"

She shushed him. "Listen, do you hear it? I think it's music. Like a flute or something."

She cocked her head and listened; Noah remained motionless. The blazing heat on his skull, the slow thumping of his heart, deafened him, but he strained to listen for the sound she heard. He wondered if it was merely wishful thinking, an auditory hallucination charged simply by her desire, and had almost given up when he finally heard it: The trilling of the sort of pipe he hadn't heard since he was a child.

"I think you're right."

A wave of relief crested, washing over him. Rachel smiled. "Someone up there must like you."

"I guess so. Come on, I think it's this way."

The sound of music had long since stopped, but that did not prevent Noah and Rachel from finding their way to the unnamed school Father Manillo had mentioned.

"Let's hurry," Noah said. "If Sonia's left him it won't be for long, and I'd like to be far away from here before she realizes Eli is missing."

The school was tiny; hardly larger than the rundown houses they'd passed, with an exterior so baked by the sun it had become porous and brittle. Running his fingers along the wall, Noah's hand came away coated with brick and dust. The remnants of childhood lay in pieces around the school's periphery—boxes drawn in chalk on the pavement, a crumbling rubber ball on the sparse, well-trodden grass. Rachel, putting her sunglasses atop her head so the tiny black arms held the chestnut hair off her face, rattled the locked door.

"This is where Eli is supposed to be? The place looks like it should be condemned."

She bent and inspected the sorry collection of desiccated flowers in the garden outside the door. The plants were merely husks, untended for far too long, and they surrounded a clay figure that looked crafted by a child's hands. The unclassifiable thing was painted pink, a colored ribbon around its neck, and had what looked like four limbs. "Look at its eyes," Rachel said, huffing as she picked it up for inspection. "They don't even seem to be looking in the same direction." She dropped the figurine, and its weight buried it headfirst in the ground. Rachel wiped her hands on her pants with disgust.

"I don't understand it," Noah said, looking through the windows at the empty classroom. "Father Manillo said they'd be here—all of them, all the children."

"Maybe he got the days wrong?"

"No, no." An overwhelming wave of disappointment swept Noah. "He was so *sure* . . ."

A noise caught his attention. He looked at Rachel for confirmation she'd heard it too, then scanned the area. There was no one in sight, yet he distinctly heard the sound of someone crying.

"Do you think—" Rachel whispered. "At the back?"

The two of them walked slowly around the side of the school, Noah in front with Rachel close behind. The sun made everything too bright, and even through squinted eyes Noah wasn't sure the shadow beside the empty playground was truly a person until it stood and looked back at them. Noah froze, motioned for Rachel to do the same, and he simply waited to see what would happen.

The shadow bolted.

"Hey!" Noah shouted, and gave chase. "Hey, come here a minute! I want to talk to you. *Por favor!*" He sensed Rachel following close behind, but as Noah's legs moved faster the distance between him and his girlfriend grew wider. When Rachel cried out his name, he was already more than a hundred feet away before he looked back and saw her doubled over. He rushed back to find her with her hands on her belly, her face contorted. His fear left him physically ill.

"Are you okay? What's wrong?" His sentences were clipped, his attention distracted by the fleeing shadow. But when he looked up, he was startled to find the shadow too had stopped and was watching them from a distance.

Rachel breathed heavily in tight, controlled breaths.

"I'll be okay," she panted. "I think I'll be okay. Go on. Go find Eli."

He looked at her and she nodded, then winced again.

"No, I'll stay," he said, hoping to any god that would listen that she couldn't see his disappointment. "I'll stay."

"Noah—"

"It's fine. I want to make sure you're all right."

"No. I mean, look."

Noah turned and saw that the person he had been chasing was no longer standing still, observing, but instead was walking back toward them. Noah stood and squinted for a better look.

"Are you okay if I leave for a minute?"

"What does he want?"

"I'm going to find out."

Noah walked toward the figure as it advanced forward. The stranger was speaking loudly in order to be heard, his arms flailing animatedly, but Noah did not understand the jumbled hybrid of Spanish and English. The man was about a foot shorter than Noah, thin with a head that seemed slightly larger than the body it was on. He had a wide, uneven mustache, though Noah wasn't sure if it was only because that was the only facial hair that would grow. The stranger sounded terrified, screaming "*¡Fuego!*" before making the sign of the cross across his chest and kissing his fingers.

"Calm down, I'm not going to hurt you." Noah held his hands up to show he wasn't a threat.

"The woman, she's hurt?" The man breathed heavily, his face red and swollen from crying. Noah shook his head.

"She's fine. We're looking for the children. For a boy." He reached into his pocket and the man flinched.

"It's okay. I'm just going to take a picture out of my pocket, okay? I'm not going to hurt you."

The man hesitated, then nodded.

Noah took the creased article from his pocket and held it out unfolded. The man cautiously leaned forward, watching Noah more than the photo, and when Noah didn't move the man glanced quickly at it. Then, for longer.

"*Si.* I know this boy. Elias."

Noah's heart stopped beating.

"What do you mean? Where's Eli? Where's my son?"

"The *madre?*" he said, pointing at Rachel. "Is she Tletliztlii?"

"What? No. Not at all. She's my girlfriend."

"Good. We must get her inside before the sun gets stronger."

They lifted Rachel and brought her inside the classroom. It was small, covered in paints. It took a few minutes for Noah's eyes to adjust to the lower light, and the first thing that came into view was a purple papier-mâché elephant that stared at them from its perch on a desk. The man kept casting nervous sidelong glances at it while he poured Rachel a glass of water. She drank it quickly and without question, then thanked him.

Noah couldn't handle waiting any longer.

"Where is Eli? Where is my son?"

The man shook, crossed himself again, and kissed his fingers before taking the folded article from Noah's hand.

"This is your *hijo?*"

"Yes. My boy, Eli."

The small man removed one of the children's paintings from the wall of the classroom and gave it to Noah. The colors were wrong, sky yellow and ground black, but it was a self-portrait of a boy, standing with a pink, green-faced animal at his side.

"This painting? This is your boy."

Noah took a second look, mesmerized by the thick-painted features. Could he tell, just by looking at the poorly constructed face, that it was his son? Was there any resemblance between that twisted figure and the boy he'd spent so long searching for? He couldn't take his eyes off of it, the first artifact of his son's existence he'd held in years. He lifted it to his face and inhaled deeply, trying to recover some sense of the boy. When he pulled the cheap paper away, he could barely speak.

"Where can I find him?"

"I don't know. Sometimes the Tletliztlii—" He swallowed, then looked out the window of the classroom. Noah glanced, but there was nothing there. Only the sun burning in the sky. "The children, they were here. Your son, too. Then today, no children. But I find that." He pointed toward the piñata on his desk, then crossed himself. *"Eso es todo lo que queda de los niños."*

"What do you mean?"

"They are gone."

Noah slumped down into one of the tiny desks, unable to keep his balance any longer. Knees up to his chest, he couldn't help but laugh, the rasps swirling in his chest before erupting volcanically from between his teeth.

"My name is Señor Alfred Muñoz. I am one of the teachers here, but I am also the caretaker. The rest, they come only when they are needed. Classes for the babies on some days, classes for the older children on other days. Between, I must make sure the school is ready. But now, maybe I'm losing my job. Today, I'm supposed to have the children, but they do not come. Maybe never again."

Noah looked around the room, needing to occupy himself to keep his heart from breaking. The walls of the classroom were covered in drawings scribbled by tiny hands, pasted upon a larger mural that swept everything else up in it—chalkboard, windows, the door. It was a row of children, their heads wider than tall, features pinched but gleeful. Each was a different color, and they danced as though floating, all in line following behind a tall musician in some sort of parade. The musician's face beamed like the sun as he blew notes out into the air, the string of them carrying across two walls. The line of happy children behind, all no more than four years old. Suddenly, Eli seemed so far away. Impossibly distant and irretrievable.

"Where would the Tletliztlii take them?" Rachel asked.

"Nobody will say. People, they are afraid of the gods, even if they don't believe in them. They are afraid of what will happen."

Noah banged his hand on the small desk.

"You have to have some idea. My son—he was stolen! I haven't seen him in years. I don't even know if he's still alive."

Rachel looked at him after his outburst in that way he hated. With well-meaning pity.

"We'll find him, Noah. Don't worry. If they'd left the village I bet Father Manillo would have known it. They're still here, somewhere. We'll find Eli somehow."

"How can you be so sure? Even I can't be sure. His own teacher can't be sure."

"I just know, Noah."

"You *know?* What do you know?" Noah recognized, dimly, his frustration was misplaced, but the fire was too great; he could not stop himself. Tinder became a blaze, and he could not turn back. "We're not going to find him. We aren't going to find Eli or Sonia or anyone from the Tletliztlii. We're—"

"Excuse," said Muñoz, careful in his interruption. "You say Father *Manillo* is helping you?"

"Yes, Father Manillo."

Muñoz did not get a chance to speak. A horrible moan, like the creaking of a massive door on rusted hinges, interrupted him as it echoed thorough the empty schoolhouse. The sound rattled

Noah, who fell silent and cold and could not understand why—not until he saw Muñoz's terror-filled eyes bulging wide. They were locked on Rachel, and as Noah turned he could feel the passage of time slowly stretch itself out. The room expanded outward until it fell away from the edges of world altogether, and all the while the distance between him and Rachel shrank to near nothing. He saw the web of veins standing from the pallid skin of her sweating face; saw the wrinkles around her eyes, her mouth, as she grimaced in agony. Tears fell onto her rigid arms as she clutched at her belly, trying to claw her way in to stop whatever was happening. Noah swallowed, his brain dully wanting to reconcile the sight, and it wasn't until Muñoz finally stood and screamed that time's normal pace resumed.

"¡*Madre!*"

Noah rushed over and put his hand on Rachel's face. She was burning, and crying uncontrollably.

"My God, Rachel. What's wrong?"

She shook her head without speaking, and Muñoz covered his own again, muttering under his breath. Noah grabbed hold of the small man so tightly he thought his fingers would puncture skin.

"Call a doctor! Do something!" he said.

Muñoz's eyes were stuck as wide as they could go, but he still managed to whisper a question.

"The name. What is the name?"

Noah didn't understand.

"Her what? Her name—her name is Rachel. What—"

"No, no. What is the *nobre del bebé*? The baby. The baby has to have a name."

"We haven't—we—what does that have to do with anything?"

"Noah," Rachel managed, her voice strained. "Help me."

Muñoz shook his head, pulling away. "*El bebé necesita un nombre.*" But Noah would not let him go. Instead, he squeezed the teacher's arms harder.

"Why do you want to know the name?"

"Noah, I need a hospital."

"Cuando la madre de gran Ometéotlitztl's estaba embarazada con su hermano, ella no le dio nombre al bebé y los dioses estaban tan enojados que le forzaron que lo abortara."

"I don't understand!"

"Help me," Rachel cried. Noah looked down at her, his daze clearing. Panic setting in.

"¡El sin nombre se quema! ¡Un lumbre que nunca se apaga!"

He slapped Muñoz hard across the face. Muñoz stumbled.

"We need to see a doctor *now*," he said, and picked Rachel up. Muñoz nodded.

"Yes, your wife. We need to help your wife."

"We aren't married," Noah muttered. It was all he could think to say.

4. The Truth Will Out

The only doctor in the village lived ten minutes away, but it could have been ten hours and the journey would have been no easier. The men carried Rachel as quickly as they could, and Noah did his best to calm her despite her delirium, while Muñoz guided them through deserted streets toward a tiny nested house.

"We're almost there," Noah said, but Rachel did not seem interested in being comforted. Instead, she continued to emit a high-pitched whine that steadily increased in volume. Part of Noah expected locked doors to swing open and shut windows to fly up, but as they passed rows of houses in the warm night nothing moved. They were more alone than they'd ever been.

The men burst through the door of the doctor's house with Rachel in their arms and called out for help. A short, dark nurse with deep-set eyes and a harelip from an ancient scar appeared and looked directly into Rachel's eyes, then at her swollen belly, then directed the two men to place her into a worn wheelchair. Noah asked if he needed to sign anything, but the nurse did not respond. Instead, she wrapped her stubby fingers around the handles of the wheelchair and pushed it forward, not waiting as Rachel weakly reached out. Before she could speak, Rachel was pushed clear of the front room.

"What are we supposed to do now?" Noah asked, eyes plastered to the door swinging unceremoniously shut.

"Now, we sit," Muñoz said. "And we wait."

Until then Noah hadn't noticed his surroundings. The stress and adrenaline had narrowed his attention until he was blind to anything not directly in front of him. With Rachel taken, that adrenaline wore away, leaving behind a cold shiver in his limbs he couldn't shake.

The front waiting room was the filthiest place he had seen since arriving in Mexico. The floor was made of press-on linoleum tiles loose from the sweat of summer heat, some missing, some cracked beyond repair. In the corner sat a small box of toys—a duck, some plastic cars—that Noah got the impression were not often played with. There seemed to be no sign of children ever having been there, which seemed appropriate, considering how oppressive the room was. But despite the small size of the room, Noah hadn't immediately noticed that he and Muñoz were not alone. There was a lonesome couple seated in the corner, their faces long and sagging, their eyes dead. They did not glance at Noah or Muñoz. They did nothing much at all except cradle a pair of twin papier-mâché dogs in their arms. At least, Noah supposed they were dogs. Bright, multicolored dogs; fat and malformed and without eyes.

"Why do they have those here?" Noah whispered.

"Here it is customary for the birth of a child. It's a *regalo*. A gift. Our people, they are too poor to afford to give anything they cannot make."

Noah nodded. They sat quietly, listening to the erratic tick of the old clock on the laminate wall, and to the sound of the couple's heavy breathing as they stared at nothing and waited. Noah was in no condition to handle the silence.

"Thank you," he whispered again. "You don't need to stay here."

"It's not trouble. I have no children. No one who needs me more. Without the Tletliztlii to teach, I—"

He caught himself, and lowered his head.

"I am sorry. Your *hijo*—your Eli—I forgot."

Noah swallowed. "It's okay. I'll find him."

Muñoz nodded.

Noah waited on word about Rachel in silence for almost two hours, but the nurse never returned. No one else entered the office either, and the long-faced couple across the room were barely more than statues, staring up at a buzzing clock, holding their plaster gifts. Noah looked to Muñoz, who sat still, eyelids closed, and Noah wondered where the teacher had taken them. A nervous itch crept across his jittering legs. Where had the nurse taken Rachel so quickly? Noah stood, started pacing, desperate to dispel his growing unease. First Eli, now Rachel—was he doomed to have parts of who he was forever disappear, plucked from his life one at a time, until he was nothing more than a set of bleached bones? Even the article in his pocket, unfolded and folded so many times, was beginning to wear.

Muñoz opened his eyes.

"You must stop moving. It is not good for you."

"I have to do something. I'll go crazy if I don't."

"You will be crazier if you do. They will come and tell us about Rachel soon. Dr. Nunio is very old, but very good."

"If he's so good, where is everybody?"

Muñoz shrugged.

"Maybe they are working. Even the poor must work, especially in Astilla de la Cruz. There is always much to do before the season ends."

"But there's no one else sick at all?"

"Maybe the people pray," he shrugged. "Maybe that is enough." Noah didn't believe it.

"The church wasn't any busier yesterday. If it was, you'd think they'd be able to fix up the place. The steeple at least needs work."

Noah stopped twitching at the sight of Muñoz. The teacher did not look well.

"What's wrong?" he asked.

"That is no church. *Manillo, él es el mal.*" Muñoz spat on the ground. Noah tried not to recoil.

"But we met Father Manillo yesterday and—"

Muñoz spat again.

"The man makes lies. Lies and half-truths. Do not listen! *El anda con el Tletliztlii y*—"

"Wait. 'The Tletliztlii'? Does he know them? He told us—he told me and Rachel that . . . He knew where they were *the whole time*? Why didn't you tell me before?"

Noah paced the room faster, hands running through hair.

"I have to do something. I can't just—I mean, I have to go. I— I have to find Eli."

"But your girlfriend," Muñoz said, eyes darting back and forth, jaw trembling to speak.

Noah had no idea if Rachel was okay. But his son needed him. His kidnapped son. How could he know what to do? No matter what his choice, he might never forgive himself. But he had to choose.

"I can't leave him there. I can't let him slip through my fingers."

Muñoz nodded solemnly and stood.

"Then I will take you. You cannot go there alone."

As he spoke, the wooden door of the waiting room opened. The small nurse entered, her stony, harelipped face long and craggy.

"*Ya puedes verla.*" Her voice was like gravel, slightly sibilant.

"What?"

"*Tu esposa. Ya puedes verla ahora. Ella está preguntando por ti.*"

"She says it's okay to see your wife now. She is calling for you."

"I told you she's not—I can go see her?"

The nurse nodded, her tired eyes already bored.

"But—"

"Go, señor. I will wait out here. I do not think the Tletliztlii will go anywhere at the moment. Unless they find out you are here . . ." He trailed off, looking at the silent couple in the room with them. They seemed oblivious to Muñoz's attention, yet Noah felt everything slipping as he was drawn further apart by opposite poles and did not know which direction he desired more.

"*Señor?*" The nurse, impatient.

"Okay. Let's go."

It took too long for Rachel's room to appear at the end of the unfinished hallway, but when it did Noah was startled. There was little equipment, and what was there appeared far too old. Light slipped past the blind slats and bisected the room, creating a staggered line across the unfinished floor. On the opposite side of the divide were a pair of single beds, but only one was occupied. Rachel sat up, her hands fidgeting absently with a small, colorful toy. It was clear from her flushed wet face she had been crying before he entered, and perhaps would continue afterward.

"They finally let you in," she said. "I was worried they wouldn't."

"I don't think they could have stopped me."

"The doctor's had a look, but he isn't worried." She sniffled, then tried to hide it behind the sleeve of her gown. "It's a bit of hysterical labor, probably caused by the stress of the trip, and maybe from some dehydration. I felt a lot better once I got some water in me."

"The baby?"

"The baby is fine, too."

"Good, good," he said, and checked the time on his watch. Rachel went quiet.

"Can't you stop looking at that thing for a second to see how I am?"

"I'm sorry. It's just that I have a lead on Eli. I think he—"

"You have a *lead*? Wait, were you going to *leave* me alone here?"

"You're safe. There's nothing wrong, is there?"

"It has nothing to do with if something's wrong or not. I'm in the hospital. Me. The woman you supposedly love. And the child I'm carrying."

"I'm here, aren't I?"

"Are you? I know you, Noah. I've been living with that look in your eyes for years. The last thing you want is to be here with me. Sometimes I wonder if you care about me and the baby at all."

"Don't be ridiculous."

She scoffed.

"Where are you going? To meet that bitch, Sonia? Do you think she's going to tell you anything?"

"She'd better."

"I love you, but you're fucking naive if you think it's going to be that easy. After everything she's done to keep you from Eli, you think she's just going to *give* him back to you? She has no intention of giving you anything. There's something *wrong* with that woman, Noah, something that scares me, and I don't want you going anywhere near her. Especially when I'm laid up in here with no idea what's going on. I *need* you, Noah. Your child needs you."

"Eli is my child, Rachel. He needs me too."

"I hate to tell you this, but he doesn't. He doesn't need you at all. He's got Sonia."

"You just told me you don't trust her. But you trust her enough to care for my child?"

Rachel was starting to cry again. Noah wanted to back off, but suddenly understood she had never wanted anything to do with

Eli, didn't even want him in her life, and she was using any weapon she could to turn Noah against his own son. The realization made him angrier than he thought possible.

"Eli is a part of me, Rachel, and nothing you say can make that different. He's my son, and he means more than the world to me. He means more to me than my own life."

"Does he mean more to you than me? Does he mean more to you than your *other* child? The one I'm carrying?"

"What are you talking about?"

"Answer me!"

"You want me to *choose?*"

"Yes, exactly. I want you to choose between your fucking crazy ex-wife and a child who has no idea who the fuck you are; and me, the woman who loves you, the woman who came down here on this crazy mission with you even though she is carrying your future child, one whom you'll know and grow close to and will love you forever. Choose, Noah. If you're half the man you believe you are, it should be easy. Choose."

Noah took a breath, but had no idea what words were going to come out of his mouth. The anger and resentment had built up to such intolerable levels they confounded him. The pressure in his head was building, struggling for release.

Who was she? Who was she to tell Noah that Eli was nothing? That he should be forgotten? Who was this woman? Not the demure girl he'd meet what seemed like only months before, the girl who once didn't know the meaning of the word "relationship." He had only been with her because her commitment to being noncommittal was so different from his that she seemed exciting, good for him. When had she become the yoke around his neck, telling him that he should no longer care about the only thing he'd ever cared about? Who was she? And who was the unborn child she said was his? Did it smile like Eli? Did it laugh like him? Was it as smart, as friendly, and perfect as his little son? It was nothing to him, nothing but a lump of flesh buried deep in a woman he didn't know, didn't recognize. She wanted him to choose between that and his perfect little boy? There was no choice. There had never been a choice.

Rachel's eyes narrowed as she glared at Noah. His skull filled with opaque fuses and felt as though it were burning. He touched his forehead; it was strangely cold.

"I have to go, Rachel. We'll talk about this later."

"Get the fuck out of here," she said, and threw the brightly colored toy at him. It bounced off his temple, catalyzing his anger before it smashed to the ground.

"With pleasure," he bellowed, then stormed out.

Muñoz was sitting in the waiting room, speaking quietly with the strange staring couple. It was clear by the look of guilt on his face that he'd heard part of the argument. Noah didn't stop. Full of burning embers, he stormed outside. Muñoz followed close behind.

"Is she okay?" Muñoz dared.

"You don't need to worry about it. Just get me to the church and to Sonia. Nothing else is going to come between me and Eli."

The sharp shadow of the steeple lay across the front of the church, cutting the path to its door like a giant razor. Noah had been anxious on the journey there from the doctor's office, still carrying his burning anger over what Rachel had said, and his nervous anticipation at seeing Eli again. He and Muñoz passed the rundown houses and saw few people outside. Most moved as if they were still asleep, staring off into space. On the stoop of a house, a woman sat surrounded by broken toys and the half-formed piñata she was building. Her hands were caked in pink plaster, and they covered her face as she wept uncontrollably.

Muñoz led Noah on without comment, along the dirt road to the towering church. Heat warped its height until the spire climbed forever into the sky. Out front, a shirtless man was working the arid ground, planting grass and flowers where it was clear nothing could grow. His back was tanned and broad, his muscles tight along his barrel chest, and it wasn't until the two men were almost upon him that Noah realized it was Father Manillo.

"You came back!" he said, his grin wide, lenses reflecting the sun into Noah's eyes. "Did you find everything you needed?"

Noah hesitated. "Almost."

"Good, good!" he said. Not once did he look at Muñoz.

"And your wife? How is she?"

"My girlfriend is fine," Noah said curtly. "But you know why I'm here, don't you?"

"*¿De verdad?*"

"My wife. My *ex*-wife. She's here, isn't she?"

Noah watched the priest's eyes, hoping the revelation would shake the man, but instead the older man dug his shovel into the ground and leaned on the handle. Then he laughed.

"What do you think is going on here? This is a place of God."

"I don't know about that, but I know you've been sheltering the Tletliztlii here. It's probably why we didn't find them up on the heath. Were they ever there?"

The priest laughed again, the sound as paternal as it was cold.

"Oh, they come and go. They come and go." Then his face grew still, the laugh lines fading back into tanned leather skin, and he grabbed Noah's arm and pulled. Noah tried to resist, but the sudden snatch had unbalanced him.

"You want to go inside, yes? I will not stop you—everyone is free to worship at Ometéotlitztl's altar—but no matter what you find you must respect the sanctity of the church. There is no anger among the Tletliztlii, only shared purpose. Do you accept?"

He held out his hand for Noah to take. Noah shook it, but his own hand felt inadequate inside Manillo's giant paw. When the priest let go, Noah wiped his fingers across his chest, trying to erase the feel of Manillo's sweat and calluses. Noah turned to Muñoz, but the teacher remained cautiously and infuriatingly mute.

Though its windows were pointed away from the sun and let

only indirect light inside, the interior of the church was an oven. There were more people in the pews, more people praying than ever before, many with plaster-covered hands, working on piñatas of various sizes and shapes; each was a colorful reminder of all the children Noah had not seen, had not held in so long. Each was a painful memory of what he had lost. He wondered about Rachel, about how she was, about whether what she'd said was true, but the thought was interrupted by the sight of the woman kneeling before the church's towering black altar.

Her auburn hair was pinned back, but wisps of it fell over her apple face. Lines had been carved where he had never seen them, and dressed in meager clothes she bore little resemblance to the woman he'd known. But the way she hung her head, the awkward turn of her nose, made it all too clear who she was. He would never forget her. Not the woman who had stolen his son from him.

"Sonia!"

Everyone stopped to look at him. A hundred eyes all staring. All eyes but two. Those remained transfixed on the altar.

"Sonia! Where is he? Where is Eli?"

The kneeling woman did not answer, did not turn. A shadow from the door spread across the room, and Noah saw Manillo standing there, filling the frame. The priest slowly wiped his hands on the cloth hanging from his belt. The church shrank to half its size. Muñoz stepped back, but Noah did not. He would not back down until he found Eli. He had come too far, travelled too long.

"Sonia! Where?"

The crowd became agitated as Noah's anger intensified. Manillo took a few steps forward, and Noah glared at him in warning. Manillo paused, but the smirk on his face was disconcerting. The shirtless old man looked more than capable of snapping Noah in two. Nevertheless, Noah carried on undeterred, his voice increasing in volume with every step he took toward his ex-wife.

"Sonia!"

She stood slowly as he stalked toward her, and her expression looked both irritated and bored.

"Hello, Noah."

He was momentarily startled. Her eyes—her eyes were bloodshot and circled with red, as though she'd been crying, but it was clear she hadn't. It had only been a few years, but the changes were immense. She'd been beaten by the sun until her face creased, and by something else that had bruised her across the side of her body.

"What are they doing to you here? Are they keeping you here? Are they keeping *Eli* here?"

"Of course not. Nobody's being 'kept' anywhere. I need you to calm down. I have to talk to you."

"Calm down? *Calm down?* You kidnap my son from me, take him to another country where you hide in case I come looking, and when after three years I find you, all you can tell me to do it 'calm down'? I ought to—" Flustered, the anger welled up inside of him, like a geyser of flame waiting to erupt. His muscles twitched; he was desperate to throttle her, but before he could act Manillo was there, chest glistening with sweat, jaw set with concrete. He stared into Noah's eyes until the younger man grudgingly backed down.

Noah sighed.

"I just want to know where Eli is, Sonia. I just want to take him home. He has no place here."

Sonia sat in an empty pew, pushing aside a crude elephant-shaped piñata, and looked down at her plastered and wrinkled hands. Noah felt a twinge of confusion, then he saw the flicker of a smile. It reignited his rage, but Manillo would not tolerate it.

"If you cannot control your emotions, Noah," he said, "I will have to control them. You are a guest under this roof. Act that way."

Noah did not care.

"I want Eli. I want to know where he is right now."

"He's fine. He's safe. Ask his teacher."

Noah looked at Muñoz, but the man would not lift his head to meet the gaze. He seemed smaller than before.

"You see, Noah," Manillo said, resting a burning hand on the back of Noah's neck that couldn't be shaken, "Eli's fine. You can calm down."

"Yes, calm down, Noah," Sonia said, a hint of mockery so slight Noah suspected only he could notice. "There's nothing wrong with Eli. He likes it down here."

"I don't care if he likes it or not. He shouldn't be here. You shouldn't have taken him. He doesn't belong to you."

"He's a boy, Noah; not a car. He doesn't belong to anyone."

"You know what I mean."

"Do I?" She glanced at Muñoz. "Haven't you even wondered why, Noah?"

"Why what? You took my son? No, I just want him back."

"You don't understand."

"Make me understand."

She looked at Manillo, who only nodded in response. Then the priest put his sweating hand on Noah's shoulder and glared at him. The message was clear.

"Muñoz," he barked at the shrinking teacher. *"Venga conmigo."*

The two men retreated, leaving Noah and his ex-wife alone. The rest of the spectators resumed their crafts.

Sonia's head was in her hands, the greasy wisps of hair falling over her unwashed arms. She did not seem capable of being awake, let alone taking care of their son.

"After we—after the divorce, I can't explain to you how lost I felt. I was doing what I could to keep up appearances, but inside I was broken. I think if I'm being fair, I was always broken; you just had the bad luck to come across me when I was hiding it better. There's always been something missing, some piece of me left empty, unfilled. I've always felt hollow, but I'd been that way for so long I thought that was how everybody felt. Do you feel that way, Noah? Do you feel hollow?"

"I can't say I do."

She looked up at him, her sunken eyes bloodshot and pleading. He'd never seen her like that before; it unnerved him. "Seriously. Think about it. Don't you feel like something is missing?"

"I do, Sonia. I've felt it ever since you took Eli from me."

She looked down again with what he hoped was a grimace, but might have been something worse.

"I had to take him. You won't understand."

"Probably not."

She stood and paced, rubbing her hands along the legs of her jeans. She moved back and forth between pews, fidgeting with one of the large papier-mâché creatures that were perched on them. She tenderly ran her fingers across the colored tissue paper.

"I needed something to fill the hole, Noah, and I found it, of all places, in the Coniston Public Library. Or at least in the newspapers there. It was a tiny article, no bigger than a column, and it laid out the plight of the Tletliztlii and their worship of Ometéotlitztl. Something about it spoke to me. Maybe because of the way they described the country, vast but lonesome, or maybe I just felt the need to fill the hole with experience. Anything to recharge my battery. By that point, there was nothing left for me anywhere."

"And some cult saying God was born from the other Mexican gods was the best place for you?"

"It's not a cult, Noah. And who told you about the child?"

"Your friend Father Manillo did. If he's even a priest."

"Oh, he is. But he didn't tell you the whole story.

"Even if I understood why you'd want to join a cult—"

"I told you: it's not a cult."

"*Even if* I understood why," he continued, "I don't understand why you'd want to steal Eli from me, too. Why did you have to take him? What good could have come from that, other than to hurt me?"

She put her hand on his, and though his skin instinctively curled away from her touch, he did not move.

"Noah," she said. "I didn't want to hurt you. Honestly, you didn't cross my mind at all."

Noah felt the baking heat multiplied tenfold across his skin, igniting the fire in his brain. He thought he might burst into flame. Manillo's warnings echoed in his clouded mind, the only thing keeping him from unleashing his fury. That, and the number of Tletliztlii around him and Sonia.

"There was something about the Tletliztlii that spoke to me as soon as I read about it. People from all walks of life came on a pilgrimage, all needing to fill the hole in their lives. Ometéotlitztl offered something nothing else did. Ometéotlitztl offered fire. But when I got here I realized it was much more than that. So much more. I don't know if I can explain it. I don't know how to make you understand what my sisters and brothers and I understand. I came down to Mexico an empty shell and found myself transformed by what filled me. I'm so much more than I once was. I like this feeling, Noah. I want to keep hold of it."

"What about Eli?"

"What about him? I've always felt a strange connection to him. Not like mother and child but something else. I can't explain it, and he's too young to do it for me, but Eli and I have a relationship that is built on different foundations. This is one of the things I realized while I waited for my life to begin again, and I wondered what that made me. Was I some sort of a monster?"

"You don't want me to answer that."

Sonia let go of his hand and paced again, lightly stroking the animal effigy. Noah watched closely for signs of the woman he'd once known, once been married to and shared a child with. But it wasn't her. It wasn't who he remembered. This woman, this person in the shape of Sonia, was a stranger, and he did not understand her. He could not predict her. She had his son hidden somewhere, and Noah knew then that Rachel was right: she would never tell him where.

"You can keep your crazy cult for all I care. I just want our son back."

"Noah, you don't understand anything. You've never understood anything. That's always been your problem. You move without thinking about what you're doing, about who you're hurting. You're like a blind bull, and I hate to tell you this but you can't always get what you want."

"Where is he?" He was becoming more agitated, his head spinning on his shoulders. "Where's that fucking Manillo gone?"

"Noah, stop it. Look at me."

"I want Eli. I need him and I'm not leaving without him. Nobody is kidnapping my son!"

"I told you: he's not kidnapped. Everything is fine. Eli needs to stay here with me. I need him more than you ever could."

But Noah was not listening. His fists clenched in rage, he screamed for Manillo to show his face. All the Tletliztlii were watching, and they started to laugh, and their laughter only further fueled his anger. He grabbed Sonia by the wrist hard so she could not struggle away and jerked her close. Her breath was fetid but barely registered through his bloody haze.

"You could *never* need him as much as I do. Take me to him now, or—"

"Or what? What are you going to do? Besides turn around and leave? Save yourself: Get the fuck out of here and take care of the *other* Eli you have on the way."

Noah stood and punched one of the misshapen piñatas with all his strength, breaking it in half.

"I don't want another Eli. I want mine!"

"You can't have him," she said. Laughing.

Noah's brain shut down, unable to comprehend what Sonia was saying, what she was doing, how far he had travelled only to be blocked by a wall of insanity. He heard the crying of children filling his mind, even though he knew their voices couldn't be real. But the cries only grew, intensified, bursting his skull amid Sonia's mocking laughter. He squeezed her wrist tighter, squeezed his eyes shut tighter still, trying to surface in the tidal wave of anger flooding over him. He was drowning in it, deaf and blind and dumb and full of hatred. He opened his eyes long enough to see Manillo had returned, and his enormous fist was travelling straight at Noah's face.

Noah remembered little after that. Just an endless series of fists and feet raining down on his crumpled body.

"Where's Eli?" he tried to spit out, but the blood in his mouth choked him, and he could barely emit a gurgling cough. "Oh, God," he cried, and Sonia laughed even harder.

"You stupid man. Don't you get it? There is no child of a hundred gods. He was aborted; never born. There is no God."

She then spat on him and kicked him hard in the face. He felt the clammy lithe arms of unconsciousness grab hold of him from the cold darkness below, and they pulled him close into her waiting bosom.

5. This Blasted Heath

Noah and Eli lay on the soft green grass, staring up at the clouds slowly moving across a picture-perfect sky.

"See that one? That's a horse, Eli. What sound do horsies make?"

Eli brayed, then laugh uproariously. Noah laughed too, the feeling of his son's body wriggling against him filling him with never-ending bliss. Noah couldn't remember how long they'd been lying there—it seemed like forever—but he never wanted it to end. Couldn't imagine the world any better.

"Are you two going to goof off in the grass all day?"

Noah rolled over and looked up at Rachel sitting on her

wooden chair. She wore a deep, knowing smile and had one hand over the edge of the crib beside her, the other wrapped around her full belly. She sat in the afternoon light, the nursery around her so bright he wondered if he should draw the blinds.

"We're seeing animals playing in the air!" Eli shouted, then cackled at his own antics. Rachel smiled too, then gently shushed him.

"You're going to wake the baby, Eli."

He laughed again.

"You don't want to do that, do you?"

Only laughter. Noah grabbed the boy around the waist and threw him into the air.

"Of course you don't. That's my favorite boy. That's my favorite Eli."

Then they both laughed, both rolled on the green grass, and Noah could smell it on them like the smell of summer, and knew that if he kept rolling nothing would ever change.

But there was a noise, the sound of a tree branch breaking. Noah put Eli down and looked at the beach but saw nothing out of the ordinary. Just Sonia walking along the shore, holding the hand of a small child he knew looked familiar, but could not place.

The park around them was crowded with people, all standing on the grass barefooted, all staring up at the sky. Some wore old clothes, worn away to almost nothing, while others were dressed in suits and evening dresses. All stared up at the clouds expectantly.

"They must be looking for the horsies too," Noah said, but when he turned he found Eli had vanished. Noah's smile faded. "Eli?" he called, looking for someone who might have his son. But no one would look at him. They each held a small child by the hands, all staring upward. Noah cast a glance too, long enough to see that the white clouds were moving past so swiftly he barely recognized their shapes.

"Eli, where are you?" he called out.

More people filled the beach, packed to its edges, some up to their knees in water, and when he called out Eli's name they gathered around him, all holding a small faceless child by the hands, cutting him off.

"Eli!" he screamed, squeezing his way through the mass of immovable bodies. Through gaps he saw Sonia in the distance, wispy auburn air fluttering as she led a small boy by the hand, a small curly-haired boy dressed in his favorite green cap and blue Oshkosh B'gosh overalls. Somewhere behind Noah was the sound of Rachel crying, the crackling sound of paper being crumpled, and a heat that blanketed everything, charring bodies and the ground to deep black ash. Noah was thrown forward by the wave, landing in the darkened nursery. Rachel had gone, the crib was empty, the shelves with nothing left. There was just a window, a large rectangle framing the blasted heath beyond. The sky was a deep blue, the air so clear he could make out every detail of the world beyond in excruciating detail. Insects creeping, rodents scurrying, grains of sand blowing though mounds of ash, and in the distance speeding toward him at an impossible rate was a column of black flame, stretching from the ground upward into oblivion. The dervish spun and spun, consuming everything in its path. And it was aiming straight toward the house Noah was hiding within. But where was Eli? A mewling sounded behind him, coming from the crib, and Noah felt the joy of relief. He turned around and put his hands into the crib, so full of shadows it was like putting his hands into a well of tar. He felt something squirm in his grip, resist him, but he struggled to get Eli free. A small body broke the surface, covered in paper and shaped like some amorphous, brightly colored animal. It mewed again, staring upward with painted-on eyes before catching fire and burning to cinders in Noah's quivering hands.

Noah's swollen eyelids did not part easily, and when they finally did he wished they hadn't. The fluorescent lights were harsh and they stung, and he turned his head from them to see where he was. Somehow he had made it back to the doctor's house, though he had no clear recollection of how or why. His half-memories were of manic and leering faces, all laughing at him. He tried to lift a hand, but it felt weighted down, and it wasn't until he gathered enough strength to move his head that he realized why. His arm, from elbow down, was wrapped with thick plaster and bandages.

The air was sour with sweat and ash, and his entire body felt overrun by a dull aching pain. He called for help, but his shriveled tongue prevented anything more than a choked grunt and cough. His chest exploded in pain.

Noah slowly pulled himself up to sit, resting every few inches to rediscover his equilibrium and to slow the shards of pain that sank more deeply with each jarring movement. He began to remember what happened and everything that had come before. He only felt sicker.

It took work, but he managed to get his legs over the side of the bed, and after a few minutes more to get to his feet. Every inch ached from his ordeal, but beyond the broken arm and his taped-up chest he seemed to be intact. His bloodied clothes were draped over an empty chair, and as slowly as he could he slipped into them. In the far corner of the room, hidden from sight until he was able to stand, was a crudely made piñata, left there by some previous patient. It looked up at him with its mismatched eyes, as though it judged him for all that had transpired. He had to find Rachel. He had lost Eli, probably forever, and couldn't face losing her as well.

His shuffling echoed in the short corridor. The nurse was nowhere to be found, but he dimly remembered which was Rachel's room and stumbled down the empty hall toward it, tears blurring his vision, heavy breathing making his ribs ache. He had nothing left without her, and as he found her room he starting apologizing before he even entered.

There was no trace of her, nor of their unborn child, just as she promised. The bed was made and the room straightened, and the odor of disinfectant still hung strong. Noah sat on the visitor's chair, exhausted, dumbfounded, staring at the empty bed. Beneath it he saw something the cleaners had missed, something small and colorful that had rolled under the bed after Rachel had ricocheted it off Noah's temple. He raised his good hand to his brow and could still feel the bruise. The pain felt good because it felt different, because it wasn't the pain that was going to tear him in two.

Astilla de la Cruz met Noah with creeping daylight and an unbearable heat that glued his clothes to his flesh. He felt vile and dizzy, and wondered if he had suffered a concussion in the assault. The broken church loomed like a vengeful spirit, and those few houses he saw along the street he hoped would lead him back to the hotel. Each window was dim, haloed by the wavering burning air, and as he slowly passed curtains were quickly drawn closed. Yet the rest of the houses seemed vacant, large paper creatures hanging from windows or sitting in the dirt outside the doors, dead eyes watching as no one walked by. The odor of something burning wafted through the air, a greasy smell not unlike grilled pork; it could have been coming from anywhere.

The bleeding had stopped, at least. He coughed, choking on the mucus that had flowed back from his nose before spitting it onto the dirt road. He felt so alone without Rachel beside him. Perhaps she was right: maybe he should never have gone after Eli. It had only made things worse. He'd waited so long to be with his son, sacrificed so much of himself, of his life, dreaming of the day they'd be reunited, that the realization he might never see the boy again was devastating. His body revolted at the thought, releasing in a flood all the unbearable emotion he'd pent up or plastered over. He dropped to his knees in the middle of the street and wept for the years of loss and hopelessness he could see laid out before him. Each hitch of his body brought a new throb of pain from his taped ribcage, but it barely registered through his grief. He'd lost everything he'd built of his new life, sacrificed on the altar of his old, and those arms he'd held wide for so long would never be filled, but neither would they ever close.

When he reached the hotel, he was a mess. Covered head to toe in dirty bandages, his clothes ripped and bloodied—had Señora Alvarez still been there, she would likely have called the police. But she wasn't there. No one was. No one but another gaudy piñata, silently watching him hobble.

With some awkwardness, he was able to retrieve his key and open the door to his hotel room. When he saw the empty hangers and missing suitcase he understood the futility of the hope he'd been harboring—Rachel had gone to Sarnia without him. What little remained of his strength dwindled, and he dropped onto the bed where springs stuck him as penance. From his pocket he removed the article he had been carrying with him so long and unfolded it. He stared at the blurry photograph of Sonia, of the heath, of everything he had tried and failed to rescue. Noah had come so far to find the piece of himself that was missing, and instead the rest of him fell apart, scattering those pieces far and wide with no hope of gluing them back together. He stared at the worn article and wondered why it should be any different, why it should be spared the same fate. He had done everything he could, and there was only one thing left unfinished. Noah took the article in both hands and tore it to shreds. He let the fragments rain down around him.

He hadn't noticed the sound at first, his head still ringing from despair, but as it cleared the scraping of burning wind against brick faded, uncovering the hush of a mumbling crowd moving through the blistering heat. Noah squinted out the window into the distance and saw flickering light dotting the gentle slope toward the blasted heath. That was where the entire town had gone, or at least those not cowering in their ramshackle homes.

They went to celebrate with Sonia and her cult of kidnappers. As if on cue, a streamer of yellow tissue paper drifted across the street, and he heard a woman's distant careless laughter.

The ground was not easy to cover by foot, even in the growing daylight, but Noah had no car, nor was Manillo's truck at the church when he passed. Dirt was hardened to rock, cracked with fissures that gaped like a series of ever-widening mouths, each hungry for him to step inside. Thirst came upon him slyly, and it wasn't until he had travelled far beyond the village's outskirts that he realized how dangerous a trek he had embarked upon. The sound of rattlesnakes thundered in Noah's ears so close he tensed for a strike. But his eyes did not deviate from where the ruins should be. He trailed the lights ahead of him as best he could, but they moved more quickly than his injured legs could manage, and the ground radiated heat like burning coal. It did not take long before he was left behind, alone under a baking sun that bore down on his unprotected body.

Had he not known where they were headed, Noah might have lost them forever, but he never questioned that the heath was their destination. Manillo had spoken so lovingly of the site that it could only have come from someone who knew it well. As well as any of the Tletliztlii, if not better. Noah wondered how long Manillo had been leading the movement, if he had always been one of them or had been turned from God once he arrived. The church had been desecrated by their cult worship, yet no one from the archdiocese had intervened. Or, at least, Noah hoped. The alternative—that the agents had been murdered to keep the Tletliztlii's secret—was one revelation too many for him. He knew he would have to tread carefully, far more so than he had previously.

He crept closer to the ruins, and as he did so he slowed, moving as quietly as his injuries allowed. He didn't know what he was going to encounter further up the increasing slope—there was virtually no noise on the heath except the crackle of flames and the howl of wind around the stone ruins. Noah crawled the last few feet to the brush that surrounded the site, wanting to keep from being spotted. He wiped the sweat from his eyes and lay still on his back, dehydrated, trying to preserve his energy and formulate a plan. From his hidden vantage point, he hoped to spot Eli once the Tletliztlii appeared and determine how best to liberate the boy from his captors. Rachel was wrong: There was no way Eli would be better off with Sonia, not while she was under the spell of that unholy cult. Noah had sworn a vow to protect his son at all costs, and would not fail again. No matter how much everything else in his life was falling apart, he would not fail again.

Noah lay still, listening for any sound that might give him an idea of what was happening. He knew he eventually had to look over the brush, if only to determine what might be waiting on the rocky heath, but he was terrified. If one of the Tletliztlii were to see him, the game would be up, and he doubted he could survive another beating. But he also knew he had no choice. Slowly he rolled onto his side, wincing as his weight rested on his broken ribs, and, getting his good hand underneath him to push upwards, he raised his head to peek over the brush. He meant to look only for an instant, but was unprepared for the bizarre spectacle that awaited him. Instead of ducking down, he simply stared, trying desperately to will the landscape to make sense.

Nothing of the heath's structure had changed, and yet when it finally came into view it was unmistakably altered. The ground was still baked, the brick surfaces cracked and brittle, and the petrified tree in the rent stone tableau at its center seemed no more or less insubstantial than ever, but instead of the bare rock that once surrounded the tree, Noah saw a series of small figurines left on the ridges of the altar openings, each staring back at the center of the heath. But what startled Noah most was what encircled the petrified tree and spiraled in a hazy pattern outward—a sight he would not have imagined was real had he not witnessed it. Around the tree, their sizes ranging up to a few feet wide, was an ever-tightening arc of piñatas. They stood, backs to him, all different shapes and sizes and colors. But they shared the same plastered appearance and the same lifeless eyes, and all were pointed toward the petrified tree that stood like a priest on a pulpit.

Eli had to be hidden somewhere close, but Noah saw no sign of him, no proof the boy was there at all. His heart sank, but he forced himself to ignore it. It was his own fear of failure trying to control him. Eli was there. He *had* to be. And yet the voice in his head remained. What proof did he have that Eli was in Astilla de la Cruz? A painting? The words of a teacher, a priest, and an ex-wife, all of whom had betrayed him? Noah had been driven on faith and nothing else, and that blinding faith had cost him Rachel and his unborn child. There was something else, though, that bothered him. Something not just about Eli, but about the children of Astilla de la Cruz as well. Had he seen sign of *any* of them since arriving at the village? He tried to recall, but his swimming head made it difficult to think. He ran through all the faces he could remember—Señora Alvarez, the waiter at the cantina, the station agent. Each was older than the last. He recalled the broken stroller, the crying women, the empty swings. All asking questions he didn't want to think about. How could they all be at the heath, hidden behind those stone ruins? He scratched his head and felt the blisters on his scalp. The world slowly rocked back and forth, and it took more concentration than he could muster to keep it all in focus under the blinding light of day.

Tiny squares of tissue paper wrapped the piñatas, and the sight of them fluttering in the waves of heat compounded the surreality of the situation, giving the plaster effigies the appearance of taking breath, but it was clear from Noah's perch that it was a trick of the light. Still, he could not shake the feeling something was wrong with them, something beyond their painted, dead-eyed stare, past that crooked tree they were facing. They were like sheep, row upon row of them, all black-eyed and still, making no noise beyond the rustle of colored paper. The sight evoked an ever-deepening dread in Noah. It silenced all sound on the blasted heath, stole so much noise from the air that Noah could not hear the sound of his own breathing. There was nothing but silence; it buzzed and burned inside his head so intensely he thought he might cry out. The only thing that stopped him was the sight of shadows moving at the entrance to the ruins.

At first, he mistook the distant thumping in his ears for the beating of his own heart, blood rushing faster as Noah stared at the scene wavering before him. Then that single muted sound intensified, came closer, and what once was background slid to the forefront of his consciousness. It was the sound of a hidden drum being beaten, old leather thwopping deep and hollow. It echoed in his head, vibrated the broken bones beneath his plaster cast, shook loose clots and stitches and ushered in near-unbearable pain. The drum was everywhere, crashing in on him, stretching the world outward from that blasted heath, from that petrified tree, from that circle of pseudo-idols, blurring it further until there was nothing left beneath the rising sun but the barren hell before him.

Noah stared, mesmerized by the radiating vision. It shimmered in the boiling sun, slowly losing cohesion, and the world slipped from one reality into another. The rocky heath took on a foreign aspect he did not recognize, some alien world of ancient creatures, clumsily moving through endless and boundless time. There was no heath, no rocky ground, but a vast barren plane that occupied numerous worlds simultaneously, one stepping-stone to many, a portal both spatial and temporal. It induced dizziness and nausea, compounded by the motion he detected in the distortion, shades of the past and future cohabiting a space that was and always would be dead deep below its surface. A place of endless nothing. He tried to wipe away the sweat that drenched his face, but his broken limb was leaden, anchored by its immovable weight.

The visions that played out before him seemed no more real than a dream. He watched hazily from between branches of the scrub, entranced by the vibration of the heath before him, the pulse of the earth, giant and consuming, fighting to maintain some hold on what he knew. He grit his teeth, struggling to ground himself in the present, and when that failed he used his own wounds against the vision, struck his arm against the ground until the razor-sharp pain focused him icily, righted the world, and threw closed doors that should never have been opened.

And in that clarity he saw what the visions had attempted to hide from him, what he was never meant to see. From between the branches of the scrub he witnessed the specter of his nightmares made flesh, loping across the baked rock. Father Manillo's bald pate was unmistakable, his thick barrel body obscured by the dried and cracked grey mud that coated his naked form. Bare feet moved in time with the ever-present drum, and Noah could not help but wonder if it was they that were the source of the excruciating noise.

Manillo, though, was only the first of the desecrated figures to appear. Close behind, an overweight and stocky man followed, his face obscured by a painted mask that revealed yellowed eyes sharp and narrow. The man's stomach protruded, blissfully hiding his member beneath rolls of stretched skin, but he used his girth to dance in a series of graceless jerks that never once drew Manillo's attention. And from behind the overweight man more figures emerged, men and women of all shapes and sizes, all naked and all chanting the hypnotic rhythm that throbbed from the ground, from that empty space beneath the petrified tree. Mud-smeared grey figures, cracked and dry, continued to dance forward, navigating through the crowd of vibrating plaster animals with reverent care, silently drawing life from what occurred before the rows of dead painted eyes.

The endless beating of the tired calloused feet continued, pounding out an appeasement to their half-dreamed Ometéotlitztl, and accompanying the sound were those faint notes of a pipe, reverberating off the stone walls, calling out with arms held wide. Their singing was like no song Noah had ever heard. The language was impenetrable—grunts and clicks as if Nature herself were in revolt, throwing off her suffocating yoke. Still more figures spilled forth from the ruins, multiplying in the burning height of day, each one solidifying into a grey, mud-covered mockery of humanity. But none were shaped like children. None were his Eli.

The discordant music elicited an orgiastic fury from the Tletliztlii, their cracked flesh drumming the world into submission. Every note, every image served to further dwindle Noah's rationality until he doubted the truth of what he witnessed. All his anchors were gone, abandoning him when he needed them most, leaving him to stare at events his sun-stroked mind could not fathom. Nothing on the heath could be trusted. Nothing on the heath could be real. There were familiar screams, but in the chaos of impossible events they retreated into moorless oblivion. A scattering of ashes, motes of dark dust, filled the air. Lifeless, shapeless piñatas vibrated, painted-on faces distorted by the blaze. Fire raged white and pure inside his skull, and yet Noah felt the cold fear of being trapped in an elaborate Goldbergian web of events. He sweated profusely as before his eyes the twisted figures danced harder, faster, and from within their multiplying childless numbers the terrified screaming resurfaced, demanding his flailing attention. It was a voice he knew frighteningly well.

Rachel was as naked as the mob that dragged her struggling from the ruins, her body covered in streaks of colored paint radiating from her swollen pregnancy, and they held her high above their heads. Noah opened his mouth wide, but nothing emerged, all sound lost somewhere inside his dried throat. He was trapped in an ever-worsening nightmare, far beyond his breaking point, and yet could do nothing but watch the woman he loved, the mother of his unborn child, as she was carried across the baked earth and placed onto that cloven altar the petrified tree loomed over. Noah stared impotently as Muñoz appeared, covered in the same cracked grey mud, and bound Rachel's hands over and over with thick loops of rope. The chanting of the others grew louder as Muñoz wrapped the rope between Rachel's arms and pulled so tight her hands slammed together. He then threw the other end over the worn branch of the petrified tree where other muddy hands waited to receive it, clamoring for a grip. Noah tried to will himself to stand, to scream for help, to do anything to disrupt the nightmare that was unfolding, but his paralysis held firm, the drone of the plaster creatures overpowering him. With a sudden jerk of the rope by the dancing Tletliztlii, Rachel was hoisted violently from the ground to hang from the branch of the tree, her mouth contorted in a drawn-out scream that Noah could not hear. Rachel's legs kicked and thrashed, her round belly thrust forward by the angle, and Noah wanted to call out to her with his every fiber, but his bruised and broken body would not comply. Even his tears dried before they emerged. He was held fast to the spot, rooted by ineffectuality and torment.

The village danced in chaotic ecstasy to the tribal rhythms and to Rachel's feeble kicking, while around them the rows of plaster piñatas continued to vibrate from the pounding of so many villagers shaking the rocky terrain. Noah felt it slipping up into his body as he lay powerlessly immobile. Each of those dead-eyed creatures stared at the proceedings, and in his sunbaked delirium Noah wished they would act, do what he could not and stop the horror. But though the piñatas shook, they took no action, not even when, from the depths of the crowd, a lone muddy figure appeared. She moved differently from the others, her limbs flailing as though in the throes of deep spasm, as though the stifling heat was consuming her from within. From beneath the tangles of mud-caked auburn hair her face flashed, revealing a darkly painted countenance blacker than was possible. And yet, within that empty void two bright eyes burned; he did not have to see them to know their owner. His battered body bucked with the strange sensation running its length, crawling into his pelvis, shrinking him in terror. "No," he rasped as Sonia's darting hand grabbed hold of Rachel's face and smeared the colored paint into chaos, her fingers leaving wet black streaks in their wake. Then Sonia stretched her head back and screamed a word into the black night, a word that echoed across the heath, a word that seemed to fracture the very air. It was a word so large Noah's mind could not comprehend it. Tears finally erupted from his eyes as though to cleanse them of the unholy blasphemies they had witnessed, but did nothing more than streak his dusty face. Sonia raised her arms toward the orb burning above and for an instant it went dark, became its antithesis, a solid ball of pure emptiness, of burning space and countless overlapping aeons. The sun burned bright, burned black, and the sound itself was like thunder rolling across the heavens. Then a glint from Sonia's upheld hands filled the sky, bursting through walls and shores like an exploding sun, and from that flash her arms emerged, swinging down in a purposed arc, one hand over the other, so swiftly Noah did not know where they had gone until Rachel's swollen belly burst open, blood and flesh spraying, the grue of his unborn child tumbling forth soundlessly to die on the heat of the ancient pedestal.

Noah found his voice then, but it was too late. And had been before he and Rachel and their unborn child arrived in Astilla de la Cruz. Before Eli had been taken, before Sonia saw any articles. The series stretched back further, each piece, each cog, tumbling in time, lined up one before the other. So far back, there was no beginning, simply causality stretching back into something else, something so distant that were Noah to scream forever the sound of the last dregs of his sanity would never reach it. Instead, they would spew into the aether until his body was burned clean through. But even the sound of his shattered sanity was eclipsed by what followed.

The rock of the blasted heath raised a foot beneath Rachel's lifeless swinging legs, a jump that shifted the earth beneath so many. The villagers stopped, the drumming ceased, and all were mesmerized by the stained altar. Even Noah, to whom words and noise had recently returned, stared dumbly at the wet mass covering the stone, at what remained of his unborn child and at the petrified tree growing impossibly from rock. The sense in the air dragged down on the world, blanketed everything in oppressive dread, and the group of villagers and their offering of piñatas could do nothing but watch as the distant thunder grew louder. And louder. And louder still. Then, with no warning, a deafening crack. As loud as the world at its end. Everything shook, the Tletliztlii stumbling over themselves in confusion, some dropping to their hands and knees as everything became unstable. The altar fell to thousands of pieces, Noah's unborn child consumed instantly by the fissure that grew down the middle of the heath, wrenching the earth apart with a horrible sound. The petrified tree tottered, its weight too much for the crumbling, receding earth, and it too fell forward into the widening chasm, the remnants of Rachel's empty body tumbling alongside. The Tletliztlii stumbled over one another as stable ground collapsed, some swallowed into its depths without a sound.

The rows of piñatas danced on the vibrations, their twisted faces smirking at the destruction. Sonia staggered across the baked uneven ground, screaming incoherently at the sky, covered in Rachel's blood. Her eyes were wide, crazed, confused by the chaos around her. Other Tletliztlii bumped into her in their mad scramble to escape, but one by one the collapsing ground took them—took Muñoz and Manillo and all the rest—until only Sonia remained. Sonia, and those endless rows of misshapen piñatas. She looked around, desperate for help, but no one was there. No one but Noah, who remained hidden. She stumbled, looking for somewhere safe she could step, and as her eyes scanned the crumbling landscape he froze, convinced she had spotted him in the midst of the brush staring at her. If their eyes locked, it was only for the fraction of a second before the ground beneath her feet wrenched open and swallowed her whole.

Noah's head continued to swim, faster and faster. Had what he witnessed been real, or had the horror and the heat finally broken him, filling his sight with the impossible? The rocky ground could not be yawning wide, swallowing chunks of the barren heath into its endless void. The ruins could not be crumbling, not after so many years of standing, crushing anything that still remained—everything but those piñatas. Those plaster abominations that shook and rattled but did not fall, not one of them into the ever-widening crack into the center of the world. Instead, they served as silent, multicolored witnesses to what Noah had to endure. He wondered how any of it was possible, any of the death and destruction that lay before him on the thundering ground, and for the briefest instant he felt hope. Perhaps he *was* mad. Perhaps nothing was real, and Rachel and Eli were somewhere else, somewhere far away from the boiling destruction, from the ground bubbling up, throwing rocks outward. Perhaps they were on that beach, relaxing and looking at the animals in the soft clouds. Noah looked up and saw nothing in the sky but a sole burning orb in endless blankness; the only animals left on the ground twisted, ugly and dead inside.

Noah's entire body was racked with pain, but as rocks rained down around him he knew he had to escape. He slid his legs to the side, then under him, enough to push himself back up. Exploding lights filled his eyes as he felt the knives of his bones slicing into his insides, but he managed to stand on a pair of unsteady legs. Stand and survey the end of everything before him.

The plaster effigies were vibrating so quickly on the quaking earth that they appeared as blurs, so insubstantial as no longer to be part of the world. Like ghosts, they hovered over the broken ground, and the sound they made was a strange-pitched and deafening howl. Deep black cracks formed across the piñatas, widening and deepening before Noah's disbelieving eyes, and from those long black cracks dark ichor flowed. It bubbled out, slow and viscous, but instead of falling to the rutted ground it moved unnaturally upward, up and across the plaster backs of the faux animals, and Noah realized it was not blood or liquid that he saw but fire. The piñatas were burning. But the flames were as black as night. They grew higher, burning clean everything they touched, destroying any life that still remained on that rocky barren heath. The brush that surrounded it lit as well, Noah's hiding spot quickly becoming an inferno, further obscuring his vision.

The flames grew higher, enveloping the entire heath, and in the center of it the deep chasm that had swallowed so many spewed something back to the above world, the world of living. It was small, the size of an orange, burnt black and still afire. The flames, those black burning flames, had destroyed everything to bring it life, and as the cold fire grew so did it. First it doubled its size, then doubled again, growing exponentially before Noah's fracturing psyche. It grew and metamorphosed as the black fire that enveloped it burned—arms that became a pair of writhing serpents, an encephalitic head perched precariously on sloped shoulders. Along its newly formed ebony back, curved spines jutted in odd patterns, each alight with burning phosphorescence. But its eyes were the most horrifying of all. Deep pits of nothing, they scoured the blasted heath that was its nursery, blind to all the horrors that had transgressed, and as that giant misshapen skull panned toward Noah those two deep wastes stayed. Though the fire burned unfettered, uncontrolled, Noah's being became ice and he averted his gaze in pain.

There was a wrenching sound then, and the thing bellowed an indescribable noise that echoed across the empty wasteland. It lifted one of its many bent legs out from deep within the earth—a pillar of black fire that filled the sky with the dark storm of night, a storm that lasted forever—and stepped over its father below and into the blistering day. Each footfall struck the ground with the force of the heavens, the first laying waste to the circle of piñatas that had acted as its host. Small bones spilled forth, some very old and some very fresh, many generations of bones all kept, all hoarded for one particular day, one particular set of events, bones no bigger than a child's. Seeds for the rebirth of an aborted god brought forth to reclaim the future it had lost. And to deliver unto all everything it had promised.

But Noah would know none of it, trapped as he was in the prison of his broken mind. Eli was there, smiling, laughing, dancing in circles around the edges of the world while Noah desperately tried to catch him before the boy was lost forever.

Acknowledgments

My deepest thanks to Laird Barron, Richard Gavin, Ives Hovanessian, Stephen Jones, S. T. Joshi, Michael Kelly, John Langan, Gary McMahon, Joseph S. Pulver, Sr., Ian Rogers, and Paul Tremblay for their help, encouragement, inspiration, and support during the writing of these tales.

This book is dedicated to those giants upon whose shoulders I stand: Robert Aickman, Ramsey Campbell, Robert W. Chambers, Thomas Ligotti, and H. P. Lovecraft.

"Dwelling on the Past" was first published in *Chilling Tales: In Words, Alas, Drown I*, edited by Michael Kelly (Edge Publications, 2013).
"Strong as a Rock" was first published in *Phantasmagorium* #1, edited by Laird Barron (2011).
"By Invisible Hands" was first published in *The Grimscribe's Puppets*, edited by Joseph S. Pulver, Sr. (Miskatonic River Press, 2013).
"Thistle's Find" was first published in *Black Wings III*, edited by S. T. Joshi (PS Publishing, 2013).
"Beyond the Banks of the River Seine" was first published in *A Season in Carcosa*, edited by Joseph S. Pulver, Sr. (Miskatonic River Press, 2012).

All other stories are original to this volume.